THE WOLF
OF
BRITANNIA

VOLUME I

JESS STEVEN HUGHES

A Historical Novel

SUNBURY
PRESS

Mechanicsburg, Pennsylvania   USA

Published by Sunbury Press, Inc.
50 West Main Street
Mechanicsburg, Pennsylvania 17055

www.sunburypress.com

For information about special discounts for bulk purchases, please contact Sunbury Press Orders Dept. at (855) 338-8359 or orders@sunburypress.com.

To request one of our authors for speaking engagements or book signings, please contact Sunbury Press Publicity Dept. at publicity@sunburypress.com.

ISBN: 978-1-62006-560-0 (Trade Paperback)
ISBN: 978-1-62006-561-7 (Mobipocket)
ISBN: 978-1-62006-562-4 (ePub)

Library of Congress Control Number: 2015932529

FIRST SUNBURY PRESS EDITION: February 2015

Product of the United States of America
0 1 1 2 3 5 8 13 21 34 55

Set in Bookman Old Style
Designed by Crystal Devine
Cover by Lawrence von Knorr Painting by Tal Dibner (www.dibnergallery.com)
Edited by Janice Rhayem

Continue the Enlightenment!

VOLUME I

BRITANNIA
AD 27-40

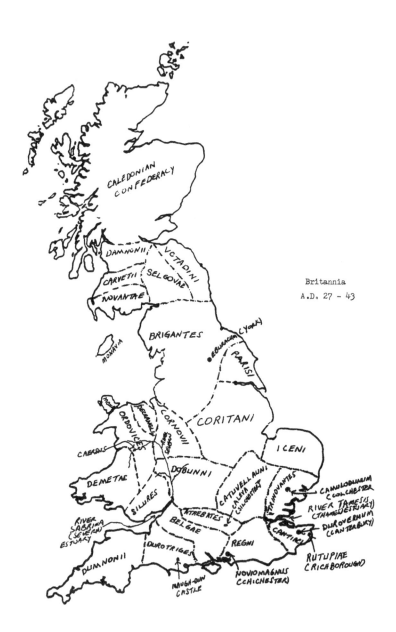

Britannia
A.D. 27 - 43

CALEDONIAN CONFEDERACY

DAMNONII
VOTADINI
CARVETII
SELGOVAE
NOVANTAE

BRIGANTES
EBURACUM (YORK)
PARISI
MONAVIA

ORDOVICES
DECEANGLIT
CORNOVII
CORITANI
CAERSUS
ICENI
DEMETAE
DOBUNNI
SILURES
CATUVELLAUNI
CALEVA (SILCHESTER)
TRINOVANTES
CAMULODUNUM (COLCHESTER)
RIVER TAMESIS (THAMES ESTUARY)
ATREBATES
BELGAE
REGNI
CANTIACI
DUROVERNUM (CANTERBURY)
RIVER SABRINA (SEVERN ESTUARY)
DUROTRIGES
DUMNONII
MAIDEN CASTLE
NOVIOMAGNUS (CHICHESTER)
RUTUPIAE (RICHBOROUGH)

DRAMATIS PERSONAE
(IN ORDER OF APPEARANCE)

THE BRITONS

* Caratacus – prince and warrior
* Tog (Togodubnos) – brother of Caratacus
  Cunobelinos (Cymbeline) – king of the Catuvellauni and
    Trinovantes and father of Caratacus
* Adminios – brother of Caratacus
* Epaticcos – king of the Atrebates and uncle of Caratacus
  Rhian – young Catuvellaunian woman
  Donn – warrior and champion
  Gwynn – wife of Epaticcos
  Clud – ironmaker and master craftsman
  Rhun - Iceni slave
  Havgan – Druid priest
  Oengus – warrior and champion
  Ibor – Druid priest
* Verica - king of the Regni tribe
  Gildas ap Caw - warrior and champion
  Gwynedd - son of Verica
  Rosmerta - Rhian's foster mother
* Dumnoveros – Brigantian king
* Cartimandua – young Brigantian woman
  Dana – young Brigantian woman
* Venutios – Brigantian warrior
  Fergus ap Roycal – clan chieftain
  Fiona - young peasant girl
  Macha – Caratacus's daughter

THE ROMANS

  Gaius Flavius Porcius – emissary and senator
  Cyrus – Persian freedman
* Aulus Plautius – general
* Caligula (Gaius) – emperor of Rome (AD 37-41)
* Claudius (Tiberius Claudius Germanicus Nero) – emperor of Rome
    (AD 41-54)
* Marcus Ostorius Scapula – general
  Marcus Valerius Bassus – centurion
* Tiberius (Tiberius Claudius Nero) – emperor of Rome (AD 14-37)

* historical character

CITIES AND GEOGRAPHICAL LOCATIONS

ANCIENT NAME	MODERN NAME
Bononia Gesoriacum, Gaul	Boulogne, France
Britannia	Britain (England)
British Ocean	English Channel
Caleva	Silchester
Camulodunum	Colchester
Dubris	Dover
Durobrivae	Rochester
Durovernum	Canterbury
Eburacum	York
German Ocean	North Sea
Maugh-Dun Castle (Maiden Castle)	Dorchester
Noviomagnus	Chichester
Portus Rutupis	Wantsum Channel
Regulbium	Reculver
River Colne	Colne River
River Danubus	Danube River
River Rhenus	Rhine River
River Tamesis	Thames River
Tanatus	Isle of Thanet
Rutupiae	Richborough
Verulamium	St. Albans

CHAPTER I

SOUTHERN BRITANNIA, AUGUST, AD 27

Caratacus's wicker chariot bucked and hurtled across every dip and rise in the track. Two lathering ponies strained at their harness as the young prince urged them ahead. Man-sized wooden targets sprinkled the course. Caratacus struck each through the heart with his casting spears. Now he raced for the finish line in a swirl of chalky dust, blue eyes ablaze with excitement.

Tawny hair whipped about his sunburned face. He sweated profusely in a woolen, short-sleeved tunic and tartan breeches, dust muting their colors. A gold collar burned his neck, but to rip it off would bring bad luck. The earthy musk of horse sweat blotted out all other odors.

Behind him, clattering wheels and thudding hooves roared in his ears. Four other chariots steadily gained on him. His horses responded to the stinging touch as he slapped the reins. Caratacus leaped from the flimsy cart onto the center drawbar between his team when another chariot nosed into the lead. He struggled for a foothold and looped the dragging reins about his wrists. Barefooted, he deftly edged his way forward on the jouncing bar and catapulted onto the back of his favorite beast. Kneeling on the bay pony, he bellowed encouragement, calling for even greater speed.

Sucking dust and screaming, urging the racers to ever greater strides, throngs of men, women, and children circled the large, rutted oval, which served as a race track below the great hill fortress of Camulodunum.

A small boy chasing a dog darted from the crowd and crossed in the front of Caratacus's path. A woman screamed. He sucked in his breath—*Damn!* In a flash he

1

kicked the pony's side, sharply swerving the team, barely missing the child. The chariot bounced, arcing one wheel off the ground and back to the earth with a thud. Violently wrenched from the beast's back, Caratacus grabbed its yoke collar and yanked himself up on the withers. A throbbing pain shot through his loins from where he caught the horse's knotty backbone between his legs.

For an instant, Caratacus glanced at the jostling throng. He caught sight of flaxen-haired Rhian, daughter of the king's champion. The young woman screamed encouragement. His team leaped ahead and stampeded towards the finish.

Caratacus heard a pop and then a rumbling noise. He turned and saw the left trace rein on his other pony had snapped loose from an iron holding lug. It whipped back and forth along the animal's side. The mare squealed, terrified by the bridle's lashing. She strained at leather bands around her girth and neck, trying to lurch free of the yoke collar.

Upset by the squealing of the frightened, chestnut mare, the little bay bucked and kicked at the weaving crossbar. Holding all the reins in his right hand, Caratacus jumped to the mare and gripped the animal's sides with powerful legs. Other riders gained on him. He grabbed the trace rein and steadied his mounts.

Hanging by his legs, Caratacus reached down his pony's side and stabbed his free hand towards the flying bridle. It snapped across his face, sending a painful shot through his eyes. For the length of a heartbeat he recoiled, trying to shake off the blinding pain that blurred his vision. Again he attempted to retrieve the other rein. The chariots rounded the last turn of the wheel-plowed course. Fist-sized clods pelted the cheering crowd. Another rider was almost upon him. Caratacus held onto the primary reins as he lunged again and snagged the end of the strap between the fingers of his perspiring left hand. As his sight cleared, he reeled in the rest of the reins. He tightened them around his left hand and held the primary reins of both animals in his right.

Caratacus guided the lathering mare back towards the center of the yoke pole and steadied her galloping to a smooth, flowing rhythm. As if on command, his bay settled down and matched the chestnut mare stride-for-stride. He kicked the side of the chestnut, exhorting the ponies to greater speed. They raced away from the other charioteers.

He crossed the finish line between two hardwood poles topped by bleached human skulls, at least six lengths ahead of his closest competitor. Horns blew. His brother, Tog, led a tremendous cheer. The riotous crowd rushed toward his chariot. A dusty, sweating Caratacus leapt from the car and tossed the reins to an awaiting groom. Grinning at one another, he and Tog clasped each other's wrists and vigorously shook them.

"Well done, Brother, victory is yours!" Tog exclaimed, "Well done! Here, take a drink," Tog urged. He thrust a large earthen bowl of corma beer into Caratacus's hands. Gratefully, he gulped it down. Hundreds of tribesmen surrounded them. It was the Harvest of Lughnasa, the first week of August. The chariot races culminated five days of celebration for the Catuvellaunian and Trinovantian Celts at their capital on Britannia's southeastern coast, Camulodunum.

When King Cunobelinos appeared, a hush fell over the crowd, which immediately opened a pathway for Caratacus's thick-chested father. Long, gray hair swept down the king's powerful back over his purple linen cloak. Cunobelinos wore a scarlet-and gold-threaded tartan tunic with matching breeches and a gold torc around his vein-corded neck. Bracelets of copper and gold circled his biceps and wrists. Sunlight danced off his longsword, made of rare and costly Damascus steel and encased in a jeweled scabbard hanging from his waist.

Caratacus's uncle, King Epaticcos, tribal leaders, and members of the Druid priesthood followed. Behind them ambled Caratacus's older brother, Adminios. Tall, ebony hair falling down to his shoulders, his pock-marked face was flushed, dark eyes watery. He had his arm around the waist of a well-known, round-face trollop, dressed in a bright-green, plaid, long tunic, girdled around the midriff with a gold-fringed sash. Adminios turned and pulled her close, and with his sensuous lips, gave her a moist kiss. A few seconds later, she pushed him away and giggled. He laughed. The two staggered to a halt by the edge of the throng, a mixture of nobility, warriors, craftsmen, and peasants, dressed in their best tartan clothing or threadbare homespun.

All of them silently watched the king stop before Caratacus. Tog stepped behind his brother.

"You do us great honor," Cunobelinos said, addressing his son. "Your victory pleases us."

"Yes, it does," Adminios said in a loud, slurring voice behind him. A vacuous grin widened on his thick lips. He stepped towards the king, leaving the woman's side.

Cunobelinos gave the eldest son a withering look. "It is not your place to speak for the king."

Adminios, his eyes going wide, looked about. His female companion shot a hand to her mouth. He bowed his large head and stepped back to the woman's side. A low murmur spread through the crowd.

Caratacus broke the tension. "The honor is mine, Great King."

The king nodded approval that his son had referred to him correctly.

Behind a sober face and clenched teeth, Caratacus hid his hatred for their forced formality and the humiliating way his father treated Adminios. Then again, his older brother had been drinking and womanizing as usual. Adminios tossed his head, shrugged, and tossed a hand as if he thought the entire scene was trivial. *You should have waited until later to celebrate, Brother.*

Cunobelinos motioned a servant forward to present Caratacus with a large, silver drinking cauldron. The cup was inlaid with intricate carvings of boar heads, wolves, and deer. The prominent relief depicted the braided head of the warrior-goddess Andraste.

Caratacus refrained from smiling as he watched his father's expressionless, ruddy face and searched the old, lined eyes for signs of approval. As expected, he found none. "This is much more than I expected, Great King."

A voice bellowed from the crowd, "Give him a drink! Let him drink from the cup!" The crowd joined the shouting, "Aye, let him!"

The king nodded. A servant hustled forward holding high a silver cup filled with Samian wine from Greece. Caratacus grasped the two handles and held high the trophy with both hands. "Although I am son of the Great King, I am still his loyal subject," he called out loudly. "I am victorious today only because he did not race against me. For surely he would be drinking from this cup of glory rather than I."

The crowd cheered wildly. The king nodded to his son, his mouth a thin line. Tog flashed a crooked grin and shook clasped hands above his head in approval. Holding the heavy cup, Caratacus tilted his head backwards and drained it, as custom demanded. Uncut by water, the wine dizzied him, but he finished without reeling or stumbling.

Caratacus handed the cup to the servant and wiped his mouth on his forearm. He noticed his father glaring at him. *I know that look. Da expects more out of me. I'm only seventeen summers, what else does he want?*

CHAPTER 2

"Look, Tog, here comes fat Porcius," Caratacus said in a voice full of contempt.

The younger brother narrowed his dark, green eyes and spat.

The small entourage of freedmen and slaves accompanying Gaius Flavius Porcius opened a pathway through the reveling throng. As he strolled among the mixture of well-dressed nobility and thread-bare peasants, he gazed at trading booths and stalls set up near the race course for the festival. Sellers, wearing a variety of clothing ranging from rags to bright plaids, hawked their wares. They did a brisk business selling souvenirs, food, and drink such as pastries, meat pies, beer, and mead to local people and foreigners alike. Porcius grinned but shook his head as the vendor reached out with hot pastries to sell.

"Damn pastry seller is sucking up to Porcius like a fool," Tog said.

"Aye, but Porcius is smart," Caratacus answered. "In the long run, it might benefit him and Rome."

"More him than Rome, I'd wager." Tog spat again. He swept back the chestnut hair that had fallen down the front of his shoulders.

Caratacus watched Porcius walk among the stands where Chaldean fortune tellers and shady purveyors of games of chance flourished. At the far end of the fair stood temporary livestock pens where cattle, goats, and sheep were bought and sold amongst clouds of buzzing flies. Two men in ragged tunics and trousers gesticulated wildly over the price of a mottled ram. In closed cubicles across the dusty pathway from the animals, prostitutes plied their trade. A gap-toothed, middle-aged woman wearing a faded but clean, tartan skirt and short-sleeve top sat outside on a stool taking money from a line of eager customers. Mixed with the sickening, sweet stench of animal dung and urine from the corrals, the smells of roasted meat and baked bread drifted on the warm, afternoon breeze.

Moving in the direction of King Cunobelinos, Caratacus, and Tog, who stood a short distance from the race track, Porcius stopped to shake hands and joke with several well-known Briton merchants and craftsmen.

"I hate giving Porcius credit for anything," Caratacus said, "but the pig knows people and what they want."

"He's a trader himself, but I can see why Rome uses him as a diplomat," Tog said. "It's a dangerous combination."

Caratacus studied the balding Roman in his midthirties. He was taller and paler than the Italian traders that Caratacus knew. Porcius's stomach bulged through the white tunic trimmed with purple, cinched at the waist with a bejeweled leather belt, and draped over shiny, blue and yellow, plaid, Celtic breeches. Yet, for all his weight, he had a quickness of foot that put many half his size to shame. However, it was Porcius's sunken, brown eyes, staring like demons carved on pillars of Druid temples, that were so unnerving. Those eyes took in everything, missed nothing, and penetrated to the deepest reaches of one's soul. He had lived in Britannia for five years, and his mastery of the lilting languages of their people was exceptional.

Porcius waddled forward and extended his meaty hand to Caratacus. "Congratulations on your narrow victory," he said in a false, honeyed voice. "Yours was as fine as any that I've seen in the Great Circus of Rome, indeed finer. I've never seen our drivers fly onto the drawbar. For a moment, I thought you might jump forward and drag your ponies to victory."

Caratacus gave Porcius a contemptuous nod, noted by the bejowled emissary.

The Roman grinned and turned to Cunobelinos. He gestured upward with a hand and returned it to his side. "You have a son worthy of your esteemed house, Great King."

"Aye, perhaps he is," Cunobelinos grunted.

Caratacus knew that he would have to take his first head in battle before his father praised him. *Great Teutates, give me patience. My time will come.*

Porcius looked about and then to Cunobelinos. "When you have a moment to spare, Great King, I would like to speak with you—in private."

The king stiffened, his cold, slate eyes glared at Porcius. "About what?"

The Roman returned his glowering look then cleared his throat. "I have received a message from the Emperor Tiberius." Porcius hesitated and glanced as the crowd drew closer, including King Epaticcos, Caratacus's uncle. "Please, Great King, this is not the place to discuss it."

"I decide where to discuss matters, not your emperor," Cunobelinos said. "Is that clear?"

"Of course," Porcius answered. A slight twitch began in his left hand. "I didn't mean to imply otherwise. I only meant—"

"I know what you meant," the king snapped. "Your emperor does not rule my people. I do." He turned and gestured to the gathering surrounding him and his entourage.

The crowd murmured in agreement.

"We have honored all trading arrangements with Rome," the king said, "and we will continue to do so. But he will not dictate the ways of my people or how we conduct affairs with other tribes in this land." Cunobelinos's ruddy complexion darkened with each word.

Porcius looked about and seemed to consider an escape. He took a deep breath and continued. "I only meant we should discuss the emperor's personal message alone as a matter of your privileged right as king. It's not as if it were an order from the emperor. Never that!"

"Very well," the king conceded. "We will go to the Great Hall."

"Brother-King," Cunobelinos said to Epaticcos, who stood a few steps away accompanied by a couple of personal guards, "join me later, and we'll discuss the message from the emperor. I'm sure it will have as much impact on your kingdom as mine."

"As ruler of the Atrebates, that's for me to decide," Epaticcos said in voice closer to a growl, glancing at Caratacus. Tall as his older brother, he stared at Cunobelinos through fierce, blue eyes. An old battle scar sliced diagonally across the forehead of his leathery face and the bridge of his crooked nose above the drooping moustache, giving the fifty-two-year-old warrior-king a menacing appearance. He dressed in an embroidered, blue plaid tunic and striped trousers and wore a short hunting dagger enclosed in a leather sheath on a bejeweled belt surrounding his waist.

Cunobelinos scowled at Epaticcos. He turned to the throng. "My people," he said in a loud voice, "important business forces me to leave you."

Cries of disappointment erupted from the crowd.

"Do not let that stop you from celebrating the God Lugh's Festival and my son's victory," Cunobelinos continued. "The day is still young and plenty of time left for feasting and drinking. Enjoy yourselves, and be merry!"

The people cheered and slowly departed, heading for the vendors' booths and tables filled with free food and drink nearby.

The king left with his retainers and Druids. Porcius followed close behind. Adminios had hovered off to the side with his woman, across the trodden pathway from Caratacus and Tog.

Caratacus shook his head and sighed at the sight of his older brother. He was about to wave Adminios to where he and Tog stood when a group of Adminios's warrior friends hurried by and surrounded him and the pasty-faced trollop. They laughed and joked, bringing a smile to Adminios's face. And with that, the eldest son of the king turned, and the group followed him through the crowded fair.

* * *

Now that Adminios was gone, Caratacus turned to Tog. Epaticcos was a few paces away speaking to his retainers who hovered about him in a half-circle. "Da insulted Uncle Epaticcos by forbidding him from seeing the emperor's letter." Caratacus said.

"It wouldn't be the first time," Tog answered.

"Da has lied about details found in other imperial messages. Why this time? I wonder what this one was about?"

The sounds of laughing, distant baying of cattle, and the playing of flutes and drums carried on the gentle sea breeze drifting in from the harbor outside of Camulodunum. A small group, mostly young people, continued to mill close by, waiting for Epaticcos to depart before approaching Caratacus and Tog. He knew they wanted to personally congratulate him on his victory.

Epaticcos rubbed his nose and closed his eyes for a second. With a hand, he waved Caratacus and Tog to his side. He nodded to his bodyguards who motioned for the crowd to back several feet away. Epaticcos said in a voice little more than a whisper, "Were my kingdom not so important in protecting his southwestern flank, your father would have gone to war with me long before now. And he still might have, except the Druids advise him against it."

"That shouldn't have stopped Da," Caratacus said.

"No," Epaticcos answered, "but your father would have risked excommunication, an unthinkable fate. No one wants their soul to wander forever in the underworld after death."

Caratacus spat in the whitish footprints left by Porcius in the chalky earth.

"Easy, Brother," Tog advised. "I know you hate the Roman and the way he influences Da, but no one can change Da's mind. Here, take a drink." He proudly retrieved a large bowl from a servant hovering nearby and gave it to his older brother. "There's nothing soothing like a little beer."

Tall and sinewy at six feet, fifteen-year-old Tog was still four-fingers width shorter than Caratacus. Beneath his long, straight nose and bright, holly-green eyes, a big, crooked-toothed grin crossed his lean, freckled face.

Caratacus grabbed the bowl and took a long swig, the sweet-sour liquid burning down his throat. He handed the big cup back to his brother. Closing his eyes, he shut out the noise swirling about him as memories flashed through his mind about his childhood. They lasted only a few seconds but seemed far longer ...

* * *

At age seven Caratacus, and later Tog, had gone to
Caleva, capital of the Atrebates, in southwestern Britannia
to live with their Uncle Epaticcos where he ruled as king. It
was a four-day journey from Camulodunum where
Caratacus had been born. Caratacus did not like this
custom of parents sending their youngsters to friends or
relatives to be raised as foster children, a custom practiced
by most Celtic peoples. At first, Caratacus hated being
away from his father. Being only four years old when his
mother died giving birth to Tog, Caratacus had almost no
memory of her. But Uncle Epaticcos had welcomed the
boys. His wife, their Aunt Gwynn, acted as the wonderful
mother they had never known. The lads followed Epaticcos
everywhere and played in the Great Hall when he held
court.

One afternoon, after a session with his council and
after everyone had departed, Epaticcos motioned them
forward from where they had been sitting in the back of the
Great Hall. They stood before him, hands behind their
backs, as he sat on his high-back throne. "You listened to
the discussions and rulings issued today by the council,
did you not?"

"Yes, Uncle," the boys answered in unison.

Epaticcos narrowed his eyes. "Good. Remember this,
one day both of you will be kings. The only way you'll learn
to rule well is by example, be it from wise decisions or from
mistakes. Blend it with the teachings of the Druids and
bards." He paused. "Always know who your enemies are. If
you do, you'll survive to be great leaders and to protect our
people from Rome."

* * *

Caratacus opened his eyes. Epaticcos and Tog were
staring at him with puzzled expressions.

"What were you thinking, Caratacus?" Epaticcos asked.

"I was remembering how you taught me and Tog as we
grew up," Caratacus answered.

His uncle grinned. "Both of you are fast learners."

"It was what you and Arch-Druid Havgan said about
the Romans that I recalled mostly," Caratacus said
through tightened lips. "Late at night around the hearth

fire, you told those horrible tales of how the Romans defeated all the armies sent by the Gauls when Caesar overran their country. How they enslaved the people."

"It's all true," Epaticcos answered with a nod of his head.

"For a long time I had nightmares about those murdering bastards killing hundreds of thousands of people." Caratacus exhaled. "And if the Druids are right, even a million."

"Unfortunately, Druid Havgan's sources are reliable," Epaticcos said.

Caratacus replied in a growling voice, "Those blood-thirsty butchers will never take Britannia while I am king!"

Epaticcos glanced at the nearby crowd being held back by his guards. "This is not the place to discuss it," he said quietly. "We'll talk more about it when we return home. This is a time for celebration." He beckoned the crowd to join them.

"Uncle is right, enjoy yourself," Tog said in a robust voice. "Join the fun."

"Aye, your brother's right," Uncle Epaticcos said. "Be merry. Tomorrow we go home. The three months you spent with your father was a long time. Too long." He grinned. "I'll see you in the morning." Epaticcos turned and, escorted by his bodyguards, walked away.

"You're the best." Tog smiled and patted Caratacus's shoulder. "Everyone knows it, and you did well in praising Da. Look around you."

Caratacus studied the multitude of smiling faces, including that of Rhian, who huddled near the rear of the group. His heart skipped a beat when he spotted her. Rhian's sandy hair, tied into a single braid, flowed down the middle of her back. He did care for her, much as he attempted to ignore her. Although only sixteen, like him, she was nearly a head taller than most in the crowd, including Tog.

As the mob grew noisier and closed in upon him, Rhian disappeared from his vision. Next thing Caratacus knew, young warriors had grabbed him by the arms and legs, hoisting him upon their shoulders. The wine Caratacus had consumed from the great cup affected him more than he realized, and his head swirled in a daze.

The band of young men jostled him proudly on their shoulders and carried him away chanting, "Drunk as a bull! Get him drunk as a bull!" He twisted his head and saw Rhian's apple-green eyes fix upon him with a level stare as he was being carried away. What must she be thinking about him now? Was she proud of his winning the race, or angry that he had ignored her afterward? Perhaps he would see her in the morning, but now was the time to celebrate with Tog and their friends.

CHAPTER 3

The following morning, while Caratacus harnessed two ponies to his chariot in the big, dusty pen for the journey home, the endless pounding within his head felt like a hammer striking an anvil. *Gods, when would it stop?* The sickening stench of horse manure scattered about the corral nearly gagged him. The buzzing of flies swarming around the filth roared in his ears like screaming banshees fleeing the underworld. The night before, after drinking what seemed like an endless amount of beer and wine, he had managed to crawl to a pile of blankets in an empty corner of the hut before passing out. Now a young groom offered to help with the mounts, but Caratacus refused and sent him away. He wished to be alone.

Caratacus heard the sound of tinkling necklaces and bracelets. He turned about as Rhian approached with a smile on her bowed lips. Her face, dominated by high cheekbones, was rouged with elderberry juice, her hair twisted into long, thick braids that fell over the back of a blue and yellow checkered tunic with little bells sewn into the fringe. A long dagger, the type carried by most warriors in training, hung from the plain, leather belt circling the waist of her azure trousers. Thrown over her shoulder was a gaudy scarlet mantle with bright, golden stripes. Beyond hearing, her two young attendants, armed with similar weapons, waited outside the staked pen.

Attempting to ignore her, Caratacus focused on the design of his chariot. She stood close and seemed to patiently wait for his notice. He glanced quickly at her then concentrated on the car's floorboard and its double-semicircular, wicker board side-panels. Despite his pounding head, it was impossible to push her from his mind. *Gods, she is beautiful.* But still, he attempted to turn his mind to the chariot, knowing that at any second she would say something.

"Caratacus, why are you ignoring me?"

Her boldness startled him, and his head throbbed all the worse. He was at a sudden loss for words. He knew what she wanted, but he wasn't about to fall into her trap.

"I'm not ignoring you." He wondered why this girl could stir his loins with no more than a purr of her soft, musical voice.

"Caratacus, I'm sixteen and ready for marriage."

"So what?" He looked past Rhian to her attendants. By the expression on their faces, they didn't appear to have heard anything.

"Next year you'll be eighteen and will need a mate," Rhian said.

He grew tenser by the moment. One of the ponies whinnied; the sound pierced his head like a screaming demon.

"You're talking to the wrong man." *Marriage. That's the last thing I need!*

Rhian shook her head. "No, I'm not. They won't marry me to someone outside our class. After all, isn't my father of the warrior class and King Epaticcos's champion?"

"He may be the king's man, but I'm in no mood to talk about marriage. My head hurts. Too much Roman wine."

She narrowed her eyes and jabbed a calloused finger in Caratacus's direction. "Ha! Drinking, fighting, and whoring. That's all you men think about!"

"It is none of your concern what a man does." He took a moment to calm his pony, which had startled at his bark. He brushed its mane with his hand. "Besides, I wasn't with any woman last night. At least as far as I know."

Rhian's face flushed, apparently embarrassed that she had lost her temper. She stepped closer and stroked the same pony, allowing her own composure to return. She took a deep breath and quietly placed a long, rough hand on his. Her nimble fingers were warm to the touch.

Caratacus jerked his hand away from hers and rubbed it along the side of his breeches.

A wounded look crept into Rhian's eyes, the sides of her lips curled downward. For a moment she left her hand hanging in midair, staring at it as though it were diseased. Then she brought it to her side and wiped it on her skirt.

15

"Don't you care about anything?" she asked in little more than a whisper. "I care about you, and I know you like me, but your pride won't allow you to admit it."

"I like horses, and drinking, and taking my pleasure when I want it," he snapped. He silently admonished himself for yelling at her, but it was too late to smooth his remark. Caratacus looked away, his muscles tight as if bunched into knots. He took several breaths attempting to relax. His pony whinnied again, and he glanced about the pen. A slave entered at the far gate with a shovel and dragged a wooden circular tub. Quietly, he started to clean up the manure.

Caratacus turned back to Rhian. "Why do you care anyway? I thought you wanted to be a warrior? You're always training with those giant twin sisters, Gwyther and Modron."

Rhian motioned in the direction of Camulodunum's defensive wall. "I want to be a warrior and wife. There are many women who are both, and they defend the fortress in time of danger."

Caratacus put both hands to his head. *I don't need to hear this, not now.* He dropped his hands to his side and looked into her pale, green eyes. "Look, I just don't want you turning into a scar-faced beast like those two."

She gasped. "How can you say such an awful thing about me?"

He knew he had gone too far. "I didn't ... I didn't mean it that way. You ... you are so ... so pretty, it's just that ... I wouldn't want to see you wounded in battle, your face sliced up like theirs. Maybe that's why your training bothers me."

Rhian smiled, showing her perfect white teeth. "I won't let it happen," she said in a soft voice.

"You may not have a choice."

She raised a hand to touch his shoulder, but he turned away. "I'd rather you chose household duties like spinning wool and baking over being a warrior. Even taking care of ponies would be more agreeable."

Rhian opened her mouth as if to respond, but closed it with a huff.

I have the right to take any woman I want or for that matter any man. I'm not ready for betrothal. He turned his back, hiding his desire.

"What's the use!" she cried. "I don't know why I waste my time." She turned on her heel and stormed through the pen's gate, brushing aside Tog, who had just entered the corral, as her two attendants followed in her wake.

* * *

Later that morning the entourage of Caratacus's uncle rode westward by horseback and chariot, leaving behind the last of the three fortified dikes of Camulodunum. They headed westward to Caleva, capital of the Atrebates and home, a four-day journey. The group traveled along the ancient, wooden trackway of the Colne River Valley, past lush wheat fields and vast herds of sheep. The party included Caratacus, Tog, Havgan the Druid, King Epaticcos, and his sixty armed retainers.

Caratacus's head throbbed with every jarring rut his chariot hit. "Damn all the gods, Tog, can't you drive this chariot any better?" He cursed for the dozenth time.

"Shut up, Brother. It's not my driving. You can't hold your wine. It's a wonder you're alive."

"Gods, I wish I wasn't." Caratacus closed his eyes and muttered another curse to himself. He grasped the wicker chariot rim and attempted to stand into the fresh wind, pretending to be stone sober.

He ignored the laughs of his comrades, who had dragged his headache-splitting body from his makeshift bed on the reed-covered floor, to his cursing displeasure. They had joked with each other, at Caratacus's expense. Still, they laughed with him, sharing the knowledge that the king's son was human. Despite the bumpy ride, he sat down and prayed before he dozed off that he would wake with a clear head. Soon his uncle's party would enter an area frequented by bandits, and Caratacus needed to be alert and ready in case of a fight.

* * *

"Ah, the gods have returned you from the Land Beneath the Earth," Tog said as they drove along the trackway.

"Watch out, or that's where I'll send you," Caratacus warned as he opened and rubbed his eyes. He yawned and stood, attempting to steady himself, and again, he placed his hand to his forehead.

"Seriously," Tog added, "are you feeling any better?"

"Much better," he lied.

"Want to take the reins for awhile?"

"Not yet." Caratacus took a gulp of water from the goat-skin bag hanging from the chariot rim. It quenched his growing thirst and soothed his queasy stomach. A refreshing zephyr swirled around his face, easing his pain. The late morning sky was a deep blue, and a cool breeze wafted in from the sea. Because of fair skin, Caratacus rarely removed his warm, sleeveless tunic. Yet the weather felt too pleasant to wear it. He pulled it off, exposing his hardened torso, and enjoyed the warmth of the sun's first rays and the crisp air. He studied the blue and red spiraled tattoos on his chest and the newly drawn circling snakes on his forearms.

"Admiring yourself again, Brother?" Tog asked.

"Don't tell me you're jealous? You'll get your tattoos next month."

Tog glanced at his long, sinewy arms and hairless chest. "Can't be soon enough."

"Easy, Brother. Tattooing is part of the road to manhood, but like Uncle Epaticcos says, so is patience."

Tog huffed and nodded.

Caratacus slapped him on the back. He turned his eyes to the edge of the distant woods, alert for marauders. They were still deep in the territory of the Catuvellaunians. He must not let his guard down.

But in spite of the danger, he let his mind wander, dreaming of taking his first enemy's head where a man's soul resided. *To possess another man's head is to strengthen my own soul. Its powerful magic.* He scanned the forest's edge. *It wouldn't surprise me if Froech and his murdering bandits were hereabouts stealing cattle and killing peasants. He's done it before.* Soon he would prove himself a warrior.

CHAPTER 4

By late morning on the third day, the night's fog melted with the sunrise and faded into a harsh glare, the weather hot and humid. They were riding through the upper Tamesis River Valley, which straddled an ancient forest of sprawling beech trees south of the Chiltern Hills. After crossing the river at a narrow ford, they headed west toward the low-lying Berkshire Hills.

Epaticcos's retinue halted when one of his scouts raised his hand in warning. He rode back to the ruler, who stood in a chariot adorned with images of deer and bear fashioned out of circular copper plates. The king wore an embroidered tunic with rich bejeweled trappings and a polished, black-iron longsword hanging from his side.

"Great King, I've discovered a large number of tracks ahead," the short-legged scout said.

Epaticcos motioned for his men to wait, but waved Caratacus to his side.

"Come with me," he ordered. Their chariots rumbled up a clearing surrounded by clumps of ancient, overhanging elms.

About one hundred paces beyond, they found the prints of many hooves. "Halt!" Epaticcos ordered. He and Caratacus jumped to the ground, leaving Tog and the king's driver to watch the mounts. Carefully, they tracked the chalky earth, occasionally glancing and stooping to examine imprints. Caratacus and his uncle studied one another for a moment. "Well ... what do you think?" the king asked.

Caratacus quickly re-examined the tracks. Crouching, he touched one of them with a long index finger, as if measuring its depth. Then he stood.

"This wasn't any ordinary cattle raid, Uncle." He motioned with his hands at the hoof prints, evidence in support of his conclusion. "At least sixty head of cattle, no doubt taken from our people. They're heading away from our lands."

From behind deep-set eyes, beneath a ridge of heavy eyebrows, Epaticcos studied his nephew for the span of a few heartbeats. "Good, my lad. What else do you see?"

"The riders. There must have been nearly one hundred. And look here." He pointed to a number of thin, parallel lines disappearing among the trees. Caratacus hesitated. A lump formed in his throat, and he swallowed quickly. "I've never seen Froech's chariot tracks, but I'd wager these belong to him and his bandits."

"Oh? How did you arrive at that conclusion?"

"It's harvest time. So he's raiding again." Caratacus focused on the churned-up soil beyond his uncle. "And those tracks," he gestured with a hand, "some of the horses are wearing shoes." Both knew only the wealthiest warriors could afford the expense of iron horseshoes. Tiny bumps formed on Caratacus's arms and back. He grasped his arms as he began to tremble, experiencing the fear of facing an enemy. The sensation was new to him, and he didn't like it. He forced himself to speak. "But why does he need so many warriors when half the number could've done the task?"

Epaticcos was about to answer when they heard a faint rumbling noise. At about a three-hundred-yard distance, a cloud of dust billowed from fast-approaching chariots. At least fifty raced toward them along with an equal number of horsemen. Caratacus exhaled as he attempted to control his fear and gazed in the king's direction to see if he would call up their warriors in defense. Instead, the broadening smile of his foster father puzzled him.

The lead car carried a burly, long-haired warrior wearing chainmail over a striped tunic. His conical, iron helmet bore a bronze raven. Hinged wings flapped violently every time the chariot struck a bump in the rutted field. Dust flew. It was Donn, King Epaticcos's champion, spurring chariots toward them. He was Rhian's father, and like Caratacus, Rhian was staying with foster parents in Camulodunum.

20

Donn pulled violently to a halt before the king. The leathery-faced, slit-eyed fighter in his late thirties raised his hand. "Greetings, Great King!" he bellowed.

"And to you, my old friend," the king barked.

Donn alighted from his rig, stooped, and examined the tracks. He stood, turned toward the king. "How long have ye been followin' them?"

"Came across the trail only moments ago, Donn," Epaticcos said. "Cattle taken in a raid, were they?"

Donn nodded, his narrow eyes fixed on Epaticcos. "Aye, right ye be, more than fifty or sixty."

Epaticcos's face tightened, giving the old battle-scar that sliced diagonally across his forehead and bridge of his nose a menacing look. "From whom?"

Donn turned and pointed his left hand that missed the small index finger in the direction of Caleva. "Five or six of your tenants."

Epaticcos narrowed his yellowish-brown eyes. "When?"

"Last night during the full moon."

"Then it has to be Froech," Epaticcos said turning to Caratacus. A grin escaped from beneath his drooping, gray moustache. "A good guess, Nephew. He's never been afraid of moon madness."

"They'll fear it soon enough when their heads be swinging from my chariot," Donn snarled. He gave a quick shove on the handle of his longsword.

"There'll be enough time for that, Donn," Epaticcos said coolly, "whatever else, it's started."

"I don't understand, Uncle," Caratacus interjected. They had cattle raids every season. It was a test of manhood. "Froech always raids on his own."

Epaticcos's eyes measured Caratacus and apparently found him worthy of explanation. "Any other time you'd be right. Except for Froech, most raiders steal no more than ten or eleven to replace their own losses. Even Froech's raids have taken no more than twenty or thirty. But this is different."

Caratacus nodded. Stealing that many cattle constituted a declaration of war.

Epaticcos explained briefly to Donn about Porcius's presence at the harvest festival.

"Does the message Porcius had from Rome for Da and you have something to do with this raid?" Caratacus asked.

"Aye, it does, but there are many details, and further explanation will wait until we are home."

"In other words, Rome has its hands in the affairs of our people again," Caratacus said with a smirk. "No doubt that pig Porcius is right in the middle of it."

"Ain't he always," Donn said.

"Whatever else, we must overtake and destroy these cutthroats before they escape," the king declared.

"We will," Donn answered. "The cattle will slow them down, and when we do—," he said with a sinister grin, "there'll be plenty of heads for all."

The king smiled in appreciation of his champion's prowess.

"We don't have enough men with us right now," Epaticcos continued. "That will come later, and then we'll fight him on my terms." He turned away and then back to Donn. "By the way, how many of my people were lost in the raids?"

"One hundred, more or less, but it's the cattle that be important," Donn answered.

Don't they realize the peasants are as valuable as the cattle? Caratacus thought. *Then again, Uncle Epaticcos and Donn have always treated them as so much fodder. A grievous mistake.*

* * *

Late that afternoon, along the forest-encrusted edge of the rolling Berkshires where pines choked with underbrush rose up the hillside, Epaticcos's and Donn's combined groups spotted mounted bandits on horseback and chariots and cattle churning up the countryside's powdery soil. Clattering hooves, jingling pendants, squeaking of leather tack and reins, and whinnying horses echoed across the field. They stirred up clouds of dry, choking dust that mixed with the sweat of man and horse.

Instead of attempting to retreat, the outlaws boldly turned, confronting Epaticcos and his men. They grouped into a central mass of horses and chariots in front of the milling cattle. From above the tree line, flocks of white-billed rooks flew skyward squawking like crows as they fled from the massing warriors. A large roebuck bounded away toward the protective undergrowth.

Nearly one hundred marauders sporting long, shaggy hair and moustaches, dressed in an array of dirty tartans and plaid tunics and breeches, halted as the dust drifted away. They pounded their chests with their fists, hurled insults, and boasted of their fighting abilities by twirling swords above their heads. One ugly, scarred villain waved a decaying head by its filth-encrusted hair. The eye sockets loomed empty in the gray-black skin hung from the skull. "Recognize yer ol' grandda, you shit eaters?" he shouted loud enough to be heard above the noise of the bawling cattle and whinnying horses. "I brought 'em along for a visit. I use his mouth when there's no woman about!" His comrades laughed boisterously.

Epaticcos's men retorted with their own insults.

Caratacus taunted as much as the next in an attempt to overcome his own fears about the impending battle. "The only woman who'd have you is your mother!" he shouted as he waved his sword.

"And your granny eats it, too!" Tog yelled in a deep voice from where he stood next to Caratacus, holding the reins of the chariot.

The outlaw turned his horse in Caratacus's direction, but his comrades blocked his way.

Caratacus and Tog laughed.

Tog scanned the enemy horsemen. "Which one is Froech?"

"I don't know," Caratacus answered. "I've heard he dresses like one of his men."

"No wonder he's still alive," Tog said. "Until it's too late, his enemies think they're fighting another warrior."

Caratacus nodded.

"Uncle Epaticcos must know his face. Ask him."

Just as Caratacus's chariot approached his uncle, the raiders charged the king's band. Epaticcos turned and quickly signaled his men forward at a run. The two sides, about one hundred each, rushed toward one another in a swarming mass. The bloody clash quickly turned into a furious, struggling mass of confusion. Metal upon metal clashed, mixed with screams of dying men, curses of the wounded, yelling warriors, clattering hooves, squeals of horses, rumbling chariots, and dust! The acrid-sweet smell of blood mixed with feces and urine from the bowels of the fallen added to the chaos.

From his chariot, with Tog guiding the ponies, Caratacus removed one of three casting spears from a socket in the car's bulwark. He took aim at the first shield-carrying horseman who crossed his path. The rider, screaming a war cry, clutched a small, round shield close to his body as he hurled a javelin at Caratacus. It missed, flying between the legs of a passing horse and sending the horseman crashing to the ground with a broken leg as the horse tripped.

Caratacus leaned forward over the side of the car, thrusting his spear above the top of the bandit's shield into his exposed throat. Blood gushed as the warrior fell to the ground. A horse crushed his skull.

"Good shot!" Tog yelled.

Tog kneeled along the front edge of the chariot and deftly guided the sweating ponies as the warriors surged back and forth in hand-to-hand fighting. He wheeled about as another chariot rider slammed into the clashing men and thundered down upon them.

"Look out!" Tog shouted as the warrior hurtled a dart-like spear, striking the top rim of Caratacus's car and just missing Tog's face.

"After him!" Caratacus ordered. The chariot lurched ahead as the ponies stretched out, straining to catch the fleeing enemy. The brothers pursued the bandit, momentum carrying them deeper into the fighting. Overtaking him, Caratacus unfurled a folded, leather sling from his waistband, seating a leaden stone from a pouch tied next to the dagger. He whirled it over his head, the weapon sounding like a "whip-whip," and hurled the bullet at the rider. It penetrated the man's skull and sent him crashing into his driver, who lost control of the team. The car crashed into a nearby yew tree, crushing the driver and rider against the huge ancient trunk.

Clouds of blinding dust blocked much of Caratacus's view. Quickly looking about, he saw a battlefield of mass confusion. Epaticcos's warriors clashed with Froech's bandits in a bloody carnage of wounded and dying men and horses. Beyond the fracas, bellowing cattle scattered.

Caratacus rapped Tog on the shoulder and pointed to his left. A broad-shouldered, hairy warrior with a heavy, protruding lower lip galloped his Gallic roan towards the young riders. For the length of a heartbeat, Caratacus's muscles tightened, and fear raced through his body. He shook it off. *I've no time for this!*

The brigand screeched as he drew next to their bouncing chariot. He slashed at Caratacus's head with his longsword.

Shit!

He missed and, with a sharp thud, splintered great chunks from the car's frame.

No you don't! Caratacus met the next blow with a shield, which savagely pushed the warrior back. Quickly, he slammed the enemy's weapon aside, jabbed another spear toward the stomach of the rider, but missed. Blocking several deadly slashes of the bandit's blade with his shield, Caratacus's arms and shoulders absorbed the shuddering impact. *You're not killing me!* Caratacus maneuvered and thrust his last spear between the rogue's shield and chest, plunging the javelin into the lower abdomen, spilling his guts, feeling the raider's body shudder. The bandit uttered a final ghoulish scream as he dropped his longsword and toppled off his horse.

As suddenly as it began, the battle was over. Few raiders escaped. Survivors were put to the sword. Then the moment of realization came.

Caratacus pointed to the body-strewn field. "Our first battle. My first kills. Heads! I can claim them!" For a moment, he trembled, but the tremors disappeared as quickly as they began. "Tog, do you know what this means?"

"You're a warrior! By the gods, that's not all. You've even been wounded!"

Caratacus eyed the small trickle of blood oozing from his shoulder. "It's a piece of splinter from the chariot." He removed the dagger needle and flicked it away. He looked about seeing other warriors collecting their share of enemy weapons and heads.

For a moment he and Tog watched as the men went from body to body, decapitating the victims and tying them to the rims of chariots or the pommels on their horses' saddles. Swords and spears were taken and piled in a location designated by Epaticcos. A number of fighters rounded up the scattered cattle.

"The murdering bastard tried to chop your guts out," Tog finally said. "Da can't deny you recognition any longer."

"Aye, now he must, even if he doesn't want to admit it."

Tog grinned. "Your friend Clud will be pleased."

"The old blacksmith would be happy even if I'm not recognized."

"He might even make you a new sword."

"His friendship is more important than any weapon. Come on, let's find my trophies." Caratacus grabbed the chariot's reins from Tog, wheeled about, and rode through the field, locating his victims. With vicious slashes, he decapitated each bloody body and tied the heads by their long hair to the double-curved rim of his chariot.

Now he was a man! A warrior. He possessed the heads of his enemies and their souls, and now, this very moment, their spirit-powers were transferring from torn heads to his. He felt it, the powers of their souls entering his body and giving him strength. The muscles in his body seemed to enlarge, and his mind became even brighter and more alert as if he had gained a new sense of learning and wisdom. Did he acquire the fighting skills and cunning of his enemies?

Epaticcos approached the two youths just as Caratacus tied the last bloody head to the chariot's rim. A wide grin revealing yellowed teeth spread across his mouth. His big hand slapped Caratacus on the back so hard that it knocked him a couple of steps forward. "Well done, boy. You're a true son of your father!"

Caratacus grinned as Epaticcos examined the blood-spattered heads more closely.

Epaticcos grabbed the long, greasy hair and lifted up the macabre head of the big, shaggy outlaw. "Do you know whose head this is?" the king turned wide-eyed to his nephew. "It's Froech, the Bone Lip! What a trophy." He pointed to the bloody head's long, protruding lip and chin. "You've done what even the most hardened warrior has failed to do, kill Froech in battle!"

Caratacus stood taller, a tight smile crossing his lips. He shook his head. "Froech? I can't believe it! Me, killing the worst bandit in southern Britannia?"

"It's true, you have," the king assured him.

Tog grabbed his brother's hand and shook it. "Wait until the people hear about this. The women will throw themselves at you!"

"I'm glad I didn't know who he was before the battle," he shuddered. "I didn't realize I'd be so scared."

Epaticcos roared with laughter. "If you said anything different, I'd see your father put you to work in the stables shoveling shit for the rest of your life." He slapped his nephew on the back. "It's natural to be afraid. Gods, that's half the fun."

Caratacus wiped his forehead and let out a heavy breath. A surge of pride swept through him. His hand rose to the newly claimed torc, the trophy taken from Froech's throat before hacking off his head. No wonder the torc was so rich in heavy gold.

"Now I'm a man like you, Uncle. When we get home, I'll have Froech's head preserved in cedar oil as fitting the great fighter he was."

"Well said," a pleased Epaticcos answered. "Spoken like a true warrior, which from this day forward no man dare deny. This is only the beginning, Nephew. Not only will you take more heads, but you will become a great leader." Balling up his right fist, he struck his open left palm. "One day Rome will fear you."

"Rome will, Uncle. And if the Romans dare invade our lands, I will crush them on the beach!"

CHAPTER 5

Home at last! Caratacus viewed the Great Fortress of Caleva with pleasure as he and Tog, along with Epaticcos and his warriors, ascended the long ramp to the tall, sturdy, oak main gate.

The fortress was smaller and more compact than Camulodunum, but just as secure. The capital of the Atrebates towered above the surrounding plain on a gravel-laden hill. A high, double rampart and ditch, constructed of heavy cross-timbers and filled with rubble and encircled by a massive dike, commanded the approach to the hill's promontory. Caratacus turned about in the chariot, scanning the surrounding countryside. In the distance were rolling hills and grazing areas for thousands of sheep. Beyond, to the north, a great forest spread at the plain's edge. The woods were so deep, a week's journey was needed to penetrate to the other side.

The heavy, iron-studded gates swung open at the approach of Epaticcos's host, and a dozen sentries and more than three hundred civilians cheered wildly. Earlier, the king had sent a messenger ahead to let the fortress know he would soon arrive and to prepare the feast. His troops cantered past dozens of warrior huts, their walls lined with human skulls, thatched, low-roofed granaries, and the homes of artisans. Women and children stood before the dwellings, waving and calling to their husbands and fathers. Barking dogs darted about the horses, cautiously keeping out of hooves range, as they happily greeted their returning masters. The aromatic smell of baking bread wafted on the breeze from the clay ovens in many homes.

"See that building, Caratacus?" Epaticcos motioned to the high-walled building of wattle and daub guarded by six warriors. "That's the new mint I told you about."

Caratacus touched his tattooed chest. "Now you have your own gold staters like Da."

"Is it wrong to take pride in my kingdom's achievements?" Epaticcos asked. "We minted the first coins just before I journeyed to Camulodunum. They're stamped with the image of a corn ear. Emperor Tiberius takes notice of anyone who mints their own coins, especially in Latin. It should help us obtain favorable trading agreements."

"But you said you were against the Romans."

Caratacus's uncle exhaled and, for a split moment, gripped the hilt of his sword. "I am. But reality says I must trade with Rome to survive and compete with your father for Britannia's trade. There's no harm using your enemies' methods to defeat them. Nothing makes friends faster than gold."

A few minutes later the retinue approached the king's home. The tall, elongated house was framed by a double-encircling wall of thick wooden posts inscribed with ornamental designs. The outer posts framed the skull-niched, whitewashed wall, and the inner wall supported the heavily woven roof of reeds.

Gwynn, Epaticcos's matronly wife, greeted her husband and the two young princes at the entrance, along with three young female slaves. From inside, a light haze of smoke drifted through the entrance. Epaticcos winked at Gwynn, who still clearly sparked his interest. Caratacus suspected this signaled a good toss in the furs tonight. Epaticcos grinned broadly at her. Tall and in her fiftieth year, his wife was clad in a short-sleeved, orange, tartan gown trimmed in white and falling to the ankles. It was a dress he favored. Tied to the girdle of her thick waist was a small, bronze dagger. Her long, silver hair was divided into two braids falling down the middle of her back. Her bejowled cheeks were the color of sunset. Despite her age, there was a sparkle in her big, sea-blue eyes.

"Welcome home, my King," she said formally in front of the warriors and glared at the shapely slaves to keep their distance.

"Enough of that nonsense, woman, I'm your husband, not your brother!" Epaticcos roared. "Give me a fat hug," he bellowed, tossing his shield to his driver and leaping from his chariot.

Caratacus chuckled as his uncle eagerly approached Gwynn, a smile on his lips. Caratacus regarded his aunt with a deep affection. Because his mother had died when he was only four, his aunt raised him and Tog as if they were her real sons.

"Humph, you treat me as if I were one of those hussy consorts you used to have," Gwynn said with a teasing smile.

"Hah! I had them all right. You were one of them." He laughed. The couple went through this charade every time Epaticcos returned from a trip. Their love was obvious and pleasing to his people.

"But I only consorted with the best of men and that is why I married you," she said, holding him at arm's length for an instant before granting him an affectionate embrace.

"So you did!"

A cheer led by Caratacus went up from the warriors as Epaticcos responded.

The king turned to his men gesturing for silence. "Tonight we celebrate our victory with a feast in the Great Hall." Another cheer erupted briefly before he waved his hand. "Now go to your homes and prepare yourselves. Show your families your new prizes!" He motioned for Caratacus and Tog to stay.

As they departed, Epaticcos turned to his wife and then to his nephew. "Caratacus has reached manhood before his seventeenth birthday. Look!" he pointed to the three bloodstained heads hanging from the side of the young warrior's mud-spattered chariot.

A grin crossed her still sensual lips. "That's wonderful." Gwynn turned and tossed her nephew a kiss. "You must tell me all about it tonight, Caratacus."

"I will, Aunt Gwynn."

Caratacus noticed Epaticcos as his uncle's eyes drifted to one of the young, ripe-breasted slaves.

Gwynn flashed a dark look in the woman's direction and elbowed his ribs. "Must you spend time with them, too?"

"You know I spend time with all my women when I return from a journey. It's my right," he said, rubbing his side.

"I know, but I don't have to like it."

Epaticcos halted. He faced Gwynn and placed his hands on her big shoulders. "Understand this, dear Wife," he said in a tender voice, "you are still my chief wife, and I shall always spend time with you first. No matter what, you are still my favorite." He gently kissed her lips.

Her face slowly relaxed. "Oh, you. How can I resist such a proposal?" she said in a lighter tone. "So long as I'm head consort, I won't interfere with your pleasures." Reaching up, she returned his kiss. "I fear that one day it's going to be your undoing."

Epaticcos laughed and wrapped his arm around Gwynn's waist. "Come on, let's go in."

Caratacus and Tog followed but stayed only as long as custom demanded. There was someone else, a good friend, whom Caratacus eagerly wanted to tell his tale of battle.

* * *

Later that afternoon, under the hot blaze of the sun, Caratacus and Tog drew up before the hut of Clud the blacksmith. His shop sat on the outskirts of the village of little thatched huts, huddled at the foot of the incline leading to the fort's gateway. The smoky forge sat outside Clud's place in the open beneath a tall, goatskin canopy.

As Clud turned from the sword he was repairing, he wiped away the beads of sweat running down from his thick eyebrows. "Ho, young Prince," he said with a brief glance at Caratacus. "I need a little more time to get this done. Then I'll join you."

"Take your time, Clud, we're in no hurry," Caratacus answered.

Caratacus noticed Clud had just fused two red-hot parts of a broken blade and couldn't pause once the iron cooled. It would no longer be malleable and would have to be re-fired in the forging pit.

Clud returned to the anvil seated on a thick, hardwood post implanted in the clay floor. With one of his calloused hands, he grabbed the iron pincers lying nearby and clamped them to the piece of searing metal. Using his other hand, he continued to hammer the weapon back into shape.

He stopped and placed the hammer on the earthen floor. Using the pincers, he dropped the iron into a tub of water. Clud motioned his Iceni slave, who swept away the cinders. "Heat up the charcoal," he ordered. "I'll finish this after I've seen my young friends here."

The slave nodded as Clud placed the weapon on the triangular anvil and laid the tongs and hammer against the nearby clay bench. He scratched an armpit and wiped his calloused hands on the burnt and stained cowhide apron. He lumbered from beneath the canopy toward Caratacus and Tog after skirting the conical clay oven that encased the forge, nearly tripping over the goat-skinned bellows. Clud brushed the sandy-braided hair from his wide forehead and shaded his eyes with a thick hand.

"Ho, young Prince Caratacus and Brother Tog!" Clud roared. "Welcome home." He turned to Rhun, his slave, and motioned for the man to keep pumping the goatskin bellows at the edge of the charcoal pit holding a red-hot strip of iron. "Keep your head away from the smoke! The fumes will kill you!"

Caratacus shook his head and grinned. "Same old Clud, terrorizing Rhun as usual." He and Tog alighted from the chariot.

"What do you expect? I've got to get my money's worth out of his useless hide before he drops."

"You've been saying that for years." Caratacus nodded to the slave. "Don't pay any attention, Rhun, he couldn't get along without you."

"You're very kind, young lord," Rhun, the thin, stooped-shouldered slave answered. He momentarily looked away from the bellows.

"Now you sound like a perfumed diplomat. Pay attention to your work!" Clud growled.

"It's true. I'm glad to be back," Caratacus said, changing the subject. "I need a favor."

Clud ambled to the young men's chariot. "For you, my young friend, anything."

Caratacus ran a hand through his freshly washed hair. He knew everyone wanted favors from Clud, his generosity was legendary. "No need of staying around Uncle Epaticcos's home after taking a bath. He's spending time with Aunt Gwynn and three of his favorite concubines."

The blacksmith grinned and brushed a fly from his drooping moustache. "By the gods, I don't know how your uncle does it. He's got a reputation for having more stamina than five men half his age. I'm lucky to satisfy one wench."

"I guess the gods bless some more than others." Caratacus shrugged. "Right now I need you to take a look at this." He pointed to the cracked iron tire framing his chariot's left wheel.

Caratacus's friend walked to the car and stooped for a closer examination. He rubbed his fingers over the jagged edges. "This has been welded before, hasn't it?"

"About two months ago."

"Who was the smithy?" Clud asked, raising the corners of his upper lip in disdain.

"Cadwal ap Nes, my father's iron maker."

"Bah, he's an iron breaker. I know him, and he's as useless as a gelding's balls."

"But our father swears by him," Tog said.

"He should swear at him and chop off his head. Take a closer look. See those edges?" he asked, pointing to the black specks around the break. "Those are traces of charcoal, impurities they are."

"So?" Caratacus asked.

"He didn't work them out like a good smith should. That's why the metal weakened and cracked. You came just in time. Had you driven another mile, it would have snapped and ripped off your legs."

Caratacus and Tog looked at one another. Tog's face paled. Heat rushed across his face.

"Don't you worry," Clud assured the young men, "I'll fix her good as new, and this time there'll be no cracking. But before I get to work, you must tell me how you won your heads, Prince Caratacus."

Caratacus related the story, only lying grandly where details were sketchy.

"If you could have only seen Tog wielding the chariot, he's as good as any veteran driver twice his age,"

Caratacus added as he finished his tale. Tog lightly jabbed his older brother in the arm with a fist.

Clud sighed and patted his hefty belly. "Aye, that I could have seen the both of you, but not now. I like food too much, and fat men are forbidden to be warriors."

"Is it true," Caratacus probed, "that twice you were fined the length of your girdle in gold for being too heavy?"

"True enough, but there's more. The Druids never told me exactly what they considered the length of a girdle."

"I don't understand," Tog said.

"After the first time I was fined, I lost weight and shortened my waist band, but they fined me again."

"They only wanted your gold, Clud," Caratacus said. "They knew you're a master goldsmith and iron maker, besides being a warrior."

"You're right, but I couldn't prove it. There are not many like me who can fight and still make jewelry so delicate that kings will pay a fortune for it." Clud looked up and down the village's dusty street. No one was around. "Although your uncle the king won't publicly admit it, he does favor me for my weapons."

Tog gestured with a hand palm outward. "It's said you make the finest swords in the kingdom."

Clud grinned, accepting the princely compliment without comment.

Caratacus had heard that Clud had an uncanny knack for finding special iron-ore bogs, from which top quality iron weapons were made. Even more unusual was his ability to make rare, steel swords, the weapons of kings. Over the years he had ingratiated himself with the warrior class and other artisans, by his craft and other favors, such as repairing weapons, free. *Free* always had its obligations though. Slovenly, he might be, but a fool he was not. If the bronze or silversmiths needed assistance in finishing an artifact in time for a wealthy patron, or the king, he was there to help. People soon forgot why he was removed from the warrior ranks. Now they conveniently overlooked his sloppy appearance and ways, knowing the superb quality brought forth by his gifted fingers.

"Anyway, I'd still take up my sword if the king called me," Clud said, snapping Caratacus out of his pensive mood. "I may be thirty-three, but I'm as good a fighter as ever. Your uncle is a good man, Prince Caratacus."

He raised his hands. "Quit calling me Prince, Clud. To you, I'm Caratacus."

"Aye, that as it should be," Tog said. He stepped closer to Clud. "The same goes for me."

"I'm obliged to both of you. Is your uncle having a victory feast tonight?" Clud asked.

"Yes, I'm the guest of honor for killing Froech the Bandit," Caratacus said.

Clud looked about and back to Caratacus. "I heard rumors he was in Verica's pay."

"That's what my uncle said."

"Then the war has begun." Clud shook his head. "Verica will be out for revenge."

"Aye, my uncle sacked Verica as ruler of the Atrebates nearly ten years ago. He fled to the land of the Regni on the south coast," Caratacus said.

"Somehow he found a way of gaining their throne," Tog said. "For farmers and fisherman, they've done real well for themselves, and Verica knows it. The people were fools to let him become their king."

Clud snorted in disgust.

"My uncle said it wasn't long before Verica organized a strong warrior class loyal to him and ingratiated himself with the Romans," Caratacus said. "And to Uncle Epaticcos's annoyance, he built up a flourishing trade."

"Personally, I wonder how long our uncle will wait before he moves against him?" Tog said.

"Have you already forgotten the message that Uncle Epaticcos told us about, the one Porcius gave our father?" Caratacus asked Tog.

"No," Tog answered.

"Then you remember that the Emperor Tiberius refused to aid Verica if he attempts to retake the Kingdom of the Atrebates, which are now these lands, Uncle Epaticcos's lands."

"So Verica has decided to retake our uncle's home without help from Rome," Tog said.

"That's why Froech stole so many cattle; it's considered an act of war," Caratacus said.

"True," Clud said. "Now you've forced Verica into the open. He'll have to lead his army against the king if his plans are to succeed."

"He won't. We'll see to that," Caratacus said.

"Unless the Roman, Porcius, interferes."

Caratacus's muscles tightened. "Why would he?"

Clud spat. "He sticks his head into anything that's in the interest of Rome."

Caratacus grabbed the handle of the dagger tied to his waistband. "I'd like to see his head stuck on the end of a pike. And I'll see it done."

CHAPTER 6

Adjacent to the king's home, the huge circular hall lit by torches was filled to capacity that night and rang with the sounds of laughter, music, feasting, and drinking. The great, vaulted interior was divided into ten wedge-shaped spaces by wooden partitions running from the outer wall to the huge, open center. The central area contained a circle of stones, forming the hearth and glowing fire pit. All parties could view and speak with one another with little effort. Nine of the ten spaces held a clan chieftain and his group of one hundred warriors and other guests. The tenth and largest wedge belonged to Epaticcos, whose walls were decorated with gold and silver plates, ornaments, hand woven tapestries, and shields of the clans.

Rulers and warriors alike sat on animal pelts upon a reed-covered, earthen floor beside ornately carved pallets heaped with steaming food. Along the high king's partitions, and around the hall's outer corridor, stood his biggest shield-bearing retainers. Behind the seated warriors sat their wives and consorts, other shield bearers, attendants, and slaves. The chieftains and warriors drank beer and uncut Roman wine, some straining the brews through grimy, long-handled moustaches. The women and others received only the wheaten beer, corma.

Caratacus sat cross-legged with the other victors, showing off their new, prized heads placed in oak boxes and preserved in cedar oil. Epaticcos's lesser bards and minstrels strolled among the guests recounting their victory in newly composed ballads. They played on small, delicately painted harps. Caratacus watched the chief bard, clutching a small harp, approach King Epaticcos.

"Great King," the pinched-face bard said, "the songs we play tonight are about your victory over the brigand, Froech. They will last for all time."

"You said that about my last victory," growled the king. He glared at the musician from beneath the bridge of his heavy eyebrows. "It wasn't much of a song."

Caratacus smiled, holding back his laughter.

The bard's face paled, and he held his harp before him. "But Great King, each of your victories is greater than the last. Unfortunately, in the enthusiasm of the greater victory, one sometimes forgets the words of an earlier battle."

Epaticcos snorted and frowned. "In other words, although it has been only four years, you don't think it was much of a victory."

The bard's hands trembled, barely holding onto his instrument. "But, Great Lord, I would never think such a thing. All your victories are great."

"For the sake of your head, you better pray that my next triumph will be the greatest yet." Epaticcos waved him away with a flick of the hand.

The bard bowed and proceeded to sing at the adjoining chieftain's partition.

Caratacus choked in a futile attempt to stifle his laughing. *It serves him right.*

During the feasting, all eyes were drawn time and again to the ghoulish head of Froech. Its matted, blood-spattered hair, gray-pallored skin, and slack jaw were made all the more macabre by the hall's flickering light. The preserved head sat displayed atop an oak box in front of Caratacus's dinner pallet. The king's nephew, dressed in a clean tunic and pair of trousers, sat to his left, the place of honor, with Tog and the other victors nearby, while Havgan, Epaticcos's arch-Druid, sat on his right. Next to the priest was Donn, the king's champion. Behind them sat the women, including Gwynn. Each time Caratacus was complimented, or someone examined his great prize, his pride puffed all the more with bragging and wine.

Caratacus heard his uncle chuckle. He turned and saw Epaticcos lean in the direction of Havgan. "Caratacus must think his prize is the greatest ever taken in battle."

Caratacus was about to protest, but Havgan said quickly, "Even greater than the two paltry heads that your champion took yesterday." The Druid's thin, ascetic face, covered by a black beard falling to his chest, studied the king with dark, piercing eyes.

"Be careful, Priest, that it wasn't yours," the king said with menace as he gulped down a cup of wine. "Caratacus probably believes he can feel the power from Froech's head," he continued, seemingly disregarding any further thoughts about the insult to his champion's prowess.

But I do feel Froech's power running through me. Caratacus couldn't understand why his uncle was mocking him.

The priest persisted. "Isn't that what you believed when you were young, Great King?"

"Of course, but no more. Power comes from within one's self and through experience."

Caratacus held his tongue. *This isn't the place to argue with uncle about it. This is a time to be merry.* He fingered the exquisite golden torc he had taken from the dead bandit. Despite the heat within the hall, he found it cool to his touch. The collar consisted of eight spiraled, gold wires, each formed of eight golden strands, the ends being soldered into sockets of hollowed ring terminals. Each end was decorated with cast reliefs of a dour-faced man wearing the antlers of a stag—Cernunnos—God of deer and other animals.

"You like it, don't you?" Epaticcos asked, interrupting Caratacus's thoughts.

"It's a beautiful torc," the young prince answered. "I'd wager that Froech sliced someone's throat for it."

"I expect you to wear it with the dignity and honor that Froech never possessed," Epaticcos advised.

"I will, Uncle, I will."

Caratacus watched Tog who sat next to him. He had given him his old torc in gratitude for his skillful driving during the battle. He was pleased that Tog wore it with pride. Caratacus's gut instinct told him it wouldn't be long before his younger brother claimed his first head in battle.

* * *

As the night wore on, Caratacus consumed several cups of beer and mead and found himself growing more boisterous and obnoxious about his feats. He staggered as he got up from the furs on which he sat. He reeled as he turned in the direction of Epaticcos's senior warriors who sat near the front. He looked at them through bleary eyes.

"If you warriors are so good," Caratacus said, "why didn't you kill Froech?"

The king's men jeered Caratacus, but none challenged him.

Caratacus grinned. *They're cowards.* "I know why you didn't kill him, 'cause I'm better than the whole lot of you!" He hiccupped.

One pock-faced warrior with a missing left ear stood and shouted, "I'll take you right now, we'll see who's best!"

"Enough!"

Silence engulfed the room as everyone's eyes turned to Epaticcos.

"Sit down, Ermid." The king motioned with his head toward the warrior. He turned to Caratacus. "You, too, Nephew."

Both sat glaring at one another before Caratacus turned his head away.

The chatting among the guests resumed, but Caratacus fumed, humiliated by his uncle. He clenched and unclenched a fist. He had promised Epaticcos he wouldn't consume too much beer or Roman wine, remembering his drunken ride in the chariot the day they left Camulodunum. But the mugs were always refilled, and the serving wenches were friendly.

A young wench carrying a small pitcher stepped between the guests and stopped at the small table before Caratacus and Tog. She stooped and refilled his cup with beer and gave him a wink and smile before moving away. He knew he would have a tumble in the hay with her after the feasting was over.

"Caratacus, you're drunk," Tog muttered. "You're damn lucky Uncle Epaticcos stopped Ermid from challenging you. He'd have killed you."

"He wouldn't have stood a chance," Caratacus muttered. He spotted his uncle watching them. "I'll fight him or anybody."

He looked about and saw Donn, the king's champion, sitting near Epaticcos. Earlier Caratacus had watched him boasting as he seemed to take measure of the other warriors for a possible challenge to a fight. Now he sat drinking beer and chatting with other warriors. *I'll even fight Donn!*

"Might happen yet," Tog said. What are you planning?" Tog asked in a lowered voice, once more flashing a glance in Epaticcos's direction, catching the older man's scowl.

"Nothing, Tog."

Tog crinkled his long forehead and snorted. "I know that look in your eyes, you're scheming something. Every time you're drunk, trouble follows."

Caratacus attempted to focus on his brother's face in the flickering torchlight—now fuzzy—now clear. *I'm not drunk.* "Nothing's going to happen. Now, shut up, and leave me alone!"

"All right, Brother, it's your head!" Tog got up, farted in Caratacus's direction, and joined some companions nearby.

Ignoring the smell, Caratacus turned and saw Epaticcos leaning toward Havgan again. "Do you see what Caratacus is doing?" he heard him saying.

"Yes, Great King, and it doesn't bode well," Havgan said. "He's measuring the other warriors."

They don't realize I can hear them, Caratacus thought.

"He's doing what so many warriors have done before him," Epaticcos said.

Caratacus was puzzled by what his uncle meant.

"Shouldn't you stop him?" Havgan questioned, his voice filled with alarm.

"Why?" the king said. "Let him challenge Donn for the right to the roasted boar's hind quarter, the champion's portion. It's time we tested his metal."

"It may cost him his life," the Druid said.

Epaticcos grinned, exposing his yellowed teeth. "We shall see."

Why shouldn't I? I killed the worst bandit this land has seen in more than one hundred years. I deserve the champion's portion! Caratacus had heard from Epaticcos that when the king's portion was served, each warrior quickly measured his prospective opponent. If he believed that he could not defeat him with a dagger, he went on drinking and boasting and issued no challenge. If he believed he could beat him, he drew more courage from drink and boast and then lived or died.

Earlier, Donn, the king's champion, had been boasting and measuring other warriors. He stopped and sat down and looked in the king's direction. Caratacus noticed Donn had stopped drinking entirely.

Caratacus heard Havgan reminding the king, "You know that you have to honor your champion with the hind quarter?"

"I don't relish the thought of my nephew challenging Donn. He is much stronger and has far greater experience as champion, taking countless heads in battle."

I killed Froech, doesn't that count for something? Caratacus balled his fists before he relaxed seconds later. *Not yet, not yet.*

Two slaves carried a roast boar upon a large, silver platter to the king. As it was placed on the short bejeweled table before him, the king inhaled the aroma of the boar, simmering in its juices. He turned to Donn, his champion, and motioned him over to carve the prized hind leg.

The Great Hall grew quiet. All eyes were upon Epaticcos.

Caratacus worked himself into a rage. The king pulled a knife from a scabbard in his waistband and raised it about his head, the signal that would lead to a challenge. Donn stood, swaggered forward, pulled his dagger, kneeled, and began carving the roast. Caratacus glared at Donn. *By the gods, there isn't any reason I can't do it. Why shouldn't I challenge Don for the champion's portion?*

He sprang to his feet, unsheathed his dagger, which gleamed in the torch light, and pointed it at Donn. "That portion belongs to me! I earned it!"

"By what right have ye earned it, puppy?" Donn laughed as he sliced the boar's hindquarter, and several warriors roared with approval.

"By taking Froech's head in battle!" Caratacus shouted. He reached down, picked up his mug, threw it at the group of laughing men, which immediately silenced them into scowls.

Donn pulled his dagger slowly from the meat and wiped it on his trousers. He calmly raised his head to glare at

Caratacus. "Powerful magic as Froech's head may be, he was a villain not worthy of your wine-soaked challenge to me. Now sit down, lad, before I'm forced to take yours."

"In a dog's eye, you fat, old son of a sow!"

With the speed of a sling stone, a gasp shot through the hall. Being called a son of a sow was the vilest insult one man could hurl at another. Caratacus looked about and realized that his remarks had been a grave mistake, but he stood taller. "If you're the king's champion, waddle over here and prove it."

Donn got to his feet and wiped the boar's grease from his hands onto his breeches.

"Very well, son of Cunobelinos, I had hopes that ye would become my daughter's husband, but now I'll have to find her another mate."

By the gods he is serious. How could I be so stupid! I'm in for the fight of my life! He and Donn squared off and slowly circled one another in the empty space between Epaticcos and the fire pit, knives outstretched, vying for a position of attack. Both glared at one another, sizing up the other's weaknesses. Caratacus made a feint, but Donn danced out of his way and jabbed his right arm, drawing a trickle of blood. Caratacus came around and attempted to get inside of Donn's long, outstretched arm. This time the old veteran's dagger flashed past and nicked his ear.

Donn grinned. "Give it up, laddie, yer no match for me. Otherwise, I'll have to get mean." With that, the subdued diners broke into laughter and jeered Caratacus.

Caratacus's eyes narrowed, and his jaw tightened. "You'll soon find out what *mean* is, Lord Champion."

Again, the crowd roared in laughter and hurled more taunts his way.

Soon Caratacus realized Donn could have killed him twice over with little effort. He could not out maneuver, let alone outfight, this grizzled warrior.

Twice more Donn darted in and out of Caratacus's reach, inflicting minor wounds that stung his right and left arm.

Then a growing number of warriors cheered for the king's foster son as Donn continued toying with him.

Caratacus received another slash to his knife arm, although the bleeding was worse than the wound itself. *I've got to do something before he kills me!*

With a lightning lunge, Caratacus slashed Donn along the ridge of his jaw and jumped away from his counter-lunge. The laughter quickly stopped. Donn's blood dripped onto his best tunic. His weathered face darkened as if to say. *This young whelp means to kill me.*

Donn quickly maneuvered to Caratacus's right side, kicked his right foot from under him, and sent him sprawling to the floor on his stomach, the wind knocked out him.

Caratacus gasped and attempted to regain his breath.

Donn was on him in a flash, placed a powerful knee in his back, and disarmed Caratacus before he could recover his stance.

Gods, is this the end?

As the champion raised his dagger, the king sprang to his feet. "Enough!" he shouted. There was a pregnant pause and again a hush fell over the hall. Epaticcos waited another moment, to make Caratacus feel the humiliation. "Donn, I declare you the victor. And an easy victory at that."

A sigh of relief erupted from the warriors.

"No one wants to see you slain so soon after taking yer first head, lad," Donn said. "However, had it not been fer the king, I'd have taken yer head off faster than a lightning bolt."

Caratacus slowly rose to his knees, shook his head, and turned towards Donn. But he kept his eyes downcast. *I'm the laughingstock of the kingdom. What a damn fool I am. I'm lucky to be alive!*

"Besides," the king said with a chuckle, "we need hotheads such as this young wolf. He has shown his bravery by taking his first heads in battle yesterday and thinks he is worthy of taking the champion's portion tonight. Such audacity is to be admired." This brought cheers and laughter from the drunken crowd.

Caratacus raised his head and locked eyes with Donn. The champion's were icy, although a tight grin crossed his face. He outstretched his hand to Caratacus.

The room grew silent. Humiliated, Caratacus wondered if he should give his to the king's champion. He paused. *If I refuse, everyone in the hall will heap scorn on me for not being man enough to admit defeat.* Caratacus reached up for Donn's hand, and the man yanked him from the ground to his full height. Donn embraced Caratacus with a bear hug, nearly knocking the wind out of him. Cheering and pandemonium broke loose. Caratacus exhaled in relief, realizing he had deserved to lose and was fortunate to be alive. *Didn't Uncle Epaticcos once say when a real man admits defeat, people will respect him all the more?*

As both Caratacus and Donn sat by Epaticcos, the ruler clasped their shoulders with spread hands and said in a voice only Caratacus and Donn could hear, "You have nothing of which to be ashamed, Nephew. Donn has lifted more heads on a ceremonial pike than the Romans have coins. And remember this: you're the only one who had the courage to challenge him, but don't make a habit of it."

The king's champion nodded and took a towel from a slave to wipe the blood from his face. Then he gorged himself with the now cold hindquarter.

Caratacus knew his uncle was right, but he swore to become a better warrior, as great as Donn. If they went to war against Verica, he must improve his fighting skills if he were to survive.

CHAPTER 7

After being assisted from the litter by two huge Libyan slaves, Porcius's body servant came forward and wiped the perspiration from his master's corpulent face with a silk handkerchief. His entourage of slaves and freedmen, including Cyrus the Persian, had halted before Cunobelinos's Great Hall. At any moment, Porcius expected the king's arrival from an inspection of his farmsteads.

"By Apollo himself, this scorching heat reminds me of Rome," Porcius said as he swatted the horse flies buzzing around his head. He waved the servant away. "Don't you think so, Cyrus?"

"Yes, sir," answered his Persian freedman in nearly flawless Latin.

"And to think I came to Britannia to get away from the heat." Porcius removed his wide-brimmed, straw hat, fanned himself, and replaced it upon his balding head.

"Although I have been in your service for five years, I still find these barbaric Britons as insufferable as the weather," Cyrus said.

Porcius raised his head skyward. "By the thundering Jupiter, they're impossible! However," he paused and motioned Cyrus closer, "once you gain their confidence they're your friends for life. You have to know how to deal with their peculiarities, something my fellow countrymen have failed to learn. Of course," he added with a sly grin, "that means more gold for me."

Cyrus scratched his trimmed, black beard, which covered a hair lip, with well-manicured fingers and searched the compound area with his piercing, dark eyes. "I still don't see why you treat these uncouth louts with such respect," he said with a click of the tongue.

"I show them respect, you fool," Porcius admonished, "because they give me trading agreements favorable to Rome. You should know that by now."

Cyrus touched a hand to his chest, covered by a tunic decorated with signs of the zodiac. "Pardon my ignorance, sir."

"Very well. Just keep in mind I receive a share of the revenue, the treasury is filled, and the emperor is happy. I intend to keep it that way." Porcius scanned the chalky path leading to the Great Hall, straining to see any signs of the king's band, hating to be kept waiting. An ox cart filled with dung creaked slowly along the way to the tanner's shop outside the fortress's outer dike, its stink drifting on the hot breeze.

"But didn't you say something earlier this morning about that young prince Caratacus upsetting things?" Cyrus reminded Porcius.

The Roman wiped his sweating hands on the side of his tunic hanging partially over his linen breeches. "Caratacus may have unwittingly ignited the flames of war between King Epaticcos and his cousin Verica by killing Froech. What better excuse could Epaticcos want to launch a war?"

"None, sir—clever indeed."

"Exactly, and that's why it could upset, how shall I say … my business?" Porcius winked.

At that moment High King Cunobelinos and his shield bearers approached the Great Hall through a whitish haze of chalky dust churned by chariots and cavalry escort. A pack of hunting hounds trailed in their wake, barking and yelping, barely staying out of reach of the horses' trampling hooves.

As he drew to a halt, Cunobelinos stepped from his chariot, scowling and slapping dust from his clothes.

"Greetings, High King!" Porcius called in his usual honeyed voice. "Allow me to be the first to congratulate you. Young Caratacus is truly a son worthy of his great father."

"Is he so courageous?" the big chieftain muttered. "The young idiot was a fool not to leave well enough alone. Instead, he had to challenge Donn, Epaticcos's champion. He's bloody fortunate he's kept his head!"

"A foolish oversight on his part, I'm sure," Porcius agreed. "After all, he's young and inexperienced." *More like stupid.*

The king glared at him. "Aye, he has much to learn. But that's not why you are here. What do you want?"

"Quite perceptive indeed," Porcius answered, clearing his throat. "I have a message from Rome," he said, unconsciously assuming an official's voice while patting a fold-pouch in his tunic containing the water-tight tube and scroll.

Cunobelinos slowly pulled off his iron conical helmet. "Another one so soon? It's only been a few days since you gave me the last one at the festival."

"Yes, Great King, that's true," Porcius said.

"Come with me, Porcius, alone," the king commanded, motioning to the Great Hall. "We'll discuss this inside." He signaled to his entourage to wait. The group included his eldest son, Adminios, Oengus, the king's champion and Rhian's foster father, and several clan chieftains. The king nodded toward his arch-Druid, Ibor, to accompany them.

Once within the cavernous building, the two sat upon ornately designed mats near the great hearth, Porcius facing Cunobelinos and Ibor. The interior felt surprisingly cool to Porcius after being out in the stifling heat, and he was only too happy to remove his hat. This intimacy was indeed a sign of friendship between him and the king. Otherwise, Porcius would have stood as Cunobelinos glared down at him from the dais. He scanned the hall, and his eyes found the new tapestry, depicting a scene of hunters attacking a wild boar, hanging from the shadowy wall. Earlier that week Porcius had given the woven cloth to the king as a gift from Emperor Tiberius.

The king called for a slave, who brought silver goblets of Greek Samian wine. The slave placed a tall bronze flagon, decorated with long-tailed monsters and a beaker shaped like a squat-legged lizard with the head of a man, on a jewel-encased pallet next to Cunobelinos. "Now, what is your emperor's message?"

The flabby Roman paused as he glanced at the Druid standing in the pulsating light of the hearth's fire.

Cunobelinos seems to sense his hesitation. "Anything you say to me can be said in front of Ibor."

Porcius crinkled his nose. *Hah! I might as well be talking to every blood-licking Druid in Britannia.*

The Roman removed the water-tight, bronze tube from his tunic pouch. He handed it to the king, who in turn gave it to Ibor. Cunobelinos couldn't read Latin. "The emperor is concerned about the secret alliance you have made with King Verica," Porcius began. "He says—"

"I have made no alliance with Verica, and if I did, it's none of Rome's concern."

"Come now, Great King, do you take the emperor for a fool? He knows you have secretly allied with Verica against your brother, and such an alliance is not in the best interest of Rome. It was dangerous enough that Froech the bandit was in his pay." Porcius surmised that the king must be wondering how Emperor Tiberius found out about it so soon, for Cunobelinos tightly gripped the hilt of his sword.

"My people are my only interest," the king responded. His eyes narrowed and Porcius could see his temple throbbing.

"The stability of Britannia is Rome's concern," Porcius said. He gestured with a hand palm up. "Are they not one and the same, those of Rome and your people? Sources close to the emperor have informed him of your connection with Verica, the Regni King. To deny that is to deny the light of day." He dropped his hand alongside his tunic.

"And I know from whom he received such lies," the king answered, maintaining an even voice while glaring at Porcius.

"You were invited to Britannia as a guest of the High King," interjected the arch-Druid, Ibor, who had opened the cylinder and removed the parchment scroll, "and you can be asked to leave ... with your tail between your legs, if not missing altogether." He smiled, contemptuously dropping the container to the reed-covered-floor.

"True, I'm here by the invitation of your High King," Porcius said, "and the will of Caesar, the Great Tiberius, who has more legions than a tree has leaves and more tails to wag than priests have tongues."

Cunobelinos roared at the Druid's expense, then cleared his throat as if trying to restore the priest's loss of face. "And leaves crumble when stepped upon and then burn easily," he warned.

"Smoke from such a fire can overwhelm the one who set the flame and scorch more than the fields and valleys and forests of your lands," Porcius replied. He locked eyes with the king, who returned his cold stare. For a moment, neither spoke.

"Your Caesar's armies would pay dearly for invading my lands!" the king advised in a cool but menacing voice.

"Invasion? Who said anything about invasion?" Porcius answered slowly, breaking his gaze and shaking his head. "Caesar has no intention of invading your lands, he simply doesn't want war between his friends. He is concerned with regional stability."

"That is of no concern to your emperor, so long as it doesn't interfere with trade with Rome," Cunobelinos warned.

"Then Caesar advises you to stay away from Verica," the emissary sternly warned.

"And I demand that Caesar stay out of my regional affairs!"

Porcius shrugged. "Very well, I regret then to inform you that Caesar will cut all trade with Britannia."

"Your emperor dares to renounce our agreement?"

The Roman answered in an even voice. "Not only does he, but your merchants will be forbidden to conduct business within the boundaries of the Roman Empire, and their goods will be confiscated. The Roman Navy will blockade your ports and commandeer all ships entering imperial waters."

A dark expression crossed Cunobelinos's face, the veiny cords tightening in his neck, but he managed to control his anger. He sat for a few moments, not out of defeat as Porcius surmised, but as was his solemn manner prior to making a major decision. Porcius knew Cunobelinos's moods well enough after spending the last five years at his court. No doubt he was raging within.

"Your kingdom and people have prospered as a result of our trading agreements," Porcius continued. "An embargo would hurt you and other Briton kingdoms far more than it would Rome."

"We would survive."

A sly grin fractured Porcius's face. "Would you?"

Cunobelinos grabbed a cup of wine from the pallet, downed its contents in one long gulp, and quietly returned it to the little table. He faced Porcius and stared through him as if he weren't there. Since coming to Britannia, Porcius had encouraged the king's love of Roman luxuries, such as wine, fine horses from Hispania and Mauretania, silk clothing from Cathay, and gold, plenty of gold. His kingdom couldn't afford the loss in trade or cattle, jewelry, tin, wool, and wheat, which he exchanged for those comforts. The king had admitted, on one occasion when he had been drinking heavily, that most of his power was derived from his people's prosperity.

Porcius poured himself a cup of wine. "To be sure, some ships would sneak through the blockade, and of course you and your fellow rulers could resort to smuggling. But your people would still suffer, and wines such as this would soon dry up."

"He talks too much, sire," Ibor quipped, though his voice lacked authority.

"Let him be! Fools always ramble." The king raised his hand as if in disgust and dropped it to his side.

Porcius sipped his wine. "You know what I say is true. You have a large warrior class to support. They have many tenant farmers from whom they derive their wealth. If the farmers have no place to sell their wheat, your warrior's wealth dries up, and you will be forced to support them from your own coffers."

Cunobelinos remained silent, glowering at Porcius. Ibor fidgeted as if wanting to say something. The king raised an eyebrow in warning.

Porcius grew bolder. "As I have said, you could resort to smuggling, but inevitably that would lead to piracy."

"Are you calling us pirates?"

"Never you, Great King, but there are others, like the Durotrigians and Verica's Regni people, who wouldn't hesitate, and Rome would lump all Britons into the same basket. A Roman blockade force could easily become an invasion fleet."

Porcius prayed that Cunobelinos wouldn't call his bluff. An invasion at this time was out of the question. There were only twenty-eight legions and an equal number of provincial auxiliaries to guard the extensive boundaries of the Roman Empire. No more than three hundred thousand were guarding an empire of seventy-five million. News had recently arrived about a rebellion in Thrace, and there was unrest among the German tribes along the Rhenus frontier. Four legions were tied down keeping the savages in check. Two legions had recently transferred from Syria to aid Porcius's long-time friend Pontius Pilatus, procurator of Judea, in keeping Jewish rebels under control.

So long as the situation remained unstable in Thrace, it was imperative that three legions remained in that turbulent province. The garrisons of the Rhenus and Danubus would have to be stripped if there were to be an invasion of Britannia. The frontiers would be left wide open to invasion by the German tribes. *No, Rome has no legions to spare.*

"Go on, I'm still listening, Roman."

The high king startled Porcius from his thoughts.

"It is in your interest," Porcius spoke again, "and that of Britannia's, that you prevent the war that is about to occur between Verica and your brother. You have the power and influence to stop it."

Cunobelinos pondered the situation for a few moments, biting his lower lip. He turned to Ibor and again to Porcius. "Very well, Roman, I will intervene, but Caesar is to call off his dogs!" The high king leaned forward, his head almost touching Porcius's face.

"Consider it arranged," Porcius replied. Cunobelinos had capitulated, a rare victory indeed. Unconsciously, the Roman wiped a sweaty hand on his linen tunic, the inside of his garment damp across his protruding stomach. Only now did he realize how draining the meeting with the king had been. He must be all the more cautious in the future. *Cunobelinos will find a way to avenge himself for this day.*

* * *

Porcius left the Great Hall, thin clouds drifted across the sweltering afternoon sun, shadowless upon the great, open field outside the king's compound. While he and his retinue hiked along the dirt path skirting the chalky turf, the Roman spotted Rhian and other young men and women undergoing combat training. Nearly a head taller and wearing an ocean-blue tunic and matching breeches, Rhian stood out among her companions. She wore her sandy hair tied in a single braid that cascaded down to the middle of her back. The youths drilled under the critical eyes of the twin sisters, Gwyther and Modron.

Sitting in his jouncing litter, Porcius motioned Cyrus, who walked alongside, to move closer. "Let's watch these barbarians for a few minutes. I find the training of women for combat fascinating and yet appalling at the same time."

"No woman should be a warrior," Cyrus said with a smirk.

"I disagree with many of your Persian ways," Porcius said, "but on this issue, I concur."

Porcius motioned his retinue to halt. They watched as one group of dirt-encrusted and sweaty trainees drilled with leather slingshots against wooden, human-shaped posts erected near the edge of the dry moat and palisade surrounding the Great Fort. A deafening staccato of thuds rolled in like hail stones whenever scar-faced Modron, dressed in a fading, red, plaid tunic and matching trousers, barked the order for slingers to fling the hard, black stones at the splintering targets.

Meantime, Porcius spied another group, including Rhian and her friend, whom Porcius recognized as Morgana, hurling javelins at a set of taller, thinner posts. Rhian threw her last weapon, barely missing the post's head.

"Gods dammit, daughter of Donn!" Gwyther, the other twin, roared. "How many times have I told you to keep your aim low! At least you'll hit his lovely crotch if you miss his heart."

Porcius raised an eyebrow while Cyrus grinned.

"Sorry, Mistress Gwyther," Rhian answered in a trembling voice, which carried on the hot breeze. She wiped the sweat from her face and brushed back loose strands of hair from her forehead.

"*Sorry* will get your pretty head on an enemy's pike, dearie," Gwyther said in a snarling voice. "Now throw another one!"

Rhian's short, stocky friend, Morgana, handed her another weapon. She balanced it in her hand until it apparently felt right. The daughter of Donn brought the javelin back and above her head. Placing the weight on her right foot, she took three steps forward and flung the deadly missile. With a heavy thud, the javelin slammed into a post center, its mass quivering from side to side.

Porcius turned to Cyrus. "Impressive—for a woman."

Cyrus curled his lips into a frown. "Undignified is more like it."

"That's better!" Gwyther said in a loud but pleasing voice. The big woman, her spiked hair washed with lime, looked about, noticing the other girls and boys had stopped to watch Rhian. She also saw Porcius and his people. She spat in their direction and turned back to the trainees. "What are you slimy turds staring at? Get back to work or I'll tie you to the backstop of this post while I throw at its front!" Gwyther stepped to her right, and taking long, lumbering strides, headed for a group of slingers.

The two amazons kept up their string of curses.

"My gods," Porcius said, "they sound like Roman drill centurions."

"Probably worse," Cyrus said.

Rhian and the other youths continued their training.

Cyrus crinkled his nose. "I wonder how long they have been training today. Even from where we are standing, they stink."

"They train at least three to four hours every afternoon during the summer, and Rhian is known to train harder than any of them. Despite that, she is also known for her weaving and horse riding skills."

Cyrus snorted. "She should stick to weaving."

"That won't happen. Rhian is a member of the warrior class, and her father is Donn, King Epaticcos's champion. She is expected to learn the art of war."

"I can't imagine a Roman or Persian woman in combat." Cyrus shook his head. "They belong at home, not on the battlefield."

"I agree, but I hear Celtic women fight like lions. It's apparently true if those two scarred, demonic twins, Gwyther and Modron, are any indication."

Porcius was aware that the Catuvellauni and Trinovantes, tribes ruled by Cunobelinos, had been at peace with the surrounding tribes for five years, but summer was the season of war, and they had to be prepared. The role of women and young men not of warrior age was to defend the tribal capital of Camulodunum from surprise attack when the men were off to war.

"Is it not true most of the boys and girls seek out Rhian's advice and leadership?" Cyrus asked.

"What you say is true, Cyrus. She may prove to be a dangerous adversary if Rome goes to war with these people."

Porcius waved forward a young, Greek slave who wiped his face with a silk cloth.

"Watch it, you lout," Porcius said. "Are you trying to gouge my eyes out?" He shoved him away.

Wide-eyed, the slave stood shaking in his sandals and stuttered, "N ... no, Master, n ... never."

"Next time it happens, I'll sell you to the Britons," Porcius said. "They are not as kind as I am. Get out of my sight!"

The slave scurried away.

Cyrus watched as the young man disappeared within Porcius's entourage. He turned to Porcius. "If you like, I could sell the fool once we returned home."

For a split second, Porcius scowled at the Persian, then a knowing grin crossed his fleshy lips. "You are very presumptuous, Cyrus, but perceptive."

Porcius pulled off his hat and wiped his eyebrows and forehead before placing the cover back on his head. "It's time to leave, I've seen enough. We shall pay a visit to King Verica. I must persuade him not to go to war against King Epaticcos. He must listen to reason. It's in his interests and that of Rome, especially Rome, not to wage war."

Cyrus nodded. "May he be wise enough to listen to your advice, but I doubt it."

CHAPTER 8

After a half-day voyage by a coastal merchant ship from Camulodunum down the southeastern coast to Noviomagnus, capital of the Regni, a seasick Porcius arrived at Verica's kingdom early in the afternoon.

In his misery, Porcius was oblivious to the numerous merchant ships tied up along the quay, the stacks and rows of goods spread along the dock, and noise from the dozens of slaves and free workers carrying and loading freight in awaiting carts and wagons. He stepped onto the dock, assisted by Cyrus and a slave, where they took off his protective linen cloak, soiled by the spray of his vomit. Thank Jove, his tunic and breeches had been spared of that indignity. His head spun and body swayed as if still aboard ship. He called for his litter, which had been unloaded, now sitting on the wooden dock. "Help me to it," he ordered. The Persian and the servant held Porcius by both sides of his corpulent body by the arms and escorted him to the cushioned chair. He sat upon the sagging seat and leaned slightly backwards within the protective shade of the sedan's canopy and caught his breath. His mouth was parched, engulfed by the sour taste of vomit. "Bring me water!" he commanded. Although a cool breeze drifted on the gray-green water of the harbor's surface, Porcius perspired, and he wiped the sweat from his face and forehead with a perfumed cloth handed to him by a slave.

Within a few heartbeats, a slave brought a goatskinned bag of water, uncorked, and handed it to his master.

Grabbing it with both hands, he gulped its contents, choking and sputtering as he did, before passing it back to the servant.

"I hate the sea!" Porcius rasped. "I hate ships!"

"I know, sir," Cyrus said in a soothing voice as he hovered by his patron's side. "I'm sorry there is so little we can do for you."

"How many times did I vomit on this wretched voyage?"

Cyrus crinkled his nose. "I lost count."

"If this journey were not so damn important, I would have traveled the long way around by land."

Cyrus fixed his dark eyes seaward. "You had no choice. Sailing down the coast was the most direct way."

"In any event, we did this on short notice. Now, I have to send a messenger ahead to let King Verica know we are here."

"You realize he will be surprised by your visit—it has been awhile." Cyrus scratched his long nose. "I hope he will be pleased to see you."

Porcius shrugged. "We get along well enough, I'm sure he will be. For him, it will be an excuse to throw a feast and more drinking on his part."

"Something for which that pig is notorious." He spat out the words.

"Agreed, but it's called prosperity. He is a Roman lackey at heart. It should work to our advantage—I must persuade him not to invade King Epaticcos's lands."

"May your gods be with you."

Porcius called for and then sent the slave ahead to notify King Verica of their arrival.

Feeling better, Porcius gave the order to move out as six Libyan slaves lifted and carried his litter, with Cyrus walking at his side, followed by the rest of his retinue of twenty freedmen and slaves. Leaving the sprawling port, which consisted of three adjoining inlets that served as Noviomagnus's flourishing seaport, they proceeded uphill toward the king's fortress. The stronghold was built in a similar manner to those of Camulodunum and Caleva, constructed with three protective dikes surrounding the fort's high walls containing the king's great hall, homes, and a supporting village of merchants and artisans.

* * *

That evening, Porcius dined with the king in the Great Hall. Built of wattle and daub, the inside was framed by ornately carved pillars, the walls lined with battle shields, animal pelts, and elaborate Roman tapestries. Two ancient ceremonial drums, no longer used, lay on their sides, one along each side of the wall. Covered with taut skins encircling their round frames, they stood half the length of a tall man. Bleached human skulls tightly ringed the top side of each drum, secured by long dried cords.

In the middle of the room a female slave turned an immense boar on a spit over the great hearth. Another young slave woman basted the meat with a rag dipped from a jar of juices, which dripped down the side of pork and sizzled in the hot coals.

On both sides of the fire ring, facing the king's table, Verica's warriors and minor chieftains sat in pairs upon wolf skins on the straw-covered, dirt floor at short-legged tables. Dressed in their best tartan tunics and breeches, they wore gold torcs about their necks and bejeweled armlets and rings. Porcius watched in disgust as the barbarians ate steaming platters of food and drank beer from cups on their tables with gusto, ripping meat from joints with bare hands or daggers, slurping their drinks, belching and farting loudly. Porcius's entourage dined among them, while Cyrus and his scribe sat together near the front.

After Verica formally welcomed Porcius, they dined together at the heavy oak table raised on a platform above the floor. Verica, tall and oxen-chested with a long face and a chin chiseled in granite, had a thick drooping moustache that covered his slit mouth. Five vicious wolfhounds lay about his feet. On the king's right sat Porcius, to his left Verica's arch-Druid. On their table sat dishes of mutton, venison, steaming vegetables, imported olives, beer, and wine. Porcius and Verica quietly conversed between bites of food and drinking of beer and wine. Porcius explained Rome's concern about maintaining stability among the British tribes if they expected Rome to continue trading with their people.

"Rome needs me more than I need Rome," Verica snapped. His baritone voice swept the hall's length, and his cruel gray eyes glared at Porcius from a face scarred by dozens of battles. At the sound of his voice, the giant hall went silent. Only the sizzling of the roasting boar echoed through the place.

A lifetime seemed to pass as Porcius considered his next words. *I don't give a damn if the king is offended, I must be honest with him.* "You are mistaken in your belief, Great King," Porcius said. "Rome doesn't need anyone." He wanted to add, *You ignorant barbarian! Compared with the rest of the empire, your trade with Rome is but a pittance.* But he kept his tongue.

"Then why do you trade with us?"

Porcius gestured toward the guests in the hall with a fleshy hand and back to the king before lowering it to his side. "Because you and your people crave Roman luxuries. Our wine, pottery, iron and copper wares, weapons, jewelry, not to mention silk from the East. Rome gives you an outlet for your wool, tin, slaves, and other goods."

The nostrils of Verica's flat, broken nose flared. "There are other ways."

"Oh, I suppose so." Porcius sighed. "It's called piracy and smuggling."

Verica swilled another bowl of corma beer and belched. "The Greeks and others have traded with us long before you Romans came."

"True, but," Porcius hesitated and glared at Verica, "now Rome controls who enters and leaves these ports. The Roman navy can blockade at will, you know that to be true. Consider this: because of us, the peoples of this land have more trade and access to goods than ever before— from all over the world. As I explained to you earlier, Emperor Tiberius will not hesitate to cut off all aid to all British tribes if you invade the lands now ruled by your cousin, King Epaticcos. Do you really want that to happen?" Porcius's spies had informed him that Verica profited from the kingdom's flourishing maritime trade with Gaul and the rest of Britannia. The king's main seaport at the base of his capital, Noviomagnus, was one of the busiest on the southern coast. Regni seamen were among the best in all the land, but many were known to be notorious pirates and smugglers.

Tossing back his head, covered by a thick crop of greasy hair, the king slurred, "I have no quarrel with Epaticcos."

"That's not what I have heard," Porcius replied.

"Eh, what do you mean?" He wiped the gray moustache with a greasy palm, then dried it on his purple and white, striped tunic.

"You say you are a friend of Rome. Are you?"

"More than you think. Why should I make her my enemy?" Verica patted the ample buttocks of the female slave refilling his bowl.

"In other words, despite the fact that Epaticcos expelled you from the lands of the Atrebates, you have no ambitions to retake your lost kingdom?"

"Why should I when I rule this land and its people?" He gestured to the chieftains and warriors present. "They are far better than the Atrebates." A loud murmur in agreement rose from the group. Verica's eyes measured Porcius's cold, steely stare, then returned to the serving woman's plump arse. He patted her again and waved her away.

"Wise, indeed," Porcius said.

"I said I'm not interested, but if I were, I would do it on my own," Verica reaffirmed, his face close to Porcius.

The Roman balled a fist beneath the table, the nails digging into his palm, to keep from grimacing at Verica's foul breath.

The king sat back in his chair and broke into a hearty laugh. He glanced along the table and to his minor chieftains and warriors sitting below him who laughed agreeably. One wolfhound howled, followed by the other four sitting by the king's chair, in an off-key, canine chorus. Verica kicked one closest to him, forcing a yelp. The others stopped and fought over the bone he threw them.

When the laughing subsided, Porcius turned his face toward the king. "It may be well and good that you are not seeking Rome's aid, but have you considered another fact?" He held a hand, palm upward.

"Eh, what's that?"

"Cunobelinos personally gave me his word that he refuses to ally with you should you move against his noble brother, Epaticcos."

Verica remained expressionless as he studied the Roman, but he had to be swelling with rage. *No doubt he wonders where I obtained my information. Even now as he scans his warriors for the informer, he won't find one.*

"Watch your tongue, Roman," Verica growled. "Cunobelinos is not my ally."

Porcius had deliberately baited him, a dangerous move. Although he was a Roman and neutral, acting as a diplomat, his head still might land on the end of a bloody pike. From this point on, he decided to choose his words carefully. Dozens of hostile faces, including Gwynedd, Verica's beak-nosed son, glared at him with hands on sword hilts.

"Perhaps I spoke too hastily," Porcius said in a milder tone. He unconsciously scratched the edge of his flabby jaw. "I have a plan that would be beneficial to you and Rome. However, I suggest we discuss it in private."

Verica turned to his chief Druid who had remained silent during the conversation. The priest nodded.

"Agreed," the king said.

Porcius had allowed the king to save face. He had been informed by his spies that Verica hated anything that interfered with his eating and drinking.

"Tomorrow is soon enough," the king continued. "Tonight, you are my guest. Drink, eat, and get drunk." He clapped his hands, and slaves appeared with jugs of corma and two huge golden drinking bowls. "To friends and Rome," Verica toasted, and both men swilled the entire contents in one gulp.

* * *

The next morning Porcius and Cyrus met with Verica and his advisors in the Great Hall where they sat at the long table. Servants served each man a cup of beer and then departed. Porcius knew Verica to be a crafty, cruel, opportunist who would pounce upon any weakness like a hawk on a rodent. Every word must be measured.

As he sat across the bench from Verica, Porcius outlined his scheme. "If you promise to leave Epaticcos and the Atrebatic territories alone, I will amend your current trade agreements with Rome to increase your profit margin."

Verica took a swig of beer from a silver goblet. He belched and, for split second, studied Porcius with a grin, a gap appearing through his black teeth. "You still believe I will invade his lands?"

"Your word is good enough for me, Great King, but it is Rome who wants assurances, that's why I am offering you an incentive in case you have second thoughts."

"What is your offer?"

"A ten percent increase in your profits."

Verica slammed his cup on the table, beer splashing on its smooth surface. "You think I'm a beggar? Your offer is fit for dogs!"

Porcius suspected it was more than Verica had hoped for.

Verica swilled his beer and shouted for a servant to refill his cup and wipe the table dry. After the servant obliged him and left, the haggling continued for another hour.

By the time Porcius had increased the offer to twenty-five percent, he thought they might have reached an impasse. The king sat silently for the last few minutes as if pondering what to say next. Porcius speculated on the crafty Verica's thoughts. A half smile formed beneath Verica's thin moustache.

"We have decided," Verica gestured to Porcius magnanimously, "that your offer is acceptable. Come, let's seal the agreement as a friend of Rome."

Relieved, but hiding his disbelief, Porcius wasn't finished. "Before we do, I ask for a token gesture to show your sincerity."

"Such as?" He lifted a mug and gulped loudly.

"Send word to Epaticcos that you pledge not to invade his kingdom."

"What!" Verica roared, spewing a blizzard of beer. "Do you take me for a liar? You dare doubt the king's promise?"

Porcius raised a hand in deference. "Not for a moment, Great King." *I know he lies!*

"We'll not send any message, unless it is through you. He can take my word as king and warrior, or there isn't any agreement with Rome."

"By your word, it shall be as you say, Great King." Porcius knew he had trapped Verica into making a public pledge. The king had to keep his vow for the sake of his people. Outwardly, Verica hid his true sentiments, but inside, there was no doubt in Porcius's mind the king fumed.

"Now we'll drink a toast," the king commanded.

As Porcius drank the warm corma, he planned his journey to Epaticcos's kingdom and prayed Verica would keep his promise.

CHAPTER 9

LATE AUGUST, AD 27

Porcius arrived in Caleva on a humid evening two weeks later. No sooner had he arrived when he and his entourage of freedmen, including Cyrus the Persian, and slaves trudged up the trackway to the fortress leading to the king's Great Hall. Halfway up the hill, Porcius stopped to catch his breath. As he shook the dust from his tunic and attempted to cool himself, he glanced back down the grade, peering beyond the squalid village to the surrounding plains and the impassible forests at its edge. *An enemy can be seen coming for miles.* The stronghold was ideally located on high cliffs with the only approach by narrow road. Unlike Verica's stronghold, were the Romans to invade, taking this hill would prove costly.

Although evening was upon them and dark shadows covered the promontory, the day's heat lingered like a hot towel from the sweat room in a Roman bath. Porcius perspired profusely in a long, white tunic and his plaid trousers. He detested this putrid weather and the foul mood it placed him in. Earlier, as the group was about to start the hike up to the king's citadel, the Roman complained out loud how much he hated climbing hills and steep roads. When a slave suggested he would be more comfortable if he weren't so fat, Porcius lost his temper, slapped, and kicked the poor wretch. Porcius realized the slave deserved punishment for being disrespectful, but he shouldn't have beaten him since he had a point. Now Porcius loathed himself even more than the heat. *I must get into a cheerful mood, otherwise, my mission may fail. I can't afford Emperor Tiberius's displeasure.*

Porcius and his escort resumed their trek up the steep road. As his party neared the hilltop and approached the stockade's main gate, Porcius reminded himself that the journey from Camulodunum to the Atrebatic capital was essential to persuade Epaticcos against waging war with King Verica. *The man was a fool to plan a campaign without the support of his brother, Cunobelinos.* Although Verica had denied any intention of attacking Epaticcos, Porcius knew Verica was a liar. That was why it had been essential for the Roman to renegotiate a more favorable trade agreement on Verica's behalf in hopes of stemming any future attack on Epaticcos. Porcius was confident that his plan would satiate the king's greed.

Unfortunately, persuading Epaticcos was a different matter. The king was planning a counter strike of his own against his hated cousin.

Porcius knew he must stop the senseless slaughter before it began. Otherwise, despite the fact the army and its resources were stretched nearly to the breaking point, he feared Rome would launch an invasion against the southern kingdoms to restore order. The money paid to him by the tribal kings to buy influence would dry up. *That* he couldn't afford.

Porcius confided to Cyrus, who walked by his side. "I've been in Britannia for more than five years, and I still can't get over how volatile these people are. It doesn't seem to matter to what tribe they belong."

Cyrus scratched his beard, nodded, and answered in almost flawless Latin, "Lord, they resort to violence at the slightest provocation. In all Persia, only the Afghans are like these Britons—barbarians."

"Confidentially, I admire the Britons' simplistic approach," Porcius said. "Kill your enemies and conquer their lands."

A crooked smile crossed the Persian's lips. "Indeed, a policy swift and uncomplicated ... if successful."

"Of course," Porcius sniffed, "it's totally uncivilized as it would put all politicians like myself quickly out of business should all countries adopt such policies."

Cyrus looked around. "You will not have to trouble yourself about that I am sure, my lord."

"Quite true. Actually, these Atrebates have a reputation for being an easygoing people, but as far as I'm concerned, they are still Britons and thus unpredictable."

Whenever Porcius dealt with any British tribe, he forced himself to portray an illusion of confidence and ease, but he kept a watchful look out of the corner of his eye, and an ear cocked for the slightest suspicious sound. For many years, Porcius had survived the intrigues of court, barbarian and Roman alike, with a glib tongue and quick wits.

To Porcius's relief, he and his entourage finally arrived at the top of the hill. They were met at the main gate of Caleva by an armed detail of twenty of Epaticcos's warriors. The Roman was used to being greeted by soldiers, so the sight of their swords and spears did not bother him. He and his people had wisely left their weapons in the supply wagons with their retinue at an inn outside of the village at the foot of the hill.

"The king is expecting you at the Great Hall," the tall captain said. Before Porcius could answer, the commander turned and said over his shoulder, "Follow me."

The group trudged through the narrow, dusty streets between the wattle and daub huts where the Britons lived. The aroma of baking bread and roasting meat drifted through open doors while smoke from cooking hearths curled upward through holes in the hovels' conical roofs. The sound of a baby crying came from a hut, followed by comforting words from the mother. Porcius skirted a pile of fresh horse dung, the disgusting smell seeping into his nostrils. He coughed and spat.

The party halted before the entrance of the Great Hall, a long building of logs, roofed with reeds.

"Your people will stay out here," the captain said. "You go in—alone."

Porcius shrugged—this was nothing new. He turned to Cyrus and told him to take charge of the retinue and then entered the building.

Inside, the Roman stopped briefly, allowing his eyes to adjust to the dim light. The hall reeked of sweating bodies mingled with the acrid smell of pitch and tar from the burning torch lights. Making matters worse, the king had ordered the chamber sealed. In the noisy, crowded hall, Porcius wiped his face and forehead several times with a silk handkerchief. *By Jupiter's balls, it's times like this that I wish I was thin. But I love luxury, pretty boys, and rich food too much.* He sighed and glanced about, sizing up prospective young warriors mixed in the assembly, but shook his head. Not one of the savages suited his taste. *Bathless wretches!*

As often as Porcius had addressed the tribal kings and chieftains of Britannia, he still felt uneasy, not of the rulers themselves, but of the glaring hostile eyes of ever-present warriors. This audience was no exception. Scores of smelly, unwashed savages stood in the chamber near the Great Hearth. King Epaticcos was holding a council of war, and only warriors were admitted. Among them stood Caratacus, nearly a head taller than the younger fighters with whom he mingled. The prince folded his arms across his sun burnt chest and glared at the emissary.

Porcius approached Epaticcos, who sat on a fur-covered chair, his chieftains and Druids standing together on both sides of his throne. The Roman stopped and bowed slightly. Silence rolled over the crowded hall like a heavy fog.

Epaticcos narrowed his eyes. "I know why you are here, Roman. Speak."

"There are rumors that you and your cousin, Verica, are about to go to war with one another." The Roman paused and cleared his throat. In the shadowy light Epaticcos's face appeared as stone, the lines like cracks in granite. Porcius continued. "If you fight, this will be detrimental to yours and Verica's tribe and to Rome. The losses incurred by both sides would be high in soldiers and revenue. Do you honestly believe you could pay your annual tribute to Rome if this happens?"

Epaticcos's warriors erupted with jeers and catcalls; the only losses would be heads of their enemies.

The king, armed with a jeweled ceremonial sword and wearing chain-mail armor over a red and gold tunic, motioned his scarred hand for silence. "Proceed."

"Wouldn't payment in cattle and gold, rather than lives, be a more acceptable solution, Great King?" Porcius suggested.

"Have you made that proposal to Verica?"

"I have. He assures me that he will not wage war on you or your kingdom."

"Verica is a treacherous liar, Great King," said Havgan, the chief Druid, who stood next to Epaticcos.

Epaticcos chuckled. "Let him finish, Priest, though I find a grain of sand has greater value than the word of Verica." As if on cue, the warriors roared in laughter.

Porcius glanced about and spotted Caratacus. He glared at the Roman as if challenging him. Porcius turned back to the king and grinned weakly. "But he is your cousin. Can't you trust a blood relative?" He already knew the answer.

"I trust no one, especially Verica. However ...," Epaticcos paused a moment as if for emphasis, "if you provide me proof of his assurances that he will pay me in cattle and gold, then I may consider the matter settled."

"The only thing Verica will understand is losing his head!" shouted Donn, the king's champion. He made a slicing motion across his throat.

One of his chieftains said, "Don't trust him, Great King! War is the only way to settle this."

Behind Porcius, the warriors shouted in unison, "Aye!"

"Please, Great King," Havgan pleaded, "don't listen to this Roman lackey's words, he's Tiberius's court-fool! My sources say Verica, even as we sit, is preparing for war."

Porcius drew a handkerchief from within the fold of his tunic and wiped his hands. "But your nephew, Prince Caratacus, killed Froech. Bandit though he was, his loss has hurt Verica badly. He was one of his best leaders. Verica will not risk war anytime soon."

"Bah!" Caratacus's uncle snapped as he tugged on his long, drooping moustache. "That was a skirmish!"

Porcius sensed Epaticcos was playing a game of words. Reports had indicated the so-called skirmish had been a pitched battle. Killing Froech was a serious matter in resolving the dispute.

Epaticcos motioned with outstretched arms toward his warriors. "What's life to a warrior? You've been among us long enough, Roman, to know that by our deaths we are glorified." He placed the fingertips of both hands and thumbs together and rested his elbows on the arms of the throne. He looked over his hands to the gathered host. "A good warrior doesn't die on his bed-pallet." The high king pulled his fingers apart and raised his hands. "That's for Romans. Death is to be met on the battlefield. It's the only real glory and pride for any warrior, no matter what his tribe."

His warriors and chieftains interrupted with a series of "Ayes!" and other affirmations of loyalty.

"If we be taking a few heads with us, all the better," Donn interjected.

A murmur interrupted the discussion. The same captain who had led Porcius into the Great Hall rushed into the chambers escorting a small, dusty man in wolves' skins. Porcius recognized the unwashed man as one of the leaders of the forest people known as the Sidhe who were spread throughout southern Britannia.

Porcius recalled that when Epaticcos became king of the Atrebates, he had found it to his advantage to treat those small, dark people well and made an alliance with their headmen to provide him with intelligence as to other enemy tribes. In return, they were not enslaved, and he conducted trade at fair prices. Epaticcos had kept his word. A wise move. After the suspicious Sidhe got over their initial mistrust, they provided the king with a wealth of information. They were rumored to perform feats of magic and cast spells on their enemies. Porcius neither had seen nor heard of anyone being the victim of their deeds.

"Great King," the captain said, "this friend of our people has a message of great urgency. Please, let him speak."

Epaticcos nodded to the shaggy-haired leader.

"Great King of the Atrebates," the Sidhe leader said, "the Regni king, Verica, and his thieves have invaded our lands, and be two days journey from here with a warrior horde."

70

Stunned, Porcius choked and attempted to catch his breath. For a moment he couldn't move. Despite the possibility of Verica reneging on the new agreement made with Porcius, he had believed Verica would keep his word. Seldom fooled, he had completely misread Verica. His sixth sense had advised him against trusting the man, knowing the Regni king was treacherous. But he had judged his movements correctly in the past. Now, Verica was marching toward Caleva.

Epaticcos gave Porcius a scathing look before turning back to the head man. "How many does he bring?"

"At least two thousand on foot and another thousand by horseback and chariots."

"You have served us well. I'll listen to the other details later." The hairy, little man melted into the shadows.

Epaticcos turned to Havgan. "Again your sources proved correct." Havgan smugly nodded. The king glared at Porcius in the mesmerizing torchlight. Silence enveloped the hall, and Porcius wiped his hands on the side of his tunic.

"There is your answer, Roman, no war, eh!" the king snarled. "You've heard with your own ears. I have no choice but to defend my people. Tell your emperor it is so!"

"I'll return to Noviomagnus at once," Porcius said quickly, desperately trying to regain lost face. "I'm sure I can persuade King Verica to go back to his lands."

"Your useless gestures are too late, Roman," Epaticcos said. "You were foolish enough to believe his lies. *I'm* not!" He dismissed Porcius with a fly-chasing wave.

"Councilors, gather round! I have no more time for fools."

The clan chieftains quickly surrounded the king. "Call out your warriors this night and bring them to Caleva. We march to battle with the rising of the sun. There'll be plenty of heads and glory for all!" An enthusiastic cheer, led by Donn, rang through the Great Hall. Standing near the front, Caratacus grinned and slapped the shoulders of fellow warriors around him. A few boasted about how many they would kill in the forthcoming battle.

Over the boisterous sounds of the chieftains, Porcius said forcefully to the king, "When your army goes to meet

Verica, I too will be there!" The warriors quieted to hear their king's reply.

"Why?" Epaticcos inquired suspiciously, squinting his eyes.

"Caesar will demand an accurate account of the battle. As you've pointed out, I have already witnessed your being invaded and forced to fight."

Havgan's lean figure turned toward the Roman and jabbed a long, bony finger. "This man must be forbidden from following our army. He is a spy."

"Of what concern is it of ours if he's mad enough to risk his life?" Epaticcos waved a hand.

The Druid colored. "He … he has no right to interfere or report our affairs or those of any other Briton tribe to the Romans. Our wars are our concern."

Epaticcos nodded and leaned slowly forward, jutting his bearded chin at Porcius. "And why is it so important that you observe our campaign, Roman?"

"As an impartial observer it is my duty to report to the emperor the facts as they really occur," Porcius replied. "It's obvious you have been provoked, and in this instance, it is time to jerk the dog to heel."

The king seemed to consider his remarks. "You came in peace, Roman," he said, "so I give you permission to follow, but at your own risk. I'll spare no warriors for your protection."

Havgan twisted his mouth as if in disgust. "Great King, if you allow him to follow, it could have devastating consequences. Should he be killed, by either side, Rome will surely invade our lands, and there would be war for a hundred years."

"I have no fear for my safety," Porcius said. "I still wield a sword as well as I did when a tribune in the army chasing Judean zealots. And I have loyal freedmen as retainers, all trained for my defense." This was a lie. Porcius unconsciously pulled on the left sleeve of his tunic. "I'm known throughout the island as Porcius, merchant and emissary, friend of the Britons," he bragged. This was true. *No one will harm me.* "Furthermore, word that you sanctioned my presence is more protection than a legion of Roman soldiers." The king sat taller at this remark. "And since I'll be wearing a Roman garb," Porcius added, "I hardly think I'll be taken as an enemy by either side. And, if need be, I'll act as emissary between your forces if there is any indication that a truce might be arranged."

"The gods damn yer truce!" Donn shouted. "This is the time fer heads!" A roar of approval erupted from the chieftains and warriors, including an enthusiastic Caratacus.

Despite the shouts and exhortations by his champion and warriors, a wry smile crossed the king's mouth. Porcius knew the wisdom of his council was not lost upon Epaticcos.

But will both sides honor my neutrality? For all his bombastic rhetoric, by following the king's army, he might not make it home alive.

CHAPTER 10

The following three days it poured. Steaming rains drenched Caratacus's tunic and breeches. He rubbed dripping water, running down his face from the hood of his woolen cloak, as he and Tog pushed their chariots out of one mud hole after another. This was weather that demoralized the soul and hindered all movement, heavy and intense. Rolling thunder exploded and thumped without end, denying sleep to everyone. Blinding sheets of rain whipped over the countryside, filling the cracked, parched earth with much needed moisture. Summer had been unusually hot and dry in southern Britannia, which spelled drought in a land where it rained throughout the year. The peasants welcomed the life-giving waters for their thirsty crops. But rain was a warrior's enemy, confounding troop movements of friend and enemy alike.

Dozens of cursing riders dealt with the chalky ooze. Following behind the charioteers, thousands of warriors on foot slogged through the quagmire as they moved towards Bagshot Heath.

"Gods, will the rain ever stop?" Tog complained.

"I hope so, even the enemy can't move," Caratacus said.

"But our warriors will die of sickness."

"Not if they keep moving. More get sick in camp than on the march. Let Verica and his warriors burn with fever."

They jumped aboard the chariot, and Tog grabbed the reins. With a cluck of his tongue and snap of the reins, the ponies lurched ahead on the muddy pathway.

"All the same, why did they have to invade our lands?" Tog asked.

"Don't you remember what Uncle Epaticcos told us?" Caratacus said. "These were once part of Verica's kingdom. He wants them back, that's why our uncle is driving the army so hard. He's looking for the most advantageous place to block Verica's advance."

At the age of twenty-three, Verica had lost the Atrebatic throne while attempting consolidation of his power. Epaticcos, allied with Druids and chieftains favorable to him, took advantage of his vulnerability and easily overthrew the young king. Caratacus had heard stories that Verica swore undying revenge against Epaticcos. The time for that vengeance was at hand.

Epaticcos drove his warriors mercilessly through the torrential downpour. Evening fell before he ordered his army to halt and pitch camp. The rain subsided to a light drizzle. The warriors prayed the weather would change by morning and watched the sky.

In the king's large, goatskin tent, lit by several smoky olive-oil lamps, Caratacus and Tog took a light meal of bread, cheese, and beer with their uncle and his champion, Donn. While they dined, a messenger arrived. His sodden clothing smelled of horse sweat and steamed in the tent's warm confines. As the warrior approached in the shadowy light, Epaticcos raised his eyebrows. He turned to Donn, who shrugged.

"What news do you bring us on this ungodly night?" the king asked. "It's too wet even for old Taranis."

The young warrior rubbed droplets from his face. "Great King, the army of Verica has been sighted."

Epaticcos put down his cup of beer on the rough pallet table. "Where is he?"

"Encamped on the edge of Bagshot Heath."

The king grinned. "I couldn't have picked a better place for battle."

Caratacus understood. He had hunted deer and boar across the wide plain. Clusters of pine and fir trees dotted the landscape. Thorn-ridden gorse and heather quilted the open stretches.

"Then Verica is ours, Uncle," Caratacus remarked.

"He is. But tonight our men must rest."

* * *

By morning the skies cleared. The ground-fog burned away as billowing white clouds fled into the distance on a light wind. The muddy earth turned a dark gray, and trees sparkled in the early sun. Thousands of purple butterflies appeared on the landscape like flower petals buffeted by the winds. The bushy undergrowth dripped with mildew, and spiny shrubs of heather turned brilliant shades of pink and yellow.

Caratacus was in the forefront of the army with the king's entourage, which had taken up positions on the edge of the plain of Bagshot Heath at dawn. Leaning forward on the chariot's front guard rail, Caratacus placed an open hand above his eyebrows to block the glare of the noonday sun. Squinting his eyes, he scanned the far edge of Bagshot Heath. He spied something in the distance. "Tog!" he said, "do you see them?"

His brother scrutinized the area. "Aye, now I do. Their army is huge!" Crowded together to the plain's south edge were Regni infantry companies totaling at least two thousand men. Spear blades and shield bosses glistened in brilliant sunlight, and colorful banners flapped confidently in a gentle breeze.

"Over there, Uncle!" Caratacus called to Epaticcos.

"Ah, now I see, exactly where I expected them."

Deployed on the Regni flanks were cavalry and charioteers bearing the nobility.

"There's Verica," Caratacus pointed.

Verica, powerfully built, stood tall, glaring at the Atrebatic army from his chariot. Even at five hundred feet distance, his long face and chin, appearing as if chiseled in granite, were unmistakable. He wore an iron helmet with a small bronze image of a wild boar welded to the top. Color-bearers trotted behind him.

Donn rode his chariot forward to the center front of the Regni companies, where the chariots of King Verica and his champion were guarded by several dozen retainers on horseback.

He halted and raised his sword in the direction of the ugly, scar-faced champion, who stood tall in his car. Caratacus recognized him as Gildas ap Caw

Verica's defender wore a patch over his right eye, kept in place by a leather thong. Two fingers were missing from his left hand. Like Donn, he wore chain mail over a tartan tunic and striped breeches. A fine bronze helmet with massive cheek guards topped by a horse-hair plume covered his head.

"Come forward, Gildas ap Caw, you fucking coward," Donn shouted at Verica's champion, "and fight me like a real man!"

"You're no real man, you son of a slut!" Gildas ap Caw yelled in return. "Your mother fucked every man in the tribe including goat herders!"

The Regni warriors burst into laughter, hooted, and shouted catcalls.

Caratacus saw Donn stiffen but refused to take the bait. Instead, he grinned.

Donn wheeled his chariot about and rode back and forth in front of the Regni formation calling them cowards and other obscenities. They jeered in return. Donn returned to where Verica and his champion waited and traded more insults with Gildas ap Caw.

"Are you going to fight me or not, you bloody whoreson?" Donn barked again waving his sword above him.

Gildas motioned to his driver to move forward.

Verica, who wore a bright green and yellow cape over his armor, turned to his champion in the adjacent chariot and shook his head. "Wait," he ordered.

The champion frowned but nodded. He placed a hand on his driver's arm.

Verica pointed to Donn. "Your bloody king has much to answer for. This will be settled here on the battlefield. Then you'll see what real men are made of."

"These are men?" Donn shouted and jabbed his weapon in the direction of Verica's warriors. "I see nothing but the son's of crotch-rotting whores. That includes Gildas's slut of a mother!"

After Donn's parting remark, he turned about his chariot as the Regni jeered and hurled more insults at his back.

He returned to Epaticcos. "Verica will settle for nothing less than full battle, Great King."

"Then he shall have it!"

* * *

Porcius and his retinue had followed Epaticcos's army at a discreet distance until they arrived in the area of Bagshot Heath. It was imperative that Porcius maintain his neutrality. The Roman ordered his entourage to camp in a clearing on a pine-clustered knoll overlooking the belligerents on the plain below who were about three hundred paces away. Even at this distance, Porcius recognized the leaders of both sides. Verica stood in his chariot, scarlet banners fluttering nearby, and in the opposite direction Epaticcos stood, surrounded by his retinue, next to emerald flags bearing the images of wolves.

Roman standards framed in colors of imperial purple and white and standards bearing the image of the Emperor Tiberius proclaimed his presence as a neutral. The emissary and his favorite freedmen and slaves sat at portable tables covered with dried meat, cheese, honey cakes, fruit, and wine in a picnic atmosphere.

As Cyrus sat next to Porcius munching on an apple, he said, "If these barbarians are the fighters they claim to be, this battle may be as exciting as a gladiator event in the Great Circus of Rome."

"The difference here is that King Epaticcos's lands are at stake."

Cyrus spat out a piece of wormy apple. "Indeed, far more important than the lives of a few worthless gladiators."

No one was happier than Porcius that the rain had passed. He hated traveling in such horrid weather, but was determined to report the battle to the emperor. Unfortunately, his best travel tunics were soiled by mud, because one of his slaves neglected to properly secure the trunk containing his clothing. The trunk had bumped out of a transport wagon, and the hapless slave received ten lashes for his carelessness. Porcius resorted to wearing a Briton tunic, hastily presented to him by Epaticcos. Barely fitting around his corpulent waist, it was a resplendent garb made of gold linen trimmed in stripes of scarlet and green. A golden pendant shaped like a spoke wheel, the protective symbol against evil, held the robe together at the right shoulder. Despite wearing British clothing, he had no fear he would be mistaken for a Briton. The banners planted by his attendants at their encampment told all the world he and his people were Roman.

The Roman rose from the table and watched the two armies draw into battle formations, now less than two hundred paces away, slowly converging upon one another. He walked along the front of the stand where his clerk sat waiting for him to dictate an ongoing report of the battle. But Porcius became so fascinated by the events unfolding before him he ignored the scribe.

He mulled on his failure to prevent the coming onslaught. The final opportunity to mediate a peace had been quashed when warriors on both sides hurled insults and abuse at one another and rhythmically banged longswords against oval shields. They waved standards to the brassy sound of upright, boar-headed trumpets. Both armies were divided into loosely knit companies. He spotted Caratacus and part of the band of eighty young warriors he was leading, riding chariots on the right flank with five hundred cavalry. The remaining cavalry rode on his left. Beyond, he saw the infantry center, containing the bulk of the fighters. As seasoned veterans, they smeared their hair with thick lime wash, pulled back and dried into hundreds of long, stiff spikes. Despite the slaying of Froech the bandit, Caratacus was still considered too young and inexperienced to be allowed the same privilege as the older men.

The tattooed, bare-chested men wore bright tartan and plaid trousers, or beaver pelts covering leather kilts. They twirled long, pointed swords above their heads in hopes of terrifying the enemy. Neither side seemed to be impressed by this manly display.

Porcius stopped beyond the edge of the tables and watched the infantry of the Atrebates rolling forward, like an incoming wave, screaming as they ran toward Verica's lines. At thirty paces, both sides discharged their javelins, and many men of both armies fell. Within seconds, a bloody clash of powerful warriors began hacking and slashing one another with hatchets, swords, and spears. The sounds of metal on metal and screams and groans of wounded and dying echoed across the field. The putrid odor of urine and feces of the slain polluted the drifting breeze. Blood spattered in wide swatches on bodies, and weapons of the slayers and slain churned the chalky ground into a pinkish ooze.

For the space of about ten heartbeats, Porcius stood rigid as if the air had been sucked out of him. He gasped, attempting to regain his breath. His stomach twisted into a knot, and bile rushed to his throat. He bent over but did not vomit. The noise of the battlefield roared in his ears like crashing ocean waves on the shoreline.

Cyrus rushed to Porcius's side and grabbed his arm. "Lord, please let me help you to a chair—you need to sit."

Porcius straightened and shoved Cyrus away. "I'm fine, you fool." He took a deep breath and staggered to a chair at the table and sat. "Bring water."

Cyrus snapped his fingers, and a slave appeared at Porcius's side with a cup of water and pitcher. Porcius grabbed the cup but cautiously sipped the water, afraid he would vomit. He rinsed his mouth and spat it out. He waved the slave away but held onto the cup. He listened again as the cries and smells of death drifted across the plain towards their camp. He looked at Cyrus, who stood before him. "This slaughter is worse than I had dared to imagine."

"No wonder you are sick," Cyrus said.

"I'm not sick!"

He noticed that despite being partially covered by a beard, his freedman's face had turned pale. "I had forgotten what the battlefield was like. Not since I was a young tribune with the Roman Army in Judea fighting the zealots have I seen killing like this." *Some man I am! I'm a Roman. I'm supposed to be immune to bloodshed!* He looked across the field. Even at a distance, Porcius made out Caratacus and his brother, Tog, riding ahead of his followers. Each warrior gripped a shield and three spears in one hand and clenched the handle of a longsword with the other, strapped at their waists. "Look, there goes Caratacus and his young warriors heading for the enemy."

* * *

Caratacus deftly kept his feet balanced in the car as Tog skillfully guided the chariot across the rutted field. Earlier he had given orders to his men to deploy as skirmishers and mount a striking probe along the enemy's right flank. Epaticcos told him spies had learned these particular companies were Verica's weakness. They were made up primarily of levies of farmers and fishermen with little combat training. Caratacus smiled to himself and looked about as the chariots turned and followed him. *The enemy won't be expecting us. We'll hit and run. It'll throw 'em into confusion.* Although Caratacus's detail wasn't dealing with hardened veterans, his warriors were still too few, less than eighty, to engage in full battle. Their best chance lay in distracting the enemy. It would give Epaticcos's main forces a chance to smash Verica's main force.

Approaching the Regni forces, Caratacus felt his muscles tighten and his mouth go dry. He licked his lips, clenched and unclenched the handle of the sword at his waist. *Teutates, give me strength. No time to be scared!* He looked at Tog, who focused on handling the ponies and chariot. He turned and watched his followers hurtling after him in their cars. *Are they as scared as I am? Uncle said it was natural. It made you more alert.*

Seconds later they were in front of the enemy flank, Caratacus's fear evaporated. With him in the lead, he and his young warriors hurled spears and short, iron darts at the enemy, slaying many. The noise of combat, screaming warriors, and horses squealing and grinding chariot wheels was deafening. Caratacus could hardly hear himself. He noticed the assault by his men had terrorized a couple companies of Regni infantry. They backed away, broke ranks, threw down there shields, and fled in rout toward the woods. As Caratacus's men were about to pursue them, the sharp tone of a carnyx, the upright, wolf's-head trumpet, sounded the order to back off. This followed Briton custom forbidding unnecessary bloodshed, except cutting off heads of the slain. Caratacus didn't like it, but waved his men back.

Instead, Caratacus ordered his men to assist Epaticcos's forces, who were fighting Verica's charioteers. They turned and soon wheeled their way among the Atrebatic cavalry squadrons. At his signal, the warriors leapt from chariots and engaged in single combat.

"This way!" Caratacus shouted. Leading his men across the dusty, torn-up ground, they slammed into a company of Regni soldiers still holding their ground. Caratacus thrust, hacked, and bashed into the Regni fighters, blood spattering his face, clothing, and weapons. Resistance by the Regni was heavy, neither side giving ground. When the trumpets of both camps sounded retreat, Caratacus had slain many enemy soldiers. The armies broke contact, withdrawing to rest, momentary reprieve to count their losses and regroup. At the moment, victory was still undecided.

* * *

Porcius took refreshment during the respite, still recovering from his shock, all but forgetting his intended report. As he sat at the table sipping a heady red wine from Rhaetia, he noticed one of his slaves had stepped beyond the table. The servant raised the front of his tunic, reached down with a hand, and urinated in the direction of Epaticcos's headquarters tent. The king had just arrived from the battlefield and stepped off his chariot. He looked in Porcius's direction. Although he was nearly two hundred paces away down the hill from them, Porcius was certain the king had frowned.

"You ignorant lout, stop that at once!" Porcius shouted. "You insult the king!" *Gods, I must own the empire's stupidest slaves!*

The slave turned, still holding his member in his hand.

"Now, you're insulting your master!"

The slave paled, quickly lowered his tunic and then his head.

"Cyrus," Porcius called to the Persian. He motioned to the slave. "Take this fool away and give him twenty lashes."

Cyrus grinned. "With pleasure, lord." He grabbed the slave by the scruff of his neck and dragged him away. Another servant followed Cyrus with a whip.

A few minutes later, from behind a bush erupted the whisking sounds of a whip and screams of mercy.

Porcius turned to the rest of his retinue who had gathered in a few knots looking nervously in the same direction. "Listen to me fools," he said to the group who turned his way, "let that be a lesson to all of you. No pissing in front of anybody!"

Soon, both sides mounted another attack, and, again, neither side faltered. Sitting in his curule chair, Porcius, now fully recovered, observed the fighting, spat contemptuously, and commented to Cyrus, who hovered nearby, "Typical undisciplined barbarians, fighting as individuals and not as an army. The victor will be decided by who has the most stamina. Now, if the Britons had fought even one of our legions, they would have been swept from the field."

Cyrus nodded. "True enough."

"The Roman Army would have countered the Briton tactics with volleys of javelins," Porcius said. "The heavy infantry would have moved forward, locked shield to shield, jabbing and thrusting short swords into the vulnerable open-stanced Britons. The legions would have been withdrawn one century at time to rest and not the entire army, as did the Britons, thereby continuing the fight."

Porcius gulped another cup of wine. The Roman turned when he heard a stirring from behind and then a scream. He saw one of his freedmen retainers, falling backwards clutching a spear sticking from his stomach.

Before he could react, a troop of British horsemen were upon his people. Several of Porcius's retainers drew swords and ran forward to defend their master.

The riders hurled a volley of javelins and four more of Porcius's men, smeared with blood, fell screaming to the ground—dead.

Heat rushed through Porcius's body as he flushed with anger. *Who are these savages? How dare they kill my people?*

"That's enough!" the young leader shouted to his men. They reined up to a halt. He turned to Porcius. "Tell your people to stay their weapons, or I'll slaughter the lot of them!"

Porcius quickly looked about and gratefully saw that the rest of his people, including Cyrus, had been spared.

"Who are you? What is the meaning of this outrage?" Porcius bellowed.

"Never mind," the young leader sneered. "Do as I say, or you're dead!" He raised an arm as if to give the order.

"Stop! Stop! I'll do it," Porcius said. He turned to his defenders. "You heard him, drop your weapons!"

They did.

"Do you know who *I* am?" Porcius demanded, his voice firmer than his confidence.

"I know who you are, Roman pig," the leader replied. His accent wasn't of the Atrebates.

Although the riders were wearing the multi-checkered, short-sleeve tunics and homespun trousers of the Atrebates, they were of smaller stature than any Porcius had known and darker, except for their leader. Their mounts were gray ponies of Spanish breed, whereas the Atrebates rode bigger Cobbs and Gallic horses. *These were Regni warriors.*

Porcius studied the young warrior's features. There was something familiar about the sun burned, elongated face, beak nose, and pointed chin. "You're Gwynedd, son of Verica," Porcius challenged abruptly. "Your father will hear from me!"

"You can tell him yourself," Gwynedd sneered. "You're coming with us for your own protection."

"From whom are you *protecting* me?"

"From the enemy. We can't risk your death."

"I had no enemies until you committed this unspeakable action. This is not like your father, I demand —"

"Do as I say, or I'll slice off your fat buttocks and use it for chariot grease! Climb aboard!" He pointed his sword to a spare horse led by one of his men.

"Very well," Porcius said, "but what of my people? They depend on me."

He ignored the question.

With the assistance of three struggling slaves, Porcius climbed on the pony, and the riders set off. But several bandits dismounted.

Headed for the gully at the edge of the knoll, Porcius heard screams and groans from his camp. He trembled, heat rushing to his face. *He butchered my people! The dirty bastard! My prized slaves! I paid good money for them. Verica will pay dearly. I swear it!*

* * *

Caratacus, taking a breather with the rest of his men, glanced in the direction of the knoll and saw the commotion within Porcius's camp. "Look!" he motioned to Tog with his head. "Something's wrong in the Roman camp."

Tog squinted in the bright sunlight. "Are you sure? Those look like our warriors."

"Uncle didn't give any orders for our warriors to guard Porcius's camp. Look closer, and you'll see Roman standards are overturned."

"Our people wouldn't do that!"

"To your chariots!" Caratacus shouted. "The Romans are in trouble!" He spotted Porcius, with what he was certain were enemy horsemen, riding down the hill. The enemy made a dash for the narrow, brush-covered gully lying along the hillock's rim. The ridge flowed downward along a slope, disappearing into the thick, impassable forest at the edge of the plain. If he didn't overtake the enemy before they reached the woods, it would be impossible to rescue Porcius. He had no love for the Roman, but he didn't want him captured or murdered.

With Tog at the reins of the chariot, Caratacus and his men raced ahead through the muck and mire of the plain. The pebble-strewn, muddy ravine, still streaming in places, was sure to slow Verica's men. Caratacus's warriors reached the edge of the sloping woods into which the chasm emptied. Its moist-earth embankment stood at shoulder height of a horseman. A large growth of bushes lined the top on both sides of the ravine as well as covering near the mouth. He ordered his band to ready their slings, and divided them on both sides of the gap.

They heard the dull clatter of noise, hooves slopping mud and water, rumbling toward them. "Here they come," Caratacus whispered to Tog as he spotted the enemy snaking down the narrow defile. "Pass it on to the men to wait for my signal."

"Right, Brother."

Caratacus raised his sword. "At my command ... now!" He slashed his weapon downward.

Fifty men slipped through the bushes, hurling lead stones from leather-thonged slings in a murderous crossfire. Rider after rider went flying from frantic mounts into the soggy mire. Shrieking warriors charged down the slopes, swords and spears in hand, furiously falling upon the enemy survivors. Several of Caratacus's warriors lost their footing on the slippery banks and tumbled beneath the dancing horses. The unhorsed survivors had even greater difficulty getting to their feet. Many were trampled by their own animals or crushed against the embankments. Those not struck by the deadly stones were killed by spears after having their mounts hamstrung from beneath them.

As Caratacus pulled a spear from one of his victims, he spotted mud-spattered Porcius on his knees, no more than five feet away. His torn garment revealed rolls of blubbery fat. Porcius attempted to stand from his knees when an enemy warrior raised a sword above his head. Caratacus shrieked, distracting the warrior momentarily, and slammed a lance into the fighter's chest. The man dropped his weapon and instinctively grabbed the shaft as the impact of the weapon toppled him backward into shallow water.

The deflecting blow from the falling enemy's sword struck blood-spattered Porcius on the shoulder, leaving a minor arm wound. Porcius grabbed the sword, sticking upright in the mud, and fell upon the victim slashing in a rage, churning the waters into a pinkish froth. Apparently, after regaining his wits, Porcius caught his breath. He turned his head, his eyes wide, and discovered his rescuer was the son of King Cunobelinos.

"I'll not forget what you've done for me, young Caratacus. I'll give thanks to all the gods, Roman and Briton alike, for your saving my life. You are indeed worthy of your father, and the emperor will hear—" Still enraged, he turned again and violently hacked the dead man's body.

Caratacus nodded in new respect for the Roman and ordered a mount for Porcius along with an escort to the Atrebatic camp.

* * *

At dusk, Cyrus and one of Porcius's scribes stumbled into camp, bearing grisly tales of death. The Persian and the clerk had managed to escape.

"I'm grateful you survived, my friend," Porcius said. "We will discuss it in greater detail later, I've just received a summons to the king's camp. Epaticcos won an overwhelming victory today, and Verica's army has withdrawn in disarray."

* * *

Porcius entered the king's huge goatskin tent just as Epaticcos was about to address his men. He hurried to one side where he had a clear view of everyone. To the ruler's left stood the cadaverous Druid, Havgan, like a ghoulish shadow in the pulsating light of several oil lamps. The Roman noticed Caratacus's bare-chested, long hair streaked with dirt and breeches caked in mud, smelling of rank sweat and blood, as he appeared before his uncle. Around his upper bicep he wore a tightly knotted piece of brown cloth. A minor wound, Porcius thought. Behind his brother, Tog mingled with the lesser chieftains, priests, and Donn.

Epaticcos noticed Porcius out of the corner of one eye. "Come forward, Roman. Here." He motioned to where Tog lingered.

Porcius gave the younger brother a terse nod.

"You showed great bravery and initiative in rescuing Porcius the Roman," the king said to Caratacus. He handed the prince a wooden bowl of beer.

"I couldn't allow Verica's men to kidnap and slaughter him, even if he is a Roman," Caratacus answered. He turned about, saluted Porcius with the bowl and drained the contents in one gulp.

"Your decision was wise, besides being humane," Epaticcos said.

"Meaning?" Caratacus asked as he faced the king.

"While saving Porcius's life, you killed Gwynedd, Verica's favorite son."

Caratacus dropped the bowl, a soft thud on the packed earth. "Are you positive?"

"I received news from one of my spies that he kidnapped Porcius by order of his father."

"But why the Roman?" Caratacus asked, shaking his head.

"Verica planned to murder Porcius and blame it on me if he lost the battle," the high king explained.

Porcius jolted. *What! Why would Verica do that?* He looked about checking to see if anyone had observed his reaction to this startling revelation.

"In revenge," Epaticcos said, as if reading Porcius's thoughts. "Rome would sever all financial support and trade. His prestige would rise in the eyes of the Emperor Tiberius, and he expected him to finance the building of another army, including mercenaries, to attack us again."

"And he failed!" Donn spat.

I have been betrayed! The emperor shall hear of this!

Epaticcos snorted. "It's not over yet." He waived Porcius forward. "Roman, when you write your emperor, be sure you tell him what has been said here today and assure him of our loyalty."

"It will be done, Great King." Porcius bowed slightly. *My report will include every detail of what took place, including Verica's treachery!* He stepped back alongside Tog.

"What else do you expect Verica to try?" Caratacus asked.

"I don't know." Epaticcos exhaled, grabbed a cup of beer handed to him by a slave, and swilled its contents in one heave. "But we must remain on guard. When you kill a man's favorite son and vanquish his army, he won't rest until he gets revenge. What he doesn't obtain on the battlefield will be gained by other, more sinister means."

* * *

When Porcius returned to his camp, he dictated his report, including his capture and rescue by Caratacus.

"In summary," Porcius dictated thoughtfully, "I am convinced the king and prince were sincere in their words regarding my rescue and loyalty to you, Caesar. As for my brief capture, I suffered minor wounds and the loss of all save one loyal freedman and scribe. But I extracted blood upon one enemy of yours, Great Tiberius. Should these ferocious warriors ever wear the colors of your legions, the world will be forever Roman. Should they unite under a Briton banner, our road to final victory, if you decided to expand the empire to this land, will be long indeed."

CHAPTER II

MAY, AD 28

"I see the *Dun*," Tog said to Caratacus. Holding the reins in one hand, controlling their chariot, he pointed with his other in the direction of the rise. Beyond it loomed the fortress of Camulodunum, shimmering in the golden glow of the afternoon sun. The two young men were part of Epaticcos's retinue of two hundred warriors and courtiers, on foot, horseback, chariots, and wagons approaching the home their father, Canubelinos, and capital of the Catuvellauni and Trinovantes. This was also a wedding party, as Caratacus was to be betrothed and married to Rhian. Caratacus's group brought with them the bride's gifts for the wedding ceremony. Epaticcos, riding at the head of the retinue, carried the maiden's fee, to be given to Rhian's mother as custom demanded.

The size of the entourage, combined with the sounds of conversations, clattering hooves, and grinding wheels bumping along the wooden trackway, drew a scattering of curious onlookers from the nearby port and village at the bottom of the hill. Here, the shops huddled along the river docks where merchant vessels from many lands moored. Goods were being unloaded and transported by wagon or on the backs of slaves up the winding trackway to the hilltop.

Three fortified dikes guarded the western approach to the citadel. Another series of defensive dikes crisscrossed the chalky hills with farmsteads and marshes overlooking the brackish Colne River Estuary. A flight of long-billed curlews glided past the noisy band as they headed down to the adjacent mudflats—their shrieking, "pic! pic! pic!" swirled on the cool sea breeze.

High hills formed embankments to protect the north and south flanks of the stockade, and the twisting river and adjacent swampland made passage nearly impassible. Within its large confines were several mini-forts, surrounded with moats and smaller farmsteads built of timber and clay. The Great Dun, although sprawling, was impregnable and foreboding. Indeed the citadel seemed to prosper, and only a fool with men to squander would dare challenge her.

The salty smell of the British Ocean, carried on a gentle wind, drifted upward and seemed to engulf Caratacus. Although he was dressed in a woolen tunic and trousers and wearing a scarlet cloak about his shoulders, he shuddered. As they climbed the trackway to the hilly settlement where his father held court at the Great Hall, the young prince pondered the official message of betrothal he had received in Caleva ...

Last month, nearly eight months after the Battle of Bagshot Heath, the courier had arrived at Epaticcos's home during the evening meal. "A message from your brother, the high king," the chief steward said to Epaticcos, who sat with the rest of his family on reed mats eating a meal of mutton, bread, and ale.

Caratacus leaned in the direction of his uncle as the steward whispered in Epaticcos's ear. Unable to hear anything, Caratacus turned to Aunt Gwynn, who put a finger to her lips. He huffed and glanced at Tog, who shrugged.

The king nodded, and the servant departed.

Caratacus's aunt, Gwynn, wore her working dress, a full-length, russet, plaid tunic, cinched around her matronly waist by a plain leather belt. Pulled tightly behind her head, her silver hair was curled into a tight bun, held in place by pins made from rare whale bone purchased from Scandian traders. The forehead of Gwynn's moon face pinched into deep lines, and her cobalt eyes squinted when she asked her husband, "What does your brother want?"

Epaticcos motioned to his wife and Caratacus. "Something we've all been waiting for, my dear. The arrangements have been finalized. Caratacus," Epaticcos said gravely, "you are to be betrothed and married to Rhian on the sixth of next month, the Festival of Beltaine, during the blooming of the mistletoe."

Caratacus bristled. "But why? I don't want to be married. I'm not ready!"

"You have no say in the matter. The union is important to the family house." Epaticcos finished a cup of ale and glared at Caratacus.

"But she's too young, so am I."

"She's seventeen and a grown woman. She should have been married by now." Gwynn pointed a finger at Caratacus and fixed her eyes as cold as a lioness on him. "You said you were a man. Part of being a man is taking on the responsibilities of marriage and being a good husband. Don't you want to keep your house alive?"

Caratacus nodded. "Aye."

"Then you will marry Rhian. She is strong and beautiful and will bear many healthy sons," Epaticcos said. "If need be, she'll fight in defense of your home or by your side on the battlefield."

The young prince glanced at Tog, who shrugged his shoulders. They appeared to be growing more muscular with each passing day. The younger brother could not say anything in his defense without being punished.

Jumping up from his mat, Caratacus tossed away the mutton joint and wiped his greasy hands on his breeches. "I know I must obey you and Da," he said to Epaticcos, "but nothing says I have to like being enslaved!" He stormed out of the house.

I'm not ready to be stuck in a hovel with a bunch of brats!

* * *

Now, a short distance behind Epaticcos's entourage, Caratacus and Tog threaded their way by chariot through Camulodunum's winding, muddy paths, a four-day journey from Caleva, capital of the Atrebates and ruled by Epaticcos. Caratacus was oblivious to the ever-present smoke permeating the walls and rooftops of the capital's many conical huts and longhouses and dissipating in the crisp morning air. He mulled over the audience he was about to have with his father in the Great Hall. Caratacus had always looked forward to seeing his father, Cunobelinos, but this time was different.

92

"I don't want any part of this betrothal, Tog," Caratacus said.

Tog, whose youthful face had begun bearing the first scraggly signs of a copper beard, turned his head to one side. He spat beyond the chariot's wicker rim. "The family demands it, Brother. It's all politics."

"I'm not ready for marriage, political or otherwise." Caratacus hawked and spat over the side of the chariot.

"But you haven't seen her since last summer. Girls grow a lot between fifteen and seventeen," Tog said, holding his hands out like cups in front of his chest as he grinned.

"That doesn't mean I have to marry her. Why couldn't she move in and sleep with me like the northern tribes' women? That's what our cousin, Cartimandua of the Brigantes, did before she married Prince Venutios."

Tog snorted. "Too bad customs get in the way. Then again, if the rumors are true, Cartimandua's been plowed by every man she could get her hooks into."

"Rumors are dangerous. But if that's the case, she went too far. It's one thing for a woman to consort with the best of men, like Aunt Gwynn did with Uncle Epaticcos, but not just anyone." Caratacus shook his head. "Still, getting a divorce is a lot tougher when there's a dowry involved and solemn invocations by Da and the Druids."

"Look, Brother ..." Tog hesitated. "You're not going to like what I say, but my gut tells me Rhian will make you a good wife." He glared at his older brother as if in challenge.

Jolted, Caratacus's muscles tightened, his narrowing eyes met Tog's stare. *Is he mad? I swear he is! Silence.* He closed his eyes and exhaled. Opening them, he wondered: if perhaps he was right, he should try to make the best of the situation. After all, she was pretty and that helped. Slowly, he relaxed, and a grin below his mustached lip revealed white teeth. He reached over and tousled his younger brother's tawny hair with his right hand and then pulled it back. "If it had been anyone but you saying that, Little Brother, I'd have smacked him to the ground. You'd best be right."

Tog smiled. "I am, Big Brother, you'll see."

"Your day will be next, Brother," Caratacus said. "I know little Ygerna has her eyes fixed on you.

Tog jutted his round, firm chin forward. "That wench will have to wait, she's a child."

"Ha! She's almost fifteen."

Tog farted.

Caratacus looked about as his senses identified the odors drifting through the huge fortress. The foul stench of blood and entrails from the slaughtered cattle mingled with the gamy smell of fresh and rotting fish. But soon the appetizing aroma of rye-grain from the bulging grain houses filled the prince's nose like a loaf of freshly baked bread.

The group forced a passage through the crowds between the maze of shops and trading stalls. There seemed to be as many foreigners as local people. Well-attired Romans and tartan-clad Gauls mingled with smelly Germans, Norsemen, and lean Spaniards. There were even Greeks and Syrians from the distant Mediterranean.

King Epaticcos's band included Tog; Rhian's parents, Donn and his wife, Rosmerta; Aunt Gwynn; Havgan, the Druid; Clud, the master iron maker and bronze-smith; numerous slaves; and two hundred escorting warriors.

As Epaticcos's party halted in front of the Great Hall, the king turned to Caratacus. A stern look crossed his bearded face. "I know you're not pleased about the betrothal; it doesn't matter. But remember this, regardless of your sentiments, you will conduct yourself as a prince and son of the king."

"I will, I promise."

"Good." The muscles in his uncle's face relaxed. "You'll see that matters here are better than you expect. After all, you are being recognized by your father for your valor against Froech and the rescue of Porcius."

Caratacus nodded. He sometimes wondered if he should have rescued the fat Roman and if Porcius appreciated this fact or took it for granted.

"Why, he even admitted to me in a message I received before the journey," Epaticcos said, "that his death would have resulted in far-reaching consequences for our lands."

"Why didn't you tell me?" *Perhaps he was grateful after all.*

"I had expected you would have seen the betrothal as a happy occasion. That should have been enough reason for the journey without further recognition. You've known each other since childhood," he reminded his nephew. "Regardless, you will do your duty well."

Inside the torch-lighted Great Hall, Caratacus squinted until his eyes adjusted to the dim light of pulsating torches. Oblivious to the murmurs of the crowded gathering, the smells of body sweat mixed with a variety of reeking perfumes, and the spicy odor of a boar roasting on a spit in the great hearth, he noticed with renewed disgust the trappings of a Roman court. This included Roman tapestries depicting hunt scenes hanging along the wall. They were interspersed with marble statues on pedestals in the images of fauns, satyrs, and other demigods from mythology. However, he was grateful Uncle Epaticcos had insisted their party wash at the stream and dress fittingly before entering the holding. Then he spotted Porcius, dressed in a flowing, white, purple-trimmed toga, along with his lackey freedman, Cyrus. He hadn't expected the Roman to be present. Porcius nodded towards Caratacus, his face expressionless. They hovered among the chieftains and their consorts, Druids, bards, and other guests of the court. Draped in their best clothing, the group wore a riot of colorful plaid and tartan tunics and trousers, gowns, and dresses. An assortment of bejeweled armlets, bracelets, torcs, and earrings complimented the clothing.

Instead of his high-backed, oaken chair, King Cunobelinos sat upon a Roman curule chair lined with furs, a gift from Emperor Tiberius. A bright-purple cloak draped his powerful shoulders, hooked at the left side by a hound-shaped, ivory broach. Beneath he wore a flashy blue and gold tartan tunic and breeches. Standing beside him, Ibor gripped his silver-plated staff and studied the approaching king and prince. Shield bearers dressed in expensive, mailed armor and carrying ornate longswords and large, oval shields, stood behind the king in a half-circle and along the sides of the Great Hall.

At least his appearance hasn't become Romanized—yet, Caratacus thought. *He'd need to layer his hair in a short haircut, an olive wreath on his head, a white and purple trimmed toga, and a boy gnawing his groin. Then he'd be like old Tiberius.* Fortunately, Cunobelinos still allowed their people to sit on the floor on cushions, as was customary, instead of requiring them to stand for hours. And yet ... yet he controlled the clan chieftains and surrounding tribes with an iron fist. Caratacus shook his head in respect, admiring the fine, fur robes and honors paid his father.

As Caratacus and Epaticcos waded through the parting crowd, the prince glimpsed Rhian with her servants and kinswomen. Awed, his heart leapt into his throat. His mouth dried in an instant, and he barely caught his breath. His body became so hot that he wanted to remove his clothes but dared not. He wanted to stop and reach out and touch her but had to keep moving.

Gods, how she has blossomed. The fullness of her face and those breasts, by gods, she's turned into a woman. He turned his head in wonderment for another glance. *By the Three Mother Goddesses, Rhian is taller than Tog.* Her emerald tunic failed to hide her curving hips. Her braided, pale-yellow hair sparkled with gold dust, a Roman extravagance.

Truly, I can bed this woman, and she will stand beside me in battle.

* * *

Porcius stood near the front before the king among the most prominent guests, which included chieftains and Druids. Next to him stood Cyrus. He watched Caratacus approach his father. The Roman studied Cunobelinos as the king formally intoned, "Caratacus, our son, you have greatly pleased us. By your brave deeds, the slaying of the bandit, Froech, and saving the life of our distinguished friend, Porcius of Rome, you have earned yourself a place in the bardic tales."

He paused and gestured toward the Roman, who bowed slightly to the monarch and to Caratacus. *I hate acknowledging I was saved by a barbarian. I know Caratacus despises me, but I am grateful and will remember his deed.*

"You have earned the right to be a warrior among warriors and leader of men," Cunobelinos continued. "To

show our gratitude, we give you a token of our thanks." He
clapped his hands, signaling drummers to pound out a
deep cadence as two spearmen brought forth his present. A
chorus of oohs and ahs from the people followed in their
wake.

Held forth in the torch light gleamed an oval ceremonial
shield of hammered bronze nearly three feet high. It was
overlaid with three large circular ridges, the center of each
inlaid with small discs of sparkling red glass, surrounded
by spiraling whorls. The design gave the shield the image of
possessing three bull's-eyes, mirroring oval rings of gold
from many torches.

"An impressive shield, even if it is only to show off the
king's wealth," Cyrus said as he watched the proceedings.

"Indeed," Porcius answered. He scrutinized the gift's
opulence and realized it was greater than he or anyone
obviously expected.

"You realize this is more than just an expensive
ceremonial shield," Porcius whispered to Cyrus. The gift
tacitly announced to all that one day Caratacus would be
king. He believed his sharp eyes detected a shudder
running through Caratacus's body. No one else seemed to
notice. "Prince Caratacus never expected to be so honored
by his father." Porcius touched the gold chain hanging
around his fat neck, a gift for a favor he'd rendered
Cunobelinos on an earlier occasion.

"This is the first time I have seen the high king show
the prince such kindness," Cyrus said.

"Exactly. At least the king now accepts him as a man,"
Porcius said. *That could be dangerous.* He pondered
Caratacus's future. His becoming king was another matter.
Adminios, Caratacus's older, but lazy, brother, was the
rightful heir to the throne. *When it comes time for a vote,
which prince would the tribal council actually elect? He is
not nearly as clever or as ambitious as Caratacus, but the
council has traditionally elected the eldest to the throne.* He
glanced to Adminios, who was in his early twenties, tall,
and with a mat of jet hair down to his shoulders. The
young man glared at Caratacus, his dark eyes full of hate.
*If Caratacus is elected over his brother, civil war might
erupt, and Caratacus would have to slay him. I have to find*

a way and persuade the king to avoid what can only be a destructive outcome.

"Rumors say that Rhian has loved Prince Caratacus since they were children," Cyrus said.

"Most likely—the wench has never made it a secret."

Porcius and Cyrus turned their attention to the dais when a clapping of hands brought two slaves forward with a long-stemmed amphora. For an occasion of this importance, the jug was filled with expensive, uncut, Roman Falernian wine that Porcius had supplied Cunobelinos at his own expense. They poured the amber nectar into two golden, ox-horned drinking cups for the king and Caratacus.

Ibor, the Druid, turned to the young prince, raised his hands, and intoned, "May Camulos, God of War and patron of this great fortress, and Taranis protect and guide you always."

The king held up his horn and proclaimed, "I drink to your coming of age as a man and warrior." He tossed the drink down his throat in one gulp. Caratacus followed suit to the cheers of the court.

When the king finished, he announced, "Tomorrow we gather again to proclaim the betrothal and forthcoming marriage of Prince Caratacus to Rhian, daughter of Donn, champion of our loyal brother, Epaticcos, King of the Atrebates." Another cheer erupted throughout the Great Hall.

Epaticcos lifted both hands. "Come, drink heartily and celebrate with your king!" Slaves served drinking bowls and cups filled with beer, mead, and wine to the throng.

"Let's enjoy ourselves," Porcius said to Cyrus, "but also listen to their loosened tongues so that I may report to the emperor their scheming plans."

CHAPTER 12

As a bard strummed a tune on his harp, Caratacus looked about the Great Hall. His father had left his side to speak to a chieftain. Epaticcos and Gwynn congratulated him before turning away to speak to old friends. In the smoky torchlight his eyes found Rhian, who stood with her father and mother, Donn and Rosmerta, at one side of the dais, speaking to a chieftain and his wife. She was so beautiful dressed in the finest of clothing and jewelry. He prayed to the gods to give him strength as he felt himself becoming aroused. *Not now!* He paused and quietly took a couple of breaths. Caratacus moved in their direction, annoyed that he could only speak to her in the presence of other people. *I have known her all my life, but now I can't be alone with her until the wedding night. What rubbish! I might as well be seeing her for the first time.* He had treated her so shabbily the last time they met during the harvest festival at the corral. Would she ever forgive him?

Caratacus halted before her. She smiled as he cleared his throat. He said formally, "I am honored to be chosen as your future husband." *Why do the words came out so stiffly. I feel like an arse!*

Rhian seemed to sense his uneasiness and responded, "It is I who am honored, Caratacus. I promise to be a dutiful wife." Her parents and the other couple nodded their approval.

"And I will be your loyal husband," he answered.

"I know," she said. "You will be the best of husbands."

Feeling a little more at ease, the young prince grinned. He hadn't expected her to be so complimentary. "You won't be disappointed, I promise." He looked about. "Now, I must move on, I'm expected to mingle among our guests. Until tomorrow, when we are formally betrothed, I will see you then." He slightly bowed to Rhian and her parents. They responded in kind as he stepped away. For a split second, he looked back in Rhian's direction, finding it nearly impossible to keep his eyes off her. He turned away.

By the gods, I hate this formality!

As he stepped away, he overheard Donn say behind him, "He better be a good husband to ye, Rhian, if'n he knows what's good fer him."

Caratacus stopped but didn't turn his head. He listened.

"Oh, Da, please," Rhian said. "Caratacus will be—he's a good man at heart."

"Yer me only daughter," Donn said. "I'll not see any harm come to ye."

"Tis true, Daughter, your father is right," Rosmerta said.

"Caratacus won't beat me, he knows better. I would fight back like Gwyther and Modron have taught me."

Caratacus grinned. He knew she would.

"Mayhap, but I want to know if'n he does, anyway," Donn said.

Caratacus turned and watched as Don, Rhian, and Rosmerta walked away. *I will treat her like a queen.*

He wandered among the noisy but merry gathering receiving congratulations as guests shook his hand and slapped his back, along with a little humorous bantering. He accepted the guests' best wishes on his betrothal to Rhian.

Porcius stepped from a group of well wishers and offered his hand, which Caratacus did not take. "May I offer my congratulations, Caratacus," the Roman said in a honeyed voice. "Rhian is a beautiful young woman—she will make a good wife."

Caratacus grunted a reply of thanks and moved on. *I saved the Roman's life, but I don't have to be friends with him.*

He glanced back and saw Porcius smiling maliciously as if saying, *You've made a big mistake.*

Caratacus turned his head and saw his brothers Tog and Adminios together with a few other young warriors nearby. Tog grinned and motioned him over. Adminios narrowed his eyes as Caratacus approached.

"Enjoying yourself, Tog?" Caratacus asked.

"Aye, that I am."

Caratacus studied Adminios's broad face. Full lips protruded over the slightly receding chin. A thin diagonal scar crossed his large forehead ending above the ridge of his left eye. His breath wreaked of strong wine. "What about you?"

"Hardly," Adminios answered. "You know I'm the one who should be the next king, not you!"

Caratacus gritted his teeth, muscles tightened. "You know damned well this ceremony had nothing to do with that! Only the king's council determines the next ruler."

"That's not what I saw," Adminios said in a voice closer to a growl.

Caratacus eyed Tog, who shrugged. He turned back to the oldest brother. "Then you're a blind arsehole. He recognized me for saving Porcius's life and killing Froech. What does that have to do with becoming king?"

Adminios's face flushed. He shot a finger in Caratacus's direction. "Everything. When I killed my first warrior in battle, he said little to me. I can fight just as good as you, better."

"Aye, that's true," several of Adminios's friends said in unison.

"Caratacus is just as good as you are, Brother," Tog said to Adminios in a sharp voice.

Porcius, who was conversing with Cyrus a few paces distant, stopped and looked their way.

Tog continued. "Caratacus led a group of us in battle. He saved the Roman's life!" He tossed a glance in Porcius's direction and nodded. He in turn bowed slightly.

"Let it go, Tog," Caratacus said. He knew he was better than his older brother, but would not give him the pleasure of an argument.

A sneer crossed Adminios's mouth. "He knows I'm telling the truth."

"I won't deny it, Big Brother," Caratacus said. "You've proven yourself in battle."

"Then why all of this?" Adminios waved a hand in the direction of the crowd.

"Ask Da yourself," Tog interjected.

"I will!" Adminios answered in a rasping voice.

"You don't have to," Caratacus said. "I can guess."

"What do you mean?"Adminios questioned.

"You spend all your time hunting, whoring, and getting drunk," Caratacus said. "Personally, I could care less. The trouble is, you've never attended the meetings held by Da and the Council."

"So what?"

"Unless you attend and learn from Da's decisions, you'll never be a good king. The cases and treaties brought to him and his councilors impact the kingdom. They also affect the common people. That's important, too, we need their support." Caratacus and Tog had always attended the court of Uncle Epaticcos, but he wasn't about to tell his older brother.

"It's a waste of time," Adminios said. "Who cares about who owns what cattle or how many fishing boats? The Druids and councilors can advise me."

"The final decision always rests with the king," Caratacus said. "Need I say more?"

"I have more to say!" Adminios lunged forward, but a couple of Adminios's friends from behind grabbed his arms and pulled him back. People among the gathering turned and looked at the young men, puzzled expressions crossing their faces. Fortunately, their father and Uncle Epaticcos were too engaged in a discussion with the Druids on the far side of the great hearth to pay them any attention.

"This is not the time or place, Adminios," Caratacus said in a low voice. "If you attack me now, Da will banish you from the tribe. You know I speak the truth."

Frowning, Adminios glanced about before relaxing. His cronies released his arms. "There will be another time." He turned and stormed through the crowd, his friends following him.

Caratacus and Tog glanced toward each other, both shaking their heads.

* * *

The following night the Great Hall was packed for the betrothal of Prince Caratacus and Rhian. Caratacus looked about and saw Porcius standing next to Havgan at the front of the crowded meeting place. He glanced to Rhian walking by his side, escorted by her parents, while next to him were Epaticcos and Gwynn. Like a ship's wake, they strolled through the opening made by the gathering of guests. It was all Caratacus could do to keep a sober face. His heart pounded, and he felt quill bumps raising on his arms and back as his eyes followed her graceful form. From the heat of the Great Hall, he sweltered in his woolen, long-sleeve tunic and trousers. Or was it his own heat at seeing Rhian? The gold torc chafed his neck, and the bracelets clamped around his wrist seemed more like hot prongs from a blacksmith's forge. He clinched and unclinched his fingers and curled and uncurled the toes within his leather boots.

In the torch-illuminated court, King Cunobelinos, wrapped in his purple, Roman cloak and matching green and gold, tartan tunic and breeches, stood before his curule chair. The Druid, Ibor, shrouded in a long, white tunic and holding the staff of his office, hovered by the ruler's side. Shield bearers lined the wattle and daub wall behind the ruler. The group approached the stern-faced king.

Rhian wore a long, emerald gown with short, white sleeves, perfumed by a light scent of rose petals. A broad, cloth belt embroidered in gold gathered Rhian's dress at the waist. Slippers of supple, bleached-white calfskin enclosed her feet. Around her smooth neck hung a small, gold-torc collar and many necklaces of gold and silver. A half-dozen bracelets covered her arms, the usual dress of a wealthy Briton woman: formal in style, yet unable to conceal her allure.

Caratacus presented Rhian with a golden, crescent brooch, exquisitely designed with concentric rings and fifteen triangle and chained pendants dangling from its base. The crowd burst into spontaneous applause.

Rhian blushed as if she wasn't worthy of such a precious gift. She turned the brooch over and over in her hands, stopped, smiled, and briefly touched Caratacus's forearm, sending a tingling sensation through his body. He grinned.

Rhian gave Caratacus a shiny, bronze belt clasp measuring half a foot long, shaped like a dagger, engraved with bulging-eyed dragons and other monsters. In the reflection of the Great Hall's torchlight, the highly polished clasp glittered like a star on a clear summer night. He fingered the superbly crafted metal fastener and put it on immediately. The young prince turned and threw his old one to a grateful Tog, hovering with other warriors nearby, a gesture accompanied by cheers and laughter from the court.

Epaticcos presented Rhian's mother, Rosmerta, the customary bride's fee, a hefty price indeed. A servant placed the small, leather bag of five hundred pieces of gold at her feet. At the king's nod, another servant opened the main door of the Great Hall. In the flickering torchlight stood five pairs of perfectly matched, white Gallic horses.

"Twenty heads of cattle will be added to Donn's herd to seal the agreement!" King Epaticcos announced.

Although Rhian was only the daughter of the king's champion, a fee for a king's daughter had been paid. In Caratacus's mind, Rhian was worth a king's measure! He knew once Rhian became his wife, his moral obligation was to her alone. Only if Rhian didn't bear any sons would he sleep with another woman, his right as a prince. He realized too many children and mothers died in birth, and it could happen to Rhian. She deserved a chance. She would be a good wife. He had to take his duties seriously and act like a man, even though it wouldn't be easy.

CHAPTER 13

The evening before the wedding Caratacus and Tog spent time drinking with their warrior companions at the home of one of Cunobelinos's retainers, a young man only a few years older than themselves.

The group sat on animal pelts circling the small, central hearth. In the glow of the firelight, they passed around a small, long-stemmed amphora full of cheap Gallic wine, splashing it into their wooden drinking bowls. Swilling loudly, they laughed and joked between gulps of the acidic vintage, complimenting Caratacus on what a fine wife Rhian would make for him.

"I heard a rumor you won't like, Caratacus," the retainer said, "but you should hear it."

"What about?" Caratacus asked. He placed his bowl down by his side and stared at the young warrior.

"Rumor says your brother Adminios wanted Rhian for his woman."

Instantly, the muscles tightened in Caratacus's back and arms, and he clinched his fists. "He what?"

The broken-nosed retainer, who was missing a left ear, raised a hand. "Easy, he didn't have his way," he said in a quiet voice.

"He better not!" Caratacus answered loudly.

"Your father, King Cunobelinos, squashed your brother's foul ambition like stepping on a bug. He heard about it and told Adminios he was too irresponsible and unworthy of a woman of Rhian's quality. She was too fine for the likes of him."

Caratacus exhaled, picked up his bowl, and took a gulp of wine. "Da is right, thank the gods. What else did you hear?"

The warrior was about to answer when a piercing scream came from outside.

Caratacus knew immediately that the sound came from the direction of the home where Rhian was staying with her parents, and that her mother and father had gone to visit Cunobelinos at his home.

"Rhian's in danger!" Caratacus blurted. More screams erupted. In an instant he was on his feet, heading for the door. "Let's go!" he shouted.

Followed by Tog and several other young warriors, Caratacus crossed the compound beneath a moonlit evening sky. In the shadowy light, he saw his father approaching along with the Druids, Ibor and Havgan and others. He darted ahead of them. As he pounded along the dusty path, he prayed he would reach Rhian in time before she was injured or, gods forbid, killed. *Why would anyone want to harm her?*

Caratacus arrived first and found Rhian and Clud, the blacksmith, standing near the entry. Although their clothing was covered by splotches of blood, he saw no signs that either had been injured. *Thank the gods Rhian is not harmed. Clud, too.* In an instant the tension drained away from Caratacus's face and body. Then he spotted the gristly sight of a severed body lying on the reed-covered floor in a pool of blood by their feet.

Looking about, Caratacus shouted, "Tog! Take our friends and search the area for any intruders or outsiders, there may be other assassins on the loose."

Tog nodded and motioned to the six warriors who had followed them. "Come with me!" They hurried off.

Tears flowed down Rhian's pale face as she looked toward Caratacus. For a fleeting moment the slightest sign of a smile crossed her bowed lips before she turned her head away and began shaking.

Caratacus stepped towards Rhian wanting to hold her in his arms, but he halted knowing that would be frowned upon, especially the night before the wedding.

Donn, Cunobelinos, and Rosmerta, who had followed behind the Druids, rushed past him to Rhian's side. "Are ye hurt?" Donn asked.

Quietly, Rhian shook her head as she wiped away the tears. She inhaled deeply and seemed to will herself to stop trembling. She nodded toward the corpse. "He was going to kill me."

When Rosmerta attempted to console her, she was brushed aside. "I'm all right, Mother."

Although Rhian had nearly been murdered, Caratacus knew because she had been trained as a warrior, she would attempt to show no fear of death. But earlier she had been weeping—who could blame her?

"Who killed him?" Cunobelinos asked, motioning with his head toward the corpse.

"I did, Great King," Clud answered.

"Good man. Tell us what happened," the king asked.

"I was sitting over there," Clud said. He pointed to the far corner in the longhouse. "I was repairing a bejeweled, golden pendant in the hearth's firelight."

Even as Clud spoke, Caratacus saw it still glowed. Wisps of smoke drifted lazily toward the opening in the center of the ceiling, giving off the pleasant scent of burning pine.

"I was repairing the broken latch pin on the ornament Rhian will give to the prince here as a wedding gift." Clud nodded to Caratacus. "It was a sorry piece of workmanship," he growled. "Earlier that day, I had gently scolded her for depriving me of the privilege of crafting it originally. Instead, she requested one of Camulodunum's inferior, all-thumbs craftsmen to make it." He glanced toward King Cunobelinos.

"As I worked," Clud continued, "one of the two slave girls," his eyes turned to the chubby, red-headed Caledonian lass, now whimpering by Rhian's side, "stayed behind while Rhian's mam and da were visiting with the king to help Rhian with her weaving." He pointed to the upright wooden loom on the opposite side of the fire pit.

"That's right," Rhian said in a steadier voice. "I was weaving cloth for a tunic." She sighed, her eyes darting to the corpse and back.

"I heard a noise and glanced from the loom and saw the outline of this thing here," she waved a hand toward the body. "Like a cat, he shot through the doorway with his sword drawn. You can see he was short and dark, but even in the dim light I saw his cruel and ugly scarred face."

Rhian paused and placed both hands to her ears and bowed her head. She trembled and took several deep breaths. The shaking stopped. For the length of a dozen heartbeats, she remained silent. Finally, she raised her head and lowered the hands to the side and faced the group. "A roar like thunder filled my ears. My two women screamed. I bit my tongue to quell my growing terror—I had to think of a way to defend myself—to defend them." She went on to explain that the intruder, apparently not seeing Clud in the shadows behind him, headed for her. "My eyes darted from one part of the room to another," she said, "searching for a way out. None. My sword hung on the wall on the other side of the hearth behind the assassin. I had only one small hope. Edging my hand along the side of my hip, I pulled a dagger from my waistband and flung it. But the stranger stepped aside, and the weapon struck the wall on the other end of the enclosure. Then he moved nearer me."

Rhian paused again as if waiting for someone to ask a question. No response.

"My attendants screamed louder," Rhian continued. "I nodded at Clud praying he understood that I was asking him to do something. Now! Quietly, Clud moved to the wall where he stowed his weapons."

Rhian further explained as the killer drew closer, she had seen a long-handled ax standing nearby. She grabbed, hurled it. The stranger stepped aside. He deflected the two-headed ax with his weapon and sent it crashing into a large stone quern used for milling flour.

"That's when I sneaked up on the bandit," Clud said, "just as he raised his sword. I grabbed the sword I had been working on and leaped for the attacker. I bellowed, 'Assassin!' With a single stroke, I sliced through the middle of his torso. The slash was so clean and swift the dirty maggot stood motionless for a second before toppling to the floor in two parts. The pig had the bal ... er, nerve to spurt hot blood on Rhian and me." He jabbed a finger towards the corpse and shook his head.

"It was sickening, I nearly vomited." Rhian unconsciously rubbed her hands along the sides of her bloodied skirt.

"Then I kneeled and examined the body," Clud said. "I checked around to make sure he was alone before I laid the bloody weapon on the floor."

"I'm not afraid to admit that I swallowed vomit," Rhian said. "I couldn't stop trembling—still am, and I cried." She raised her arms and folded her hands across the elbows and held them tightly. "I didn't care about holding in my fears any longer, I was terrified, just like the two sobbing girls huddling about me. I guess I was more afraid than I wanted to admit."

"Ye have nothing to fear now, Daughter," Donn said. "I'll see to that."

Rosmerta stepped to Rhian, who now allowed her mother to give her a hug.

"So will I," Caratacus said.

"I can't in the name of the Mother Goddess understand why anyone would want me dead? What have I done to deserve this?" Rhian asked.

"Nothing, my Child," Rosmerta said. "'Tis an evil person who would do such a terrible thing."

Ibor, Cunobelinos's chief law giver, whose duty it was to investigate violent deaths, stepped forward. "I will take charge of this inquiry as my position requires." He kneeled and examined the body. He looked up and asked, "Does anyone recognize this man?"

They all shook their heads.

"He is a Regni by the looks of his clothing," Ibor said.

"And the blunt end of his sword further confirms it," Havgan added as he looked on. "We saw enough of those devilish weapons when we fought them last year at Bagshot Heath. Correct me if I'm wrong, Great King," he nodded to Cunobelinos, "but unlike the Regni, most kingdoms in southern Britannia use swords with pointed tips."

"Havgan is right," the high king said.

Caratacus spotted the crimsoned weapon used by Clud. "This isn't your sword, Clud. Whose is it?" Even the blackening blood could not hide its splendor.

For a moment, Clud stood silent. Then a sheepish grin crossed his face.

"Well?" Caratacus demanded.

"I ... ah, the truth is, this is your wedding present ... from me. It's made from rare Damascus steel, the best. I hate the bastard for spoiling the surprise."

Caratacus gasped. In wonder, he stooped and wiped the blade upon the straw. Carefully, he fingered the blade's edge, drawing an unintentional line of blood. He stood and held the weapon in his left hand, feeling its perfect balance.

"A magnificent sword of this quality requires a great deal of work and much expense," Ibor said in a demeaning voice. He stood and moved away from the dead assassin. "Why did you place so much time and effort into this?"

"I will not insult Prince Caratacus with shoddy craftsmanship," Clud answered sharply. "He deserves a present fit for a king, nothing less will do. Always has he treated me with respect."

Caratacus grasped Clud by the shoulder. "Thank you, my friend. Much as I appreciate this gift," he said, "I'm more grateful that you used it to save Rhian's life. I'm in your debt."

"Your thanks is enough for me, young Prince," Clud answered, apparently embarrassed by the attention. "I shall always serve the king and his family with sword or bare hands."

"But the question remains," Caratacus said, turning to his father, "Why would anyone want to slay Rhian? And *who?*"

"We will investigate this matter thoroughly, Son," the king said. "With your pending marriage, I already consider Rhian as my daughter." The king reached out to pat Rhian's arm.

Rhian bowed her head. "You're very kind, Great King."

"This is the work of Verica, I'm sure of it," Havgan concluded.

Donn scowled. "If it be so, it be a coward's way."

"It doesn't make sense," Cunobelinos said. "The question remains, why didn't the assassin go after my son?" He nodded to Caratacus.

"Maybe he did," Caratacus said, "and when he found I was drinking with too many of my companions, decided Rhian was the next best target. Our betrothal was no secret." He stepped to Rhian's side and looked into her eyes. A rush of heat swept through his body. "Your death would have pained me as much as if he had slain my prize gelding—more so," he said softly.

A smile flashed across her lips. Rhian grazed his wrist with her hand. "You honor me, Caratacus," she said formally. "I know being compared with a prized horse is the highest compliment that a warrior can pay to a woman."

"You are an accomplished rider, you deserve such praise and more," Caratacus said.

Cunobelinos glanced to Ibor and back to Caratacus. "Still the attempt on your life puzzles me."

Caratacus looked at his father and nodded. "It's because I killed his son, Gwynedd, at Bagshot Heath. He wants revenge. He'll take it in any way possible, by any means."

"We will never be certain, Great King," Ibor said. "The assassin's death leaves that and many other puzzles forever unanswered."

"Too bad he wasn't taken alive," Cunobelinos said, "then we'd have pulled the bloody truth out of him!" He motioned as if ripping a tongue from the dead man's head.

"The assassin figured he could kill and flee amid the panic," Cunobelinos continued. He eyed the two whimpering slaves with disgust. He motioned the iron maker forward. "Not only does our son, but all of us, owe thanks to our friend Clud, the iron maker and master craftsman," Cunobelinos proclaimed. "Had it not been for his courage, one close to all of us would have died a needless and savage death."

A chorus of "ayes" and "well done" came from the grateful group of onlookers.

Caratacus stepped towards Clud, reached out, and shook his hand. "I won't forget what you did for Rhian today. I swear one day you will ride by my side into battle."

* * *

The next day, Caratacus and Rhian stood beneath a knotted tree in the Great Forest of oaks near Camulodunum, waiting for Ibor to complete his prayers to the gods.

111

Rhian, bejeweled with gold bracelets and torcs, wore the great, gold pendant given her on the night of the betrothal. A deep-blue, woolen cloak covered her green- and gold-trimmed, silk dress. Tightly drawn into a braided crown upon her head, her hair was encircled by a wreath of purple and white wildflowers. Caratacus found her more beautiful than he could have ever imagined.

Caratacus wore a deep-brown-and-white-striped, long-sleeved tunic and trousers. A belt of gold-ornamented leather, clasped by the dagger-shaped buckle given by Rhian, was wrapped around his waist.

When the priest finished his incantations, he gathered up his flowing robe and sprightly climbed the tree. With a bronze sickle, he chopped the tough stem of a mistletoe branch growing in one of the clusters. The mistletoe tumbled below, caught as planned in a white cloak held by Havgan and a young, female acolyte. Returning to the ground, Ibor blessed the poisonous berries containing medicinal and magical qualities. He held the plants above the young couple and chanted the indecipherable words of a long-dead, ancient language. When finished, two white bulls tied to a nearby tree were led to the altar. As two acolytes held the beasts tightly by ropes, Ibor approached and slashed the drugged beasts' throats as an appeasement to the gods. Blood spurted on Ibor, the acolytes, and the altar—a good omen.

After Ibor's invocation, Cunobelinos came forth to give his fatherly blessing. The king wrapped a leather cord around Caratacus and Rhian's joined wrists. He intoned loudly the blessings of the Three-Mothers that the marriage be prosperous, long, and fruitful. "May Rhian be blessed with many children. Henceforth," he proclaimed, "you are a daughter of the House of Cunobelinos!" The crowd cheered.

A weight seemed to roll off Caratacus's shoulder as his muscles relaxed throughout his body. He hadn't realized how nervous and tense he had felt. He turned and grinned at Rhian who gave him a loving smile. Caratacus wanted to hug and kiss her, but custom forbade any show of affection during the wedding ceremony. Despite his earlier doubts, he was proud that Rhian now belonged to him. She would be a good wife, and he prayed that he would be as good a

husband. He silently prayed to the Three Mother
Goddesses that all would go well in their marriage.

* * *

The glowing embers of the hearth cast a soft light on
the wolf-skin blankets covering the bed-pallet. Caratacus,
lying naked beneath the cover, waited for Rhian as her
attendants adorned her for the wedding night. She
emerged wearing a revealing blue and white, woolen gown.
In the fading light, he fixed his eyes on her graceful body
scented with sweet jasmine. As she knelt beside him, the
warmth of her closeness seeped into every pore of his body.
Rhian slid down alongside her new husband, but
Caratacus sat up, the blanket falling to his waist.

A moment passed before Rhian forced a smile through
tightly-set lips.

Caratacus softly touched her rouged cheek, smooth
and warm. He let his hand linger a second longer. "Let's
talk for a while."

"Could we?" she asked. The tension drained from her
face. "I'm not afraid to admit that I'm a little nervous."

"I know."

"Is it so obvious?"

"Aye, but I guess that is to be expected. What would
you like to talk about?"

She thought for a moment. "You. We've known each
other since childhood, but I really know little about you."

Caratacus sighed and his breath made a tickling,
exciting feeling in his chest. His loins ached, but he had to
be patient. Rhian mustn't be rushed. "There isn't that
much. I need to know more about you."

Rhian softly kissed him on the mouth. "What about
me?" She smiled and snuggled closer. "I think I'm a little
boring, don't you?"

"Hardly," he said in a husky voice and kissed her soft
lips. "If you're not busy in the household, then you're out
training horses or drilling for battle."

"Well ... I suppose so. That's just the way I am." She
raised her free hand and stroked the bridge of his nose.

"There is nothing wrong with that."

"Maybe, but ... but I want to be a good wife. I've ... I've loved you all my life!" she blurted. Her face flushed. "Now, I've said it. I hope you don't think me too bold."

"I wouldn't have it any other way."

"I usually don't hold in my thoughts, except ... except that sometimes I have when you were around. I don't know why."

"Then don't. Always be honest with me, always."

"One of these days you will be king, a great one."

Caratacus pushed the thought of being king to the back of his mind. "Perhaps. Either way, you'll be at my side as my queen—a warrior queen."

She smiled. "I just want to be a good wife and bear your children, that's all I really want."

Their conversation progressed, they said more with fewer words and greater intimacy. Even in silence, the feelings they conveyed seemed to reach one another in the dark shadows of their bed-pallet.

* * *

Caratacus awoke. Where had the time gone? The night had rushed by faster than he remembered. He and Rhian had been touching and kissing with increasing passion and soon were making love. Now, as dawn approached, he looked about and saw Rhian leaning on her elbow watching him. She brought one hand to his cheek, reached over, and kissed him. But his curiosity about where she had learned her lovemaking skills, and from whom, stirred again.

"Gods, you were so good, Rhian, where ... how? I'm almost embarrassed to ask?"

Her green eyes looked deeply into his. "Please believe me, you are my first, my only man."

"I believe you, but how?"

"Mother sent me to the tribal wise women, the crones. They taught me how to please a man. And they said not to be afraid and hold back nothing!"

"You didn't."

"I didn't want anything to spoil our first lovemaking. If I thought it would have brought you to me sooner, I would have offered myself long ago."

"Why didn't you?"

"Mother said it wouldn't be the same unless we were truly husband and wife. She said it was better to wait."

"She is a wise woman."

"Did I please you?"

He grinned. "Mother Goddess Anu couldn't have pleased me more."

She snuggled next to him. "Do you think that you can ever love me?"

For a moment Caratacus was silent. What were his true thoughts about her? He cared for her more than he realized. His face contorted as he attempted to find the right words. "I am in many ways like my father. Sometimes I have difficulty expressing my true feelings. But I know now that I love you, and I want you to be the mother of my sons. Truly, you are a joy to me."

Rhian kissed him. "That is more than I have dared to hope. I've always wanted to be your wife and have your children. They'll be the most beautiful in all Britannia, because you'll be their father."

They loved again, more gently, and slept, arms embracing. *How long before we can love again?* Caratacus thought. He wanted the memory of this time together to last forever.

CHAPTER 14

JANUARY, AD 29

Seven months later as a dreary, afternoon fog rolled in from the channel, Caratacus and Tog left the Great Hall where Cunobelinos and the High Council had held court. Caratacus smirked as he recalled Adminios demanding that the king give him a command in the next campaign. As the eldest, he had said it was his right. The king refused. "You are a good warrior," Cunobelinos admitted, "but you are not a leader of men. You are too lazy and incompetent."

Adminios had stormed out of the council meeting.

As they trudged along the muddy path, dressed in woolen tunics and trousers and wrapped in heavy cloaks against the chill, Caratacus and Tog discussed the high king's decisions. Out of the mist, between wattle and daub houses, Adminios, along with a couple of his friends, crossed the trail a few paces away. A dog barked. Adminios and his companions stopped and glared at his two younger brothers as they halted.

"Satisfied, Brother?" Adminios's nostrils flared as he faced Caratacus. His hand dropped to the hilt of his sword.

"About what?" Caratacus said, returning Adminios's foul stare.

"Don't play me for the fool, Caratacus," Adminios answered in a snarling voice. "You know Da will give you a command in the army when the time comes."

You're an arsehole, Caratacus wanted to say. Instead he answered, "You know damn well it's his right as king, not mine. I haven't asked him for anything."

"Liar!" Adminios lunged forward.

Instantly, Caratacus's muscles tightened. He planted his feet firmly, and his hand gripped the handle of his sword, waiting for Adminios to strike. Out of the corner of his eye, he saw Tog readying himself.

Quickly, Adminios's friends intervened and pulled him away, urging him to calm down.

Tog squared his powerful shoulders and took one step forward. He gripped the hilt of his sword. "You'd better listen to your friends, big Brother," Tog advised. "Don't you ever learn? You've been warned by Da. If you injure Caratacus, let alone kill him, you'll be banished for life."

"You don't stand a chance against me," Caratacus said, staring into his brother's venomous, dark eyes.

"Wouldn't I?" Adminios growled as he struggled himself loose from his friends.

"He's right," one of them said. "Harm your brother, and you'll never command the army or become king."

"Listen to your friend, Adminios," Caratacus urged.

"One of these days," Adminios said, "when Da is no longer with us, then I will take the kingdom for myself."

Caratacus balled his hand into a fist and raised it above his head. "That day will never happen, I'll see to it."

"Oh, will you? If I have to, I will seek Rome's help." Adminios turned and hiked away, his companions following behind.

Caratacus immediately thought of Porcius. Would the Roman aid Adminios? It would give Rome the excuse it needed to invade southern Britannia. They would exploit his brother's ambition to their own ends. Should they invade Britannia, they would never leave. Adminios would be fortunate enough to survive as a puppet ruler. He would be at their beck and call like a pet dog.

* * *

Later, after supper, Caratacus and Rhian warmed themselves by the hearth against the cool autumn night air. Relaxing, he drank corma beer from a wooden bowl and contentedly glanced about their circular, thatch-roofed house. The aroma of venison stew and baked bread still lingered in the air. The empty, black cauldron, earlier filled with their dinner, casually swayed on an iron chain above the hearth. To its side sat the bee hived clay oven where Rhian baked loaves of flatbread. On the wood poles, framing the house's wall and holding up the straw roof, his battle shield and spears hung, along with a half-dozen tartan blankets and tunics. Behind him, framed between two poles, stood Rhian's upright loom with a bundle of raw wool piled nearby. Along the wall lay the bed-pallet where he and Rhian, now with child, spent many nights making love. Because she was seven months along in her pregnancy, lovemaking had become too uncomfortable for her. Reluctantly, Caratacus agreed they would stop until after the baby was born. He knew it was for the best.

Rhian, dressed in a brown and white woolen shift, sat next to Caratacus quietly sewing a rip in a work tunic.

"I heard Adminios nearly attacked you," Rhian said. "Is that true?"

Caratacus wiped the beer from his mouth on a tunic sleeve, wondering how women found out such news so fast. "Aye, but his friends stopped him."

She pricked herself with the metal sewing needle and instantly brought the forefinger to her mouth. After sucking for a few seconds, she pulled it from her lips and blew on the tip. "Why did he act so stupidly?"

Caratacus explained about the king's decision at the council meeting and the confrontation afterwards.

Rhian dropped the tunic onto her lap and glared at her husband. "You know this will only get worse. Be careful, my love, Adminios will try to kill you."

Caratacus placed his hand to her warm cheek. "I'll take care. I fear more that he will seek the aid of Rome."

"Could we defeat them?"

He shook his head. "I don't know. They have a reputation for defeating all who stand in their way. Look what happened to our Gallic cousins, and they numbered in the millions."

Rhian huffed. "Whatever comes our way, my warrior women and I will do our part. Gwyther and Modron have taught us well. After I have the baby, I will train again."

Caratacus squinted his eyes, studying Rhian. "What about the child?"

"Don't you worry, the baby will come first. Always." She paused. "But I will still have time to drill with the others. Gwyther says I should take command of one of the companies when I return."

He nodded in approval. "Then she thinks very highly of you."

"I suppose. Gwyther isn't one to give anyone leadership unless they have earned it." She motioned with a hand as if it were obvious. "You know how harsh she is with us?"

Caratacus chuckled. "She's a hard one all right."

"She is, but she is also fair. But right now I don't feel like a warrior." She looked down at her stomach. "I feel so big with child."

Caratacus grinned as he remembered how pleased he had been when Rhian first gave him the good news. He prayed it would be a son. He reached over and gently stroked her swelling abdomen. "You're not that big, and you're more beautiful than before."

Gradually, a smile appeared on her rouged face. "You really think so?" She looked down at her dress and shook her head. "Sometimes I feel so ugly and fat."

He leaned toward Rhian and gently ran his hand through her hair. "Trust me, you're not ugly and never will be in my eyes. I'm the luckiest man in the kingdom to have you as my wife."

Rhian hugged Caratacus. "Every day I thank Mother Goddess for making you my husband."

* * *

Since their marriage, Caratacus and Rhian had lived in his father's realm, the kingdom of the Catuvellauni and Trinovantes. He preferred to be with Uncle Epaticcos and the Atrebates, but custom must be honored. He wasn't one to rebel, not without good cause. His father had given him several tenant farms from which he derived a steady income. Caratacus lived outside the fortress, his holdings on the plain near the edge of the forest. A small, circular, defensive bank and wooden palisade enclosed the home. The inner yard near the house contained several structures, including lean-to-sheds for stables and dens where his blacksmith and other craftsmen worked. When he required their services, three oval, thatch-roofed buildings for storage and quarters for servants and warriors, straddled the base of the fence. The prince's retinue of warriors were in turn given smaller farms. And

Clud the blacksmith had become his faithful friend and unofficial advisor.

"Da is giving me the command of a small raiding party," Caratacus said to Clud after a private meeting with Cunobelinos. It had been three days since the confrontation with Adminios. They ambled along the rutted path between the cluster of huts leading from the Great Hall, the day cold and overcast. Both men held woolen cloaks tightly around their shoulders.

"Who do we strike?" Clud asked. He scratched his shaggy face, killing a flea between two dirty fingernails.

"Iceni outlaws." He motioned with his head to the north, the direction to where the tribe shared the border with the Trinovantes, an area constantly in dispute. "They're attacking our people's lands along the border and stealing cattle. We will find and destroy them. If we don't, it'll mean war between the tribes. The king of the Iceni denies his people are involved. But he conceded it might be a couple of isolated clan chieftains raiding on their own."

Clud hawked and spat. "Your da's right. A war would be too costly for either tribe, especially since it involves two Roman clients. Neither kingdom can afford a Roman invasion. We'd never get rid of those bastards."

"Da didn't say anything, but Ibor told me later he felt the same fear. At least he's giving me the chance to make my mark as a leader."

The two stepped around a pile of horse manure as they ambled between a couple of stock pens. "It's about time," Clud said. "You've proved your worth."

"Not yet," Caratacus said, "but if we wipe them out, he promised to give me another command."

Since the battle at Bagshot Heath more than a year before, Caratacus had fought bravely in two other skirmishes against enemy raiders. In both instances, he received minor wounds to his arms and legs, badges of honor.

Clud patted the large belly overhanging the leather belt of his gravy-stained, yellow and gray tunic. "A good start it is."

"I'll need your advice if we're to succeed, Clud."

"Ho, you have it, gladly, but it's the same as the last time: kill the men and plow the women." Clud laughed.

"Then we'll smash our enemies, sure," he said, joining in the laughter.

Clud stopped laughing and faced Caratacus. A dog barked nearby, and the sound of angry voices of a man and woman arguing came from a distant hut. "What about Adminios? In everything but name he's threatened to kill you. What plans does your father have for him?'

Caratacus scanned the shadows of the little homes within the fortress. No one lurked about, and the pathway was deserted. He continued to walk with Clud at his side. "Da will give him a command where he can do no harm."

"Aye, but the trouble is, he's not clever and that shit-eating Porcius will use him for his own purposes. Wouldn't be surprised if he didn't persuade him to seek Rome's help."

"Da will see it doesn't happen."

"Maybe, but your father grows old, and he won't live forever."

Caratacus exhaled. "I know. I will deal with the problem when the time comes. Right now, I must succeed in this new command."

In less than two weeks Caratacus and his warriors discovered the outlaw's encampment. Surprising them with an early dawn attack, they killed every man before they were fully awake. To Caratacus, cowardly bandits who slaughtered innocent peasants weren't worthy opponents of a face-to-face battle with real warriors. Clud agreed.

* * *

One month later, Cunobelinos gave Caratacus a larger command. This time he was instructed to crush a rebellion among the Cantiaci, a tribal vassal of farmers and fisherman in the southeast part of Britannia. In one month he returned home in triumph to his father's acknowledgement.

"Your victory pleases us," Cunobelinos said to Caratacus before a gathering of clan chieftains in the Great Hall. "You acted with bravery and ability as a leader in battle. Indeed, you are a warrior befitting our house."

A cheer echoed through the court. Caratacus barely contained the pride he felt in gaining his father's recognition. All that remained to complete his jubilation was the birth of a son. And Rhian was expected to deliver their child within the week.

He turned and saw Adminios among the front row of the court's onlookers. Even in the shadowy torchlight, his brother's eyes blazed with hatred.

Is he foolish enough to try and kill me?

CHAPTER 15

Within days of the confrontation between Caratacus and Adminios, Porcius returned from a visit with one of the northern kings. He lived in a small villa outside of Camulodunum and was thankful that Cunobelinos had allowed him to build a Roman-style home in his lands—every brick and tile imported from Italy. In gratitude, Porcius made a substantial *gift* of gold and expensive Setinian wine to Caratacus's father—a token of his gratitude.

Porcius smiled when he recalled how his friends in Rome accused him of being mad to live in such a remote and gods-cursed land as Britannia. He had calmly informed them that although the Britons were savages, they were forthright, and you always knew where you stood with them—most of the time. Whereas, in Rome, you never knew from one day to the next if you would keep your head.

Upon his arrival, the Roman had reported to Cunobelinos that he had been on a *trading* mission. *A future alliance was more like it.* However, if Caratacus did succeed the old king, Porcius wanted to make sure that the new ruler was surrounded by allies of Rome. That part he kept secret.

On a cold rainy afternoon, three days after his return, a servant approached Porcius in the library, where he was dictating a letter to a slave secretary, and told him Adminios was at the door.

"Escort him to the atrium, I will receive him there," Porcius said. *What does that lazy fool want from me?* He dismissed the scribe.

As Adminios entered the reception room, Porcius stood. "Welcome to my home, Prince Adminios, please be seated."

Adminios grunted his thanks and handed his cloak to the slave. Both sat in the small atrium on basket-weaved chairs, warming themselves by a smoky brazier. A light shower fell outside.

For a split second, Porcius studied Adminios, whose long, black hair straggled down the side of his stubbled face, and his breath smelled strongly of wine. His mud-spattered tunic wreaked of a sour odor.

Porcius wore a heavy, woolen cloak over his tunic and long, Celtic trousers. Woolen socks and leather boots covered his feet.

A slave brought silver cups of calda, a warm spiced wine.

"What brings you to my humble home?" Porcius asked after taking a sip.

"It's about my brother, Caratacus."

This might be interesting. "Go on, I'm listening."

Porcius quietly sipped the wine as he listened to Adminios complain about the confrontation with Caratacus.

"I am rightful heir to my father's throne, not Caratacus," Adminios said in a mildly-slurred voice. He grabbed his cup and loudly gulped its contents.

The Roman studied the younger man. *The drunkard hasn't shaved or washed in at least three days.*
"Remember, it is the Council and the chief druid, Ibor, who will make that decision."

Adminios's full lips pursed into a thin frown. "The men of the Council are fools!"

"Why do you say that?"

"They do the bidding of the Druids. Pay them enough gold, and they will elect me as king. They'll listen to you, especially Ibor."

Porcius raised his eyebrows. "You give me too much credit. The Druids hate the Romans. Why would they listen to me?"

Adminios exhaled, his alcoholic breath nearly gagging Porcius, shook his head, and gestured toward Porcius. "Everyone knows you are friends with Ibor. He's as corrupt as a week-old, dead eel."

"Whether he is or not makes no difference." Porcius shook his head. "The truth is, your father is in excellent health. He may live for many years."

"Caratacus's influence with Da will grow if nothing is done to stop him." For a split second, the younger man balled his fists.

Porcius, wine cup in hand, motioned to Adminios. "I heard you threatened to kill him, is that true?"

"Aye, it is," he answered in a defiant voice.

By Jove himself, this may work out better than I had expected. Rome needs Adminios on the throne where he can be easily led—a perfect lackey for the empire's purposes. Porcius noticed that Adminios's cup was empty and called for his servant, who scurried into his presence. After ordering him to bring more wine and dismissing the slave, Porcius turned back to Adminios. "I advise patience—your time will come." Porcius took another sip of calda.

"But I have already tried once and failed."

Porcius choked on the wine and sputtered. "You what?"

"Aye. Remember the night before Caratacus and Rhian's wedding when an assassin was killed by Clud the Iron Maker?"

The Roman coughed, drew a deep breath, but coughed again before placing his cup on the small table next to him. "I remember," he finally answered.

Adminios scanned the atrium and viewed the entry and exit to the garden. "That was my idea." His self-satisfied smirk irritated Porcius.

Porcius gasped. "How?" *What in Jupiter's name was this fool thinking?*

"I went in secret to King Verica," Adminios said in a voice above a whisper, "I told him my father was planning to make Caratacus king—" At that moment, the servant returned with two more cups of calda. When he departed, Adminios took another swill of wine and continued. "I convinced him I am the rightful heir. If he wanted revenge for his son, Gwynedd, I told him there was a way and where he could find Caratacus. But the fool assassin went to the wrong house, and Clud killed him."

Porcius inhaled deeply. "Why are you telling me this?"

"Because you know as well as I that Caratacus hates Rome and would expel all Roman traders, including you." He paused. "I have heard you do not want to see him become king."

Porcius snorted. "Don't believe everything you hear. Nevertheless, you are fortunate that your part in this attempt on his life wasn't discovered."

"Who would tell?"

"Spies, of course. Who do you think?" Porcius answered with growing impatience. *Doesn't he realize the implications of his acts?* "You are fortunate they didn't tell your father. And since you visited Verica in secret, he could have gotten rid of you, and no one would have been the wiser."

"I didn't think of that."

That's because you never think. Porcius narrowed his eyes. "I strongly suggest you refrain from any further reckless attempts on Caratacus's life."

Adminios leaned closer. "Then I need your help, Rome's help."

"Not at this point." Porcius waved his hand as though swatting flies.

Adminios raised his black eyebrows. "Why not? Rome has conquered our Gallic cousins. Why not invade our lands and place me on the throne when my father dies?"

One day you will be Rome's puppet. "At this time, Emperor Tiberius has no interest in sending an army to Britannia. It seems, if the rumors and secret reports I have received are true, he lives in self-imposed isolation on the Isle of Capri. He has been indulging himself in lusting after little boys and girls—disgusting."

The nostrils of the young man's big nose flared. "The pig! We have laws protecting our children from monsters like him. Can't the old bugger be replaced?"

Porcius glanced about the reception room and lowered his voice, "There is one who would like to do just that—Sejanus, his Praetorian Prefect. He is in everything but name the ruler of the Roman Empire. Tiberius believes his every word whenever Sejanus accuses anyone of treason, lies though they may be. Unfortunately, he too has no interest in invading Britannia."

"Why not?"

"It's called power. He's waiting for Tiberius to die or the right opportunity to kill him so he can rule as Emperor—he has the backing of the Praetorian Guard."

"But how long before he takes power?"

Porcius threw both hands upward. "Who knows? The true heir to Emperor Tiberius is young Gaius Caligula. Now, if he manages to survive any of Sejanus's murderous attempts on his life and succeeds Tiberius, then possibly he would intercede on your behalf." He paused and jabbed a finger toward Adminios. "However, under no circumstances are you to link my name with any hint of a Roman invasion—I will deny it to the world. Do you understand?"

Adminios nodded.

"Until then, you must wait."

Adminios glared at Porcius. "I will, but not for long."

* * *

Late afternoon, early in March, in the cold gloom of overhanging, slate-gray clouds, Caratacus, Tog, and Clud had left the king's chambers, split up, and proceeded to their respective homes. As Caratacus neared his, a lone rider cantered his bay horse down the muddy path, the sounds of muffled hoof beats growing louder as the rider approached him. He reined up in front of Caratacus, the horse drenched in sweat, white foam dripping from its mouth. Caratacus immediately recognized the scar-faced warrior as Llew, one of Epaticcos's younger retainers. He wore a cloak around broad shoulders. A longsword hung from a baldric running down the front of his tunic to his waistline on the left side. *Why did he come to me and not Da? Is something wrong with Uncle Epaticcos or Aunt Gwynn?*

"Llew, welcome," Caratacus said. "Do you bring news from my uncle?"

He dismounted and stepped toward the prince while holding the horse's reins in one hand. "I do, Prince, but it's not good."

"What? Speak, man."

He gulped. "The king's wife is gravely ill. He asks that you come at once. He is afraid she is dying."

"Aunt Gwynn's dying? No!" Caratacus's muscles tightened. He took a deep breath and struggled to keep a sober face.

"That's what he fears."

"All right, Llew, I will make preparations to leave with you in the morning. I will tell my father and Tog—my brother will ride with us. In the meantime, I will see that you get something to eat and drink and a place for you and your horse to rest. You must be exhausted." *Why did this have to happen now?* He and Rhian hadn't seen Epaticcos or Gwynn since the wedding. They had planned to visit them next summer after the baby was born.

After seeing to Llew's needs, Caratacus informed Cunobelinos, who said his pressing duties as king would not allow him to travel to Caleva. However, he prayed for Gwynn's recovery, but if she went to the gods, he'd send his condolences. Caratacus then found Tog, explained the circumstances, and hurried to his home.

Caratacus returned home and spotted Rhian, her growing belly outlined by a flowing tunic, standing at the hearth. She watched as one of her young serving women stirred a pot of stew, the spicy aroma enveloping the room.

Rhian turned and smiled as he approached, but it disappeared, her eyebrows raised. "What's wrong, Caratacus? You look as if an evil spirit has crossed your path."

He huffed. "It's Aunt Gwynn, she's dying."

She gasped. "What? How do you know?" She stepped a few paces in his direction.

"I just received a message from Llew, one of Epaticcos's retainers." He explained in greater detail.

"Then you must go, darling," Rhian said when he finished. "She was like the mother you really never had."

"My real mother died when I was four—I hardly remember her."

"When will you leave?"

"At first light with Tog and Llew." He placed a hand on her shoulder. "Will you be all right? You will deliver our baby soon, and I want to be here when you do."

Rhian gave him a reassuring smile. "Don't fret, Fand is an excellent midwife. Besides, you'll be back before the baby arrives."

Caratacus hugged his beautiful wife. "I pray I will. I also pray I will arrive in time to see Aunt Gwynn before she leaves this world."

"As do I," Rhian said.

"She was Uncle Epaticcos's favorite consort and wife." Caratacus stared beyond his wife as though looking into empty space. "He's bound to take her death very hard."

* * *

For the next three days, Caratacus, Tog, and Llew rode hard, only stopping when it grew too dark to ride. They arrived in Caleva, capital of Epaticcos's kingdom, on the evening of the third day.

Llew had been dismissed. Caratacus and Tog were greeted by the captain of Epaticcos's retainers after the guards at the hill fortress gates had already passed on the word of Caratacus's arrival.

"Where is my uncle, the king?" Caratacus asked. "How is my aunt, Gwynn?"

"The king is at his house," the captain said. "He will answer your questions, Prince Caratacus. Follow me."

Inside in the gloom of Epaticcos's home, Caratacus and Tog found him wrapped in a heavy, woolen cloak, sitting on a high-backed, cushioned chair by the smoky, central hearth. The pulsating light of the central fire and four olive-oil lamps on a couple of small adjacent tables illuminated his ashen face. Deep lines crawled down the side of his leathery features and across his forehead. Sunken, black pouches shrouded the area beneath his lower eyelids. Caratacus's heart leapt into his throat. He glanced to Tog, who nodded. Both knew.

"Uncle?" Caratacus asked.

Epaticcos slowly looked up at Caratacus and Tog, who stood before him. "Leave us," he ordered the captain hovering behind the two young men. He gestured to the two stools opposite him. "Be seated."

When the captain departed, Caratacus asked, "Is she," he swallowed. "Is she gone?"

Epaticcos's lips tightened, and he inhaled through his nose and exhaled. "Yes ... I am afraid so." He inhaled again and, for a second, turned his face away.

Tog paled and sniffed. He cleared his throat. "When did she die, Uncle?"

"About three hours after I dispatched Llew to fetch you two."

Quickly, Caratacus calculated at least six days and more had passed. "I take it you have already buried her?"

Epaticcos nodded. "Aye, we couldn't wait. I hate to say it, but much as I wanted to wait for your arrival, her body quickly started to decay. I had no choice. We buried her two days after she died—with all the honors due to a queen."

The muscles in Caratacus's body tightened, his face grew hot. As much as he wanted to weep, he couldn't. He bit his lip, swallowed, and asked Epaticcos for the details. "What did she die from?"

"A wasting disease."

"So soon?" Tog asked. "She seemed healthy enough when we went to Camulodunum for Caratacus and Rhian's marriage."

Epaticcos looked into Tog's and then Caratacus's face. "Remember the night the assassin almost killed Rhian?"

"How could I forget," Caratacus answered.

"If you recall, Gwynn and I weren't there when you and your father and the others ran to her aid."

For a second Caratacus and Tog turned to one another. "Now that you mention it," Caratacus said, "that's true. I thought you were visiting friends."

"We weren't. Gwynn began spitting blood that day and fainted."

"Why didn't you tell us?" Tog asked.

"She didn't want anything to spoil the wedding," Epaticcos answered.

"Still we should have been told," Caratacus said.

Epaticcos raised a hand. "She wouldn't hear of it. When we returned to Caleva, she grew worse, spitting more blood. Your aunt started losing weight and wasted away quickly. At the end, she was little more than a skeleton."

"But so fast? She was a big-boned woman, who would have thought it could have happened so quickly," Tog said.

Epaticcos nodded. "I know, she wanted to live long enough to see the both of you one more time—it wasn't to be. Now," he paused, "she is in the underworld and at peace."

Caratacus's body ached. He wanted to weep, but knew it would be considered unmanly. He had to wait until he was alone.

"Enough of my loss," Epaticcos said, pulling Caratacus from his grief. "How are you two? More importantly, how is Rhian? I hear she is with child."

"She is due in little more than a month," Caratacus said.

Epaticcos managed a weak smile. "Then I won't keep you long. Despite my loss and my sorrow, there is important news I must share with you now. In the morning we will visit your aunt's tomb, and then you can return to your homes."

"What is your news?" Caratacus asked. *What is so important that it can't wait until later?*

"I have heard rumors that your traitorous brother, Adminios, has been in touch with Verica."

Caratacus and Tog glanced to one another. "Dirty bastard," Caratacus huffed. "I can't say I'm surprised." He stood and began pacing back and forth in front of the hearth.

"But why?" Tog asked. "As if I couldn't guess."

Epaticcos shook his head. "There is no firm evidence that it's true." He watched Caratacus. "A couple of passing traders, whom I've done business with on a regular basis, told me. They heard the story when they were in Noviomagnus. Have either of you noticed Adminios being away from Camulodunum for any length of time?"

"I haven't paid any attention to his movements," Caratacus said. He stopped and eyed his uncle. "I figured he was probably out hunting again."

Tog pulled on his scraggly moustache. "He wouldn't have used a messenger as a go between with Verica, would he?" Tog asked.

"I don't know," Epaticcos answered. He adjusted his cloak, wrapping it tighter about his shoulders. "Adminios could have used a merchant as a go-between, but that could prove risky as the person might think it more profitable to inform Cunobelinos."

"Unless Adminios paid him a large fee," Caratacus added, not liking the conclusion he reached. He paced again.

"Either way, it seems that he made contact with Verica," Epaticcos continued. "He probably went to Verica in disguise, otherwise, he would have been recognized."

"I didn't think he was that clever—must have had help," Tog said. He cracked his knuckles and sat straighter on his stool.

Caratacus halted and sat down. "Well, what did he and Verica discuss?"

"He asked his help in overthrowing your father."

"Damn him!" Caratacus blurted. "He's a fool if he believes Verica would aid him in overthrowing Da. Verica would murder Adminios in return."

"I always knew Adminios was stupid, this proves it," Tog said. He turned to his older brother.

"My thoughts, too," Epaticcos said. "However, there is no proof. Both would deny the accusations."

"Then I'll confront Adminios as soon as we return to Camulodunum," Caratacus said, his voice full of determination. "I'll wring the truth out of him!"

Epaticcos narrowed his eyes and studied Caratacus. "You would do that based on what? Rumors? Your father would never tolerate it. All you would accomplish is to alert Adminios, and he would hide all further treasonous activities. He would plead innocence with Cunobelinos accusing you of being a liar, because you crave the kingdom for yourself."

"Why couldn't he be tortured?" Tog asked.

Epaticcos's eyes met Tog's. "Your father would never torture his sons, you know that. It's not his way. His outside enemies—yes. Besides, your father was counting on Verica as an ally to war against me. Cunobelinos would probably kill Adminios outright if he believed he sought

Verica's help to overthrow him. Still, you need hard evidence before your father will move against Adminios."

"Then what should I do?" Caratacus asked. He slapped a hand on his thigh.

Caratacus's uncle surveyed him with is hawk-like, brown eyes. The old battle scar slicing diagonally across his face gave him a menacing look. He jabbed a finger toward Caratacus. "Wait, but keep a close eye on him. I will send spies, traders I know, to Noviomagnus to learn more—to see if the rumors are true."

"All right, but it will be difficult to refrain myself from slicing off his stinking head." Caratacus placed a hand tightly around the hilt of the dagger tied to his waist.

Epaticcos turned to Caratacus and then Tog. "Stay away from him—both of you. Keep level heads and your eyes wide open."

"Both of us will keep a watch," Tog said through clinched teeth.

"Then wait until you receive word from me before moving against your brother."

Caratacus paused, frowning. "Where has Porcius been through all of this?" he asked. "I wouldn't be surprised if he were somehow involved."

"He has been traveling throughout Britannia speaking with the tribal kings, looking for more favorable agreements for Rome."

"Favorable not only for Rome but for Porcius," Caratacus said. "I swear it's only a matter of time before Rome invades our lands. Just like in Gaul, they'll slaughter our people if we don't stop them."

"Calm yourself, Caratacus," Epaticcos said. "If it comes to that, our armies will drive the Romans into the sea."

Caratacus shot a fist into the air. "And I will lead the charge."

"Do you think Porcius might have anything to do with Adminios and Verica's plotting?" Tog asked.

Epaticcos shook his head. "I wouldn't think so, considering Verica's son attempted to murder the Roman and failed," Epaticcos said.

"Aye, and Gwynedd paid with his life," Caratacus added.

"If anything, he probably would counsel your brother to wait until Cunobelinos was dying," Epaticcos added.

"May that not happen for many years," Caratacus said. "But I doubt if Adminios will wait that long to make his move against Da."

CHAPTER 16

MARCH, AD 37

As Caratacus waited with Tog outside his home most of the evening, he prayed that Rhian, in labor again, would finally give birth to a healthy child. The two brothers, both wrapped in heavy, woolen cloaks, huddled by the small bonfire waiting for word about her. Would the gods curse Rhian again? Tense muscles and tightness in his chest confirmed his fears. These were the same feelings he'd experienced prior to the deaths of the other two children. Were the gods against him? Was Rhian under a curse? He prayed he was wrong. Exhaling, Caratacus breathed on his fingers, warming them against the frigid air.

Shaking Caratacus out of his thoughts, Tog said, "I still say you should come inside my house with me instead of freezing out here, Brother." His teeth chattered. A couple of finger widths shorter and leaner than his older brother, Tog was now a grown man. A drooping moustache hung down the sides of his wide mouth.

"I'm not keeping you from your warm bed and wife, Tog," Caratacus said. His younger brother had married a comely, raven-haired lass, Ygerna, about two years ago. Now, they had a six-month-old baby son. Caratacus regretted he hadn't been as fortunate. He prayed that would change now that Rhian was about to give birth again.

Caratacus rubbed his hands together again. Despite the fire, a chill penetrated his body, and his hands and feet like icicles. "I've got to stay for Rhian's sake."

"I won't desert you," Tog answered as a wisp of warm air shot from his mouth, "even if they have to cut off my black, frost-bitten toes." He glanced to his feet layered in thick, woolen socks, wrapped inside and outside, over the top of his leather boots. "Too bad every time Rhian gives birth it's like going to battle. I've never known a woman who's struggled so much."

"Nor I. And thanks for the company." Although grateful, he couldn't hear Rhian's birthing pains through the thick wattle and daub walls of their house, Caratacus was too embarrassed to confide his feelings to Tog. Only women shared their worries, not men.

"Prince Caratacus," came a woman's voice behind them.

They turned as Fand, the head midwife, approached. She wore an ankle-length, tartan tunic, covered by a light, woolen apron, splattered with blood. Furrows lined her sallow face, and the sour smell of birthing fluids oozed from her slimy hands. "I'm sorry, my Lord Caratacus ... the child ... he ... was born dead."

Caratacus clinched his fists and kicked one of the wooden braces of the thatch-roofed house, oblivious to the pain that shot through his foot in spite of the padded boots. "Damn! The third death in eight years! What went wrong, woman?"

Frightened by his outburst, the stout, middle-aged woman stepped back a couple paces and looked away, then back. "The same as the last. The babe strangled on its own cord. By the time his head came through the birthing canal it was too late."

"The son I wanted." He exhaled, "By Lugh, I know babies die at birth, but why ours? Are we cursed?"

Curse all the gods! Caratacus's body shuddered. Tears rolled down his cheeks. *I don't care who sees them. But of course I do.* He sighed. Before the woman saw his face, he wiped them away and rubbed his nose on his sleeve. Shame rolled through him for such an unmanly display. *Yet, how else should I feel about losing my son and the other children?* No answer.

"Easy, Brother," Tog said, placing a hand on Caratacus's shoulder, "the midwife did all she could."

"I know that," Caratacus said in a reassuring voice. He glanced at her wrinkled face, pale with fright. "How is the Princess Rhian?"

"She's resting, my lord," Fand answered. She pushed back the gray strands of hair from her wrinkled face. "The babe wore her out. It wouldn't be wise to see her yet."

"Why?"

Fand shook her head. "Just like after she lost the last two babes, she would weep and feel so ashamed that she didn't give you a live son. Wait 'til tomorrow when she's feeling a little better."

He nodded and Fand returned to the house.

Somehow I've offended the gods. They've placed a curse on me, and it must have passed through my seed into Rhian. Gods forbid!

He shook his head. Three babies dead before he realized how much he loved her.

By custom, he could have taken a concubine or another wife to sire a child after Rhian lost her first child. Yet, he felt he would have betrayed her. He couldn't do that, not yet.

He wondered if this is why Adminios had turned into a drunkard. His older brother had always been lazy, preferring hunting over learning the affairs of state. However, when he was younger, he had been married twice. Unfortunately, both women died with their babies in child birth. It was after his second wife died, a women whom he especially liked, that Adminios went on a drinking binge that never stopped. Caratacus remembered his brother saying, "The gods have cursed me, why should I marry again? I can have any woman I want—I don't give a damn who rules after me."

While Caratacus understood Adminios's grief, he wouldn't excuse his excesses and outrageous behavior.

Caratacus stooped and placed another pine log on the fire. He sat staring as the wood flamed and blazed skyward. The heat warmed his face, and the fresh smell of resin seeped into his nostrils. Gradually, the muscles of his body relaxed. "It's as if Rhian had been cursed," Caratacus said. "If true, it should have been me, not her. Gods, I wonder if we'll ever have any children?"

* * *

Caratacus slept little that night. Early the next morning, a servant awakened and informed the prince that his father wanted to see him immediately. He wanted to see Rhian first and console her, but it would have to wait.

Inside the Great Hall, the shadows of smoky torchlight reflected eerily on the high king's drawn face. Black circles that Caratacus hadn't noticed before ringed his father's eyes. The long moustache had turned into a clump of gray, his ruddy complexion fading like the last rays of the setting sun. Despite the glowing warmth from the nearby hearth, Cunobelinos slumped in his Roman curule chair, his purple cloak drawn around his shoulders. Except for the shield bearers standing at a discreet distance in the shadows, no one was present.

"I'm sorry to hear Rhian bore you another dead son," Cunobelinos said.

"I've been up most of the night." Caratacus yawned and rubbed his eyes.

The king leaned forward. "I see it in your face. It's my desire to someday bless the son of my son. I pray the gods are kinder when she has another child."

"So do I," Caratacus said. His father had expressed his condolences in the past but never one bit of sympathy. Before, he had shrugged off the deaths as the way of the gods and a hazard all women endured.

Stifling another yawn, Caratacus asked, "What do you want, Da?" Normally, his father never summoned him at this early hour. "Has another conspiracy been uncovered?"

"Fortunately, not this time."

"Aye, the discovery of two conspiracies on your life in as many years is enough." *Too bad neither involved Adminios. I know he is a traitor.* Since the day he and Tog had been warned, nearly eight years ago by Epaticcos, Adminios had not made any move to overthrow their father. But Caratacus was always at the ready to stop Adminios should he make a move against their father.

"Don't forget your friend Clud who learned from friends about the second one."

"And you showed confidence by allowing Clud and me to arrest the traitors." Caratacus recalled it had been four years since he led a contingent of hand-picked, loyal warriors that caught the rebels. Under torture administered by old Ibor and his Druids, they extracted confessions from the chieftains. It had served the traitors right when they were excommunicated and put to death for planning the overthrow of Cunobelinos and allying with Verica.

"I received a message," Cunobelinos said, arousing Caratacus from his thoughts, "that Dobunni raiders are stealing cattle from the outlying settlements again and killing our people. You're to take a company of riders and go after them."

"Didn't you warn their king that we'd retaliate if they didn't stop raiding?"

His father snorted. "I did."

"Why didn't he stop them?"

"They're his trouble-making clansmen," Cunobelinos answered with a growl. "He wants us to get rid of them so he can keep his hands clean."

Caratacus motioned as if that were obvious. "But then he'll have an excuse to war against us."

"He won't." A crafty grin crossed the old king's wrinkled face. "Not only do I have his promise, but a hefty sum in gold for the favor."

Caratacus wasn't surprised. His father knew how to negotiate the best terms for himself when it involved gold. He had the riches to prove it. "Very clever, both sides profit. He's rid of a nest of vipers, we save our peasants and cattle and get paid in the process."

"Aye, we would've anyway, but the gold greased my axle." Cunobelinos opened and closed his hand as if holding something of value. "He's desperate. And we profit in another way."

"How?" Caratacus asked.

"Our slave trading has declined in recent years." He pointed to a row of skulls sitting in niches along the wall. "This time I want prisoners, not heads. They'll be sold as slaves to the Romans."

Caratacus shook his head. "My warriors aren't going to like it, especially if they're sold to Rome."

The king narrowed his eyes and glared at his son. "I don't care what they like, they'll do as they're told. You'll see to that."

"I will, but heads are important to them, for their souls. You can't win a battle without deaths."

"You'll get your share of heads. But right now, the kingdom needs the money. I'm holding you responsible for the acts of your men. Kill no captives and behead only the dead."

Caratacus recalled what Uncle Epaticcos had said years ago, and he was right. There is more to being a great leader and warrior than taking heads in battle. He no longer found decapitation a thrill as he once did. He took one occasionally, only to maintain his reputation as a fierce warrior. Because his own followers wouldn't understand his changing outlook, Caratacus kept his thoughts to himself.

"The slave trade has dropped only because Porcius was recalled to Rome four summers ago," Caratacus said. "It's a shame you need a Roman to deal with slave traders to make our profits."

Cunobelinos straightened his back and pulled the cloak tighter about his shoulders. He turned and spat onto the rushes placed around the foot of the throne. "I'm aware of your loathing for Porcius and Rome, but they are a necessary evil. Porcius knows how to make money for us."

"Not to mention for himself."

The king snorted. "He's a typical Roman merchant, and one day he'll return. He's too greedy to stay away forever."

Caratacus nodded. He recalled that shortly after he and Rhian had been married and established a permanent home in Camulodunum, his father gave him a minor command in the army. He was dispatched to search for and attack the raiders from a neighboring tribe whose chieftains were stealing cattle from farmsteads near the other's border. He successfully carried out the campaign, killing the raiders and recovering the livestock.

Cunobelinos had shown his pleasure by giving him greater responsibilities and placing him in charge of a warrior company in a couple of campaigns against the rebellious Cantiaci to the south. After the successful conclusion of the war, Caratacus was publically recognized as a warrior and a man, much to the consternation and animosity of Adminios.

Prior to this, Caratacus had brought to his father's attention the rumors about Adminios's conspiracy with Verica to overthrow him. His father had refused to believe him.

"The rumors are lies," Cunobelinos had said. "No son of mine, not even Adminios, would betray me."

"Da, this is too serious to disregard. You should at least send spies to verify. Epaticcos did."

"Bah, do you expect me to believe him? He wants my kingdom as much as Verica."

"All the more reason to send your own spies. To standby and do nothing is madness."

"I'm doing no such thing." Cunobelinos paused and, for the length of a few heartbeats, stared beyond Caratacus toward the entrance of the Great Hall. "Even as we speak, my spies are in the field. Should Adminios turn on me, I will know about it and deal with him."

At least Da is taking some action.

* * *

Caratacus's mind returned to the present when he saw his father giving him a puzzled look. "I'm flattered you've given me the responsibility of going after this Dobunni vermin, Da," Caratacus said a moment later.

"It's because you earned it," the king said gruffly. He raised his arm and pointed a finger. "Don't let it go to your head."

"I won't." For Caratacus that was compliment enough.

"The time will come when I'm no longer here," Cunobelinos continued as he lowered his arm, "there is no room in the kingdom for a ruler who has a big head, only one who rules wisely."

"What about Tog and Adminios?"

"Your younger brother learns from you. As for Adminios, you know he can't be trusted with this responsibility, that's why I gave you the command." The king shook his head as if disappointed with his oldest son.

Caratacus tightly gripped the hilt of his sword. "He'll object."

"Let him. He will abide by it if he knows what's good for him."

"Do you still believe he wouldn't overthrow you?"

The king paused, his scarred ruddy face studying Caratacus. "You haven't presented me with any substantial proof. Until then, I will not act. My spies watch him, and he has not shown any signs of betrayal. I'm no fool, which is why I only give him minor commands for token raids."

"There are members of the council who would elect him as king so they could rule through him."

"Not while I live," Cunobelinos answered in a voice more like a growl. "I have the right to choose my successor."

Caratacus released the grip on the hilt, raised his hand, and gestured in the king's direction. "You have many summers left."

Cunobelinos lowered his eyes, which were surrounded by black pouches the color of a burnt stick, and exhaled. "My aching bones tell me that they pass by faster each year."

Suddenly, the king snapped his head back, his eyes alert, and straightened in his chair. He smiled at his son. "Enough of this nonsense. Have you seen your wife today?"

"No, I slept at Tog's last night."

"Then it's time you see her. Go and be with her for now. Soon, you'll be setting out against bandits."

* * *

Arriving at his home, Caratacus headed for the goat-skinned, partitioned area inside, situated at the far wall where Rhian was now bedded. He entered the enclosure, dimly lit by three candles. He quickly scanned the room and saw that it had been cleaned, the birthing stool used by Rhian was gone, along with blood-stained garments or any other evidence of her ordeal. The air smelled of vinegar, used for cleaning and the reduction of infection, one of the few Roman ideas that he approved of. Caratacus spotted Rhian sitting upright, propped up by pillows, but still covered in furs. A female slave, using a wooden spoon, was feeding Rhian from a bowl of porridge. She took small bites. Her face was drawn and pale, eyes reddened, lids swollen. Loose hair draped her shoulders.

Rhian turned, watched as he approached, only seemed to recognize him as he drew closer. A weak smile crossed her lips. Caratacus eyed the slave and nodded toward the entrance. She placed the bowl on a small table with stubby legs near Rhian and departed.

Caratacus knelt by Rhian's side. He grinned as he reached over and lightly stroked her cheek.

She tightened her lips and looked away. Her body quivered before turning towards him again, tears running down her face. "I'm sorry, I've failed you again."

He moved closer, taking Rhian into his arms, her body seemed lighter than before.

She buried her head into his chest and sobbed.

Caratacus stroked her freshly washed hair, the scent of chamomile filled his nostrils. He said in a soft, compassionate voice, "You didn't fail me. Not this time, not ever."

"I didn't give you a son," she said in a muffled voice. "I haven't given a child, not even a daughter. You must hate me."

Caratacus shook his head. "Hate you? Never. It isn't your fault the gods have been against you, that's how I see it."

Rhian turned her head to one side of his chest. "The gods have nothing to do it—it's me, only me—how can you love me?"

He remained silent for a short time before he answered, "I will always love you. No matter what the future brings, even if you don't have another child, you will always be the number one woman in my life."

"You mean that? Honestly?"

"I do."

Rhian snuggled closer. "I pray to Mother Goddess that one day I will bear you a child, even if it is only a daughter."

Caratacus pushed her slightly away from his chest so he could look into her tear-stained eyes. "I would be content with a daughter."

* * *

On a chilly evening, a month after Rhian's latest stillbirth, Caratacus returned from a patrol along the tribal border with the Dobunni. The previous week they had caught the raiders his father had told him about and managed to take most as prisoners to be sold as slaves, pleasing Cunobelinos to no end. This particular foray was to search for any who had escaped—there were none. After reporting to his father, he returned home. He entered and handed his cloak to a young, female servant. She nodded in Rhian's direction, who stood in the dim candle light by the weaving loom a few paces from him.

"What's wrong?" he asked.

Rhian moved towards him, a frown on her bowed lips. "You tell me," she answered and tossed him a small leather pouch, which he grabbed in midair by one hand, its weight heavier than he expected.

Caratacus moved to the hearth where the light was better, followed by Rhian. Both sat side by side on fur pelts spread beside the fire pit. "I don't understand what this is all about," he said while untying the cord around the pouch.

"It's a message from Cartimandua," she answered in a huff.

He turned to Rhian, studying her rouged face in the shimmering light as the fire crackled and popped. Smoke drifted upward to the small escape hole in the center of the straw-packed roof. "My cousin?"

She glared at him. "Is there another one? Are you keeping something from me?"

Caratacus shook his head. "Don't talk to me like that, woman. No, I have no idea what this is about. Who brought this?"

"A merchant friend of your father. He sailed down from Eburacum and was instructed to deliver you the message. Since you weren't here, I received it. I would have read it if I knew how."

"If you knew how to read, I would have forbidden you to read my dispatches without my permission," he growled.

"Humph!"

Caratacus pulled out a packet containing several thin, curved sheets of birch bark tied together with a leather string. He said to himself while he untied the bundle, "Strange, the last time I saw her was eleven years ago when I was twelve—she was seven."

"Oh, really?" Rhian surveyed him through squinting, emerald eyes.

Does she think I'm lying? "Yes, King Prasutagus brought her and the rest of his family for a visit while he negotiated an alliance with Da. The two of them are half brothers. Da seems closer to him than to Uncle Epaticcos. Still, that doesn't explain why she would send me a message. "

"Read it and learn for yourself," she said.

Pulling the sheets apart, one by one, he perused the lighter, smoother sides of the sheets, which were written in Latin.

"Well, what does she say?"

"Cartimandua sends her condolences on the loss of our child."

Rhian sniffed. "She sent a letter all this way for that? The woman never sent one when I lost the first two."

Caratacus held up a hand. "There's more." For a moment he silently read. He looked at Rhian. "This is interesting. She says that I have the right to take another wife, if the first one—obviously meaning you—cannot bear me an heir."

Rhian jolted, her face flushed. "How dare she say that? It's none of her business what goes on between us."

He exhaled. "I agree, but she is right—it's the custom."

She slapped a hand against her thigh. "Custom be damned!" she blurted so loudly that it startled the nearby servant grinding flour in the stone quern. "You wouldn't remarry, would you?"

He moved closer, grabbed Rhian by the shoulder, and pulled her to his chest. He gave her a lingering hug. "No, you're the one I love, you're my joy." He released her and moved slightly away.

"Truly?" Rhian asked. A grateful smile crossed her lips.

"Aye." He hesitated. "But there's more."

Rhian shook her head, strands of tawny hair fell across her face. "I've heard enough."

He raised his hand. "Patience. It's important that you hear the rest."

"If you must." She crinkled her nose as she pulled the strands away from her cheeks.

"Cartimandua has heard rumors that I will inherit the throne."

"Where did she hear that?"

Caratacus shrugged. "The gods only know. Even I haven't heard that story."

"Well, you should be the next king and not Adminios."

"Be that as it may. Listen to this," he said. "She married Venutios three years ago."

"I remember you saying he is a good man, I pity him."

"So do I."

"Better him than you."

"She has other ideas."

Rhian gave him a questioning look. "Meaning?"

"If I gave the word to marry her ..." He hesitated.

"Go on."

"She would divorce Venutios."

A long gasping sound escaped her mouth. "How dare she? If the stories are true, she is nothing but a slut. You once mentioned Aunt Gwynn said a woman should consort with only the best of men. Cartimandua consorts with all sorts, even the vilest. Well, she's not going to have you. I'll kill her first!"

Caratacus held up a hand. "Calm yourself, my love. I will never marry her."

"Then tell her."

"I will," he said softly, "first thing in the morning when I send for Da's scribe. In the letter I will say I have no interest in her *generous* offer and advise her to stay with Venutios."

"I pray to Mother Goddess she will take your advice and keep her prying hooks off you."

"She will," he answered in a confident voice.

"The question is, for how long?" Rhian twisted her head, looking toward the entry to their home as if half expecting to see Cartimandua at any moment.

Had Cartimandua appeared, Caratacus wouldn't have been surprised if Rhian took a dagger to Cartimandua's throat.

CHAPTER 17

MAY, AD 39

Porcius leaned over the ship's rough, wooden rail and vomited. He hated the sea and had dreaded the voyage from Gaul to Britannia, even though it took only five hours. He retched so hard he was certain he'd puked his guts inside out. His mouth flooded with the foul taste of bile as he slumped to the oaken deck, exhausted. Deathly pale and sweaty, Porcius wiped his puffy face with a silk handkerchief. "Bring me water," he moaned.

A smiling slave brought him a pitcher.

The Roman turned and grabbed the jug from the slave, rinsed out his mouth, and spat. "That's better. Now, if Neptune will quit kicking my guts, I can rest." He grabbed the swaying ship's oak railing. Cautiously, he stepped in the direction of the vessel's protective canopy near the stern.

"Lord, please let me help you." Cyrus placed a hand on Porcius's shoulder.

"I can manage!" Porcius shoved his freedman's long, muscular hand aside. "I'm not dead yet." But after stumbling, he extended his hand for support. "If you really want to help me, beat that grinning, fool slave. No one smiles while I'm dying."

After resting on a bench beneath the goat skin-covered deck, his cramping muscles relaxed, the aching pain within his stomach lessened. "Now you know why I hate voyages," Porcius told Cyrus. The Persian turned away from the ship's railing and stepped to the Roman's side. "Even when the crossing is this close. I pray that one day another means of traveling will be found. Unfortunately, I'll have crossed the River Styx, and old Charon, the boatman, will laugh at my suffering the entire way."

Assisted by Cyrus, Porcius stood again and peered landward into the light breeze. A sluggish haze lay like a clump of gray ashes on the gentle, rolling swells of the channel. He squinted in vain, searching for the chalky outline of the British coast. The beamy merchantman slipped in and out of a drifting fog bank, midmorning, late in May. Finally, there was a break, and the ship sailed into warm sunlight. The ocean changed from a drab gray-green to a brilliant blue, and an earthy breeze encouraged him with the scent of land.

"Look, there is Mersea Island," Porcius said. "I'd know those slimy mud flats anywhere." Little skiffs dotted the shallow waters beyond as hardy fisherman slowly dredged the bottom for oysters. "Behind the island is the Promontory of Camulodunum. From there it's five miles up the Colne River estuary to the great fort itself."

Partially covered in fog, the fortress's massive, stone dikes pierced the shrouding mist like a floating monolith: gray, grim, and foreboding, as if it were a prehistoric island adrift in a becalmed sea.

"I hadn't realized until now how much I'd looked forward to returning to this bleak isle, even though I bribed my way into the Senate while in Rome."

Cyrus cricked his mouth into a sneer. "It is a shame you had to cater to that group of insufferable, perfumed snobs."

"The members of the Senate hate new money and self-made millionaires, especially those who are wealthier than they are."

"No matter, you had far more than the one million sesterces needed to qualify for the office. That is a sum many of those buffoons no longer have."

"True, a number of the senators are lingering on the edge of poverty, hanging onto the vestiges of ancestral glory."

"It didn't take long before they came crawling on their knees begging you for loans and your friendship."

Porcius chuckled. "Indeed, Cyrus. If I recall correctly, at least ten of them came *crawling*, as you put it, before we left Rome. Strange how all of a sudden new friends appeared out of the brickwork like flies on dung."

"Lord, it was more like vultures feasting on carrion." Cyrus turned to the ship's rail and spat overboard.

Porcius sighed. "There is more truth to that than you might believe, my friend. Indeed, I *shared* with a few of the most influential members and the emperor's secretary. It's a wonder I had anything left when I was finally appointed to that lofty position. That is why I have returned to Britannia—I need to make more money through my trading contacts." Porcius looked seaward and studied the fishing boats. Sometimes he envied the Britons' lives, even the dangers and hardships they suffered. At least they knew what faced them on a daily basis. He wished he could say the same.

"Eight years is a long time to wait," Cyrus said.

"Quite so, but I'm happy to be back. The pain and retching have been worth it."

"This land," Cyrus said as his bulbous nose flared, "is so cold and remote. In all the years I have served you, I have never grown used to it." Bigger than most of his countrymen, the Persian wrapped his woolen cloak tighter around his husky shoulders.

"For your Persian blood, perhaps," Porcius said. "Then again, it should be for me, but it isn't. You see those nightingales." He motioned skyward. "We have something in common: Britannia is a second home for both of us. Since Caligula became Emperor of Rome, I am eager to be out of the man's sight," Porcius continued, "and, hopefully, out of his mad mind. That is why I'm all the more grateful in returning to Britannia. I would think you would feel the same way, too." The thin and placid face of Caligula, Tiberius's twenty-five-year-old nephew, reminded Porcius of a goat. His looks belied the fact he was a monster, who consumed friends and opponents alike at a whim, and for no reasons other than simple amusement.

Cyrus gave him a quizzical look.

"Don't despair, Cyrus," Porcius consoled. "You know I could not do without your services. You've flogged my unruly household into submission, and I'm pleased. We're as remote as one can get from Rome, but we'll still live in comfort."

"The great Ahura Mazda must have smiled upon you to achieve such a miracle in this foggy land," Cyrus answered. He absently stroked his black, curly beard.

Porcius had built the small villa before he left Britannia the last time he and Cyrus went to Rome, importing every brick and stone at great expense. Porcius added, his voice trailing away, "Whether it was your God or some other that helped, I managed. I was determined to have a little bit of Roman luxury in this barbaric land."

Unexpectedly, a huge swell slammed across the bow of the ship lifting the vessel and flinging it down like a piece of wet laundry on the rocks. A drenched Porcius found himself sprawling on the deck, shivering from the wet and cold. He cautiously got to his knees, grabbed the railing, pulled himself to his feet, and looked about. Most of the passengers and crewmen had suffered the same fate.

"Are you all right, lord?" Cyrus asked, helping Porcius to stand.

"Just freezing wet. Get me a dry tunic and a blanket."

A moment later, Cyrus returned. "I should have been more alert," Porcius said as he changed his clothing. Only the ship's crew and his entourage were on board. The Persian placed a woolen blanket over the senator's dry, ankle-length traveling tunic and around his shoulders. "This swell was a warning from the gods to keep my wits about me. I'll need them now that I'm back among these temperamental Britons."

"Is Prince Caratacus as hotheaded as he was in the past?"

"He used to be, and the reports I've received say he still is to a certain extent. However, it's been a long time since I've seen him. Maybe the whelp has mellowed." Porcius paused for a moment and wondered if he really had. "He's been married to that Amazon wench, Rhian, for eleven years, and marriage tends to settle a man, even Caratacus."

Porcius leaned on the ship's rail again and, for a moment, closed his eyes. As the overhead sun drenched his face in warmth, he snuggled further into the woolen blanket feeling like a caterpillar in a cocoon.

It may have been inevitable that Caratacus would take another woman, and it was his right if his wife didn't bear children, but it hadn't begun that way. Thankful for having an original copy of his report to Tiberius at the time, Porcius had refreshed his mind on all matters such as this during the channel crossing.

Recalled to Rome eight years earlier, the Senate had tried Porcius for embezzling tribute. His responsibilities had included collecting gold and other precious metals from the Britons and sending it to the imperial treasury in Rome. Although exonerated, Emperor Tiberius had decided to keep him close to home for further scrutiny.

Now, after a long absence, the emissary was returning to Britannia. Many of his compatriots accused him of madness, but he disregarded their pleas to stay in Rome. News reached Porcius that Cunobelinos's rheumatism grew worse with each day, and he suffered from swollen, aching joints, but only recently had it impaired his movements. Nevertheless, he tenaciously clung to power. Porcius learned that during the last five years, three conspiracies against the old king's life had been uncovered, the conspirators ruthlessly ferreted out and butchered. His son, Caratacus, had defeated the Dobunni in another round of skirmishes and fought brilliantly against the Iceni Tribe.

Remarkably enough, Adminios had refrained from any attempt to kill his father or Caratacus. *Thank Jupiter he has heeded my advice. But how much longer will he wait?*

But Cunobelinos's archenemy, Verica, has increased power at an alarming rate, long since recovering from defeat by Epaticcos. Verica formed an alliance with the king of the Belgae, Epaticcos's neighbor. Intrigue enough to merit Rome herself, Porcius surmised.

Indeed, southern Britannia was mired in turmoil, and Porcius and Rome liked it that way. He was determined to continue sowing the seeds of disenchantment. Constant political strife kept the Britons weak and vulnerable to outside intervention. In the past, he had used that as leverage for obtaining very favorable trading concessions for Rome and would do so again.

When he originally drafted the report, he'd dismissed Tiberius's insatiable appetite for details of Britannia's power as just another quirk or perversion. Nevertheless, when he went into self-imposed exile on the Isle of Capri, he lost interest in Britannia. That changed when Caligula came to power upon the old ruler's death. The young emperor's interest was nearly as intense as that of his old uncle, Tiberius. Now, such details of love and hate between various parties might prove invaluable, as old wounds could be reopened if necessary, and he had an ample supply of salt.

* * *

"We have arrived, lord," Cyrus said.

Porcius snapped his head about and watched deck hands as they threw mooring lines to the dock workers below. "Something's not right, Cyrus."

"Lord?"

"King Cunobelinos hasn't sent his usual contingent of counselors and Druids to greet me as is his custom." Porcius scanned the bustling crowd of warehousemen, merchants, and sailors scattered along the stone quay. "He hasn't sent anyone. I have been away for a long time, but I don't think he would have changed that much, or would he? By now he should have received the message I was returning. There must be something wrong with the old king."

CHAPTER 18

Three days before Porcius's arrival, Caratacus, accompanied by Clud and Tog, had been summoned to the Great Hall for a council of war with his father. Outside, a freezing, afternoon rain fell, while inside, it was cold and dank. The smoky, center hearth, smelling of pine resin, emitted little warmth. The three made their way through a group of warriors and clan chieftains hovering about the fire pit. Bundled in furs, the haggard king sat on his Roman throne surrounded by clan chieftains, Ibor the Druid, and Caratacus's older brother, Adminios. Dressed in a sour-smelling and mud-spattered, striped tunic and breeches, the older brother's face reddened into a scorching look. He spotted Caratacus, and his dark eyes narrowed and full lips curled in disgust beneath his drooping moustache. Fists bunched at his side.

"Your father belongs in bed," Clud whispered as they approached the dais.

Caratacus grimly nodded. "No doubt Adminios wants my father's death."

The nostrils of Tog's long, pointed nose flared. "Not to mention yours," Tog added.

After the usual salutations, Cunobelinos turned to Ibor. "Is everyone present?" he asked in a voice that sounded like a sword being sharpened on a grindstone.

"Yes, High King," Ibor said.

"Come closer, Prince ..." The king paused, and Ibor whispered something in his ear before stepping back a few paces. "Prince Caratacus ... Son. My eyesight grows worse with each passing day." He coughed hard several times and spat on the straw-covered floor. "We have decided that you are to lead our army north to Brigantia and aid our noble half brother, King Dumnoveros, against the Caledonians."

153

"Is this in response to the message you received this morning?" Caratacus asked, his eyes narrowing.

"Aye, he urgently needs our help. His forces are not strong enough to repel the invading Caledonians and Picts, who are pillaging the kingdom's northern lands."

Caratacus stood silent, feeling nothing. *Strange, I should be honored. For ten years I have waged war and led our tribal forces in many battles defeating our enemies, bringing honor to our tribe. But the enormous loss of life sickens me. My warriors have been slaughtered. Such waste. The supply of good men is not inexhaustible.*

Then he realized the king and the rest were staring at him, awaiting a reply. "I am honored you have chosen me from so many worthy chieftains," he responded formally.

"You were chosen because you have proven yourself a leader among leaders," the king said. "You are also my son and will represent us in Brigantia."

Adminios turned to his father, puffing out his chest. "But Da, Great King, what about me? I can lead."

Before Cunobelinos could answer, Caratacus said, "Does our father have to draw you a picture? You're unfit to lead pigs."

"You shit eater!" Adminios shouted. "I'll show you who can lead!" He lunged toward Caratacus, only to be restrained by a couple of chieftains.

A loud murmur of disapproval erupted among the gathering in the court.

"I'll gut you first," Caratacus answered. His hand dropped to the hilt of his dagger, which he pulled instantly from the scabbard and pointed at Adminios.

"Enough!" Cunobelinos roared, his voice echoing throughout the hall. He coughed several times and spat on the floor before giving both his sons a withering look.

Caratacus shoved his knife back into its holder, while Adminios shook off the hands restraining him and stepped back.

The king gestured to Adminios. "You are only capable of hunting cattle thieves, nothing more."

For a split second, Adminios's mouth opened as if to speak before closing it again. He looked about; the eyes of the court seemed to be focused on him. "But ... but, Da ..."

"For years," Cunobelinos continued, "I have given you minor commands, leading our warriors on raids against our enemies, in hopes you would prove yourself a worthy leader. Although you have shown bravery, you displayed no leadership. You chose to allow your captains to lead while you followed."

"That's not true, I swear it," Adminios said.

Cunobelinos studied the older son. "The reports I have received said otherwise." He jabbed a finger in Adminios's direction. "Most of the time you were drunk. Only by the benevolent gods have you survived."

Too bad you weren't killed, it would have saved Da a lot of grief, Caratacus wanted to say but held his tongue.

"Isn't it enough that my warriors won the battles?" Adminios asked.

"Chasing cattle thieves doesn't count for much of a victory. You must lead from the front, not through your captains."

The king's eyes swept the battle-hardened men and then Adminios for signs of challenge. None was seen or voiced. "There is more. Instead of taking a proper wife, you still waste your time as a womanizer. You have no heirs."

Adminios glared at Caratacus. "What about him? He doesn't have any."

"Not from lack of trying, and he has a worthy wife," the king answered, his mouth set in a straight line.

Caratacus grinned. *Yes, Rhian is the most worthy of all women and has the makings of a great warrior.*

Adminios's face flushed. "I have tried, but my wives died giving birth, and the babies were lost with them."

"You should try again instead of spending so much time in drink and whoring." Cunobelinos glared at Adminios. "There is nothing wrong in getting drunk once in a while, even whoring, those are the rights of any man, but not all the time. Find a wife."

"You wrong me, Da," Adminios said. He shook his head.

"Do I?" He paused. "No, I haven't. You will remain here in Camulodunum where I can keep an eye on you. I will not embarrass the kingdom by sending you as leader on such an important campaign."

"But Da—"

"Silence!" the king ordered. "One more word out of you, and I will put you in chains." The old king's eyes surveyed the Great Hall, and then he raised his hand. "Except for Prince Caratacus, leave us, all of you!" he commanded as loudly as his raspy voice allowed.

Ibor protested, "But Great King, your health."

He raised his hand, pointing to the Druid. "You may be the chief law giver, but I am still king. I'm not with the gods yet, though you crave it."

Ibor shrank back, casting a quick glance to his side.

The king motioned to the rest of the court, including a sullen Adminios. "I talk to my son in private. Now, get out! All of you!"

Once the hall was cleared, Cunobelinos waved Caratacus to a chair next to him. He noticed the deep fissures erupting on each side of his father's nose. Crow's feet spread from the eyes like a river delta. His once powerful shoulders appeared to have shrunk and now rounded, giving the king a stooped appearance. The breath escaping through his thin lips smelled of rancid meat.

"My son," the king whispered, "those vultures think I'm dying. I'm not, though my joints grow more inflamed."

"Except for Adminios, they feared saying anything in your presence."

A smirk crossed his father's lips. "Adminios is a fool who cannot be trusted. He will stay here where my spies and I can keep a close watch on him. As far as the rest, it is well they should keep their mouths shut. But the truth is, I might as well be dying."

"I don't understand."

"It's time you knew. You're the only one I can trust." He coughed into a cupped palm then wheezed.

After seeing the speckles of red in the phlegm upon the king's hand from the retching cough, the prince wondered, *Was he suffering from the same sickness that killed Aunt Gwynn? How long will he live?*

"I'm afraid," he continued, "that I'm losing my memory."

Caratacus suspected his father's health had been deteriorating, but his candid admission shocked him. His muscles tightened. "Impossible!"

"But I am. I have difficulty remembering things, simple things. I forgot your name just as I was addressing you before the assembly."

"Does anyone else know?"

"Ibor ... but I don't know if I can trust him to keep it secret, if he hasn't already told others."

"Is there anything I can do for you?"

Cunobelinos shook his head. "No one can help me. Usually, I have full recollection of my thoughts, but there are times when I don't. It happens more often. I'm afraid I'll soon babble like an idiot," he said softly. "And when my enemies—your enemies—find out, they'll use me." He stood, his mind seemed to drift, and Caratacus caught the name, "Ibor."

The king paused and stared blankly into the hearth's fading coals and sat again. "That's why I'm sending you north," he continued. "I can't go. I don't trust myself, and I trust no one but you. You've served me well during the last eleven years. I have some unfinished matters I must attend to before I die."

"It isn't that severe—it can't be!" Caratacus protested.

"It is. It is." Cunobelinos slumped in his chair.

If Caratacus forced the issue, he could stay, but he respected his father too much to disobey. There was the danger of Adminios taking advantage of the king's failing health. Although by no means as clever as he or Tog, Adminios was bound to learn sooner or later. *At the same time, if I remain, the people will whisper that the king has grown weak and is losing his authority. That must not happen. There must be a show of unity.* "All right, I accept command of the army," he said. "But Ibor must keep Adminios away from you—he's grown too dangerous—you know I speak the truth."

The king nodded, obviously relieved of a heavy burden. "Ibor will keep him away, I promise."

Although he never felt close to his father, Caratacus hadn't wished to see the old monarch degenerate into a mindless hulk. In the old days, the Druids condemned failing kings to death. They were brought before the people, stripped naked, and stabbed in the back. As they lay dying, naked priestesses, tattooed with purple woad, studied their death throes for omens to learn the future of the tribe.

Caratacus realized it was his right, when his father reached that moment, to slay him quickly and cleanly. To live his remaining years like a helpless baby was not the way of a warrior or a king.

He touched the hilt of his dagger. *I can't kill my father, but I'll be damned if I allow anyone else either. When I take the throne, I'll care for him.*

His father had proclaimed him ruler in everything but name, but he still must be elected by the council of clan chieftains. Some favored Adminios. Caratacus would have to overcome their opposition, their allegiance being essential. He had proven himself in battle, but to be king required more than being a good warrior. He knew that from the political squabbling, constant bickering, and testing of strong wills at the king's councils. His people prospered, and he wanted to keep it that way. Somehow he must break the economic stranglehold of the Romans on the kingdom.

The Romans considered his father a client-king.

Caratacus resented the close relationship. To be client-king meant that Da would take up arms on behalf of Rome. *Would Cunobelinos fight at Rome's side if they invaded the lands of our neighbors? Was he fool enough to believe that the Romans would leave their people alone once they got a toehold in Britannia?* His father must surely see the folly of being a Roman ally.

* * *

The rain stopped, and Caratacus gathered the chieftains outside the Great Hall in the cool evening light and issued orders for marching. He needed three days to gather warriors and supplies from around the tribal confederacy.

Caratacus returned home at supper time. Helping a servant, Rhian removed freshly baked bread from the domed clay oven. The aroma permeated the room. He savored the tangy fish stew boiling with vegetables in the cauldron over the hearth, not realizing how hungry he had been until now. He kissed Rhian and asked her to cut a slice from one of the round, flat-bread loaves for him.

"How did the meeting go with your father and the council?" Rhian asked as they seated themselves on reed mats around a low table.

Caratacus told her the news between mouthfuls of food.

She gasped. "This is the opportunity my women and I have been waiting for. You must let us ride with you!"

"I must?" Caratacus's hands froze half way to his mouth, placing the bread chunk back down on the table. He turned and locked eyes with hers. "There is nothing I *must* do."

Rhian placed a hand on his bicep. "I know you don't have to do anything, but for once, please don't deny me this. We deserve the chance to prove ourselves."

Since they had married, Rhian had prodded him to let her go to war. Although she had proven herself on the training field, under the stern supervision of those masculine, female twins, Gwyther and Modron, Caratacus had refused her permission to go on campaign. He feared she would lose her life before bearing him a son. Now, Caratacus doubted she'd ever bear children again. It was time to let her prove herself, something he understood.

"All right," Caratacus answered after a moment.

"There hasn't been an attack on Camulodunum in years. We're eager to use our skills before we lose them," Rhian continued, her hand gestured broadly.

"I said you may go, woman. What more do you want?"

For the first time since she'd begun her campaign to go, she was speechless. Her sea-green eyes searched his for the span of a couple of heartbeats as if making sure she heard him correctly. Slowly, a smile, revealing her still-white teeth, evolved across her bowed lips. She threw her arms around him and kissed him.

"I'm not going to repeat myself. Choose one hundred of your best women riders. I'll find a use for them."

"As long as they have a chance to fight, they'll do anything," she cried.

He struggled to loosen her arms from his neck and laughed, pleased that she seemed happy. "A chance to fight, huh? Before we return, there'll be enough bloodshed to satisfy even your lust for combat. But as you're willing to do *anything*." He glanced toward the partitioned goatskins walling off their bed furs from the rest of the home.

"Oh, you're terrible. Don't you think about anything else?" she said, slapping him playfully. "But what about dinner—aren't you going to finish?"

"That can wait, and so can the rest of the world."

* * *

Later, as they lay side by side on their bed furs, Caratacus stifled a yawn. He turned and smiled at Rhian, whose brows were furrowed deeply, as if lost in thought. "Something bothering you?"

She turned toward him, strands of hair partially covering the side of her face, which she brushed aside. "I was thinking ..."

"And?"

"Most likely, Cartimandua will be in Eburacum when we arrive."

"So? Remember, she is King Dumnoveros's daughter and Venutios, her husband, is one of the king's chieftains."

"Don't you understand?"

"What?"

"With her vile reputation, she may throw herself at you, tempting you to leave me for her."

Caratacus lifted himself up on one side, reached over, and touched her shoulder. "Woman, you're mad. It's been four years. Don't you remember I sent a letter in reply to her message that I had no intention of leaving you for her or any other woman?"

She pouted. "I remember, but she may well try anyway."

"She will fail miserably. I will refuse her advances."

"Promise?"

"I promise." He kissed her, and they made love again.

* * *

Early the following morning, on the same day Porcius landed in Britannia, Caratacus departed from Camulodunum leading an army of four thousand, enroute to Eburacum, capital of the Brigantes. They rode northward on worn trackways through rolling, green hills and thick forests. He sent messengers to the wooded lands of the Coritani, vassals of the Catuvellaunians, to provide food at designated intervals.

The army marched all morning. After passing through a heavily wooded area of birch and yew, they entered a wide meadow with a small stream snaking across its center. Caratacus ordered the army to halt for a short noon rest. During the stop, he decided to check on Rhian and her women. Being inexperienced as warriors, Caratacus assigned them to guard the supply wagons. Some grumbled, but Rhian quickly silenced their chatter. It was as if she realized they had to crawl before walking. Earlier, her unit struggled to keep a tight formation around the wagons. The men who guarded the flanks, the front and rear of the army, seemed uneasy with women among them. But the women steadily improved, and they needed praise.

Shielding his forehead, Caratacus squinted into the noonday glare as he approached Rhian, who dismounted at the water's edge and allowed her horse to take a long drink. She looked radiant in the bright afternoon sun, and he smiled at her beauty. Caked with dust and sweat, the other kilt-clad female riders, who wore ankle-length breeches, paid little attention to personal appearances as they watered and rested their animals. Not Rhian. Caratacus watched as she kneeled and dipped a piece of woolen cloth in the cool stream and then place it to her sunburned face, wiping away the grime. She reached for the berry juice, which she kept in a small vial in a pouch tied to her waist, to touch up her lips, but apparently resigned to the fact everyone was filthy and smelled of horse, she drew back her hand. Despite her appearance, she looked nearly as beautiful as the day they married; more so, in spite of being twenty-eight.

He reined up next to the stream and dismounted. "The women have improved a great deal since this morning."

Rhian stood and a weary smile formed on her lips. "Do you really think so?"

"If they hadn't, I would've told you." A nearby horse whinnied and Caratacus's mount answered with a loud, grating sound.

"Yes, you made that clear earlier." Rhian now used the cloth to wipe her sweaty hands.

"Have to whip the women into shape in a hurry if they're to survive against the Caledonians."

Rhian's eyes narrowed. She grasped the handle of the dagger tied at her waist. "They'll fight as well as the men."

"That's the spirit," Caratacus answered with a grin. "Other than that, how are they faring?"

"One of them, Mugain, is suffering from morning sickness." She clapped her hand to her mouth.

"Why did you allow her to come along?" Caratacus grasped the hilt of his sword.

"I didn't know." Rhian hesitated. She stared at the dusty ground beyond her horse and back to Caratacus. "Mugain was afraid to tell me and thought it would pass. She's one of my best riders and didn't want to be left behind. What should I—"

"You decide," he snapped. "You're a leader, make the tough decisions!" Then he said in a softer voice. "I'm sorry if I sound so harsh, but now that we're in the field, where others can see us, I have to treat you in the same manner as I would other warriors. Otherwise, I would be accused of favoritism, not to mention being considered a weak leader. You must understand. When we are alone, it's different."

Rhian pondered only for a moment. "I know. As commander of the army, you must be firm. Of course, Mugain must go back. We have no room for pregnant women. Did she really think I would allow her to fight in her condition?"

Caratacus nodded approval, pleased by her decisiveness. She had passed her first test.

"But Mugain will be all right. My women will see to it."

"Good, because I won't allow anything to slow our march. She'll return by your orders. I remember how you suffered from the sickness."

Rhian narrowed her eyes at her husband. "You think I've forgotten? I lost three babies."

"I know," Caratacus answered gravely. "I'm sorry for you and the three little ones."

She leaned toward him and whispered, "But the memories ... I can't forget."

And neither can I.

162

"You're right, Caratacus," Rhian said, pulling Caratacus out of his thoughts. "I never really thought some of these young women, most of them just girls, really, might be killed. There is no place in battle for a woman with child."

"None whatsoever. Have an escort of women take Mugain back to the last village we passed. When she's well, the peasants can return her safely to Camulodunum. Here's an incentive for them to help." He handed her five newly minted gold coins. They contained the image of a half-naked, Druid priest holding the decapitated head of a sacrificial victim. Beneath, the Roman letters CVN, the Latin abbreviation for Cunobelinos, were inscribed.

"For that fortune they would protect her from their own mothers," Rhian answered.

"I'll see you later when we make camp." Caratacus remounted and rode away. He looked back at Rhian one more time. *She and her women still need to prove themselves as warriors. When that day arrives, I pray Rhian and her women will be worthy of my confidence.*

CHAPTER 19

After landing at the Port of Camulodunum, Porcius headed on foot for the house of Cunobelinos to request an immediate audience. *Why wasn't I met by the king's representatives? Something smells rotten, and it isn't dead fish!*

As Cyrus and his entourage followed, he trudged up the low hill to the stockade, huffing as he went.

Despite the cool sea breeze, his face grew hot, and his mouth turned dry as a desert—not from any apparent thirst but from his growing concern about the king.

Passing through the fortress gateway, Porcius approached the Great Hall. He told Cyrus and his party to wait outside. He entered the audience room, illuminated by smoky torchlight and the large, center hearth, and approached the ruler who sat on his throne upon the dais. Ibor stood by the king's side and whispered into his ear. The king nodded. The once powerfully built ruler now sat stooped-shouldered, draped in his purple robe, as if the years of rule and responsibility weighed down like a heavy, oxen yoke.

His face was now withered, skin sagged around his cheek bones and jaw like a plucked fowl. Porcius sucked in his breath, alarmed by the old king's appearance. Watery eyes sank into deep hollows as if stagnant pools, and his once flaxen beard was now scraggly white. Cunobelinos shifted in his chair and Porcius heard the sound of passing wind. A fetid odor radiated from Cunobelinos and lingered, as if he had soiled himself. To Porcius's disgust, the smell seeped into his nose.

Great Jove, how much longer can the king rule? When Porcius had left Britannia, Cunobelinos had been a robust, middle-aged ruler. *If this is a virtue of growing old as Cicero preached, then I would rather be dead. If I play my dice right and throw the cast of Venus, Rome will greatly benefit from this state of condition.*

Cunobelinos motioned the Roman closer. Porcius stepped to the foot of the dais about three arm lengths from the king and bowed slightly. He forced himself to keep his nose from twitching.

"Is this our old friend, Porcius?" Cunobelinos asked in a rasping voice.

"Yes, High King," he answered. "After many years, I have returned to the land I consider a second home."

"Indeed, you are welcome." Cunobelinos turned to Ibor, who hovered at his side. "Why ... why wasn't I informed of our friend's arrival?"

"You were, Great King," the Druid answered. "I advised you that a delegation should be sent to the port to greet him, but your permission was not forthcoming."

Cunobelinos seemed to hesitate. "Oh yes ... I forgot to tell you, didn't I?" He faced Porcius. "Forgive me, old friend, my memory is not what it used to be."

"No apology is required, Great King," Porcius said. "I'm certain you had more important matters on your mind." Quickly, he glanced to Ibor, raising an eyebrow. The Druid shrugged.

Besides a deteriorating mind, what other weaknesses did Cunobelinos have? Ibor would know. His love for Roman gold and gossip always outweighed loyalty to his office and ridiculous tree gods. *Too bad there weren't more Druids like him.*

* * *

Later, after the audience was concluded, Porcius approached the Druid and slipped him a leather pouch.

A fine mist sprayed Camulodunum that evening, but Ibor's warm hearth soothed Porcius's chilling bones. The high king's closest advisor could not leave the king until dusk. Now the two powerful men sat in fur-lined, oak chairs by the fire. The Roman sipped Gallic wine from a bronze cup embossed with red- and green-enameled spirals. He waited as Ibor greedily counted the gold Roman *Aureii*.

Ibor finished and placed the last of the coins back into the bag and tied it to his sash. He turned to Porcius, his gaunt cobweb-lined face studying the Roman. "You saw and smelled the poor state of the king's physical condition, did you not?"

"Is he that ill?"

The Druid nodded. "And he is slowly losing his wits. He grows more feeble minded with each passing day."

"Then something—"

Ibor held up his hand. "Wait, there is more. The king knows he is failing and is determined to remove his brother, Epaticcos, as tribal leader of the Atrebates before his mind is gone. He has formed a secret alliance with Verica against his brother."

Porcius started, aghast by the revelation. "But why?" he stammered, his mind feverishly sorting the ramifications this could have for Rome.

"Epaticcos is too anti-Roman, and the Atrebatic Kingdom rightfully belongs to Verica." Ibor labored in his best but butchered Latin.

"But that will shift the balance of power. Verica will challenge Cunobelinos for the dominion of southeastern Britannia."

"Perhaps," Ibor said, "but the king has his reasons, and Epaticcos must ... will ... be destroyed."

For a moment Porcius pondered those words as he glared at the wrinkled, white-bearded face of the Druid. Porcius shook his head. "You know very well that although Verica and Cunobelinos are pro-Roman, neither will tolerate a Roman Army in their lands."

The Druid shook his head. "I know and have attempted to advise the king of that fact."

"Then try again." Porcius narrowed his eyes. "There is no way Cunobelinos will allow the anti-Roman faction under Epaticcos to threaten his throne."

"I agree."

Although he and Ibor were alone, Porcius leaned close to Ibor and said in a lowered voice, "If Verica takes the Atrebatic throne, southeastern Britannia would be ringed by pro-Roman tribes."

"But Cunobelinos is still the dominant ruler and keeps the minor tribes in check," Ibor said.

"Yes, and Rome has benefited commercially from his rule, and *I* am determined to see this continues after his death."

"But there is something else, noble Porcius ..." Ibor paused, as if dangling a juicy tidbit, until Porcius almost begged him to continue. "Verica has agreed to support Adminios's accession to the throne."

The Roman sucked in his breath. A chill shot up his back and through his arms. "Surely you're joking?"

"On the contrary, Adminios is a fool and easily manipulated, and we need a pro-Roman ruler. That is why he must be placed on the throne. We will use Adminios as a puppet, and through him Verica will rule the Catuvellaunians and the Trinovantes."

"What about Caratacus?" Porcius asked. "He was promised the kingship."

"Only in so many words and never officially. The bronze shield, the rank of office he received when he was seventeen, means nothing until he is proclaimed by the Council."

"You mean—"

"He hasn't been informed. The king isn't that foolish— yet. But he has decided Adminios should succeed him. Caratacus is too anti-Roman, like his uncle, Epaticcos. Who knows? Caratacus might be slain in battle."

"Caratacus will revolt if the Council follows through. When he learns of this, the next battle will be with an army of warriors who support him. They are many."

Ibor lifted the pouch of coins, then opened his palm as if to convey that its weight was becoming less than the value of the information.

Porcius slipped him a small, gold-studded ring from his left index finger, while mumbling under his breath, "True friend of Rome."

Ibor continued, "We plan to appease Prince Caratacus by giving him lands in the southern part of the kingdom."

"The poorer part of the country," Porcius said sarcastically. "That won't be enough, it's betrayal." He jabbed a finger at Ibor. "I warn you, he will rebel and line the walls with our heads."

167

"*Our* heads, Roman, not yours. He's not foolish enough to kill a Roman and force the emperor to send troops. But we'll deal with the situation when the time comes." Ibor studied the gold ring in the poor light then examined the one upon Porcius's other hand, as if comparing the value of the two.

Porcius narrowed his eyes. "The time is now."

"Leave it to the king," Ibor said.

"The king will be dead!"

Ibor looked away slowly and nodded.

The sincerity of Ibor's concern surprised Porcius. He should have given him the other ring, he thought, fingering the orb. No, he decided to save it for a more propitious time. In the meantime, he would leave for Noviomagnus, King Verica's capital. Porcius was determined to learn if he could use Verica's ambition to Rome's advantage. Ironically, it was Caratacus who saved Porcius's life when Verica's son tried to murder him at Bagshot Heath. He prayed he no longer has any plans to try again.

CHAPTER 20

Early one sweltering afternoon, as Caratacus, Rhian, Tog, and Clud rode together at the head of the army column, a scout on horseback galloped down the path, muffled hoof beats growing louder until the rider drew up his foaming mount before them. The earthy smell of horse filtered the air, drifting into the noses of Caratacus and his companions.

The scout pointed to the north. "Prince Caratacus, Eburacum is just over the rise."

"Good man," Caratacus said and dismissed the warrior.

Sitting on his large bay gelding, Caratacus turned to his companions. "Not much longer now. We'll see what kind of reception awaits us." He motioned them forward.

"It should be friendly," Rhian said as she trotted on a piebald mare by his right side. Dirt smudged her sunburnt face, and a trickle of sweat ran down her neck. "Shouldn't it?"

"You never know with so-called allies," Clud said as he and Tog rode their shaggy horses along Caratacus's left. Clud hawked and spat, muttering something about dust in his mouth.

"We'll keep a sharp eye out just in case," Caratacus said. He wiped a perspiring hand along the right leg of his breeches.

"Our cousins have been friendly to Da, no reason they shouldn't be with us," Tog said. "Otherwise, why ask for our aid?"

"King Dumnoveros requested our help, but I'm not taking any chances," Caratacus said.

"That can work both ways," Rhian added.

"Betrayal is a fact of life." Caratacus's eyes searched the tree-lined hill to their right. A flock of screeching jackdaws flew above the ridge heading west. "The king's scouts have been shadowing us for days, so he knows we have a big army."

"Aye, that he has," Clud added. He motioned toward the same area. "They've done a sorry job of hiding themselves, my old ma could've done better. Our men have spotted them a dozen times."

When Caratacus reached the crest of the hill overlooking Eburacum, the capital of the Brigantes, he spotted a group of horsemen racing toward them, hooves pounding the ground in a thundering drumbeat, a cloud of dust billowing behind. They were less than five hundred paces away and closing fast.

"Looks like an escort from the king," Caratacus said as he placed a hand on the hilt of his sword tied at the waist. "We take no risks."

"Aye, they be armed," Clud growled.

"They're Dumnoveros's retainers," Caratacus said. "Their clothing and weapons are too well made to be ordinary clan warriors."

Every rider wore conical helmets and chain mail-covered tunics with long, embroidered sleeves. The warriors wore striped breeches, carried spears, oval shields, longswords, and daggers.

Caratacus twisted around on his horse. He motioned to the detail of fifty escorting mounted warriors, who rode a short distance to the rear of his group, to move up just behind them. He waved the captain in charge forward to his side. "I don't expect trouble from the king's men, but be ready to fight."

"Yes, Prince," the captain answered and returned to his men.

"They wouldn't be stupid enough to attack us," Tog said. "We're too many—there can't be more than thirty of them."

"Stay alert," Caratacus warned. "Stay by my side, Rhian."

"I'm not going anywhere," she answered and gripped the handle of her sword. Clud and Tog followed suit.

The clatter of hooves and snorting horses drifted away like the powdery earth behind them as the riders drew to a halt before Caratacus and his companions. Nonetheless, the churning dirt roiled into Caratacus's eyes and nostrils causing him and everyone to choke and cough. Once Caratacus stopped his hacking and cleared his throat, he took a cloth from his waist band and uncorked the goat skin water bag tied to the same. He doused water onto the rag and wiped his eyes and face. He deliberately made the riders wait while he turned to Rhian, who was using a plain scarf to clean her face.

"I will live," she said. "I should be used to this after all my years working with horses."

"You're a good woman," he said quietly.

She managed a smile.

He turned about and saw that his cavalry escort were spread behind him, all with hands on their swords.

"Welcome, Prince Caratacus," said a large, pock-marked warrior covered in grime. He briefly raised a hand in salute and moved his sweating mount forward, a few steps ahead of his band of warriors. "I am Rhodri, captain of King Dumnoveros's retainers. He sends his greetings."

Caratacus took a swig of water from the container, rinsed his mouth, and spat. Once he had recorked and retied the flask, he turned back to the rider and raised a hand in return. "And how is the king?" he asked formally.

The captain looked beyond Caratacus and then back to his own men and answered, "Well, indeed. He has instructed me to say that you and twenty of your companions are to follow me to his fortress. He will greet you there, and you will dine with him as his guests. In the meantime," Rodri motioned to the broad plain south of the settlement's fortified walls, "the rest of your army will camp out here beyond the town."

"I'll join you once I've picked my companions," Caratacus said. He motioned to Rhian, Tog, and Clud to follow him back to the army's advance column, which had halted a short distance behind. Summoning his couriers, Caratacus sent them to his clan chieftains, captains, and lieutenants with orders to report to him immediately.

"What do they mean by allowing only twenty of us to escort you?" Rhian asked after the messengers had been dispatched.

"Because they will outnumber us," Caratacus answered.

"Ha! A lot of good that will do them," Clud said. "By the scrawny looks of 'em, the plague has had its way. We would slice through 'em with no problem." He straightened on his mount and, in a mock gesture, swiped a finger across his throat.

"You're right," Caratacus said. "Nonetheless, the clan chieftains and captains will stay with the army. If I brought them, King Dumnoveros may be treacherous enough to spring a trap and kill us along with our best leaders. Yet, I don't believe that is his intention."

"May you be right, but I'll be ready," Clud said with a grin. He tapped the hilt of his sword hanging from his bulging waist.

"Let me guess, you're bringing the lieutenants with us," Tog said.

"Not so loud," Caratacus warned. He twisted around on the back of his horse surveying the king's retainers a short distance away before turning back to Tog. "You're right. In case this turns out to be a trap, the clan chieftains and captains know what to do."

"Aye, wipe 'em out," Clud said as he pointed to the town. "Then our army would sack the town and claim it for your father's kingdom."

"That's right," Caratacus said. "But I doubt King Dumnoveros will kill us. He would gain nothing from it. He won't risk losing Eburacum, it's a major trading center. The kingdom has made a fortune in port fees and taxes."

Caratacus knew merchant ships from Gaul, Germania, and the Mediterranean brought goods up the meandering Ouse River in trade for wool, iron ingots, finely made jewelry, leather goods, and more. Trackways from Caledonia to the north, and from lands to the west and south, led to this bustling region.

No wonder the Caledonians raided the area.

A few minutes later, Caratacus was joined by all his subordinate officers. He explained the situation and picked the men.

"All right, let's join the king's men and go to the feast." Caratacus kicked the side of his mount, rode ahead, his party following.

* * *

The entourage, escorted by King Dumnoveros's retainers, bypassed the main part of the town spread along the edge of the river, lined with a muddy beach, docks, and small warehouses framed in wood and stone.

As the group trekked up the road leading to the fortress, Caratacus appreciated the commanding view of the town and river to the north and broad plains and farmlands to the south. *Any army foolish enough to attack these heights would be doomed to failure, including ours.*

"Do you remember what Cartimandua and her sister Dana look like?" Rhian asked pulling Caratacus from his thoughts.

He shook his head. "No, it has been several years since I last saw them. They were very young. Cartimandua was seven and Dana was six."

Despite the tramping hooves, jingling of metal pendants on the horses ridden by the king's retainers, and the bantering among the men, Rhian leaned toward Caratacus. "We've both heard that Cartimandua is ambitious," she said in a lowered voice. "If the rumors are true, Dana has no interest in being a ruler."

Caratacus kept his face forward, eyes fixed on the riders ahead of him. He didn't believe they could overhear the conversation between him and Rhian but kept a cautious look out and his voice low.

"She doesn't," he finally answered. "Dana is looking for a husband to replace her first one who died of the plague."

"Is that right?" Rhian asked in a voice full of interest.

"It's what I've heard, she wants children."

"Any woman would," she murmured.

Caratacus cupped a hand to the side of his mouth and leaned toward Rhian. "I pity Venutios. If the tales about Cartimandua bedding everyone are true, he should have never married her."

"Only a fool would stay with her," Rhian said.

"Although Venutios is consort to a king's daughter, I hope he is smart enough to realize that he will never succeed Dumnoveros on the throne."

"That would be a grave mistake, wouldn't it?" Rhian said.

"When her father dies, no doubt Cartimandua will find a way to get the council to vote her queen," Caratacus said. He dropped his hand to the side, straightened his body on the back of his mount, and watched the riders ahead of him.

"Yes, and to get her own way, the bitch will sleep with all of them," Rhian said. She readjusted herself on the hand-woven riding blanket of her mare.

The king's men and Caratacus's retinue halted before the Great Hall, built of un-mortared, close-cut stone that stood in the fortress center.

After dismounting, everyone dusted off their clothes before entering.

"I look and feel so dirty, Caratacus," Rhian said, wiping a smudge of dirt from her face. "I wish the king would have allowed us to wash ourselves and change into clean clothing before he received us."

"I agree," Caratacus answered. "Apparently he won't be bothered by our appearance. No doubt he's seen his share of dusty riders. We'll just have to do the best we can."

She sighed. "I suppose so."

Caratacus touched her forearm and grinned. "Even through the dust, you're still beautiful."

Rhian smiled but lightly slapped his hand. "Liar."

The captain, Rodri, dismissed his warriors.

A good sign, Caratacus thought.

Rodri turned to Caratacus. "Follow me."

Tog, Clud, and his lieutenants followed Caratacus and Rhian, who entered the stifling court behind Rodri. Inside, they stopped to adjust their eyes in the dim light. Burning torches hung in wolf-headed iron casings along the wall, illuminating the interior. Focusing on the interior, Caratacus realized the Great Hall was large and cavernous, far greater than he had ever seen before. Compared to this building, the one at Camulodunum seemed no bigger than a mud hut. Tall and thick hardwood posts framed the thick walls of wattle and daub, while at least another dozen going down the center held up the vaulted, wood-framed roof tightly packed with straw. He noticed several side doors opened to allow in fresh air and light, but it wasn't enough. The noisy crowd of lesser chieftains, captains, warriors, and wives dressed in their finest clothing grew quiet as Caratacus and his retinue slowly approached in the hazy light across the stone floor, covered with furs and rugs in a riot of colors and patterns. They walked past several rows of long, rough-cut, wooden tables set up for dining. A gathering of clan chieftains, Druids, and bards stood before the king at the far end of the court. The place was bigger than Caratacus had imagined.

A big man past fifty, King Dumnoveros sat on an ornately carved, wooden throne upon the low dais. He wore a heavy graying beard that Caratacus found more appropriate for a Druid priest. It cascaded down the ruler's chest in front of his broad but sagging shoulders. Pink cheeks surfaced above where whiskers did not cover his face. And yet there wasn't a single hair on his leathery, sunburnt skull. A bulbous nose pushed out from between small but alert, grey eyes that studied Caratacus and his party.

"I don't like seeing all these guards lining the walls," Clud whispered as he and Tog walked behind Caratacus. Rodri was taking his time moving through the crowd toward the king.

"Smells like a trap," Tog added in a low voice.

"They could kill us easy enough; though we be armed— the king's guards surround the place," Clud affirmed. Standing along the wall in the murky shadows lurked Dumnoveros's retainers, armed with shields and swords.

"I doubt it," Caratacus whispered. "King Dumnoveros's forces are too weak, he lost many of his best warriors to the plague. That's why we're here."

"Do you really think so?" Rhian whispered as she looked about. "Is that Cartimandua and her husband, Venutios, sitting on the king's right?"

"Yes," Caratacus answered

"She appears to be already playing the part of a queen," Rhian said.

At twenty, Cartimandua was a striking woman who appeared older than her age. Light freckles covered her full, pleasant face. Her lips were the color of rowan berries, and her hair appeared like that of a shimmering sunrise, tightly woven like a net and combed in a wave along the sides of her head. She was clothed in a garish, cardinal and aqua, tartan gown with long sleeves trimmed in silver. A twisted, eight-strand, gold torc collar surrounded her neck.

"You think so? What about Dana?" He nodded in her direction where she sat to the king's left. "If anyone looks the part, it is she."

No more than age nineteen, Dana's large, hazel eyes and a slightly turned up nose radiated a gentleness about her countenance. A narrow, gold diadem crowned her wiry brown hair. She wore a long, scarlet tunic trimmed in silver and three jeweled torc collars around her long neck.

"Hmph, maybe so, but it doesn't look as if she is trying to be one," Rhian answered. "Her appearance isn't smug like that of her older sister."

Rodri looked back, scowling.

King Dumnoveros fixed his gaze upon Caratacus and raised his bushy eyebrows.

"The king is waiting for us. Let's proceed to the front before he grows impatient," Caratacus said to his retinue.

They approached the king.

Rodri presented Caratacus and his party to King Dumnoveros and then disappeared among the courtiers.

"Welcome Prince Caratacus, your wife, Princess Rhian, and your allies," King Dumnoveros said.

"We are honored, Great King," Caratacus answered formally.

"It is mine," the king replied. "We are grateful that you have come to aid us in our fight against our common foe, the Caledonians. But we will speak more of that later." He turned to Venutios and Cartimandua. "My daughter, Cartimandua, and her husband, Prince Venutios."

Caratacus and Rhian gave them a slight bow. "Prince Venutios and Princess Cartimandua, my pleasure," Caratacus said.

Cartimandua's alert, emerald eyes locked on Caratacus. A smile crossed her ample mouth and her eyelids dipped invitingly as she nodded to him.

Venutios nodded, his face expressionless.

Caratacus studied the younger man, who appeared to be in his mid-twenties. Venutios's jet-black hair was tied back with leather thongs, usually worn when hunting. His shoulders were strong and supple, outlined by his short-sleeved tunic. The youthful chieftain's deep-set, chestnut eyes appeared to be intelligent but savage. He looked like a man who could make trouble. A thin scar crossed from the left side of his forehead, across the bridge of his thin nose, and disappeared along the right side of his jaw line.

"I'm so pleased to see you, Cousin Caratacus, after all these years," Cartimandua said. "We have much to talk about. Of course, if your wife," she crinkled her nose, "doesn't mind. Some women are so jealous."

Rhian gasped as did the rest of the court's guests, the sound echoed through the chamber. She turned and looked at Caratacus, who frowned.

Caratacus shook his head. "My wife is my closest companion and confidant, Cartimandua. She has no reason to be jealous of you or any other woman."

"My husband speaks the truth," Rhian said and touched Caratacus's arm.

"These are our guests," King Dumnoveros said. "Your rude behavior will not be tolerated, Daughter."

Venutios nodded to Rhian and then gestured toward Cartimandua. "Apologize, wife."

Cartimandua's face flushed and she huffed. "Yes, you're right. I apologize, Rhian, please forgive me. Sometimes I speak without thinking."

A momentary pause passed before Rhian said, "Of course."

"Prince Caratacus, my daughter, Cartimandua, has always had an independent streak," the king said. "But that does not excuse her poor behavior."

Cartimandua gasped. "Father ..."

"You heard me, Daughter," the king said sharply.

"I agree with the king," Venutios said.

Cartimandua seemed to squirm in her chair and turned her head away.

"Cartimandua has apologized to my wife, and that is enough, Great King," Caratacus said.

Dumnoveros turned to his left. "I present Dana, my younger daughter."

Dana smiled demurely and nodded.

"You may have heard that she was recently widowed," the king said, "losing her husband to the plague."

"So I have. My condolences, Dana," Caratacus said.

"Thank you, Caratacus," she answered in a meek voice.

Caratacus had heard she was widowed the year before when her husband died in a smallpox epidemic that decimated the Brigantian Kingdom, killing many of the king's best men. This had been the major reason Dumnoveros requested Cunobelinos's warriors. Dana had been fortunate, not only in escaping death, but also its pock-marking blight.

"Dinner will be served shortly," the king said. "Prince Caratacus, you and Rhian are to join me upon the dais as honored guests. The rest of your party will be seated among the other guests. Please, join us now."

Rhian and Caratacus sat to the king's left. Dana, who had been sitting on the same side, excused herself, stood, and mingled with the other members of the court.

During dinner, Caratacus watched how Dana reacted with everyone. She floated from person to person saying kind words. She carried about her an aura of quiet strength, her head held high while telling stories in soft, confident tones and finding a kind word for everyone, including the attending slaves. More than once, the chief steward consulted with her about the dinner arrangements to which she offered advice. To Caratacus, Dana appeared to be an intelligent woman, not afraid to speak her mind. The tables were close enough so that Caratacus listened as Dana told a few noblemen what she thought of their opinions on various matters of state. But she did it in a manner offending no one. A peacemaker, Caratacus thought.

After a moment, Caratacus realized he had been staring at Dana and a couple of times she turned in his direction.

Each time she smiled briefly and moved on to the other guests. *Why did I look at her like that?*

Caratacus had learned earlier that the young princess, as the king's favorite daughter, had been taught to read and write Latin. Few men and almost no women were taught the letters. That explained Dana's ability to converse intelligently with the king's men.

About midway through the meal, Caratacus asked Dumnoveros where he could relieve himself and asked to be excused. One of the king's servants showed him to a wooden privy outside the Great Hall and left him to find his way back. Upon doing his duty, Caratacus returned and entered the hall's shadowy recesses at the back of the court. He stopped when he overheard the voices of two women in conversation. Out of curiosity, he quietly moved forward staying in the shadows. In the dim light of a single candle he saw Cartimandua, who appeared quite animated in her gestures, and a soft-speaking Dana responding.

"Trying to catch another husband, are we?" Cartimandua said.

"What are you talking about, Sister?" Dana asked.

"Oh, come now, let's not be coy, I saw how you watched our cousin, Caratacus."

Dana shook her head, exhaling as if in disgust. "He is married to Rhian, and she seems very devoted to him."

That's true, but what about Dana? Had she given me the eye as Cartimandua had accused? I thought she was only being polite.

"You can tell by the way she looks at Caratacus," Dana said, "which is more than I can say about you."

Cartimandua arched one of her thin eyebrows. "Oh, how would you know?"

"I have eyes, Sister," Dana replied, "Who are you sleeping with this time, one of father's retainers?"

A smirk crossed Cartimandua's lips. "Jealous, aren't you?"

"Of what? I'm not the one making a fool of myself." She paused. "I've heard … I've heard stories that you are not that good a lover."

Cartimandua narrowed her eyes and extended her long fingernails. "How dare—"

Dana placed a hand to her mouth, but not quick enough to hide her smile.

"Nobody will laugh when I become queen, especially you," Cartimandua said.

"Oh, what will you do, kill me?"

Cartimandua glanced to the shadowy entrance leading to the Great Hall. "The thought has crossed my mind," she said in a low, sinister voice.

Dana gasped. "You wouldn't! Your own sister?"

"Why not, you'll only make trouble for me."

Dana gestured with a hand. "You know I have no ambitions of being queen, I only want another husband and children."

"So you say." Cartimandua paused and once again looked towards the hall entrance. "I've noticed how father's councilors and clan chieftains hang onto your every word."

"About what? I just compliment and make them feel at ease in father's presence, you know how stern he can be sometimes."

Cartimandua's nostrils flared. "Rubbish, they'll listen to you when father dies. They'll vote to make you queen, but I *won't* let that happen. That's why you must go."

Dana shook her head. "May that day never arrive. If so, may I be far from your grasp."

"You simpering fool." Cartimandua sniffed. "You are even more naive than I imagined."

"Sister, you are vile." Dana turned and walked into the Great Hall.

Neither woman seemed to realize that Caratacus had been close enough to have overheard their entire conversation. He didn't like the revelations by Cartimandua. Indeed, if Cartimandua succeeded Dumnoveros on the throne, she might prove to be a force to be reckoned with. Perhaps, more to the point, she might eventually ally with Rome. Caratacus waited until Cartimandua had left before returning to his place by Rhian.

* * *

Next to his wife, Caratacus looked about and noticed Cartimandua was still gone from the dining table. *Probably bedding one of her lovers already.* For a moment he mulled over the conversation he had overhead between her and Dana.

Rhian turned to Caratacus. "Is there something wrong?" she whispered. "You have that strange look in your eyes you get when there might be trouble."

"You may be right," he answered in a low voice. "I will tell you about it after the evening meal when we are alone."

After dinner the king invited Caratacus, Tog, Clud, and his lieutenants to join him, Venutios, the Druids, and his chieftains into another room to form plans for the campaign against the Caledonians.

Before Rhian could object to being excluded, Caratacus shook his head and leaned toward her. "Never mind about the meeting, I have something more important in mind for you."

"Does it have something to do with the possible trouble you mentioned earlier?"

"Aye, I couldn't tell you at dinner, but on my way back from the privy, I overheard a very heated conversation between Cartimandua and Dana."

Rhian's eyes widened.

"I don't have time to go into all the details, but Cartimandua threatened to kill Dana."

Rhian jolted, slightly opening her mouth.

Caratacus half rose, glanced about, but no one seemed to notice. He whispered in Rhian's ear, "I know this is a shock, but try to stay calm. I don't want this getting out."

"All right, I will," Rhian said as she took a few shallow breaths.

"I promise to tell you everything I heard when we're alone. Right now, I want you to speak to Dana."

"What about?"

"Initially, anything to place her at ease. Then ask her about Cartimandua—learn anything you can."

"You think it will tie into her threat against Dana?"

"It might. It could also determine the future of King Dumnoveros's kingdom." Caratacus hesitated. "When Cartimandua's father dies, she wants to be the next ruler."

Rhian shook her head. "That doesn't surprise me one bit." She looked past Caratacus's shoulder. "Dana just took a seat by the wall. I'll go to her and see what I can learn."

Caratacus lightly brushed her jaw line, stepped away, and followed the rest of the leaders into the king's chamber. He knew Rhian was a resourceful woman. The question was, would Dana reveal to Rhian Cartimandua's true intentions? The same answers she gave Dana? Or would she inform her of something ever more sinister?

CHAPTER 21

Caratacus, Clud, Tog, and his lieutenants gathered with King Dumnoveros, his clan leaders, and his Druid advisor around the oaken table in the stonewalled council chamber adjacent to the Great Hall. On the table stretched a long, sheepskin map depicting the Brigantian and Caledonian territories. Crude drawings suggested major landmarks.

Surrounded by eighteen of his followers, Caratacus scanned the crowded room, briefly studying the faces of the Brigantian leaders. For a moment, he locked eyes with the young chieftain, Venutios, his dark eyes radiating defiance.

"This is our land," Venutios said, almost spitting out the words. He turned to Dumnoveros. "Prince Caratacus is here by your invitation, Great King. His army is much bigger than our own, but it still must come under your command."

Caratacus had heard that the king's muscular son-in-law of twenty-four years rose to that position at the age of seventeen, upon his father's death. He is still maturing, Caratacus thought. The temperamental, young man will eventually become a great warrior if he uses his head more and his dagger less. Strange how familiar those words sounded.

A sneer crossed Venutios's face as he glared at Caratacus and his men from across the table. He turned to King Dumnoveros standing next to him. "As chieftain of the Brigantian Uplands and kin to you, Great King, I claim the right to lead the armies against the Caledonians."

"Why?" Caratacus bellowed and pounded a fist on the table. "So that more of your sickly warriors can be slaughtered?"

Venutios glared at Caratacus, his eyes full of venom. Although the room was cool, sweat rolled down the side of

Venutios's face, which became redder as if he were thinking. *This son of a scorpion deserves a knife between his ribs.*

If he was a man, Caratacus thought, Venutios would admit he had been driven from the uplands by the invaders. But it was true, despite the ravages of epidemic, the young clan leader and his small force had fought a heroic, delaying action.

Venutios stabbed a finger on the Caledonian part of the map. "Give me enough men, and the Caledonians will wish they'd never left their cliffs and goats!"

Caratacus gestured toward the group. "If you had more warriors, you'd lead us like mindless sheep. To defeat those stinking shit eaters, we have to fight as an army: your warriors, the king's, and mine." He realized he had cast down an unspoken gauntlet between them. Venutios would never willingly withdraw his claim without spilling blood.

"My men take orders only from me," Venutios said, his voice like an angry bear.

Caratacus stared across the table into his dark eyes, searching for any weakness should there be a fight. "And *you will* take orders from me," Caratacus said, glaring at the young leader.

"Who gave you the right to give orders to anyone?" Venutios asked coolly, balling up his fist.

"Your king!" Dumnoveros said, raising a calloused hand and bringing it to his chest.

Venutios twisted his mouth as he turned toward the grizzled ruler, but pointed a finger toward Caratacus. "But Great King, he's a foreigner, he has no—"

"Enough! He has the right if I command it."

"Aye, 'tis the king's right!" shouted several clan chieftains.

Dumnoveros motioned to Venutios from the head of the table. "Your forces are too weak. His are large and powerful." He made a sweeping gesture with both hands in Caratacus's direction. "More important ... he has proven himself a worthy warrior."

Venutios winced, but remained silent. His mouth twisted into a crooked frown.

"He is not a foreigner," the king said. "You forget, he is my nephew and cousin of your wife, the Princess Cartimandua."

"As you say, Great King, but I have the ancient right to challenge him for command. I now claim that right!" Venutios flashed a dagger and spun toward Caratacus, who followed suit. The king, clan chieftains, and Caratacus's followers quickly moved to the sides of the room along the stone walls and shouted support to the fighter they favored.

Venutios leaped on top of the wooden table.

Caratacus instantly shoved the table over, forcing Venutios to jump clear.

The younger man grabbed a wooden stool and hurled it at his opponent. It missed and crashed into the wall, nearly striking King Dumnoveros and several chieftains, who side-stepped. The hollow sound echoed through the room.

Caratacus hurled his weapon, missing Venutios's broad shoulders by a hair's width. The knife careened off the back wall. The blade struck with such force that it bounced back, sliding along the stone floor to within his reach. Again, he grabbed the dagger. He looked up as Venutios slashed at his face. Caratacus dove to the left and snatched the younger man's right ankle, yanked, and toppled him.

But Venutios was quick and jumped from a backward somersault to his feet.

Caratacus rose as Venutios slashed again. The prince deftly stepped aside, catching Venutios's right ankle with his hand, sending him crashing to the floor.

Instantly, Venutios recovered and lunged again.

Caratacus slid sideways and kicked him in the groin.

Venutios howled as he doubled over and fell, writhing to the floor. "Dirty bastard!" he moaned. "Bastard!"

"There are no rules in claiming the right to lead men in battle," Caratacus snarled.

He grabbed Venutios's jet hair with his left hand and yanked him to his knees. Caratacus stomped his left foot down on the back of the young warrior's calves and with his right hand held a dagger to Venutios's throat. "You

shouldn't have challenged me, Cousin—you're no match."
Caratacus drew a shallow cut, and a trickle of blood ran
down the side of his victim's neck.

"Son of a sow!" Venutios gasped as he licked his dry
mouth. A look of terror crossed his twisted face. He
trembled. "Gods damn it! Kill me and get it done!"

For a split second, Caratacus pondered the situation. *I
could easily kill the young prince, and probably should, but
to do so would drive a wedge between both our armies. I
have humiliated and defeated him. Now I must restore
Venutios's dignity.*

"I could kill you, but who would win? The Caledonians!
Your death, or mine, could only divide us further."
Caratacus glanced to King Dumnoveros and the gathered
chieftains. "You have led brave warriors, and although
driven back, you were never defeated. For every man lost,
your enemies bled two. And every man knows the truth;
that disease carved away the strength of your forces as no
worthy army could."

He studied Venutios, keeping a tight pull on his hair.
"The simple truth is, the king's army, not yours, not mine,
needs your warriors' bravery and loyalty and your proven
leadership ability and knowledge of the Uplands! We, you
and I, don't have the right to challenge to the death. The
times are too serious. ONLY the king shall choose who will
lead, for victory is not assured in any event." Caratacus's
voice rose. "Even now, should the king choose another to
lead, I pledge to follow."

Caratacus slowly withdrew the bloodied knife, alert to
any sign of resistance, and released Venutios, who fell to
the floor. The prince stood towering over the prostrate,
young chieftain. No one spoke a word. For a moment,
Venutios lay on his stomach. Slowly, he rose upon his
elbows, seemingly puzzled as to why he was still alive. He
dropped his head, but did not touch his wound. Yet,
Venutios seemed to feel the trickle of blood and must have
guessed that it symbolized his defeat for all to see.
Gradually, he stood.

King Dumnoveros and the assembly of clan chieftains
roared their approval as Venutios and Caratacus extended
their hands simultaneously and grinned at one another.

"Even facing death, you're not afraid, are you? A true warrior," Caratacus complimented. He kept his hand extended to the young chieftain. "The king needs all the good warriors he can get, especially you."

"Aye, that I do," King Dumnoveros said.

"You're a brave man and a valued warrior, Venutios," Caratacus said.

Venutios nodded painfully. "I'll not forget this. I owe you my life."

"I prefer to have you as a friend rather than an enemy."

The young chieftain stared at Caratacus as if considering his remark and slowly nodded.

The situation had come full circle. Caratacus had no intention of killing Venutios, only disabling him at the most.

King Dumnoveros, followed by Caratacus and the other chieftains, reentered the main assembly room of the Great Hall where the guests were still congregated, including the women. As they appeared, a hush engulfed the assemblage, who gathered before the king's wolf-skin throne. Dumnoveros sat down and raised his arms for silence. He turned to the petty kings, but addressed Caratacus. "Prince Caratacus! I charge you with leading my armies against the Caledonians."

The chamber rocked with shouts of approval. Caratacus's eyes locked onto Dana and Rhian as they hugged one another. Obviously, Rhian had been successful in befriending Dana. *What had she learned that had brought about such a friendly embrace?*

CHAPTER 22

After the meeting with the king, Caratacus was curious to learn what information Dana had revealed to Rhian. He turned to Clud, Tog, and his lieutenants and motioned for them to stay where they had halted by the king's dais and wait for him. Although a few of the king's guests milled about the Great Hall, most were departing.

Caratacus grinned, stepped forward, and approached Rhian and Dana. "Well, it seems that you two ladies have become friends, if your hugging one another is any indication."

Dana smiled and nodded. "Yes, Caratacus, Rhian has been telling me all about you."

"Indeed?" He quickly glanced to Rhian.

"It wasn't all you, Husband," Rhian said. "Dana told me much about herself."

"I am interested in hearing more of Dana," Caratacus said. For the first time, he noticed the tiny mole on the right side of her delicate face.

Dana blushed. "Oh, it's not all that much—being a widow isn't really the life I want."

Caratacus raised an eyebrow.

"I'll tell you the rest after we have returned to our new bivouac," Rhian said.

Dana touched Rhian's arm with her long fingers. "Yes, I will leave it in your hands, Rhian." Dana turned her head to Caratacus. "I am so happy to see you again after all these years, and I hope we shall see more of one another soon." She turned away and followed the other departing guests out of the cavernous building.

Caratacus's eyes followed Dana's willowy figure as she disappeared through the main door. He moved to Rhian's side. "I'll wager your conversation with Dana was about more than just Cartimandua, wasn't it?"

"Much more," Rhian said softly.

Caratacus motioned to Tog, Clud, and the lieutenants to follow him and Rhian. "Let's find where they've quartered our army."

Darkness had enshrouded the countryside when they reached the army's site beyond the walls of Eburacum, down by the Ouse River. The heat of the day was finally receding, leaving a breath of cool air on a gentle breeze. Caratacus, Rhian, and his retinue had been guided there by a couple of the king's retainers by the bright light of the full moon and sky full of countless stars. There was no organization as to the camp's construction or layout. The hodge-podge of tents and lean-tos, lighted by a mixture of campfires and torches, surrounded the larger tents of the clan chieftains and captains. Their banners hung limply in the night's heat on hardwood poles before their leader's quarters. Guards posted on the perimeter challenged Caratacus's party upon their approach and passed them through.

Caratacus's headquarters tent was the largest, located in the center of the campsite. Once inside the well-lit, goatskin tent, Rhian said she must wash up before telling him about Dana. Caratacus mentioned he would do the same.

Later, when both had cleaned themselves, Rhian and Caratacus sat side by side on the fur-covered pallet. She had changed into a russet, linen gown, while Caratacus, bare-chested, wore a pair of home-spun, buff-colored breeches. The servants were dismissed after dousing all the lights, save a small, olive-oil lamp.

"Now tell me, what did you learn from Dana?" Caratacus asked. He placed a hand about her shoulder, which still felt firm and smooth even under the material of her garment.

Rhian leaned against Caratacus's muscled chest. "Tell me first about what you saw going on between Dana and Cartimandua. Then when I tell you about Dana, it might make more sense to both of us."

"That's right, I forgot I was going to fill you in," Caratacus said. He explained the confrontation between the two sisters.

"Strange," Rhian said when he had finished.

"Why?"

For a split second, Rhian twisted her head toward Caratacus. "You'll see when I tell you what Dana said about her. But you should know what she said before I asked her about Cartimandua."

"Is it that important?"

Rhian nodded, rubbing her warm, smooth face against Caratacus's chest. "I believe it is."

"Then tell me," Caratacus said.

"When you departed with the king and the rest, I approached Dana and gave her a hug. I thought she might resist, but she didn't. In fact, she returned the greeting."

Rhian related how Dana was so pleased the two of them were finally getting a chance to talk and know one another. A smile had crossed Dana's lightly freckled face, and she commented how she hated formal gatherings. "I told her I felt the same way," Rhian said

Caratacus grinned.

"Dana told me," Rhian continued, "her father put her in charge of arranging tonight's feast."

Caratacus furrowed his eyebrows together. "Isn't that the responsibility of the chief steward?"

"My thoughts, too," Rhian answered, "but Dana said her father believes she organizes things like a Roman, whom she loathes. Why, she even mimicked her father's gruff masculine voice, 'If you were a man, you'd be my top general.' Dana admitted she hardly knows one end of a sword from another, but King Dumnoveros wanted to leave nothing to chance."

Caratacus smiled.

"Actually, I chuckled," Rhian said. "But I considered it a compliment, because everything had gone so smoothly at the feast."

"Thank the gods it did," Caratacus said. Gently, he caressed Rhian's shoulder.

"There is more," Rhian continued. "Dana told her father she wouldn't do it again. From now on, her talents were for the household only, not for using at the king's banquet. She hated being compared to those horrid Romans. Then we both laughed."

"That wasn't all you talked about?" Caratacus asked, growing impatient.

"I'm getting to that," Rhian said. She explained that Dana seemed embarrassed talking about herself and touched Rhian's arms with the tips of her fingers. "Her hands were rough from work, but not calloused like my own," Rhian said. "She wanted to talk about me, because she had heard so much and believed everything people had said was true."

"What did she hear?" Caratacus asked.

"She didn't say, because I quickly replied I hope what she had heard wasn't all bad. I admitted that I had a frightful temper," Rhian answered with an uneasy laugh. "I mentioned my greatest desire is for children—and to be a warrior."

Rhian related how this seemed to surprise Dana. The younger woman couldn't believe she had a temper. Dana had heard Rhian was the most loving of wives and more beautiful than anyone could have imagined. And no doubt she would still have children.

"I told Dana that while I still wanted children, I had little hope, but that you still needed an heir."

Rhian turned her head and looked up at Caratacus. "That's when I asked myself, what does this woman really want? She seemed too kind, too good to be true."

"What did Dana say?" Caratacus inquired.

She sighed, snuggled against Caratacus, and continued. "She said it was true, that I was a good woman. Then Dana gestured with her hand and said she heard I was a great warrior, and you must be proud."

"You have yet to prove yourself in battle," Caratacus said.

"That's what I told her." She explained that Dana believed Rhian would fight well when the time came. "As for Dana, she demeaned herself saying she could barely mount a horse. For a moment, there was a pause, and then Dana grabbed me by my arm and pointed to the wooden bench by the hearth in the center of the Great Hall. While other guests milled about, no one else stood near the enclosed circle of stone. She led me over there where they could talk with a little privacy," Rhian said. "It had been years since she had seen you, not since you were little children. She urged me to tell her all about you and, more importantly, myself and the women fighters. We strolled to the planked seat and sat side by side."

Rhian paused and pinched her eyebrows together.

"What else?" Caratacus asked.

"At that point, I realized Dana must be interested in you," Rhian said. "Was it because you are cousins or was there something else? I needed to learn more." Rhian described the conversation. "I told her about the hardship of field marching, you, myself, our marriage, and the tragic deaths of our three sons while giving birth.

"When I had finished, Dana had said how sorry she was. She told me she was certain I would have babies. She leaned over and softly touched my hands.

"I felt the sincerity of Dana's contagious optimism," Rhian said. "But I could not help but feel a sense of hostility toward her. I don't know why I felt so jealous." Rhian exhaled. "Then she told me she would love to have children."

What is Rhian hinting at? Does she want me to take Dana as a wife? I know the time will come since I want sons, but now?

"At that point I hesitated to ask, but my curiosity got the best of me," Rhian said. "I asked why didn't she and her husband have any?"

"Why didn't they?" Caratacus inquired.

"According to Dana, it was a long story and few people knew the reason. That's when Dana paused and her face tightened. I understood if she did not want to go on. But Dana bit her lip and said it was strange, she barely knew me, yet found herself thinking of me as a good friend, even as a sister."

"What was your reaction?" Caratacus asked.

"Somehow, I had the same feeling I told her," Rhian answered. "I didn't really, but Dana didn't have to know that."

Rhian returned to her story. "Dana brought her face closer to mine and asked me never to tell anyone. She sighed," Rhian said. "She admitted she did not grieve when her husband died a horrid pox death. I was surprised by

192

her calloused answer and told her I couldn't believe she had meant it. But it was true." She took a deep breath. "Dana's husband was very cruel and had beaten her countless times.

"When I asked her why she stayed with him despite his abuse, she said she feared her father would lose face for mismatching the two of them. Like a fool, she endured the loveless marriage. Then a devious smile formed on Dana's lips. She took deliberate pains to prevent any pregnancy," Rhian added. "Dana used medicinal herbs prescribed by a healing woman. I agreed she had done the right thing.

"Dana partially turned about," Rhian said, "and glanced toward the entry to the room where her father, you, and the others were conferring about their plans to fight the Caledonians. No one was present. She turned back to me and, in a low voice, said when she returned to her father she told him she had the right to choose any man she wanted, her privilege as a widow. However, she would be content to marry a man of his choosing again with one stipulation. The groom must agree never to beat Dana upon pain of losing her and the large dowry that came with the marriage."

"Was there more?" Caratacus said, interrupting Rhian's story.

Rhian paused, pulled herself from Caratacus's grip and sat up. Her aqua eyes peered deep into those of Caratacus. "When Dana finished, it was then I remembered the argument you and I had about a second wife last month as we dined one evening at home. ...

"I knew you had the right to take another woman if I didn't bear you children," Rhian said.

Caratacus took a swallow of corma beer from his bronze cup and sat it back on the short-legged table at which they sat on the rug-covered, earthen floor. "By custom, the second marriage is temporary, until the woman bears her first child," Caratacus said. "Then it becomes permanent. If no children result, the marriage is dissolved."

"Yes, I know children that came from the couple had the same rights as if born by the first wife." Rhian took a sip of beer from her cup, carved with the image of the horse goddess, Epona, sitting on the back of a mount.

"Nevertheless," Caratacus motioned to Rhian, "even if I remarried, you would be the chief-wife, and respected all the more."

"Your intentions may be well and good, but will you still love me?" The firelight of the center hearth a few feet from where they sat ebbed and flowed, bright one moment, showing the concern in her face, and the next moment nearly hiding her face. "Or is respect all that I will have?"

"What do you want me to say?" Caratacus answered impatiently. "Of course I love you."

"You could show a little more sincerity," Rhian said in a sulking voice.

"Rhian, I will always love you."

"But sometimes I feel like a piece of property, not your wife."

"How can you say that? I have never regarded you as a piece of property." Then, in a softer, more conciliatory tone, he said, "You are the first woman of my life—the first I truly cared for—and always will. I have loved and honored you since marriage, and I do love you now."

Rhian appeared to be pouting, her nose crinkled, lips drawn tight.

Caratacus reached toward her and slipped a hand about her waist. "I do love you."

She grimaced, eyes filling with tears, and wept for the first time since the death of their last child.

"The time has come for me to look for another woman," he said softly, "only to bear an heir, not to replace you in any way."

"You still mean that, don't you?"

He nodded silently. Moments passed.

"Very well, if you must find a woman, then I want a say in her choosing."

"Done."

Knowing the choice was his privilege alone, Rhian seemed taken aback by Caratacus's quick reply.

"You heard me, Rhian," Caratacus said. "You look surprised."

"I didn't believe you would be so quick to respond."

For a split second, Caratacus pursed his lips. "I agree, the time has come. You may choose whomever you want, but I do hope she will be comely." *Perhaps Rhian has concluded that she will never bear another child.*

* * *

Rhian brought Caratacus back to the present; while they sat on their bed-pallet, she continued Dana's tale. "You were still in conference with the king when Dana finished her story. There was a burst of laughter that broke the moment. As Dana looked toward the merrymakers, I noticed a maturity despite her youth, her eyes ... yes ... she had born her fate well. I thought for a moment. Dana could be the answer. You had said you would still honor me, but I wondered if you really meant it?"

"You know I do," Caratacus answered.

"But I don't want to lose you to this woman. Yet you need an heir. I thought what were your other choices? A mindless daughter of another chieftain? No, your children cannot be dim-witted or self-indulgent."

"No, I don't want a son like Adminios," Caratacus said.

Rhian chuckled. "No, never." She exhaled and continued. "As much as I hated the thought, Dana must be the one. She might be content with the role of second wife and bearer of your children ... the thought that brought forth the realization I would remain barren all my life. Then I watched the younger woman's profile, so cheerful now and careless, and it blurred through my own tears."

Caratacus brought Rhian close to his chest again and she continued her story.

"Dana touched my hand," Rhian said, "and asked what was wrong. Had she said something to offend me? She hadn't, but I had to wipe away the tears and compose myself. I looked about and then softly asked Dana if the thought had ever crossed her mind about sharing another woman's husband?

"For a moment, Dana dropped her hand and studied me. Then she asked if I meant you? I said yes.

"Then she sighed," Rhian said. "Dana hesitated before saying that if I did truly mean what I said before about feeling almost like a sister, then she believed ... she knew ... she could share you with me as a husband. Dana smiled and reached out to me, and we touched hands. I thanked her."

"I believe you have made a wise choice, Rhian," Caratacus said. "I have liked my cousin since we were children. I'm sure this will work. But remember," he looked into her eyes, "I still love you. You are my first love and wife—always."

"I'm so glad you feel that way about me. I prayed you would."

"But there is still another question," Caratacus said. "When did you ask Dana about Cartimandua?"

"I was just getting to that," Rhian said. "I changed the subject and asked her about Cartimandua." Rhian shook her head. "For some reason I don't understand, she refused to say anything negative about her sister. It's strange she wouldn't talk about it, especially after what you heard between them. At that point, I asked Dana if her willingness to marry you had anything to do with getting away from Cartimandua? She denied it and said she wanted to become your wife."

"Then we must meet with Dana tomorrow before we leave on campaign. I need to learn firsthand how sincere she is about marrying me and see if I can persuade her to change her mind in telling us about Cartimandua."

Although Caratacus hardly knew Dana, what he had seen tonight at dinner and overheard during the confrontation between her and Cartimandua led him to believe that Dana would make a good second wife.

CHAPTER 23

At dawn the next morning, Caratacus and Rhian, followed by a small entourage including Clud and Tog, arrived outside the king's home by horse. Nearly half the size of the Great Hall, the wattle-and-daub building, whitewashed with lime, stood encircled by a small moat filled with muddy water and a tall, wooden palisade. Guarded by two sentries, the house was about one hundred yards from the Great Hall. A thin, blue line of smoke and the perfumed smell of pine seeped through a hole in the center of the thatched roof and disappeared in the shimmering gold and crimson glow of morning sunlight. Sounds of barking dogs, whinnying horses, and baying cattle drifted from homes and the animal pens outside the fortress.

Although still early, Caratacus and Rhian wore only short-sleeved tunics and striped breeches with daggers and swords strapped to their sides.

"Wait for us here, we won't be long," Caratacus told his retinue after they had halted. He and Rhian dismounted, crossed the short bridge over the narrow stream, and approached the sentries. "Princess Dana is expecting us," he told them.

"Stay here," the taller of the two guards said. He headed for the house.

A moment later, the king's man returned and waved Caratacus and Rhian through the oaken gate.

Accompanied by a female servant, Dana met them in front of the home's covered porch. A vivid, short-sleeved, cobalt tunic fringed in gold, which the Brigantians called a leynah, and held together at the shoulder by a bronze pin encrusted with sapphires covered her willowy frame. Around her long, delicate neck clung a beaded, amber necklace that plunged below the gown's neckline. Silverhooped earrings, glistening in the early-morning sunlight, hung from thin ear lobes. Gold armlets, the shape of serpents, clasped above the elbows circled her slender arms.

Dana smiled. "It is so good to see the both of you again, especially you, Caratacus." She nodded to him. "I regret that we had so little time to speak to one another last night."

"Aye, that was unfortunate, but your father had important matters to discuss that wouldn't wait." Caratacus grinned. "Regardless, I'm here now."

"I would invite you inside," Dana explained, "but father is still asleep. He drank too much last night—again."

Caratacus chuckled.

"We can talk out here." She turned to her servant. "Leave us." The woman disappeared into the house.

"Did Rhian explain my situation?" Dana asked once the attendant was gone.

Caratacus turned to Rhian, who raised an eyebrow.

"Rhian says you are willing to become my second wife," Caratacus said. "I am honored, but is it truly what you want? We have not seen one another in years."

Dana moved closer to Caratacus and touched his calloused hand. "I meant it when I told Rhian that it was my desire to become your wife." Dana paused and glanced to Rhian, who nodded, and back to Caratacus. "Rhian is a charming woman, and I was so pleased that she would ask me."

"I wouldn't have told him if I didn't believe you were worthy, Dana," Rhian said in a soft but firm voice. "But remember, I still will be his first and chief wife."

"Yes, I know," Dana answered. She turned from Caratacus, stepped to Rhian, grabbed her hand, and peered into her emerald eyes. "You gave him something that I can never give."

"But you can give me children," Caratacus said.

"If the gods bless me, yes, I will," Dana said. She removed her hands from that of Rhian and faced Caratacus.

He looked about and then asked Dana in a voice bordering on suspicion. "What about Cartimandua? I overheard the conversation between the two of you last night outside the Great Hall."

Dana jolted, her eyes widened. "Did you hear everything?"

"I heard enough," Caratacus replied. "I know she threatened to kill you. Could that be the real reason why you are willing to marry me?" he said in a stronger tone. "To get away from her?"

Dana shook her head, earrings swinging from the lobes. "No, not at all. When you and Rhian first arrived at the Great Hall, my heart nearly jumped to my throat. Then I remembered years ago asking myself why hadn't my father arranged with your father for our betrothal before you married Rhian?" Dana stopped, visibly swallowed and for an instant, tightened her lips. "I knew ... I knew then I wanted to be your wife, but it wasn't to be so. And then ... when I saw Rhian by your side, I understood. She ... she is the most beautiful of women."

Rhian's face reddened. "You ... yourself, are a most elegant and lovely woman in your own right, Dana."

Dana paled and for a few seconds bowed her head.

I had no idea Dana thought of me this way, but would it have really mattered? Just as Rhian said, Dana is a "lovely" woman, I have to be sure. "So your decision had nothing to do with Cartimandua's threat?" Caratacus asked.

"Nothing whatsoever," Dana answered. She brought her hand to her chest. "If I had not been chosen by Rhian, and believe me I had no idea that I would, I had already planned to leave the kingdom. This is not the first time she has threatened my life. It was after seeing you and Rhian that the idea of leaving came to me. And when Cartimandua threatened me again last night, I decided that enough was enough. My idea was to take ship to Camulodunum and ask political asylum from your father."

"Then we would have met again in any event," Caratacus said.

"If that had been the case, yes. Once I had arrived, it was my hope the king would be sympathetic to my plight. I cannot believe your father would have sent me back here to Eburacum to be murdered by Cartimandua."

I believe her. She will make a fine wife. I need children, and if Dana is willing, then so am I. Caratacus turned to Rhian, who smiled and touched his elbow.

"Rhian, do you truly want Dana to become my consort and second wife," Caratacus asked.

A brief smiled crossed Rhian's bowed lips. "It is my wish, honestly."

I find no deception in her eyes, Caratacus thought. *Surely she meant what she said.* He faced Dana. "All right, I will take you for my second wife—it will be my pleasure to have you as part of my household. I know you and Rhian will get on very well, and I will honor both of you."

"Thank you, dear Caratacus," Dana said. She stood on her toes and kissed his cheek. Dana turned, stepped to Rhian, and did the same. "I know I will be happy to be your sister-wife."

"I feel the same about you, Dana," Rhian said as she and Dana braced one another by the forearms.

"Now, we must see your father, the king," Caratacus said, "to receive his permission and blessing."

Dana touched his arm again. "Before we see him, please do me a favor?"

Rhian gave Dana a questioning look.

"What is it?" Caratacus asked.

"Don't tell him of Cartimandua's threat against my life."

"Why not?" Caratacus asked.

"Despite the way my sister acted last night when you and Rhian were presented to father, she is still his favorite, not me. You may have heard Cartimandua accuse me of that last night, but it is not true."

For an instant, Caratacus looked beyond Dana's shoulder and focused on the house's entrance. "Don't you think your father would believe me?"

"He never believes Cartimandua can do any wrong," Dana said. "Father thinks she is just a strong-willed girl."

"He's a fool," Caratacus said. He came to a decision. "All right, I'll say nothing for the time being, but if there is the slightest hint that Cartimandua is scheming against you, I want you to immediately send me word by a courier you trust. Anyone harming you will see the point of my dagger."

Dana bowed her head. "As you wish."

"Let's go inside and wake your father," Caratacus said. "It's time he got up."

They entered the house, dimly illuminated by the light from the fire pit. Wisps of smoke curled upward and seeped through the straw-roofed ceiling. A female slave stood over a small cauldron stirring porridge. The aroma of baked bread wafted from the earthen oven at one end of the room. The woman glanced at Caratacus, Dana, and Rhian before returning to her duties.

Loud snoring drifted from an area cordoned off by tall, goatskin hides. Dana motioned for Caratacus and Rhian to wait by the pit. She dismissed the servant.

Dana stepped within the cubicle. "Da, wake up, wake up," her voice carried outside.

A loud groan erupted from Dumnoveros. "Not yet, the gods are stomping me head."

Caratacus and Rhian looked at one another and smiled.

"Get up, Da, we have guests," Dana said.

"Send them away, leave me alone."

"No, I won't, Da, Caratacus and Rhian are here. Get up!"

"Ooh, the gods hate me!" He exhaled loudly. "They've clubbed me with a thousand hammers."

"What did you expect? You were drunk again."

Dumnoveros moaned. "Alright, alright, I'll get up."

Caratacus and Rhian snickered.

"Serves the old sod right," Rhian whispered.

Regardless of the king's condition, Caratacus was concerned about what his reaction would be when he asked permission to allow Dana to become his consort. He remembered that Dana had told Rhian that as a widow she had the right to choose whomever she wanted as consort or husband. However, she would allow her father to pick her next man. Caratacus wondered if he should have waited for a time when Dumnoveros was in better spirits.

Dana rejoined Caratacus and Rhian who remained standing together.

Caratacus shifted his weight from one foot to another. He noticed Rhian did the same. The muscles in her face tightened as if trying to hide the growing tension in her body.

A rustle came from within the cubicle as if someone was putting on clothes.

Dumnoveros staggered through the cubicle flap, his face flushed, eyes blood-shot, and his breath reeked of beer and wine. Dressed in a pair of faded breeches and a wrinkled tunic, he approached the three waiting for him. Before the flap closed, Caratacus saw in the shadowy light a young woman, probably one of his concubines, still lying within the bed furs, her face partially covered by hair strands.

The king plopped on a stool by the hearth. He coughed and winced as he placed both hands to the sides of his face. "Gods, my head!"

Caratacus knew the feeling. "Sorry about your pain, Great King."

"Do you, now?" Dumnoveros exhaled. "I suppose you do. It's a man's right to get drunk."

Dana sniffed. "Perhaps, but the gods make you pay for the *right*, Da."

He grunted and scraped his feet on the hard-packed, dirt floor.

Dana went to one end of the house and returned with an earthen bowl filled with a dark liquid. She handed it to her father. "Drink this, Da."

"What is it?" he asked, grabbing the bowl.

"You should know by now, it's for your hangover, willow bark in cold water."

"Ugh, that miserable swill?"

She pointed a finger at her father. "Drink it, Da, it's the only remedy that cures your aching head."

Dumnoveros raised the bowl to his mouth and noisily downed the contents, loudly slopping liquid out both sides of his mouth into his matted beard. He handed the container back to Dana, coughed, and spat. "Terrible stuff, like drinking mud."

Despite the king's description, Caratacus thought the mixture might be worth trying the next time he had drunk too much. His eyes glanced to Rhian and noticed, even through her long tunic, the tightened muscles in her arms and shoulders. She slowly clenched and unclenched her hands.

Dumnoveros didn't offer them seats, even though there were stools nearby. "I've taken my daughter's putrid tonic, and my head is clearing—barely. What brings you to my home at this early hour?"

Puzzled by the king's lack of courtesy, Caratacus knew this could be a bad sign. Would Dumnoveros refuse his request for Dana's hand? He took a step forward. Yet, he didn't feel any pangs of nervousness in what he was about to tell the king. "I'm here to ask your permission for Dana to become my consort and one day to be my wife."

The king rubbed his forehead and shook it as if to clear his mind. He faced his daughter. "Is this true, Dana?"

Dana bent over and touched her father's calloused hand and then straightened up. "It is, Da."

He snorted and stared at Caratacus through bloodshot eyes and towards Rhian. "You have a wife, does she approve?"

For a moment, Rhian's bowed lips tightened into a thin line. She sighed and nodded. In a low, raspy voice she answered, "I do, High King. Caratacus needs an heir, I cannot give him one, and I believe Dana can. When she does, my husband will have the right to take her as his second wife."

Dumnoveros winced. "Ooh!" He rubbed the side of his head again. Slowly, a smile emerged showing brown, jagged teeth framed by his graying whiskers. He turned to Dana. "You know Rhian will remain Caratacus's chief wife. Are you sure this is what you want?"

Dana nodded, touching his hands a second time. "Yes, Da, need I repeat myself?"

"No, you don't," the king answered. "Very well, as a widow you have the right to choose any man you want for a husband."

The king turned to Caratacus. "With pleasure, I give my permission and blessing to take my daughter as your wife." He shrugged his shoulders as if it mattered little to him.

"I thank you, Great King." Caratacus turned to the smiling women.

Dumnoveros stood and approached Caratacus. Rhian stood back a step next to Dana. The two men shook hands. Dumnoveros turned and kissed Dana on the cheek. "He's a good man."

Afterwards, the two women hugged one another.

The king addressed Caratacus, "The ceremony will be performed once you and the armies have returned from the campaign against our enemies, the Caledonians. Bring us victory."

Later that morning, Caratacus, Rhian, and their army, along with the forces of Venutios, departed Eburacum and marched northward in pursuit of the Caledonians.

* * *

Stifling heat hung over the land like a low-drifting fog the day Caratacus and the allied army departed Eburacum. Nearly six thousand warriors strong on foot and horseback journeyed north through the fertile valley of Brigantia, a green land crisscrossed with rushing streams and creeks and filled with a smell of iron-red, rich earth, plowed into meandering furrows.

White waters of many streams plunged swiftly from the iron cliffs and crags of the hills into the Rivers Swale and Ure, which flowed into the Ouse, a river gracefully wandering around the edge of Eburacum, draining into the broad Humber near the British Ocean. It was a land more accustomed to frequent, cool, summer rains and winds rather than breath-sucking heat waves.

Columns of bare-chested warriors, caked with dust, snaked across the countryside, grouped in loosely knit companies. Woven banners bearing images of black boars, red stags, and gray wolves hung limply from poles tilted at lax angles. Including Rhian, the women, riding large ponies, sweltered in colorful, hot, woolen tunics and breeches. Custom forbid their stripping to the waist.

Abandoned housesteads, whose occupants had been victims of plague, grew more numerous as the army moved further north. Caratacus's warriors soon trekked across hundreds of barren acres of now-fallow, dusty farmlands, a land pimpled with newly constructed burial cairns and old defensive dikes. Every now and then the army encountered pockmarked peasants, men stripped to their waist, and women dressed in itching, woolen cowls, toiling on small plots of land. The parched earth belched little dust clouds with the blows hacked from each hoe. One of the men complained that even if the farmers plowed and planted, what would they use for water when it hadn't rained in months. The survivors were a grim reminder the countryside had not recuperated from the epidemic.

In the best of times, less than half the children reached the age of five. If a king lived to age forty, the kingdom considered itself fortunate for such a long rule. And if a man reached fifty, people would wonder how he did it. Now, most of the survivors had been swept away by the great sickness. Warriors, who would have otherwise plundered the homes, left them alone in fear of catching the dreaded pox. Even more, they feared the wrath of Caratacus, who ordered his fighters to stay away upon pain of death. His men were little better than the brigands from the north.

The army tramped on, drawing closer to the rocky, northern uplands.

Caratacus received word the Caledonians fled just ahead of them, flushed with booty and vulnerable to attack. Determined to destroy the redheaded demons before they reached their homelands, he dispatched orders to all companies to pick up the marching pace. The raiders would pay for the destruction wreaked upon the Brigantes.

Caratacus's sweltering host slogged along the cobblestone remnants of an ancient trackway, hugging the western slope of the eastern Brigantian Hills, gradually leaving behind the narrowing plain of the Brigantian Valley.

* * *

Early afternoon of the second day of the march, a minor clan chieftain drew up his mount before Caratacus and reported his scouts had spotted the Caledonians less than five miles ahead approaching the River Tees. Upon dismissing the leader, Caratacus rode his gelding toward the front of the column. If the enemy successfully crossed, their army would scatter and disappear into the mountains and thick forests of the Northern Pennines. Hunting them down would be impossible.

The combined armies of Caratacus and Venutios ascended the steep trackway carved into the sides of a mountain cliff. Strung out like a hunting snake, the army slithered and twisted its way up the mountainside and through a narrow defile toward the pass that would lead them down into the Tees Valley. Familiar with the terrain, Venutios's scouts rode far to the front of the loosely formed companies of infantry and cavalry squadrons searching for signs of the enemy.

Caratacus sat tall on his horse at the head of the main body of warriors with Clud riding at this side. Tog rode at the rear to check on stragglers and keep the army moving.

In the center of the vanguard trundled the baggage and supply wagons escorted by Rhian and her mounted warrior women. The high cliffs on one side and sharp ravine and thick forest falling away to the other side of the trackway, left only a narrow road wide enough for six files of men to pass.

A scout riding a piebald gelding through the file of tramping warriors pulled alongside Caratacus. "Lord," he said, "one of our advance columns sighted Caledonian bandits in the Tees River Valley below."

"Very good." Caratacus grinned. "We'll make quick work of them."

A deafening roar jerked them about. Huge, gray boulders, followed by rocks and dirt, trees and shrubs, tumbled down the craggy cliff sides above the narrow road. The murderous, crashing avalanche drowned the screams and moans of men and horses. Choking clouds of dust engulfed not only the survivors but the victims trapped in the crushing mound of debris.

"Get back! Get back!" Caratacus barked. "It's a trap!"

"I'm not leaving you!" Clud shouted.

Caratacus turned about and caught a glimpse of the baggage train and the escorting women. They were far to the rear, out of harm's way.

Finding it impossible to circle around the flying boulders, hundreds of Caratacus's warriors on foot and horseback fled from the direction of the onslaught back into the still-advancing column.

Just as quickly as it began, the great din subsided. Screams and groans and cries for help shot through the receding dust cloud from about five hundred warriors pinned by boulders and logs. Bloody, lifeless limbs stuck through the rubble as if buried in a refuse pit.

A flood of warriors rushed forward to pull free their trapped comrades.

"Look out!" Clud shouted. From the great scarp above, a murderous stream of arrows and sling-stones rained down, killing many would-be rescuers and scattering the rest.

A stinging pain slammed through Caratacus's bronze helmet onto the back of his head and knocked him off his mount. Just before he struck the ground, he instinctively brought up his hands in front of his face. As he lapsed into unconsciousness, two more black stones hammered his back.

Moments later, he awoke, his head and back aching as if horse kicked. Still on his stomach, he turned his head to the side and discovered a blood-smeared warrior sprawled on the ground nearby, dead, with arrows sticking from his back and neck.

"You're alive!" Clud exclaimed as he pulled alongside Caratacus and jumped from his horse. He dropped to Caratacus's side. "I figured sure you'd be dead."

Caratacus nodded and with a scraped and bloodied hand touched his aching head, still enclosed by the helmet. "Thank the gods this stayed on my head, it saved my life."

"Can you get up?" Clud asked.

"Let's see." Again, pain shot through Caratacus's back and head. He flung off his burning-hot helmet allowing the cool air to caress his skull. He winced as he pulled his hands to his side, straightened his arms, pushed up, and came to his knees. Nausea roiled within his throat and stomach and for a second he thought he would vomit. But the sensation quickly fled. He struggled again before he eventually stood.

Tog galloped out of a cloud of billowing dust and pulled his mount up beside his older brother. "Thank Lugh and Teutates you're alive!" He dismounted, his body and long chestnut hair covered with grime, and stepped closer. Tog checked Caratacus's face and head. "That's a nasty knot you're developing—it'll stick through your hair like the bloated belly of a dead horse. And there's four or five welts on your back."

"Thanks for the encouraging remarks." Caratacus gasped. "The gods must have danced on me—I feel sore all over."

"You're lucky it ain't worse," Clud said.

"Aye, when this is over, I'll sacrifice to the gods," Caratacus said. He stood and, for a few seconds, allowed the dizziness to pass before pulling himself up onto his horse. He took a few breaths and shook his head. "Let's get out of here." Caratacus dug the sides of his heels into the horse's flanks and kicked the animal forward.

Caratacus found that the survivors of the advance companies had retreated on their own to the last bend in the road just beyond the range of the archers.

Boldly standing on the steep escarpment above, the Caledonians hooted and taunted the survivors below.

Sitting on his horse out of range of the enemy's arrows, Caratacus studied the band of ragtag outlaws on the cliff above. "They think we're trapped, but they're mistaken," Caratacus said.

"Are you daft? This is a choke point," Tog said as he and Clud sat by Caratacus's side. "We can't get through!"

"You're right," Caratacus said, "but the Caledonians should have kept going instead of attempting to stop us."

"Aye, the prince has something else cooking up there." Clud touched the side of his head.

"You're not thinking of climbing directly up the cliff? It's impossible," Tog said. "No, another way."

One of Venutios's men, a native uplander guide, approached Caratacus on foot. "Did you find it?" the prince inquired.

"Aye, Prince Caratacus," he said, looking up at the prince. "Long has it been since I used it, but it wasn't hard to find."

"There's a little used trail on the other side of the ridge circling the Caledonians' backside," Caratacus explained to Tog. "This man hunted here as a boy. I sent him out this morning to find another way through. I hate having one choice through any pass. Now, we'll bring the fight to them."

Caratacus sent runners to his captains with orders for his troops to keep drawing the enemy's attention. At any given moment, one of his clan chieftains and his followers would step out on the road, just beyond the range of Caledonian arrows, and taunt the enemy. And Caratacus's archers will engage them in duels from behind the protective cover of the huge rocks.

He sent runners to summon Venutios, who arrived moments later in his chariot. "I want you and Tog to take a small group of warriors and scout back the way we came," Caratacus said.

"Good as done," Venutios answered and rode away.

"Clud, you stay with me," Caratacus ordered.

The iron maker grinned. "Aye, someone has to keep you from getting another skull cracking."

CHAPTER 24

In the suffocating afternoon heat, Caratacus, Clud, and his warriors remained out of arrow range of the Caledonians, who harassed them from the overhanging cliff more than one hundred yards away. Occasionally, boulders thundered down the landslide that had previously fallen upon his men, gray, choking dust settling over the area.

"It won't be long now," Clud said as he sat sweltering on the back of his mount next to Caratacus, "until your brother, Tog, Venutios, and their men are in position to launch the surprise attack."

Caratacus, his head still aching from the stones that had struck him earlier, turned northward and surveyed the outcropping. He watched the bearded raiders, dressed in leather breeches and variegated kilts, yell challenges and shoot more arrows. He looked to the left toward the path, which Tog, Venutios, and the detachment had used to hike up into the mountains behind their attackers.

"If all goes as planned," Caratacus said, "our men will rush them from the rear and cut them to pieces."

A trumpet blare from above echoed down the canyon.

"That's it," Clud said, "the assault's underway."

Caratacus turned to the captains waiting behind him. "Get the men ready to move forward and clear the rocks once those bastards on the cliff have been wiped out."

A thunderous crack erupted. Caratacus looked toward the rocky outcrop again. Dozens of screaming Caledonians tumbled down the landslide, bouncing along the rocks like rag dolls, dead by the time their bodies smashed upon the debris-strewn road.

Seconds later, Tog and Venutios appeared above on the outcrop waving their hands in Caratacus's direction. They shouted something he couldn't understand.

Caratacus assumed they were saying they had slain the raiders and raised a hand in acknowledgement.

"By the un-named gods, they did it," Clud said. A wide grin spread across his face.

The prince raised an arm and waved his men forward. They raced along the road and quickly cleared the remaining obstructions.

A short time later, Venutios and Tog returned down the mountain trail, their clothing and faces splattered with blood, the odor a mixture of copper and salt. Their men followed close behind.

A crooked grin flashed across Tog's sunburnt face. "We slaughtered the lot."

"Aye, we caught them by complete surprise," Venutios added, thrusting his sword upward, stained with drying, brownish-red spots of blood.

"Excellent," Caratacus said. "Give me the details later. Right now, take your warriors and halt the enemy down there." He pointed to the demons from the north as their army spread themselves along the foot of the valley. "Cut them off."

The main Caledonian force, which had remained idle down in the Tees Valley to the northeast, had a clear view of the pass and the avalanche their men had sprung on Caratacus's army. But when they saw their kin were now being destroyed, they yelled bloody war chants and swarmed to engage Caratacus's forces as they reached the valley floor.

Tog and Venutios motioned their men to follow.

Caratacus shouted, "Follow me!" and waved his warriors forward with his blade.

Like a raging torrent, Caratacus's army flowed down into the valley. A great head-on clash ensued involving thousands as warriors hurling their javelins and slamming into the carnage before them. The sounds of metal upon metal swords, screams of the wounded and dying as limbs and heads were severed and smashed to the churning earth, echoed across the plain. Choking dust, the coppery, salty smell of blood, and vile odor of urine and feces drifted from the battlefield. Caratacus was in the middle of it all hacking, chopping, and stabbing with his massive, double-edged, steel sword. He ignored the stifling heat, while from his mount he deftly blocked and parried the enemies' blows with shield and sword, the impact of their bodies barely shoving him back. Awash in blood and gore, he sliced through the warriors like a hot knife through lard.

As Caratacus raced around the battlefield exhorting men to butcher the Caledonians, his huge frame appeared in the Caledonian's midst and reinforced Caratacus's warriors' enthusiasm to keep fighting.

Broken and defeated, in less than an hour the scattered Caledonians fled, leaving over one thousand bodies on the field, a fortune in booty, and hundreds of cattle and horses scattered throughout the countryside.

Signaling the trumpets to sound recall, Caratacus ordered his men to gather the spoils and animals and move them to an open area and wait for Rhian and the supply wagons, which he expected to arrive shortly.

Covered in more blood, Tog and Venutios reported back to Caratacus after regrouping their men, and together they rode toward the caravan.

"All right," Caratacus said, "backtrack and fill me in on the details of your attack on the cliff."

Before answering Caratacus, the two wiped blood from their faces. They looked at one another and grinned.

"It was like this," Venutios said. "Tog and me led the men as quietly as possible along the path through the woods. The climb was steep, and the place riddled with bristled gorse—damnable stuff—jagged rocks, and small boulders. Then the Brigantian guide, who was a short distance ahead of us, signaled a halt."

"Aye," Tog interjected, "we heard laughter and curses and an occasional bark of a crashing boulder—careless buggers they were."

Venutios took up the story. "Me and Tog crept to the guide's position, and through an opening in the bushes, we spied the Caledonians along the broad ledge." Venutios said that several of the raiders dug at the base of a gigantic boulder with daggers and makeshift shovels, while others worked it with a long, thin log. At the same time, many of the three hundred used slings and bows and arrows to harass Caratacus's army."

"We didn't expect so many," Tog said.

"That's when I whispered we'd carve them down to size," Venutios added. "We returned to our companies, and I gave instructions to the group leaders. Then, quietly, we spread along the forest's edge. I raised my hand, and the trumpet sounded the signal."

Caratacus smiled as he pictured the fight in his mind, wishing he could have been there with them.

Tog tapped the hilt of his sword. "We hurled ourselves upon those stinking bastards with a fury," Tog said, "like banshees from the underworld, wielding and hacking our swords, slicing through the lot."

"The rear Caledonians panicked," Venutios said. "We cut off our enemy's room to maneuver and pressed the attack. Our men shoved and crowded the Caledonian shit eaters to the cliff's edge. Out of about three hundred, only their first few ranks could fight us."

Venutios continued the narration explaining that although the Caledonians defended themselves with longswords and small rectangular shields with cutaway edges, they were no match against the ferocity of his and Tog's warriors, whose quick advance had negated the defending superior numbers.

"Within minutes, we'd cut the enemy to half their numbers," Venutios continued. "Dozens fell to their death over the cliff, as you probably saw."

Caratacus nodded. "Served them right."

"Venutios butchered many of the enemy with his great, iron sword," Tog said.

The young chieftain shrugged. "You did pretty good yourself, Tog." Turning to Caratacus, he grinned. "Your brother hacked nine or ten of the slimy bastards to death."

"What happened next?" Caratacus asked.

"It wasn't long before the survivors fled, screaming down the cliff pathway in a ragtag mob," Venutios answered. "You know the rest."

"I do," Caratacus said. He recalled the clash of warriors head-on, the war of metal on metal and leather followed: screams, yells, the thunder of hooves, blood and gristle, disembowelment and decapitation; the demons from the north were slaughtered without mercy. "Still, many got away. We will reorganize and strike them again." He twisted his body in Venutios's direction. "Then you and your men can hunt down the enemy remnants and avenge your fallen warriors."

"We will make them pay dearly," Venutios said.

* * *

Later that afternoon, Caratacus was about to lead a large contingent of horsemen and hunt down the last of the Caledonians, when he spotted a tired and blood-spattered Rhian and her cavalry detail approaching with the supply wagons. Instantly, Caratacus felt his heart shoot up into his throat. He realized that Rhian had led the caravan behind the army as they had advanced down to the valley to cut off the Caledonians. It was a terrible blunder on his part for not ordering her to stay behind until the battle was over. He had been so absorbed in pursuing the enemy, he had completely forgotten her. He realized they could have been destroyed. He had entrusted Rhian and the women to protect the wagon supplies. To his relief, they survived.

Rhian rode her mare triumphantly forward with five heads hanging from her saddle. "See what I bring you, my Husband!" Rhian exclaimed as she drew up before him and held up a bloody head by its stringy hair. She appeared eager to receive his acknowledgment that now, she too, was a real warrior.

"Well done, dear Wife," he said formally, smiling broadly, proudly. "Their spirits will become part of your totem, making you even stronger. You've earned the right to be called warrior."

Instead of tying the head by its hair to her mount, she tossed it to the churned-up ground.

Why did she do that? Caratacus puzzled. *I'll ask her later when we are alone.*

Rhian described their encounter with the raiders. "My riders and I left the baggage train behind. True to your orders, I led my horsewomen and harassed the enemy's flanks."

Good gods, no wonder why she rode on ahead, I failed to change the order.

Rhian said that the Caledonians fought like demons, but the women struck back slashing the enemy footmen to pieces with spears and longswords.

"I hate to admit it," Rhian whispered, "but I was horrified the first time I saw one of my riders die. When she was struck by spear to the chest, I ... I wanted to weep, to kill, to wreak revenge. Instead," she said in a louder voice, "I hardened myself and refused to dwell upon my fallen friend. I gored the Caledonian demon in the eye with my lance and sent him screaming to the trampled ground." Rhian thrust her hand forward as if holding a dagger. She added that she quickly bloodied herself as she chopped down those attacking her warrior maids. "I drew pleasure from seeing the surprised expressions on the enemies' faces as if they were saying, *How could a mere woman kill me?* Revenge was all the sweeter." She grinned.

"I had predicted that you and the warrior women would get share of heads by the end of the battle," Caratacus said. "Well done."

"Thank you, my lord," Rhian answered, bowing her head.

Caratacus's remarks seemed to please her, considering he could only address her in an official manner in front of his warriors.

For a split second, she held her breath and pointed towards him. "Your head and arms."

"Oh, those?" he said. "Minor injuries, nothing serious, they'll heal. However, I must ride out and finish the enemy once and for all."

"What about us?" she asked, motioning to her surviving seventy-plus horsewomen. "As your consort and captain, I have the right to fight along your side."

"As prince and leader of the army I decide who fights," Caratacus answered stiffly. "You will stay behind and guard the booty and wagons."

Rhian winced and grabbed her shoulder before dropping her hand to her side. "Why us?" She shook her head and wiped the sweat and blood from her face and mouth. Glancing down at her legs, she looked at three hairline slashes slanting across the left leg above the knee.

Through the caking dust, tiny rivulets of blood dribbled from each.

"Those we hunt will fight like the desperate savages they are," Caratacus answered.

She waved back towards her mounted detachment. "My women fought like wildcats, doesn't that warrant them another chance!"

"They fought bravely," he answered quietly. "But your losses were too high, almost thirty. If you join us, you'll lose more. King Cunobelinos and the Council will prohibit the women from fighting again. Is that what you want?"

"Of course not!"

"Then you will obey my orders," he said evenly.

"As you wish, my Lord Caratacus," she answered in a tight voice and turned her horse away, riding back to her troop.

As he watched Rhian leave, Caratacus shook his head. She hadn't realized how fortunate she and her riders were to have survived the skirmish. He may be marrying Dana when he returned to Eburacum, but he wasn't ready to lose Rhian. Not now, not ever! He turned about and gave orders to his men and set out to smash the remnants of the Caledonians.

* * *

That evening when Caratacus returned, he saw Rhian speaking to Morgana and her other leaders outside the headquarters tent—all of whom were covered in blood. He told Tog and Venutios to see to their men. Beyond his wife, he spotted the bodies of Caledonians lying about the wagons. Flies noisily swarmed about and feasted upon the macabre figures. Caratacus dismounted and approached his wife.

She thrust her chin forward and smiled in triumph. With a sword in one hand, she pointed to the corpses. "The Caledonians attacked the wagons, and we destroyed them to a man."

"They will sing songs of your feats for a thousand summers!" he exclaimed. He gave her a hug, blood and all.

"Tell me how it came about," Caratacus said.

Rhian shoved the weapon back into her scabbard as she and Caratacus stepped a few paces away from the women.

"It happened about an hour after you and your men left us," Rhian said. She explained she'd been on her mare, surveying the perimeter they were guarding, when Morgana, her squat-legged second in command, rode up beside her. "Morgana said one of the scouts reported seeing a small band of Caledonians sneaking through the forest. They had spotted the wagons and were about fifteen minutes away."

"What happened next?" Caratacus asked.

"I told Morgana I wanted them closer. When they saw that we were women, I wanted those demons to think it would be easy to slaughter us. Morgana said they would be disappointed."

"An understatement," Caratacus said.

Rhian nodded. "I drew my sword and ordered the women to the wagons." She nodded toward one of the bodies on the ground. "The Caledonians were so reckless. They came out of the woods right in front of the wagons like they owned them—the nerve. Their leader was an ugly cur. His scummy face was full of scars and had a head of dirty auburn hair. He stood in front of his ragged thieves, like it was going to be an easy fight, and screamed an order to attack."

She turned towards her leaders. "I gave the signal, and my women and I swarmed from behind the wagons. We caught them by surprise. We slaughtered the pigs." Rhian described how her women hacked and jabbed the marauders and wielded swords and spears with deadly skill. She hurled a javelin at the leader. The iron blade plunged deep into his chest and nailed him to the iron-red earth. "Like Banshees, we wiped out the whole band."

* * *

That evening as the sun set, glowing crimson and orange, in the valley where Caratacus and his warriors defeated the men from the north, he ordered the construction of a victory trophy for transport by wagon to Eburacum. His men slapped together two large, wooden crossbeams crowned with the silver eagle helmet of the Caledonian chief warlord. They decorated the arms of the cross with his shield and those of lesser chieftains. The chain mail and tunic of the leader clothed the upright part of the beam, while the base was stacked high with the swords and shields of his best warriors, symbols of triumph over the enemy.

The prince gathered his forces and stood before the torch-illuminated trophy. He held his hands skyward. "Behold your enemy. No more will he raid our lands; not in our lifetime. Your bravery and valor made this possible and will be rewarded. Because the people to whom this booty rightfully belongs were butchered and cannot be given back, you have right to its claim. When we return to Eburacum, all will share!" The trumpets sounded, and five thousand warriors raised a tumultuous cheer.

* * *

Late that evening, a cool Brigantian summer rain drifted in from the German Ocean to the north, sweeping away the month-long, simmering heat wave. As Rhian lay in Caratacus's arms in a corner of the brightly painted headquarters tent, she wept, no doubt Caratacus suspected, with memories of the day's lost friends.

"What's wrong, my Wife?" Caratacus asked softly.

"I'm ... I'm almost ashamed to say it, but I find no joy in taking heads or seeing you injured in battle."

So that's it. Now I know why she tossed the head away.

"You don't have to be ashamed," Caratacus said, "you fought as bravely as any man. But I'm puzzled about your trophy heads."

"At first, I was so proud and wanted your praise. Then I looked at my trophies and thought, *why do I need this!* It did nothing for me except bring back bloody memories."

"Of what?"

"I kept thinking of the night before we were married when the assassin nearly killed me. And I remembered how Clud sliced him through with your new sword and seeing the bloody corpse on the floor. Today's battle wasn't what I had expected. I saw hundreds of the same bloody stumps, some by my own hand."

"What did you expect?"

"That it'd be as simple as slaughtering pigs or cattle, and the glory and honor of conquest over our enemies would be rapture. This was not the glory promised by the bards or portrayed by old warriors," she said as she wiped tears from her cheeks. "Close friends of mine died today. The bards lied! The warriors lied! Men lie!"

Caratacus exhaled. "True enough. There is no glory in what happened today. Just bravery, death, and driving out invaders. Do the other women feel the same way?"

"I think so. Most of them won't admit it, but I saw it in their eyes and faces. Oh, at first they were very excited, showing off their heads to one another. Some of the women surprised me, like Morgana."

"What about her?" he interrupted.

She exhaled. "I expected great feats from her, but she vomited after lifting her first head. And timid little Brigit was a demonic badger. She refused to give ground or quarter when the bandits charged, thrusting herself suddenly in their midst and now, she's ..." Her voice drifted off.

"It's always so," he comforted.

She continued softly, "But soon they grew weary and tossed the heads aside. Some wet themselves or ran into the forest. I saw others vomiting behind bushes while more hid their tears. I don't know if it's because they realized it wasn't as glorious as they had expected or if they were grieving for their lost friends or both."

Again Rhian cried and Caratacus held her tightly and stroked her soft hair.

"Wars are so wasteful." She sniffled. "If there's a warrior's paradise, it's a place for men, not women!"

He considered her remarks. "From what you told me, most of the women fought like hellcats. The feelings of a first battle are to be expected, even of men. As for the bards, years from now when they sing a ballad of this day, you'll remember fondly those who fought bravely and fell, and yes, of the glory and honor the women warriors brought to our clan."

Rhian only sighed as they embraced beneath the furs.

Later, Caratacus awoke and found her lying fully awake. "Is yesterday's battle still bothering you?"

Rhian took a deep breath. "I had been resolved to be a great warrior and make you proud of me. But right now, my only consolation is in the comfort and safety of your warmth."

Caratacus reached over and brought Rhian closer to him.

"Perhaps that is the only truth of victory," she said, "returning to the arms of loved ones, something the accusing, dead eyes of my trophies never can."

Rhian snuggled next to his warm body. "I wish this night would last forever."

"I wouldn't mind, either, Rhian, but why now?"

"Because tomorrow we return to Eburacum, and you will marry Dana."

"That's what we agreed upon," Caratacus answered, feeling a little annoyed. "Are you having second thoughts?" *Are they going to get along? The last thing I need is a house with tension festering just below the surface.*

"No, actually not. I guess I'm concerned ... I'm more concerned about our return to Camulodunum. You must be ready to assume your father's throne—you said his health was failing. But will he honor his promise to you?"

"Why shouldn't he?"

She pulled away from Caratacus's embrace. Even in the darkness, Caratacus knew Rhian's emerald eyes were fixed upon his. "He might change his mind. The king's council of clan chieftains and Druids can easily manipulate Adminios. He could receive their votes over the objections of your father and be elected the new king. If that happens, then what? Will you fight your brother in a civil war?"

"Adminios thinks only about Adminios. He is no friend of our people, not even his own family. I will have no choice but to kill him."

CHAPTER 25

LATE SEPTEMBER, AD 39

Three days after Caratacus defeated the Caledonians, he and his warriors crossed the Ouse River, east of Eburacum at a shallow ford. Earlier he had sent a messenger ahead to inform King Dumnoveros of their impending arrival.

A scout, part of the advanced skirmishers, returned to Caratacus. "The fortress is over the rise, less than three miles away."

The prince nodded and ordered him to inform the clan chieftains and captains leading the companies behind him.

Riding her piebald mare, Rhian trotted along Caratacus's right side with Tog and Clud on his left. The soft clip-clopping of hooves echoed in his ears, and a light cloud of dust drifted up from beneath their mounts. The pungent smell of horse sweat swirled through his nose and gritty dust filled his mouth. It had been a long day's ride.

As sweat poured down his muscular shoulders and stained his tunic, Caratacus turned to Rhian, then Clud and his brother. "It may not be home, but it's good to be entering friendly lands."

"Aye, they should be," Tog said, "we sent the Caledonians like dogs running with tails between their legs." His gelding whinnied, and one from behind answered.

Clud wiped perspiration from his beefy face with a calloused hand and nodded. "Still, I'll be glad when we set eyes again on Camulodunum."

Rhian pulled down the bandana covering her nose and mouth and spat. "I've been eating dust all day—I will be so happy to clean up. It's been a long three days since I last washed."

Caratacus grinned. "You'll have your chance, Rhian, and so will your women—they've earned it."

Smiling, Rhian brushed dirt-caked, stringy hair from her sweaty face. Then she sobered. "It just occurred to me, you haven't mentioned Dana once since we left Eburacum."

Caratacus cricked his head and eyed her skeptically. "Why? My mind was on the campaign, no time to think about her until we returned to Eburacum. Does that bother you?"

She shrugged. "Not really, I guess."

"You chose her to be my consort," Caratacus reminded her.

Clud and Tog looked at one another, nodded, slowed their mounts, and allowed Caratacus and Rhian to ride ahead of them at a discreet distance.

For a split second, Rhian turned away from Caratacus. "I know, but now that we are almost there, I was wondering if you really wanted her as your wife?"

Caratacus rolled his eyes and frowned. *Why is she acting this way? This was her idea.* "I have no doubts about Dana," Caratacus finally answered. "You picked a good woman for me, but ..."

"But what?" Rhian's muscles on her sunburnt face tightened.

"Now that you mention it," Caratacus said in a strained voice, "when we arrive in Eburacum, I will make it a point to see Dana, alone."

"Is that necessary?"

"Dana told me in your presence she wanted to be my consort, but I plan to find out if she was telling the truth."

"She told you the truth," Rhian said in a huff. "But if you feel you must do this, go ahead."

Caratacus studied her for a moment. "You don't sound like you want her for my second wife after all."

"Yes, I do, you need sons, but ... but now that it's about to happen, I can't help but feel a little jealous."

He raised his head toward the hazy sky and loudly exhaled. Lowering it, he focused on Rhian and said, "Look, I can postpone this if you have any doubts."

Rhian vigorously gestured. "No, please don't. Dana would be humiliated, and the king would lose face among his people. We need his alliance."

"You're right, we do, but," Caratacus raised a hand and pointed in the direction of Eburacum, "I don't need a house in which the two of you will be at each other's throats like cats." He dropped the hand to his side. "Once we reach Camulodunum, I will have to deal with Da's failing health, and ..."

"What's this about your father's health?" Rhian asked. "You haven't said a word to me about it."

The prince hesitated. He twisted about and looked back toward Clud and Tog, who were still riding a short distance behind. Slowly, he turned and leaned toward Rhian. "I know," he said in a lowered voice, "he made me promise not to tell anyone, but you might as well know. If I can't trust you, then who else?"

Caratacus explained about his father's deteriorating mind. When finished, he added, "I can't help but wonder how much worse he has grown since I last saw him. Another question, has Ibor been able to hide his condition from the High Council?"

"I don't see how he can if it's that serious," Rhian finally said, hunching her shoulders.

"Aye. And this brings up another problem. My lazy, scheming brother Adminios."

She raised an eyebrow. "What about him?"

"I have no doubt he is attempting, with the Druid's assistance, to influence the Council into making him the next king."

"Then would Ibor bother shielding your father's condition from the Council?" Rhian questioned. "It seems to me he would make it a point to aid your brother."

"Ibor may be behind the whole scheme. That's what troubles me," Caratacus answered through tightened lips.

"Given those circumstances, I will do everything I can to see that Dana and I get on very well. I promise," Rhian said. "You need be free of any worries in our household so you can deal with your brother and the Druids."

Still leaning to one side of his mount, Caratacus kissed Rhian's perspiring cheek, the salt coming away on his lips. "Good, I'm glad to hear that. You are still my first and chief wife. I rely more on you than you realize." He straightened his body. "Now, let's ride on to Eburacum to be welcomed as the victors we are."

* * *

As the army approached Eburacum, Caratacus's mind still dwelled on the troubles he had discussed with Rhian. He forgot to mention how his father might react to the union with Dana, but he believed Cunobelinos would accept her based on Caratacus's need for an heir. That was about the only issue that seemed to be in his favor.

The warriors approached Eburacum in triumph. A large group of cheering people gathered outside the city gates to welcome them. King Dumnoveros stood on a dais surrounded by his councilors, Druids, Cartimandua, Dana, and retainers. They waited at the base of the road leading up to the fortress, who's stone wall loomed behind them.

Caratacus, Rhian, Venutios, Clud, and Tog dismounted and approached the dais and bowed slightly to the king.

Dumnoveros raised his hand in greeting. "Prince Caratacus, Prince Venutios, and your companions, I welcome you and the victorious army to Eburacum. You have crushed our enemies in a great victory. Songs of your valor will be sung for all time."

A cheer rang out from the gathering crowd.

"On behalf of our brave warriors," Caratacus said, "and my brave companions and leaders, I thank you, Great King."

The king stepped down from the dais, followed by his entourage, and approached Caratacus. "You, Prince Venutios, your wife, your brother, and your friend, Clud, will be my guests at the feast given in your honor." He turned in the direction of the rows of dozens of tables situated outside the city walls filled with food. "Follow me."

Dana went over to Rhian and hugged her, then turned to Caratacus and did the same. As they made their way to the table where they would dine with the king, she added her own personal welcome. "Dear Caratacus and Rhian, I'm so pleased you returned safely."

"So are we," they said in unison.

Just before being seated, Caratacus noticed Venutios approaching Cartimandua. A cold, blank expression crossed her rouged face as they embraced. Caratacus shook his head, pitying his younger friend.

Hundreds of tables filled with food and drink awaited them on the open field. Dozens of fire pits had been dug and spread about the area. A variety of meats were roasting on spits, the savory aroma drifting on the gentle breeze. Vendors had set up tents and stalls filled with items and souvenirs of all kinds to sell the warriors flushed with booty and the spoils of war. A noisy but happy crowd feasted and drank their fill.

After the banquet, Caratacus and his followers, including Rhian, Tog, Clud, and Venutios, who now escorted Cartimandua, along with Dumnoveros, Dana, the king's High Council, and Druids proceeded to the Great Hall. Inside, Tog, Clud, and Venutios took their places behind Caratacus. Rhian took her place by his right side and Dana to his left as they stood before the king. Dozens of other guests gathered behind them.

In the flickering torchlight of the sweltering hall, King Dumnoveros, now seated on his throne, formally announced, "My friends, earlier we gathered and feasted, celebrating a great victory over the Caledonians led by Prince Caratacus and our combined armies."

Loud murmurs of agreement erupted from the crowd filling the meeting room.

"Now, I am pleased to announce another happy event, one much closer to home." The king eyed Caratacus. "Prince Caratacus has asked for, and it is the wish of my daughter, Dana, to become his consort."

Another murmur resounded from the guests.

"Should a child result from their union, they will formally marry. I give them my blessing and may they have many children."

A loud, enthusiastic applause and cheering filled the hall.

Caratacus saw Cartimandua jolt but quickly turn stone faced. *No doubt she is shocked and angry that Dana will be my consort. Too bad. She's a fool to believe I'd want her for my woman.*

When the king had finished speaking, the group gathered around the great hearth. Caratacus, Rhian and Dana, Clud and Tog all huddled together.

"Congratulations, Dana," Rhian said. "I'm pleased you are part of our family."

Caratacus nodded his approval.

"Thank you, Rhian," Dana answered. "I look forward to being with you and Caratacus." For the space of several heartbeats, she turned and gazed admiringly into Caratacus's eyes.

Cartimandua and Venutios broke away from another cluster of people and moved forward.

"Congratulations to both of you," Venutios said to Caratacus and Dana. He nodded to Rhian. "I wish you the best for the future."

A tight smile surfaced on Cartimandua's lips. She embraced Dana. "Congratulations, dear Sister," she said in an icy voice. "May you have many children. It is what you want, isn't it?"

"Yes, it is," Dana answered, pulling away from Cartimandua. "Although by your cold voice, I doubt if you really want me to have children."

Venutios locked eyes on Cartimandua, his nostrils flared.

Caratacus raised a hand. "No, Venutios, don't. I'm certain Cartimandua's compliments are sincere, aren't they?" he said glancing in her direction.

A crooked smile crossed her mouth. "Of course, my Lord Prince. I look forward to the day when I learn that Dana has given birth to a healthy son—or has died."

Rhian gasped.

Dana smiled at Caratacus and then turned to Cartimandua." I'm sorry to disappoint you, dear Sister, but I plan to live." She sniffed.

"May the gods be so kind. That, too, is my wish," Cartimandua said in a facetious voice.

"Enough, woman," Venutios warned his wife. "At least she wants children, something you loathe."

"Being tied down to suckling brats and changing dirty, swaddling clothes is not my idea of living," Cartimandua answered. She glared defiantly at her husband. "I'm not the mothering type, everyone knows that. That is not my role in life."

"What is?" Caratacus asked. The muscles tightened in his shoulders. *Cartimandua has no business treating Dana or Venutios like dirt. If the king weren't here, I'd tell the bitch what I really think of her.*

Cartimandua smiled. "One day you and the rest of those here will learn."

"If you mean ruling the kingdom, that is for me to decide," King Dumnoveros said in a voice of warning. He stepped towards Cartimandua from a group of councilors and Druids. "If I hadn't been talking to my arch-Druid, I would have ordered you to keep a civil tongue in your head! Your ambitions are dangerous, and you insult not only our guests but your own sister."

Stunned, Cartimandua's lips opened slightly. "Father, I only meant ..."

"I know exactly what you meant. This is not the place to discuss it. Dana is being united with a great man, one who saved our kingdom from destruction. We owe Prince Caratacus everything including Dana's happiness and the chance for him to sire an heir. That will benefit both our kingdoms."

Cartimandua's face turned crimson. She narrowed her eyes and glared at the king. "You mean to make Caratacus the next king of the Brigantes!" She turned on the heels of her shoes and fled the Great Hall.

Venutios huffed and clenched his fists. He shook his head, excused himself, and followed her.

Caratacus turned to King Dumnoveros. "It has never been, and never will be my intent to become king of your people, Great King, you know that."

The king gestured as if waving away the remark. "Aye, I do. Cartimandua is an ambitious, young woman who will say and do anything to get her way."

At that point, Caratacus nodded to Rhian and then to King Dumnoveros. "With your permission, Great King, I need to speak to Dana in private."

"Permission granted," the king answered with another wave of his hand. "After all, tomorrow before you leave, I will give the both of you my official blessing."

Dana furrowed her eyebrows then relaxed. "I know a place." She turned to Rhian. "Will you please excuse us?"

Rhian raised her eyebrows, looked to Caratacus and then Dana. "Of course, soon you will be my sister-wife."

Yes, she will, Rhian, get used to the idea, Caratacus thought. *Learn to get along with Dana, I need her.*

"This way," Dana said.

It was the same dimly lit hallway where Caratacus had first observed the confrontation between Cartimandua and Dana when he had originally arrived in Eburacum.

Before Caratacus could say a word, as they stood facing one another, Dana spoke. "I could not say it in public, Caratacus, but I prayed the gods would bring you back alive and well."

Caratacus grinned. "The gods were kind to me and my warriors."

"I'm so happy you wanted to be with me," Dana said. "Even though I told you in front of Rhian that I am willing to be your consort, I want you to know I truly meant it."

"I'm pleased to hear that, because that's the main reason I wanted to see you alone. I didn't want you to go through with this just for the sake of pleasing me or your father."

"Oh no, it's what I wish. Honestly, I ..." She hesitated and blushed. "I have loved you since I was a little girl. Even when I had heard you had married Rhian, that feeling never vanished. I do hope you don't think me a silly woman for thinking such a thing." Her pleading, hazel eyes looked upon his. Slowly, she raised her hand, long fingers touching his jawline.

Caratacus reached out and took Dana's soft hand into his. He brought the fingers to his lips and lightly kissed them. She shuddered, a low gasp escaped her lips. In that moment, his entire body relaxed, the tension in his muscles draining away. He hadn't known what to expect.

Caratacus moved her hand a few inches away from his and said, "No, you're not a silly woman. Now that I'm with you, I'm happy you feel that way."

"So am I," Dana answered. She placed her other hand on Caratacus's shoulder.

"I hope you and Rhian will become good friends," Caratacus said. "I'll see that she treats you well."

"I'm sure she will. I respect the fact that Rhian is still your first wife. It won't have any affect as to how I feel about you."

Caratacus moved closer, and with a couple of fingers he slowly lifted her delicate chin. He slid them along her jawline and curved them across her lower lip. He pulled them away and bent his head and softly kissed her soft, smooth lips, lingering for a moment.

She sighed as he pulled slightly away. He hugged Dana, her face brushing against his.

"I will cherish you as much as I do Rhian."

"Promise?"

"I promise." *I pray she will believe me, I mean it.*

Dana smiled, looked toward the entry to the Great Hall, and sighed. "We better return to the rest of the group."

"Yes, I suppose we must. They'll be wondering what happened to us."

"By tomorrow it will no longer be any of their business." *I wonder if Rhian will feel the same way.*

CHAPTER 26

Earlier that day, word was received that Caratacus's army would arrive in Camulodunum in the evening. King Canubelinos immediately ordered preparations for a welcoming feast for the prince and his warriors.

Still seeking answers about the succession to the throne, Porcius hoped to learn more from King Cunobelinos before Caratacus's homecoming. Now, in the king's private chambers as Ibor stood to his right side, Porcius voiced his concerns. "Great King, you must realize that Adminios is lazy, scheming, and too irresponsible to rule alone. He is easily manipulated. Caratacus won't stand by idily—he'll drive his older brother from the throne. If the reports are true that Caratacus will arrive this evening, shouldn't the issue of succession be settled?"

Bright-eyed and alert, the king seemed more lucid than at Porcius's last audience with him. Cunobelinos focused on Porcius and seemed to listen intently to what the Roman was saying.

The king glanced to Ibor before answering, "How dare you tell me what I should do, Roman? You are stretching our friendship too far."

Porcius cleared his throat. "I mean no disrespect, Great King, I cherish and honor your friendship above all others. It has always been my intention to act in your best interest."

"And that of Rome," the old man growled.

"Of course, but yours, too."

"Nevertheless, Caratacus is too anti-Roman. This is why Adminios should rule under the control of the Council. They will do as I command. As for Caratacus, he is my son, and as long as I rule, he will obey me," Canubelinos said. "As strong as he may be, he will not go against his father."

Porcius's lips tightened into a thin line. *Surely he can't believe that.* "But that doesn't answer the question about Adminios."

"My Druids and clan chieftains will guide his rule."

Porcius nodded to Ibor. *It is obvious this fool king in his vulnerable state is being manipulated by Ibor. How can I convince him that his own Druids will betray him? Ibor being the first. They'll chose Caratacus. He hates the Romans as much as they do. Still I need Adminios on the throne, not Caratacus.*

"You are aware, of course," Porcius said, "that Caratacus's victory over the Caledonians has strengthened his reputation as a leader and his claim to the throne? He may use that situation to unite the anti-Roman factions under him. Is that what you want?"

The old king snorted. "Your concerns are exaggerated. My spies and Druids tell me the opposition is weak and will be easily smashed. And I repeat, Caratacus will not disobey my commands."

Porcius scanned the smoky, torch-lit hall and frowned. *Your Druids lie. Ibor lies. I know he took my gold.* The Roman kept the information to himself and shook his head. He knew the time would come when Caratacus consolidated his power among the clans, a threat to Roman influence in Britannia. As this and other thoughts rolled over in his mind, Porcius turned back the king. But if he told this to Cunobelinos, he wouldn't believe him. But he was determined to do what he could to prevent the inevitable. He must find a way to make Adminios the next ruler of the kingdom. If not, Porcius had no doubt that Caratacus would drive Adminios out of Britannia, and in so doing, the tribes of Britannia would be at the mercy of Rome.

The king's eyes narrowed and a twitch of his lips could have been that of a fox. With a wave of a hand, he dismissed Porcius.

* * *

A severe storm swept in from the British Channel at midday, catching Caratacus's army a half-day's journey from Camulodunum. In the cloak of an early winter's death, long rolls of thunder rumbled across black clouds shadowing the fertile Colne River Valley. A vicious rain surprised the warriors, who quickly donned seldom-used tartan cloaks. Exposed chain mail suddenly doubled in weight and many men, exhausted from trudging through the clay quagmire, threw their woven armor into the supply wagons rather than bear the burden. A pelting, icy wind needled them with sharp bits of dirt, bark, and rock.

Caratacus braced himself against the onslaught, determined to reach the Great Fortress by nightfall. He urged, cajoled, and ruthlessly drove his shivering, soaking warriors forward. Gusting winds swept both his curses and praise among their ranks. His own body screamed for rest as it failed him in bursts of uncontrolled shaking and chattering teeth. He willed himself to obey his commands and demanded as much from his men. The tall prince squinted into the gray, waning light until he sighted the pale, somber silhouette of Camulodunum's huge outer dike. Home! At last.

A contingent of Druid acolytes on horseback met him inside the main gate. "Greetings, Prince Caratacus," the chief acolyte said. "Arch-Druid Ibor sent us to escort you directly to the Great Hall."

"My warriors and I are drenched and tired. Can't it wait?"

"Your father commands it. A massive feast is being served in your honor, and he waits impatiently."

Caratacus turned to Dana and Rhian, who had halted their mounts next to his. The women's faces and clothing, including the cloaks draping their bodies, were soaked, muddy, and smelled of horse.

"Dana, Rhian," Caratacus said, "you heard the acolyte. I will go with him to the hall."

"What about us?" Rhian asked through chattering teeth. "Dana and I are filthy, we can't be seen like this. What would your father think of Dana?"

"Rhian's right, Caratacus," Dana said. "We must look our best."

"I said *I* was going to the hall," Caratacus answered. "You two go on home, clean up, and join me later."

"Thank you, dear Caratacus," a grateful Dana said.

Rhian added her thanks and the women departed.

Caratacus motioned forward Tog, Clud, and his six clan chieftains, who reigned up on both sides of him. "Lead on," he said to the chief acolyte.

They moved through the downpour.

Tog held his hood tighter as he rode next to his brother. "At least we'll get out of this shitty rain and warm up."

"Aye, it's cold enough to freeze a banshee's arse," Clud said, riding along Caratacus's other side.

Futilely, Tog attempted to wipe away the rain dripping down the front of his hood onto his face. "I'm looking forward to seeing my wife, but I need a hot meal, my stomach's growling."

"And plenty to drink," Clud roared. "I'm cold and wet. Maybe I can get one of them serving wench's to warm me up later on."

Caratacus chuckled. "Both of you will get what you want and more."

Caratacus looked forward to the warmth of the hearth in the Meeting Place and wasn't disappointed. Once inside the Great Hall, the sight and smell of a large boar roasting on a spit made his mouth water. Indeed, eating a big slice of ham would be a savory consolation for not being allowed to clean up first. Nobles and warriors alike hailed the prince as he made his way through the throng of admirers. Many reached out and shook his hands or slapped his back.

In the smoky torchlight, Caratacus saw Porcius standing along with minor chieftains before the king. The Roman's return to Britannia caught him by surprise. For the space of a couple of heartbeats, he halted and stared at the Roman. *Why had he returned to Britannia now?*

Now in his late forties, Porcius looked the part of a Roman emissary wearing a white, linen toga, his left arm bare. Tufts of gray hair surrounded Porcius's nearly bald head, but his face remained almost free of wrinkles, his pig eyes still alert. Porcius had been in his father's favor many years.

As he approached his father, who sat on his Romanized throne, Caratacus sensed something amiss. Then he knew. Dressed in a long, bright, purple and gold tunic, his older brother, Adminios, sat beside King Cunobelinos. Warm furs draped him from the lap to his feet. Upon seeing his younger brother, Adminios's hand twitched, but his cruel eyes stared defiantly. His mouth twisted into a sneering frown. The light from the hearth's fire and pulsating torch lights lining the walls gave Adminios's face a menacing appearance.

When Caratacus halted before his father and saluted, he noticed the tightened skin around the king's face, a deathly pallor. How he had aged in less than four months! Ibor, a spider of a man, stood slightly to the rear of the king.

"Welcome home, Prince Caratacus," Cunobelinos said. "The news of your great victory proceeds you. Through your bravery and leadership, your army destroyed the barbaric Caledonians."

Applause erupted from the guests in attendance.

"It will be many years," the king continued, "before they dare attack our cousin and ally, King Dumnoveros, again. You and your warriors are to be commended for a job well done. Songs of your victory will be sung for all time."

Another round of applause accompanied by cheers resounded through the meeting room.

Caratacus's chest swelled with pride. He glanced to Clud and Tog, who grinned and nodded.

"Not only you, Prince Caratacus," the king said, "but Prince Tog, your friend and advisor, Clud the iron maker, and your loyal clan chieftains will receive gifts for valor and leadership."

Cunobelinos nodded to three slaves hovering nearby. "Bring forward the gifts for the noble clan chieftains." The servants stepped forward and presented each of the six men with golden armbands, a symbol of heroism. The chieftains accepted the tokens and saluted the king.

Clud was presented with a solid, gold torc, a gift normally reserved for nobility. Clud saluted the king. "You do me great honor, High King."

Caratacus grinned and turned to Clud. He whispered, "You deserve it, friend."

Clud shrugged.

Tog received a longsword made of the finest steel, with a handle carved from rare, imported ivory. He pulled it from a scabbard, quickly inspected, and shoved it back. For a few seconds, he remained speechless before he saluted and thanked his father.

Clud gave a sly grin and winked at Caratacus.

Tog apparently caught the look and whispered, "You knew? Did Da put you up to this?"

"Well, ah, he did," Clud replied. "He commissioned me to make it. Hard to keep the damn thing secret."

"You knew, too, didn't you, Brother?"

"I did," Caratacus whispered.

"And now for Prince Caratacus," Cunobelinos said. "Bring it forward."

A husky slave stepped before Caratacus with a large, linen-covered packet, followed by another slave with a small bench. The package was placed on the table. The servants bowed and padded away.

Caratacus bent and opened the bundle. Stunned, nearly losing his breath, he pulled out an expensive, highly polished, iron-ring mail shirt—fit for a king. He lifted up the heavy, protective armored shirt, turned, and showed it to the audience, who cheered again.

Caratacus turned back and saluted his father. "I am honored that you have presented me with such a valuable gift, Great King. May I prove worthy of it."

Cunobelinos nodded and then looked toward Adminios. "Before the feasting begins," he announced, "we will make one more proclamation of great importance to the entire kingdom." He turned to his eldest son. "Adminios stand before us!"

Adminios looked around and smirked. His head stopped as he viewed a heavily made-up woman, dressed in a scarlet and silver, tartan gown. Known to be a notorious prostitute, she brazenly smiled at Adminios. He slowly stood, but not before Caratacus caught the brief nod of approval from Ibor to Adminios. Not just something wrong here ... danger. Caratacus's older brother, shoulders back, stepped before his father.

"Kneel!" Cunobelinos commanded. Two Druids stepped forward with a bronze ceremonial shield crisscrossed with oak leaves engraved in gold and a long, iron sword. The king presented them to Adminios and proclaimed, "I anoint thee king of our tribal brothers, the Cantiaci."

A stunned silence ringed the Great Hall. Then a polite applause rippled, led by Ibor and the Druids.

Caratacus's body tightened. *Fucking betrayal! I'm the one who crushed the Cantiacians. I should be their king.* He gnashed his teeth and clenched the hilt of his sword. His cold skin flushed in rage as his eyes seared those who dared meet them. *Will Adminios's sluggish mind understand the significance of this title?*

Caratacus understood. Becoming ruler of the Cantiaci, a small kingdom on the southeast coast of Britannia, was one step away from becoming king of all the Catuvellaunian and Trinovantian territories. *Unfortunately, Ibor will make sure Adminios understands the meaning of his new title.*

Caratacus turned, glaring at Porcius, who lingered about five paces away. "This is your doing, Roman," he snarled. "Only you could persuade my father to choose Adminios over me." Low gasps rippled through the Great Hall.

Adminios's eyes flashed in defiance, thin lips twisting into a frown. "The noble Porcius is a friend of our father and our people. He knows who should be the rightful king."

Caratacus looked about and snorted. "Rightful king? What rightful king? I see only our father."

"You know what I mean, Brother," Adminios answered.

"Damn right I do. Porcius is a Roman lackey," Caratacus said as he jabbed a finger in Adminios's direction. "He works for Rome and his own interests, not ours."

Porcius shrugged and answered dryly, "I admit your father sought my advice, Prince Caratacus, but the decision was his alone."

"In a boar's eye." Caratacus raised a fist in the Roman's direction. "You're like an eagle circling over a victim, waiting from the right time to kill it. You preyed on his weakening mind, filling him with lies." Murmurs rose from the court guests behind him.

The Roman sighed. "My dear, young Prince," he said in a voice full of sorrow, "were that the case, I would have persuaded him to invite the Roman Army to Britannia to protect his interests. But I didn't, nor will I."

The prince tightened the grip on his sword hilt. "You won't live another day if you do."

There came shouts of agreement.

"Silence!" the king bellowed. He glared across the room before nodding to Porcius.

"The king's decision is his *alone*." Porcius bowed his head.

"What he says is true, Prince Caratacus ... Son," Cunobelinos said. "The noble Porcius had no part in our decision." Caratacus caught Ibor's slightly negative shake of the head. A warning unnoticed by Porcius.

"But why, Noble King?" Caratacus asked in an incredulous voice. "Why?"

"For the sake of the kingdom."

His eyes full of contempt and loathing, Caratacus stared at Porcius and then Adminios. "You mean for the sake of Rome!"

"This is neither the time nor the place to discuss it," his father said firmly.

"There will never be a time so long as we lick the slimy paws of the Roman she-wolf." Caratacus turned and stormed out of the hall.

* * *

Outside, the rain had stopped, and the wind scattered bruised clouds. A half-moon and countless stars lit up the crisp heavens. Caratacus left the Great Hall but wasn't ready to go home. He walked aimlessly through the village. A short distance ahead, two dogs wrestled and snarled playfully in the muddy pathway. But their actions so irritated Caratacus that he picked up several stones and pelted the animals. "Get out of here you mangy curs!" he shouted as he found his mark. The startled dogs yelped, turned, and ran into the darkness.

Caratacus peered down the blackened pathway. *Why did I do that? Get a grip on yourself.* After several deep breaths, he slogged through the muddy way between Camulodunum's wretched wattle-and-daub huts, oblivious

237

to the smells of barley soup, roast pork, and fish stew wafting from the cooking fires from within and the sounds of laughter of his warriors now home with their families. A horse whinnied from a nearby pen.

He pulled his cloak tightly around his shoulders and peered upward. A series of shooting stars streaked northward across the black, curving sky from the direction of Gaul. *Omens? Ha! I don't place value on streaks of light. The gods are just playing games.*

"You better take care, my friend."

Caratacus was so lost in his thoughts he didn't hear the intruder approaching from behind. Startled, he whirled and drew his dagger, relieved to see only Clud.

"I could have stuck you quicker than a frog flicking a fly," Clud said, grinning. He hurried to Caratacus's side as he continued moving along the path.

"Quieter, too. I wasn't alert. I didn't realize how angry I am."

Clud turned his head to Caratacus. "You should be. Adminios hasn't the wits to be king of anything. Your father's councilors got their brains in their arses to go along with his decision."

"I know, but I shouldn't have left the Great Hall. It was an act of a witless youth."

"Yes … it was. But more important now, what are you going to do about it?"

"I won't do anything rash."

"That's wise, but you must act before your shit-brained brother does."

"I will, but I have to make alliances first. I spoke to Tog about it yesterday. He feels the same way. There are others inside and outside the tribe who are willing to support me." He further explained his plans to Clud.

"You're taking a great risk," Clud said when Caratacus finished.

Caratacus halted and faced Clud. "It's either that or wilting in my scheming brother's shadow while the Romans grab a foothold in our lands. I won't tolerate it. But I'll take my time and nurture my contacts."

Although Caratacus hated the Romans, he had more respect for their army than any other Britons. He knew the awesome powers they wielded through might of arms. If the mad Emperor Caligula committed his legions to invasion, it would be like trying to hold against the forces of a hurricane. He had to unify the south and form alliances with other anti-Roman tribes.

An acolyte approached the two. "Arch-Druid Ibor requested your presence at his home at once."

Caratacus and Clud met with the old priest in a small, sparse room used for private meetings. Ibor approached as they stood near the smoldering, little hearth. He stopped and lifted his hand in peace and dropped it wearily to his side. For a few seconds his eyes studied the hard-packed floor in front of Caratacus's riding shoes. Grimly, he brought his gaze back to the prince's face.

"I bring you sad news, Prince Caratacus. Your uncle, King Epaticcos, is dead."

Stunned, Caratacus's heart jumped into his throat. His mouth went dry, and he licked his lips. He stood motionless for a moment. *My uncle? How can that be?* He glanced at Clud, seeing his look of disbelief and turned to Ibor. "When did he die?" he asked as calmly as his voice would allow.

"Nearly a month ago."

Caratacus stiffened. "Why wasn't I sent word?"

"King Cunobelinos prohibited the sending of any messages. He wanted nothing to interfere with the war or the strengthening of the alliance with King Dumnoveros."

"Damn him! If the rumors I heard are true, he always wanted Uncle Epaticcos dead!"

Ibor's dark eyes narrowed. "Your father denies having any part of it. Epaticcos caused his own demise. But your father would have played a sinister role had not fate interfered. Your uncle's womanizing in the Sacred Grove destroyed him before your father could."

"In the name of the holy gods, he had no business going into the Sacred Grove. Why?"

Ibor explained that Epaticcos and his entourage had journeyed to the Holy Shrine by the River Itchen to negotiate a peace settlement with Verica.

He continued, "Late on the second night, while everyone was sleeping, your uncle sneaked out of his quarters and found his way to the grove. He met with a young female novice. They were discovered in a compromising position by King Verica and his chief Druid. He was arrested, and the novice was executed on the spot."

"How did he die?" Caratacus asked, his voice dropping to little more than a whisper.

"He was found dead the next morning in his quarters. He took his own life rather than face the Druid's tribunal."

Caratacus turned his head, not wanting them to see tears. "My uncle was always more of a father to me than the king," he said after regaining his composure. "Damn Verica to the underworld for this!" He added in a bitter tone, "He always hated my uncle."

"Don't be too harsh with either one," Ibor cautioned. "Your uncle committed a grave sacrilege and sealed his own fate."

The prince concluded the death of Epaticcos had been planned months ago. Yet, it seemed too coincidental that Verica would discover his uncle and the young woman so easily. No doubt Verica had planned to expose and bring Epaticcos's downfall by exploiting his weakness for women.

But without proof, Caratacus could not say a word. Ibor was right. In his heart, he knew Epaticcos acted incorrectly, and he himself was a coward for not admitting likewise. If he were to be king, he was determined never to allow outside influences to cloud his emotions or his judgment.

He must form new alliances. Now!

CHAPTER 27

Five days later, Porcius and his retinue arrived late in the afternoon at the busy port of Noviomagnus, Verica's capital, from where he ruled the Regni people. The half-day voyage down the southern coast from Camulodunum by a small merchant ship had been cold and wet but otherwise uneventful. *For once I didn't suffer from seasickness,* Porcius thought when he stepped off the wooden gangplank onto the dock. His legs still swaying from the voyage, it took a few minutes to steady himself and adjust to being on land again.

Porcius and his entourage journeyed by foot up the low-lying hill to the king's fortress overlooking the harbor and protected by three defensive dikes of packed earth and rock. Once inside the stockade, the king's steward welcomed Porcius's group. He led them to their quarters, a small, circular, wicker-framed house covered by a thatched, domed roof. A small, smoky center hearth, its sunken basement made of clay, contained a fire that barely illuminated the home. Goatskin hides partitioned the place into several small rooms.

Having time to refresh himself in the largest of the rooms, Porcius rinsed his face and hands in a bowl of tepid water and changed into a clean tunic and breeches, assisted by Cyrus. "Thank the gods for the change of clothes," he said. "I can't believe that only a half-day aboard ship would stink up my clothing so much."

"The same here, sir," Cyrus said. "Mine smell of harbor sewage, dead fish, and bilge water." In the flickering light furnished by several tapers, the Persian's gaunt face appeared like a mythical specter from the underworld.

"See that you change, too."

"I will, sir."

"And when you are finished, I want you to do something for me."

Through his well-trimmed beard, a sly grin formed on the Persian's hair-lipped mouth. "I think I have an idea of what you want."

"Indeed?" Porcius chuckled. "If you recall, the steward said I will be seeing King Verica alone, and he ordered you and the rest of the retinue to remain behind."

The Persian nodded.

"However, he didn't prohibit any of you from wandering about the compound."

"And I am to assume that's what you want me to do?"

"Exactly," Porcius answered in a low voice. Ever cautious, the Roman looked towards the partitioned entry, cocked his head, and listened. Nothing. He turned to Cyrus. "Stroll about and stop and chat with the people, innocent like of course, especially with the guards. See if you can pick up any useful information."

"Anything in particular?"

"Everything. However, keep an ear out for any rumors of war."

"Do you suspect King Verica will launch a war upon Caratacus or King Cunobelinos?"

A good question. "Perhaps. I don't want to be caught by surprise like I was before the battle at Bagshot Heath."

* * *

Hiking across the small courtyard, Porcius took the wooden bridge over the shallow moat and arrived at the Great Hall. A heavily woven, thatched roof covered the elongated building constructed from waddle and daub.

The Roman was greeted again by the king's steward. He led Porcius toward the great hearth where Verica and his chief Druid were seated. As Porcius followed the servant, his eyes adjusted to the gloomy light. He noticed five retainers, discreetly out of hearing, standing in the shadows among the ornate pillars along the wall lined with battle shields. The Roman halted before the ruler and priest. At that point, the king's servant disappeared beyond the light of the fireplace. The glowing flames from the fire pit radiated warmth and illuminated the faces of the king and priest. Pine scented smoke drifted lazily upward, percolating and then disappearing among the packed rushes in the ceiling. Next to the chairs of Verica and the Druid and an empty one, stood small tables containing silver bowls of corma beer, Verica's favorite drink, along with large, earthen pitchers.

After the usual salutations, the king motioned to Porcius to sit in a chair by his left side.

Tall and broad-chested, the ruler wore a *brat,* an open, woolen cloak edged with a fringe of gold, and clothed in a similar tunic and blue and white striped breeches like those worn by Porcius. A thick, gold torc circled Verica's muscular neck, silver armlets surrounded his powerful arms, and a bejeweled sword hung from a baldric on his left side. His face was scarred from countless battles, a long, drooping moustache covered his thin mouth, and his breath smelled of stale beer. Black, greasy hair, now receding half way across the top of his head, draped his shoulders.

Ignoring the corma on the table by his side, Porcius got down to business. He turned and leaned toward Verica. "Great King, if you haven't heard already, King Canubelinos has chosen Adminios over Caratacus to rule the Cantiaci. Do you know what that means?"

Verica gave his Druid advisor a sidelong glance as if both knew something. The priest bowed his head.

"Aye, he will rule once Cunobelinos is dead," Verica said in a deep voice. The king grabbed his drinking bowl and swilled beer. He pulled off his cloak, which landed on the hard-packed, dirt floor, and wiped his mouth on his tunic sleeve." The big Celt faced Porcius. "I know I can persuade that fool Adminios to ally with me. And when the time is right, I will kill him and take his kingdoms for myself."

Porcius's chest tightened as did the muscles in his shoulders. *I was afraid it would come to this. I should never have wasted my time traveling here. The Council and I should manipulate Adminios, not this dog.* "Caratacus will resist," the Roman warned. "He will go to war. The prince knows Adminios can be manipulated by the Druids and you."

A sneer crossed Verica's mouth. "And by you."

"Yes, I can, but in this matter I played no part; it was the decision of King Cunobelinos and his Druids." Porcius glanced toward Verica's priest.

"No matter, Roman." Verica gestured with an uplifted hand before dropping it to his side. "Bring Caratacus on—he will lose. I welcome the chance to kill the bastard and revenge my son's death."

"Why did you order Gwynedd to kidnap me at Bagshot Heath?" Although Porcius had asked him on an earlier occasion, he brought up the same question again, knowing Verica would probably lie.

Verica furrowed his eyebrows together into a thick, black line. "I told you before," his voice nearly a growl, "I did not give him the order. One of his surviving friends told me Gwynedd got the stupid notion that it would please me. He hated Rome as much as Caratacus."

Porcius pressed his lips together. *Liar!* "Except, Caratacus knew that killing me might have been the excuse Rome needed to invade your lands and those of his father, something neither of them wanted."

The king jabbed a hand in Porcius's direction. "Gwynedd knew that—I told him. Had he survived and brought you to me, I would have released you and punished him."

I seriously doubt that.

"It doesn't matter," Verica said, interrupting Porcius's thoughts, "my son paid for his stupidity. Caratacus killed him, and that is all that matters to me. I want him to fight me like a man." For a split second, he raised the hand pointing toward the Roman and turned it into a balled fist. Then he dropped it to his thigh.

By the gods, he's mad. Porcius reached down to the table along his side, picked up the bowl, and sipped the bitter-tasting corma. He winced before he set the cup down. He licked his lips and took a deep breath. "Caratacus has built a solid reputation for himself among many tribes as a fearless warrior and leader. He believes many tribal leaders will come to his aid should he put out the call to arms."

"You're exaggerating—he isn't that strong."

Porcius vigorously nodded his head as if he were a nervous horse. "Oh, but he is, especially after his victory over the Caledonians. And while he was in Eburacum, Caratacus took King Dumnoveros's daughter, Dana, as consort with marriage in the future."

"Hmm, I wasn't aware of that." Verica gulped down the remaining contents from his bowl and belched loudly.

"No doubt King Dumnoveros would send aid if Caratacus requested it," Porcius said. "If rumors are true, so would the Iceni."

Verica eyed his Druid once more. The priest nodded.

The king crinkled his flat, broken nose. "The Iceni can be easily bought—they won't lift a spear to aid him." He paused and for a few seconds closed his eyes before reopening them. "In the meantime, I will meet with Adminios and his Druids."

Porcius's chest tightened as if his heart had leaped into his throat. Outwardly, he managed to keep a straight face. "Is that wise? I think you are moving too quickly."

Verica's watery eyes studied Porcius as if he were staring through a rock. "You said Caratacus took this woman as his consort. He expects to grab the kingdom of the Brigantes as well as the tribes here in the south. My lands would be surrounded. He means to destroy me and rule all of Britannia. By Teutates, I'll crush him first. When I control Adminios, Caratacus will be left vulnerable. His reputation with the other kings will mean nothing. I will command the southern kingdoms."

"Making it easier to assassinate him," Porcius said.

Verica gestured toward his chest. "Me, assassinate him, Roman?" He shook his head. "It's manlier to kill him in battle. But," he hesitated, "Caratacus has his share of enemies. Given the chance, they would oblige me in taking his head."

"Naturally," Porcius agreed. "A little gold, I'm sure would be incentive enough."

A black-toothed grin crossed Verica's thin, scarred mouth. A deep, guttural laugh escaped his throat. "This will be far easier then when I reconquered the Atrebates, which rightfully belonged to me."

"So I heard," Porcius said. He had received news that Caratacus's uncle, Epaticcos, had committed suicide after being caught with a female Druid novice in the Sacred Grove. Within weeks of the death, Verica sent an army against the leaderless Atrebates in a surprise attack and overwhelmed them.

Donn, father of Rhian and Epaticcos's former champion, had been forced to flee, along with Havgan the Druid, to Canubelinos's court where both were given asylum.

Damn that stupid barbarian! If Verica moves now, Rome's interests in Britannia will be totally disrupted. It might be enough for that mad Emperor Caligula to launch an invasion. Britannia can't afford that and neither can I. If the Roman Army lands on British soil, I would be arrested and sent to Rome for execution by the emperor.

Beneath the table, Porcius balled a hand into a fist.

CHAPTER 28

LATE FEBRUARY, AD 39

Side by side, on a damp, chilly afternoon, Caratacus and Tog rode their horses back to their homes after meeting with their father and the tribal council. Both shivered despite wearing heavy, woolen cloaks hooked tightly about their shoulders, which draped down to their thighs. Caratacus rubbed his hands together as he held his reins. The breath escaping from his mouth evaporated into a patch of steam in the frosty air. While they passed through drifting patches of fog, Caratacus glanced about the bleak landscape of skeletal oak and walnut trees barren of all leaves on both sides of the muddy trackway. Drab fields, gray and fallow under patches of snow, laid waiting for spring plowing. Caratacus attempted to distract himself from the foul weather by reflecting on the events that had occurred since his return from Eburacum.

Despite the humiliation he'd suffered five months earlier when Cunobelinos proclaimed Adminios future ruler of the Cantiacian kingdom in all but name, Caratacus still served his father, but for how long? The old king still showed flashes of awareness, even brilliance, but it became more difficult for Caratacus and Ibor—whom he didn't trust, to shield Cunobelinos's infirmities from the council. Caratacus suspected the chieftains had already guessed his father was losing his mind.

Caratacus recalled that at today's meeting when he and Tog entered the torch-lit Great Hall. They saw Cunobelinos on his Roman curule chair on the dais with his eleven councilors, clan chieftains, sitting around him in a semi-circle. As always, Ibor stood by his side. While Tog had waited in the shadows, Caratacus approached his father and stopped at the foot of the dais.

The king wore a heavy, fur cloak about his sagging shoulders. His face appeared blank, a far-off look in his eyes. Caratacus knew what that meant. His father grew feebler with each passing day. Nevertheless, the information he possessed couldn't wait.

Ibor whispered into the king's ear.

Cunobelinos looked in Caratacus's direction, appearing more alert, eyes wider. "What do you want from us, Prince Caratacus?"

Thank Teutates, he recognizes me. "I bring important news, Great King."

The king grunted, "Tell us."

"As you recall, your spies learned five months ago the Roman, Porcius, met with King Verica," Caratacus said. He paused, glanced to the clan chieftains making up the High Council, also wearing heavy furs. All eyes turned to him, including those of bald-headed Fergus ap Roycal. "We have just learned Adminios has agreed with Verica's plan to invade our lands."

Cunobelinos flinched. "He what?"

A loud murmur erupted from the High Council. "That's outrageous!" one member said, followed by similar outbursts.

Fergus ap Roycal raised a fist and shouted, "He's a fucking traitor!" His raven eyes darted from one chieftain to another and back to Caratacus.

Good. No sympathy for my rotten brother. Caratacus slowly nodded before continuing. "That's not all. The Romans may support Verica and Adminios. We know Emperor Caligula is currently with the Roman Army along the River Rhenus."

"But that is far away from the Gallic Coast," Ibor said.

"Ibor is right," Cunobelinos said in a lucid voice. "What does that have to do with us?"

Good, Da is alert.

"I sent spies, disguised as traders, to check on possible troop movements," Caratacus said. "It was the right move. They discovered and followed two cohorts of Roman legionaries that moved from the River Rhenus to the coast of Belgica on the channel."

The king scowled and gestured with a hand toward Caratacus. "Gaul has been occupied by Romans for many years, what difference do two cohorts make?"

Caratacus bowed slightly to his father. "You're right, but these troops are from the River Rhenus Fleet. They are well-trained in crossing rivers and ocean landings. They came to Gaul to train the legions in what they call, *wet landings*—for invasion by boats."

"If they plan to invade us, they will need hundreds of boats," Fergus ap Roycal said.

The other councilors murmured in agreement.

"And they'll have them, Fergus," Caratacus said. "My spies discovered flatboats being built for transporting troops nearby at the port of Gesoriacum."

"It has to be for an invasion," Fergus said. "I hear the rivers near the port are already crisscrossed with bridges or can be easily forded. They don't need that many boats."

"How can we be sure that Adminios is part of this plot?" A pock-marked chieftain said.

Fergus ap Roycal stood and took one step in Cunobelinos's direction. "Great King, I suggest that Adminios be summoned before this council and questioned about his part in this treasonous scheme against our people."

Ibor whispered in the king's ear. He nodded.

Cunobelinos stood and all members of the council followed suit. "Adminios, our son and king of the Cantiaci, is hereby commanded to report to our presence to answer questions regarding his collusion with King Verica and the Romans." He turned to Caratacus. "If what your spies say proves to be true, then Adminios will be charged with treason."

The councilors bowed.

Cunobelinos faced Caratacus again and narrowed his eyes. "Know this, if your spies have lied, they will lose their heads!"

Caratacus grabbed the hilt of his sword. "If that is so, Great King, I will personally execute them."

The king nodded and seemed to be satisfied with his answer. He motioned to Ibor with a hand. "See that the message is sent to Adminios at once."

"Yes, Great King."

Fergus ap Roycal tugged at his long, bushy moustache and asked the king, "What about the Roman, Porcius? The pig-sticker should be seized by the balls and made to answer his part in this scheme, too."

Cunobelinos stared at the chieftain, his eyes seemed to have glazed over. His face turned expressionless, flat. "Porcius who?"

Fergus jolted. He eyed Caratacus and then Ibor. Caratacus shook his head.

The councilors looked at one another, about half of them sighing in disgust.

Ibor paled as he momentarily raised a hand up in dismay.

Caratacus stared at his father. He couldn't believe how quickly his father had relapsed into a feebleminded state.

Cunobelinos turned his head toward Ibor and slurred. "I know Porcius—he's our friend—so is Adminios."

Ibor whispered to the king once more, who nodded. The Druid faced the chieftains. "I ask that you leave us for now. Prince Caratacus, you may stay."

"But High King, there are many issues to be discussed," Fergus ap Roycal said. "If Verica plans to attack the kingdom, we must prepare for invasion."

"Aye," the others murmured their agreement.

"Those and other matters will be handled in due time," Ibor said. He cocked his head and glanced to the hall's entrance. "Now leave us."

After a short period of grumbling, the chieftains departed.

Caratacus studied his father as Ibor stepped to him and away from the king. He whispered to Ibor, "This situation is becoming untenable. The Council isn't stupid. We were lucky his mind was clear enough to order Adminios to the court. They know Da is growing feebleminded."

Ibor shrugged, his cobweb-lined face glazing at the king and then Caratacus. "I know. I don't know how much longer I can keep them at bay."

"Especially if either Verica or the Romans launch an invasion."

A smirk crossed the Druids thin lips. "I don't believe their information is correct."

Caratacus raised his eyebrows. "What do you mean? My spies *saw* the Romans constructing landing barges."

"It may be just a diversion, a facade," Ibor said. "My sources tell me that Porcius tried to persuade Verica to wait. He fears a Roman invasion as much as we. After all, your father is pro-Roman. I know it would not be in Porcius's interests anymore than ours."

It wouldn't be in yours, either!

"Regardless of Porcius's interests in this fucking scheme," Caratacus said, "you know my brother is involved up to his ears in this mess. He wants to take Da's kingdom and kill me and Tog."

Ibor grimaced. "That part is true."

"See that Da gets back to his home—safely," Caratacus said and departed.

* * *

Caratacus's mind returned to the present as he and Tog continued riding toward their homes. Besides sending spies to Gaul and Germania to watch the Romans, he had sent spies to the land of the Cantiaci, where Adminios now ruled, to keep an eye on his activities. He'd also sent agents to Verica's kingdom. No doubt his older brother and King Verica planned to get rid of Cunobelinos and him.

Caratacus could depend on Clud and Tog to be his allies, and there were other tribal chieftains who might aid him, such as Fergus ap Roycal. The victory over the Caledonians had sealed his reputation as a fighter and leader of men. Now that Rhian's father, Donn, was in Camulodunum, along with Epaticcos's former arch-Druid, Havgan, Caratacus's chances for support had been strengthened. Those two men were still highly regarded by other tribal kings.

"Do you believe Donn and Havgan will support you?" Tog asked. He turned about as if searching the bleak land for something before returning his gaze to Caratacus.

"Donn and Havgan are not fools. They know Da is failing and have no love for Adminios, especially Donn." Caratacus pulled his cloak tighter about himself as they continued trotting along the muddy path.

"Your father-in-law and Havgan have known us since we were boys. They know you are the best one to succeed Da."

Caratacus grunted and blew on his hands. "Don't forget Verica. Ever since he reclaimed the Atrebatic throne, he has set his eyes on this kingdom. He will use his influence with Adminios and the Druids to take it for himself. Then he'll kill Adminios and come after us."

Tog Smirked. "If Adminios doesn't attempt to murder us first."

"Not to mention our families—he'll slaughter them as well." *I have to protect Dana and Rhian at all costs, especially now that Dana is with child. Nothing must happen to her or Rhian.*

Caratacus and Tog had learned that Verica had gained the throne of the Atrebates through a betrayal by their council. The chieftains had invited him to Caleva after their Uncle Epaticcos's death and proclaimed him king of the Atrebates. The irony wasn't lost on the brothers. Epaticcos had ousted Verica from the same position twenty years earlier.

Caratacus twisted in his saddle toward Tog. "I still can't get over how Uncle Epaticcos got caught with a woman in a grove sacred to the Druids. It was stupid."

Tog's face tightened. "Our uncle was a known womanizer. I wouldn't be surprised if he had been lured into the Sacred Grove as part of a plot to get rid of him. Being found there with a woman is a sacrilege. He had no choice but to kill himself."

Caratacus balled the fingers of one hand into a fist and opened it again. "Verica must have bribed the council—it's the only way he could have been made king, short of waging all out war," Caratacus said.

"Donn must have objected to the council's decision, along with Uncle's arch-Druid, Havgan."

"Thank Teutates they fled before being murdered," Tog said.

"Considering how loyal they were to Uncle Epaticcos, they were lucky not to be murdered before the council voted for Verica."

"At least Da had his wits about him at the time to grant Donn and Havgan asylum."

Darting from behind a roadside bush, a thin, mottled fox crossed their path a few paces away and disappeared into a nearby drainage ditch. The animal startled Caratacus's gelding, who whinnied and reared up on its hind legs. Instantly, Caratacus clamped his legs tightly around the horse's girth and leaned forward, bringing the animal down on all fours. He calmed the horse with soothing words as he stroked its neck. After settling the mount, they continued riding.

Caratacus remembered how happy and grateful Rhian was to hear her father, Donn, had escaped from certain death at the hands of Verica and had arrived safely into his father's kingdom. Now, Caratacus and Cunobelinos would have to deal with Adminios's treachery. Again, he clenched and unclenched a fist.

"What are you thinking, Brother?" Tog asked. "You've been quiet these last few minutes."

"We'll see if Adminios will heed Da's summon to come to Camulodunum and answer his questions about the rumors."

Tog shook his head. "Don't be surprised if he fails to appear—that's something he would do."

"I'm aware of that," Caratacus said. "However, if he obeys the order, will Da have a clear mind when he arrives?"

"He better be alert. If our arsehole brother has been conspiring with the Romans, Da must remove him from the throne."

Caratacus's hand gripped the hilt of the dagger tied to the belt around his waist. "If I had my way, I would cut his throat and be done with it."

Tog winked. "I'd help you, but no chance of that. Banishment and losing all rights as a tribal member is what he'll get. Besides, it's more disgraceful."

"Adminios is supplying the Romans with information about our people, lands, and warriors. That's why the bastard traitor shouldn't be spared." He paused, hearing the sounds of hooves as his and Tog's horses trotted along the path.

"Adminios has more ambition than I gave him credit for. He intends to replace Da sooner than I expected," Caratacus continued.

"By murder you mean." Tog blew on his hands. "The Druids are leading him by the nose. He's too lazy to do anything on his own. I can't believe they would work with the Romans, knowing they hate Druids."

"If the Romans invade, we fight to the death," Caratacus said, squeezing the handle of his knife, knuckles turning white. "I will not see our people enslaved by those butchers. I still remember the tales Havgan told us as boys of how the Romans murdered more than a million people when Caesar conquered Gaul.

"No matter who the buggers are behind Adminios, we've got to stop them from taking the kingdom." Caratacus's jaw tightened.

"There is no way we can allow him to do that—it would be a disaster for the kingdom and us," Tog said. "Then he will invite the Romans here for sure."

"I'm not waiting for Adminios's arrival; it's time to learn who our real allies are," Caratacus said. "I'm sending secret messages to the kings of the Iceni, Durotrigians, and to others to seek help."

* * *

The brothers parted as they approached Caratacus's wattle-and-daub house, which loomed out of the patchy fog. Tog's place was about a half-mile further away.

Upon returning home, he dismounted his horse at the stable. As he took the short walk to his home, he remembered how Rhian had grown increasingly hostile to Dana after they had returned to Camulodunum from Eburacum. The situation came to a head one night about a month later. It was a late afternoon like this, a pale and watery yellow sun trying to pierce through a foggy mist. The air silent, heavy with a chill. He had returned home from a training exercise with his warriors. Upon entering, he spotted Dana and Rhian by the hearth, the fire's illumination filling the home's interior with shadowy light. A small cauldron, cooking a tangy venison stew, sat on a grill at one end of the spit. The aroma made his stomach rumble.

At first, the women didn't see him. It was just as well, because at that moment he saw something he didn't like.

Caratacus stepped forward into the light

Startled by his appearance, the women stood.

"Rhian, why are you treating Dana like dirt?"

Dana shook her head. "No, she isn't, Caratacus."

Caratacus glowered at Rhian. "I think otherwise."

Rhian crinkled her nose and returned his glare. "What are you talking about?"

"I saw the dirty look you gave Dana when she offered to help with the sewing. You threw my tunic at her."

"Honestly, Caratacus, she didn't—it was an accident," Dana said as she raised a hand up toward him.

"Really? I'm surprised you didn't throw it back," Caratacus said. "I saw how your face flushed and the frown that crossed your lips."

Rhian sniffed and turned to Dana. "Why didn't you, dear Sister-Wife?"

Dana slightly lowered her head and answered quietly, "I'm trying to keep peace in this family, Rhian, that's my way."

Caratacus stepped to Rhian and looked down into her apple-green eyes. "You've treated Dana like dog-meat ever since our return from Eburacum. Why?"

Rhian sucked the bottom of her lip, glanced to Dana and back to Caratacus. "Since we have returned, you have spent nearly every night with her but no time with me. I'm the one who is dog-meat!"

Heat rushed into Caratacus's face. His ears filled with roaring sounds like ocean waves crashing upon the surf. The muscles tightened in his shoulder and back. He raised his head and stared at the ceiling as wisps of smoke from the fire pit drifted upward and disappeared between strands of straw in the thatched roof. He loudly exhaled, lowered his head, and glared at Rhian and then Dana. "For the love of the gods, is that what this is all about?" Caratacus realized what Rhian said was true. He had spent most of his nights with Dana enjoying the passions of their newly formed union, all but ignoring Rhian.

Dana dropped the tunic she held to the hard-packed, dirt floor. She glanced to Rhian and back to Caratacus. "Rhian is right. I have watched her anger growing with each passing day. You have spent too much time with me. She is your first wife and deserves your attention and respect."

Caratacus paused, allowing himself time to relax, the tension draining from his body. The two women watched him patiently as if waiting for him to make a decision. "You're right, Dana," Caratacus finally said. He turned to Rhian. "From now on, I promise to give you the attention and respect due to a chief wife, my Wife." He looked from Rhian to Dana. "I will divide my nights equally between the two of you. Is that agreeable?"

Dana nodded.

"It is, Husband," Rhian answered.

Caratacus pulled Rhian close and hugged her tightly, holding her for the length of a dozen heartbeats before releasing her.

Rhian smiled. "Now I can turn my energies to other matters. I need to recruit and train more warrior women to replace the losses we suffered against the Caledonians."

Relieved, Caratacus glanced to the stew cooking in the small cauldron at one end of the hearth. He remembered his grumbling stomach. "Good, now if there isn't anything else, I'm hungry."

Fortunately, since that night, it appeared to Caratacus that Dana and Rhian, if not good friends, were at least getting along with one another.

* * *

Within a few minutes, Caratacus had reached the front porch of his home and entered. Instantly, he felt the warmth from the center fire pit seep into his body, starting with his face, rushing through his arms, down his torso and legs, and into his toes. He allowed his eyes to focus on the interior as he handed his cloak to a female servant, who disappeared into the shadows.

Beyond the firelight of the hearth, he spotted Dana and Rhian by the clay oven. The aroma of fresh-baked bread filled his nostrils. He hadn't realized he was so hungry. Dana looked up for a split second and saw Caratacus. She smiled, but raised a finger and nodded to the bread. He understood. She used a heavy rag to remove the flat loaves of bread from the oven. An overhanging, wooden plank deflected the last remnants of smoke from a hole in the oven's domed top toward the center of the house's straw roof. She placed the hot dishes on the clay ledge next to the oven. The fragrant smell permeated the household. Nearby, a young slave woman sat on a mat grinding corn into flour in a stone bowl.

Finished with the bread, Dana got up and straightened the sleeves of her dark-green, tartan tunic and shook out the lower part clinging to her slender legs. Both women stood. Rhian kissed him on the cheek followed by Dana as he came over to the fire pit. He grinned and gave both a quick hug. "It's good to be here."

Caratacus's eyes drooped. He decided to wait until he had eaten and relaxed a bit before telling Dana and Rhian about Adminios's treachery. There was no rush as it would be at least a week before he arrived in Camulodunum. *If he comes at all, which I doubt!*

He turned to Dana. "How was the trip to my client villages? Are the people well?"

"They prosper," Dana answered with a smile.

Caratacus grinned. "Good, I'm pleased."

"There is more," Rhian said. "We need to talk with you." She nodded to Dana.

"Oh, by the looks of you two, it must be serious," Caratacus said. *They couldn't have heard the reports about Adminios and the Romans.*

"It is," Dana said.

He exhaled. "Give me time to get my wits together. The council session was grueling. I promise to give you my full attention."

Dana and Rhian nodded.

He closed his eyes for a few seconds and took a deep breath. *I may have to tell them about Adminios's treachery sooner than I planned.*

Caratacus opened his eyes about the same time his stomach growled. "I'm hungry, but dinner can wait so long as I get a piece of that bread to chew on while I listen." He motioned to a servant hovering nearby and ordered her to bring him part of a loaf and a cup of warm mead. The women ordered chamomile tea.

A servant appeared in the firelight with a wooden platter holding a partial loaf of the flat bread, which she placed next to Caratacus's side and left to retrieve the women's beverages.

Caratacus tore off a small chunk and chewed the warm, savory bread. The growling in his stomach ended.

After the slave returned with their drinks, the woman was dismissed, and the three of them settled on fur skins by the fire pit. Caratacus and his wives sat silently, savoring their drinks. The warm liquid warmed Caratacus's insides, and he shut his eyes again and allowed the tension to drain from his shoulders, arms, and even his calloused hands. He took another bite of bread, chewing it slowly.

"Now, tell me, Dana," Caratacus said. "I have a sneaking suspicion your news is worse than I can imagine."

CHAPTER 29

Rhian and Dana looked at one another.

Dana nodded. "It's a long story, Caratacus, please hear us out."

"This better be worth it." Caratacus took another gulp of mead.

Rhian sat quietly, staring past Dana towards the wall of the hut. Within a few heartbeats, she turned her head toward Caratacus. "When I have ridden with you," she said slowly, "on days you inspected your holdings, I have heard the peasants praise Dana's name, especially the women."

Dana blushed. She set her cup of chamomile tea on the hard-packed floor beside her. "It's Caratacus they praise." Her eyes focused on Caratacus. "I know you want to help them, but you've been distracted by tribal affairs and your father's worsening condition."

"You're right, but I still should have done more," Caratacus said.

"It's not your fault," Dana said. "That's why I tell the people when I visit them, I come on your behalf."

Rhian shrugged. "I have heard the same thing from the women warriors I have recruited from among the villagers. It was Dana who persuaded them to join me."

Caratacus raised his eyebrows and turned to Dana. "You have become my extended hand, Dana," Caratacus said. "Because of you, they are more loyal to me than before."

Dana's nose flared. "If you say so. But you don't see the little things that make all the difference in the lives of people. A little extra piece of cloth for a new tunic, or a fur to line their clothing against the cold, and an additional portion of grain to feed a growing child means a great deal to them. Rhian has seen that."

Caratacus bristled at her comment, but kept his tongue. *Unfortunately, you are right.* "What does any of this have to do with your serious news?" Caratacus asked, his impatience growing.

Rhian touched her heart and glanced to Dana, whose hand momentarily covered her mouth. "We suspect Adminios and the Druids are practicing human sacrifice."

Caratacus jolted, nearly spilling his drink. His back tightened. He sat straight. "Are you certain of this? What proof do you have?"

"He was seen riding through the village of Usk and the surrounding hamlets on several occasions," Dana answered. "People saw him disappearing into the woods."

"Adminios could have been hunting," Caratacus said in a dismissive tone. "He's bragged enough about being a great hunter."

Dana crimped her mouth in annoyance. "The people reported strange sounds and omens."

"They are probably signs from the gods," Rhian said. "We must respect them."

"They do, and so do I," Dana replied. "However, from what the villagers have told me, I believe there may be more than just the gods at work." She paused and glanced to Rhian and Caratacus. "Both of you know the village of Usk is closest to the great forest of the River Tamesis basin. It's a logical choice for conducting secret, human sacrifices. Rumors abound that this area had been such a place in the past."

"I'm familiar with the place—a small fortified village," Caratacus said. "I wouldn't put it past Adminios to bribe the Druids to perform human sacrifice." *True. Why didn't my spies uncover it?*

Dana blanched. "If he did, then he's an animal. But why here? Why not do it in the land of the Cantiaci?"

"If he is involved, it means he plans to kill me and Da," Caratacus said. "The sacrifice must be performed in the land where the murder is meant to happen. In other words, the territories ruled by Da, not his."

"If your horrid brother practiced human sacrifice, why so far from the fortress?" Rhian motioned toward the entry of their home.

"It must be done in secrecy," Dana said, "away from any populated area. Usk is remote, and the peasants are very fearful of the gods and the wrath of the Druids." She touched her chest as if warding off a curse. "They told me as much and wouldn't dare interfere."

"How would they really know that was going on?" Rhian asked. "If Adminios hunts there, the villagers would be used to his passing through their midst. After a while, the people would think nothing of it."

Dana took up her cup from the floor and, holding it with both hands, sipped her tea. She lowered it to her lap, her hands around the cup. "I believe I found the answer on my last visit."

"Finally, we get down to the matter." Caratacus took a drink of mead and wiped his mouth on his sleeve. *I have a sneaking suspicion this ties in with the Romans.*

"As usual," Dana said, "I took a couple of female attendants and ..." She paused and glanced to Rhian before continuing, "a small escort of Rhian's warrior women when I traveled to Usk yesterday.

"If sacrificial rites were still being held there," Dana continued, "I made it a point to be careful of what I said and did. I feared there might be followers living there who would inform on me if they believed I was attempting to learn of the acts."

Dana explained Usk was her best hope for discovering any information about them. She had aided the villagers in the past, and would be welcomed, especially since she arrived during the Festival of Imbolc. The holiday celebrated the time of lambing and the year's renewal and purification.

"After paying a brief visit to the village chieftain," Dana said, "I rode to the sacred oak outside the compound. As I expected, I found only women praying before the image of Brigit."

Dana went on to say that in the cool, afternoon, winter light, she had observed about a dozen women offering wooden bowls of ewe milk to the tall, weathered, wooden statue of the goddess. A larger group of women had stood about in little knots gossiping. Dana commanded her escort and attendants to stay behind and carefully slipped off the back of her chestnut mare and approached the group.

"And?" Caratacus asked.

"Two young women stood apart from the rest by a bush I was walking past," Dana answered. "I overheard the red-haired one say to the smaller girl of about fourteen that she shouldn't speak evil in the presence of Brigit's sacred statue that she's the goddess of life, not death."

"What evil?" Rhian asked.

"The younger girl, Fiona, said she saw the sacrifice of a baby eight months ago."

Rhian's hands flew to the side of her face. "No!"

Caratacus clenched his fists. "Go on, Dana."

"The other girl, Aife, looked around to see if anyone was listening. The other women continued chattering. She turned and warned Fiona to keep her mouth shut."

"Why?" Rhian asked.

"Otherwise, she would be accused of lying and punished," Dana said.

"Then I was spotted by several women who called my name and flocked about me. They chattered all at once and asked me dozens of questions."

Dana explained that she stepped to the idol and bowed and then walked among the scattered groups of colorfully clad women wearing tartan tunics dyed in the hues of the rainbow. The material had been supplied by herself on her last visit a month earlier. At the same time, she kept an eye on Fiona and her friend.

After a bit of small talk and complimenting their appearances and devotion to the goddess, Dana had handed out small gifts of sweet meats. She said a brief prayer to the goddess and asked Fiona to walk with her. The others murmured about her good fortune in being favored by Dana.

"The mottle-faced girl froze in her steps," Dana said. "She turned her head toward the women drifting back to the village."

Dana paused and took another sip of tea.

"She was frightened of something, wasn't she?" Rhian said.

"Indeed," Caratacus added. "Continue, Dana."

Dana pursed her lips. "I told her she could trust me and assured her I wouldn't betray her confidence. At first, she hesitated, but I said if she didn't confide in someone, she might go mad. I promised she would have your protection."

"She will," Caratacus said with a gesture of his hand.

"We continued our walk," Dana said. "That's when Fiona described the horror she witnessed in the forest."

About eight months before, Fiona had gone searching for a lamb that had strayed from the flock into the woods. She was afraid of wandering accidentally onto a secret rite and being murdered. Her mum and da had warned her the forest was full of dangers—evil spirits who killed people. Fiona's curiosity overcame her fear, and she went farther into the woods, although she stayed to the bushes. She heard a chant in a language she didn't understand. It grew louder with her every step.

"At that point," Dana said, "Fiona seemed hesitant to say anymore. I encouraged her to continue.

"Fiona reluctantly went on. The young woman caught the light of a glimmering fire and stopped to peek through the underbrush. At first, Fiona was afraid she had made too much noise rustling the branches. But the droning chant was so loud she didn't believe anyone had heard her. She paused and looked about before continuing. Then she saw five or six men or women dressed in homespun robes. One was an old man who wore a golden crescent moon, and like everyone in the village, Fiona knew only a Druid could wear that symbol," Dana added.

"Did she recognize the priest?" Caratacus asked.

"She gave me a description." Dana told Caratacus what he looked like.

"It's Ibor!" Caratacus said. "I would know his cobwebbed face anywhere. What else did Fiona tell you?"

"Close by, Fiona spotted a dark-haired, young man dressed in a rich, tartan tunic and breeches, wearing a long, drooping moustache," Dana answered. "Fiona had seen him ride through the village before with a hunting party. At the time, he was only another rich nobleman to her. But later she saw him again on another hunt. So she asked her father, and he said it was Prince Adminios."

A chill shot through Caratacus's body. "Was she certain?"

"As certain as I'm sitting here, Caratacus," Dana answered. "I asked her again to be sure."

"Go on," Caratacus urged. He took a bit of bread, chewed, and swallowed, followed by another drink of mead.

Dana explained that Fiona spotted something near the altar she had never seen before, four trees growing out of one trunk. Next to it stood a young mother holding a baby in her arms. The child couldn't have been more than three or four days old. The woman was squeezed between two acolytes, who were making sure that she didn't escape.

"The mother pleaded for their lives, but it was no good," Dana said. "The poor woman screamed, but the two acolytes muffled her, and the priest drove a knife into her chest, killing her.

"At that point, Fiona stopped speaking, her dark eyes took on a haunted look. She turned away and halted."

Dana sighed and glanced to Rhian, who shook her head. "I saw tears running down the sides of her face and placed an arm around Fiona's shoulder and drew her close as she quietly wept."

"It must have been a horrible experience for her," Rhian said in a rasping voice. "Just listening to the story makes my blood turn cold."

"I know," Dana answered in little more than a whisper. "I barely contained my own horror and disgust."

"No one should witness such things," Caratacus said. He cocked his head. "There must be more. Normally, sacrificial victims are volunteers from the nobility."

"Fiona wiped her face, and I asked if she was feeling better. She wasn't but needed to finish the tale."

Dana explained that she scanned the oak-filled woods about them and, not seeing anyone about, told Fiona to continue.

The girl had watched as the priest drained the blood from the baby's jugular vein, and then both he and the mother were beheaded. The acolytes dismembered the child and placed the parts between the feet of the mother in a shallow grave. The Druid raised the wooden bowl with the baby's blood skyward and recited words Fiona didn't understand. When finished, the priest drank the blood and poured the rest over the burial site.

"All this time, Adminios watched the horrible rites and didn't say a word," Dana said. "When it was over, he gave the Druid a silver, triple-headed horse amulet."

Caratacus held up a hand.

"What is it?" Dana asked.

"I know that amulet, it belongs to Adminios."

"How do you know?" Rhian questioned.

Caratacus nodded. "There isn't another charm like it in the kingdom. Adminios received it from Da when he officially reached manhood." He gestured to Dana with a hand. "Go on with your story, what did the Druid do with it?"

"He placed the charm in a small, gold box with a finger bone from the baby and gave the container to a female acolyte," Dana said. "He ordered her to bury it next to the bodies.

"I told Fiona that you must be informed about Adminios's misdeed," Dana added. "Fiona understood, but I gasped when she told me what the Druid said next."

Rhian took a breath.

"What did Ibor say?" Caratacus asked.

"He turned to Adminios and spoke the following words: 'Oh, Great Prince, I foresee that within one summer the kingship will be yours alone. You shall have the blessings of all the Druids.'

"Then Fiona said Adminios placed a curse on you, Husband, and swore to kill you."

Rhian gasped and shook her head.

Caratacus slapped his thigh with the palm of his hand. "Adminios is a dirty traitor—I knew it! Damn him!"

"What an evil man," Dana added.

"He is more than that," Rhian hissed. She drew a finger across the front of her neck from one side to the other. "This is what he deserves."

Caratacus took a deep breath, opening and clenching his fists several times before the muscles relaxed. "What else did Fiona hear?"

"Nothing, Caratacus," Dana said. "Fiona had been hypnotized by the gruesome rites, but finally came to her senses and fled the woods before she was discovered."

"Thank Mother Goddess Anu that she wasn't," Rhian said.

"Fiona said the experience was so terrible that she didn't tell anybody until the day I saw her," Dana added. "She was afraid of being kidnapped and sacrificed. She is certain her friend, Aife, will keep her mouth shut."

"She better," Caratacus said. *Fiona's story must not spread. As much as I would hate to do it, she would meet with an accident.*

"I assured Fiona I was the right person to help her," Dana said. "I admit I was shaken by Fiona's ghoulish revelations." She drew a deep breath and remained silent, apparently composing herself.

A roar-like, crashing surf on the beach filled Caratacus's ears. Heat burned his face. He wanted to growl like a bear. *If this Fiona is telling the truth, Adminios will pay for this outrage, and pay dearly.*

CHAPTER 30

"I have something to tell you," Caratacus said to his wives. He described the council meeting and the reports that Adminios was conspiring with the Romans who planned to invade Britannia.

"Until you told me that Fiona heard Ibor's proclamation that Adminios would be the next king, I believed this sacrifice might have been a separate piece of treachery— simply my murder. Now that the Romans are involved, it is important that Da and the High Council are warned before he arrives."

"But Ibor must not be told," Rhian advised.

"He won't, I'll see to that," Caratacus answered. "Can Fiona find the sacrificial place again?"

"I asked her the same question, and she believes she can," Dana answered. "I told her not to say a word to anyone, not even her people, until I sent word we were ready to help her."

"Tomorrow we'll go out and search the area," Caratacus said through tight lips. "If Adminios and Ibor are involved, they will pay for their treachery and murders of the poor woman and her child."

"Then you believe us?" Rhian asked.

"About the sacrifice and amulet, yes. I'd say the peasant girl told you the truth. Adminios is always hunting. So the peasants might have seen him in the area of Usk."

"Fiona has no reason to lie," Dana said.

"Probably not, she'd be afraid of being punished," Caratacus said. "It's worth a look."

"All I ask is that you make a real effort," Dana said. "But please, the girl must be protected."

"I agree," Rhian said.

Caratacus stared at Rhian and then Dana. "The girl will be protected. You have my word. Only Clud, Tog, and a few of my trusted men will go with us. As far as anyone will know, I'm taking my wives on a hunting party."

"I'll send word for Fiona to be ready." Dana laid down her cup.

Caratacus shook his head. "No, Dana. I don't want Fiona to know until we arrive in the village."

"Why?" Rhian asked.

"News of our journey will spread soon enough," Caratacus answered. "A large welcome by the peasants is the last thing we need. Some would become suspicious, especially when we take one of their girls with us."

Caratacus gestured to Dana. "The word must be spread that you want a female guide."

"And it's true," Dana said. "The village knows I favored her, and we need her to show us the tree."

"Good. That'll alleviate suspicions. The old clan chieftain will be appeased and honored."

"I hope she stays quiet," Rhian added.

"Fiona will," Dana said. "She's afraid she'll be next!"

* * *

The following day Caratacus's band of twenty hand-picked warriors, including Tog and Clud, along with Dana, Rhian, and Fiona, searched the cold gloom of the great, oak forest on horseback. For several hours they scoured the woods near the village of Usk looking for the hidden sacrificial site.

"So far we've found nothing. Are you sure about the location?" Caratacus asked in disgust. He glared at Fiona's pinched face. "Four trees out of one trunk, indeed!"

"But it's true, Great Prince," Fiona pleaded as she walked alongside Dana's mount. Fiona's close-set, dark eyes seemed fearful of his possible wrath. "It is around here, I know it. It's just that everything looks the same in the forest." She ran ahead a short distance.

"The afternoon is growing late," Rhian said, "but let's search for at least another hour, Husband. I believe the girl. My heart tells me what she says is true. The bodies are here, somewhere."

Caratacus spat. "The trouble is, where? There are hundreds of square miles of forest."

"Look, Prince Caratacus," Fiona called. "Over there, I think that's the place." She pointed to an oak with four trees growing out of one trunk. "The altar was next to it."

Caratacus halted. For the length of a half-dozen heartbeats he stared at the warped tree. *By Teutates, she told the truth.* Carved into one was the discolored shape of a crescent moon.

"This has to be it," Rhian said. "No one but a Druid uses the sacred crescent."

Caratacus snapped out of his thoughts. "Let's take a closer look. I doubt if we will find another tree like this." Caratacus studied the surrounding area. "If there was a sacrifice, the altar must have been in this clearing."

"Obviously, they tore it down and destroyed any evidence of its existence," Rhian said. "You can see where branches and limbs were cut to make room." She pointed to the darkened limb stumps close to the trunk.

Fiona pointed to an opening covered by rotted leaves and other decaying vegetation. "I think that's where the woman and baby are buried, Prince Caratacus."

Caratacus nodded to his party. "All right, we'll not take any chances. Get down on your knees and start probing."

The men and women formed a line, shoulder to shoulder, slowly moving forward as each probed the soft forest earth with sword tips and daggers.

After excavating for about fifteen minutes, a warrior waved to Caratacus. "Over here, Prince Caratacus, I found something." He gouged the object to the surface with his sword. "A rock!" Some of the men laughed.

Dana and Rhian scowled at the men. Dana's hands were stained from digging. "Are you sure there was a box?" she asked Fiona.

Caratacus hiked to the spot pointed out by the man. He slid his sword from the scabbard on his belt at the waist and shoved it into the ground. He felt a thud against his probing sword point. The others turned at the sound and watched. With a few sharp prods of Caratacus's weapon, the handle shot back into his palm from the impact. He dropped to his knees, laid the sword next to him, and dug with a dagger. Carefully, he clawed the dirt away revealing the skeleton of an adult covered in rotting clothes, and the tiny dismembered parts of another one between its legs.

He motioned for everyone to gather round and pointed to the remains. "You were right, Fiona. Human sacrifice."

Fiona trembled. Dana came to the girl's side and held her close.

Rhian and the others looked at the remains and made signs with their hands to ward off the evil spirits.

"What now?" Clud asked.

"I'll cover them up," Caratacus answered. "We don't know who they were or where they came from. They are with the gods and no longer suffering."

"What about the amulet?" Tog questioned.

"We'll search a little longer. It must be close to the bodies," Caratacus answered.

After a few minutes of digging, Caratacus's knife struck something through the leaves covering the earth, emitting a cracking metallic sound. Everyone stopped, their heads turning towards the sound. Even through the chalky earth, its golden luster, so long locked beneath the ground, shone through. His heart pounded as he pulled it free. Cautiously, he scraped away its sides.

Using his dagger on the encrusted top, Caratacus popped open the frozen latch. "Here's the finger bone," he said aloud. Then a gasp shot from his lungs. "By the Great Teutates, it's Adminios's amulet, I'd know it anywhere." He held up the silver ornament, the three horse heads glistening in the fading sunlight, shining through a gap in the trees. He stood.

Caratacus turned to Fiona and his wives. "You were right all along—Adminios is involved. This fits with his helping the Romans, especially if they promised he would be the next king." He paused. "My brother will pay dearly for his treason. He must!" He turned to Fiona. "I will see that you are rewarded, Fiona, you deserve as much."

Fiona bowed her head. "Thank you, my lord."

Dana, Rhian, and Caratacus's warriors murmured their approval.

Rhian stepped toward Fiona. "Would you like to become one of my warriors?"

Fiona's eyes widened and a smile crossed her full lips. "Oh yes, my lady, you have a reputation as a great leader. It would be an honor to my family and me."

Rhian blushed. She turned to Caratacus. "With your permission, Husband, I will enroll her into my ranks of warrior women and see to her training."

"Granted," Caratacus said. "That will be your reward, Fiona."

Caratacus glanced from one person to another and raised his fist. "Hear me now! I will do everything in my power to drive Adminios from our lands."

CHAPTER 31

Riding through a near-blinding snowfall, Caratacus and his entourage returned from Usk to Camulodunum late the same night. Fortunately, the shivering group arrived at the fortress before high drifts clogged the trackway.

Dana, in her fourth month of pregnancy shared his bed that night, slept undisturbed, her breathing steady. He had kept his promise of dividing his time equally between his wives. The prince tossed and turned as he thought about his next move against Adminios. Sliding from underneath the warm blankets, he grabbed an extra fur at the foot of the bed-pallet. He got up shivering and wrapped the covering around his naked body. He stepped along the cold, dirt floor to the hearth. The fire had been banked for the night, but was now little more than glowing embers in the shadowy darkness. Kneeling, Caratacus picked up a few slivers of wood and placed them next to the coals. He blew on them until they ignited and little flames shot upward. Small logs immediately caught fire. The wood crackled and popped as flames licked against the bark like a tongue savoring a sweet honey cake. Soon the heat warmed his face. At thirty-one, Caratacus realized his appearance was of a man who spent most of his time outdoors exposed to the ravaging elements—he had seen his image with its ruddiness and wrinkles enough times in clear ponds and his wives' expensive, copper mirrors. *So what? It's part of being a man—a hunter, leader, and warrior.*

Caratacus's mind turned to the revelations by Fiona of Adminios's involvement in human sacrifice and reports of his plotting with Verica to invade Cunobelinos's lands. These charges when brought before the king's council should be enough to bring his traitorous brother down. His hand gripped the edge of the blanket with white knuckles. *I need the backing of the tribal council if I'm to accuse*

Adminios of treason. Most of them hate him, and will side with me. During the past several months since he had returned from Eburacum, a number of the king's councilors, all clan chieftains, had secretly told Caratacus they wanted him as their next king. Now, Caratacus had to journey to their respective holdings to confirm their fealty and request their support. *Will they side with me against Adminios or were their words nothing more than empty gestures?*

* * *

The next morning Caratacus summoned Tog, Clud, and Donn to his home. He explained to them, as well as to Dana and Rhian, his plan to contact members of the council. He trusted them and would learn if they would agree to his plans once Adminios appeared before the king. "We still don't know if Adminios will comply with Da's order, but we must be ready if he does."

Rhian's father, Donn, scratched his bulbous nose. "Remember, the councilors be yer Da's men. Do ye think they'll see the wisdom of yer plan?"

"The chieftains hate Adminios and have no love for Ibor," Caratacus answered.

"Not all hate yer brother or the Druid," Donn said. "They be the kind who smell treason in every shadow." Donn, Epaticcos's former champion, was now honored as a brave and distinguished warrior among Caratacus's fighters. Although an outsider, he had a good reputation. Now loyal to Caratacus, he pledged to serve him in any capacity.

Clud raised his arm and balled his hand into a fist. "Donn's right. I don't trust some of them buggers. There's a couple I'd take a dagger to before I'd tell 'em anything." He lowered his arm and relaxed his hand.

"I know who you mean, Clud," Caratacus answered. "I won't waste time on them."

"If Adminios does obey Da's command," Tog said. He jabbed a finger in his brother's direction. "You'll have to make sure the chieftains get word before our brother arrives so they can be here to meet him."

"Aye, if they're not here in time, the Druids will block the meeting," Clud said.

A frown crossed Tog's sunburnt face, now scarred from numerous skirmishes with bordering tribes. "We can't let him get away," Tog said.

Caratacus furrowed his brows and pulled on the end of his drooping mustache. "My spies will bring word in plenty of time. Then I'll send messengers to the chieftains to report immediately."

"If not sooner," Donn said. The old warrior stared at Caratacus, his craggy face filled with determination.

"Have you heard from the Iceni or Durotrigian kings?" Clud asked.

"Nothing yet," Caratacus said. It had been less than a week since he had sent messages proposing an alliance with the two rulers to aid him should Verica invade the lands of the Catuvellaunii and Trinovantes. By taking it upon himself to contact these rulers, it would be seen as an act of treason. He was certain they would back him once Adminios was driven from power. He banked on at least King Unig of the Durotrigians to respond in his favor. They, too, were vulnerable to attack by Verica.

Caratacus turned to Dana and Rhian, who had quietly listened while the men spoke. "While we are gone, it will be your duty to be on the lookout for anything unusual."

Rhian hunched her shoulders. "What shall we tell people, especially Ibor, if they ask where you have gone?"

"Tell them I'm checking on my holdings—they know that's part of my duties as son of the king," Caratacus answered.

"Should Rhian and I wait until you return home before bringing Fiona from Usk for her training?" Dana asked, looking to Rhian, who nodded.

"Yes," Caratacus said. "I'll know more by the time I return if her presence will be required at the session."

"You promised to protect her identity," Dana reminded Caratacus.

Caratacus nodded. "So I did. The only person Fiona will tell what she witnessed will be Havgan. He will use the information in a way that will not implicate her."

Dana's shoulders relaxed as a smile crossed her lips. "Thank you."

Tog gripped the handle of his dagger hanging from the iron-chain belt on his waist.

"All I can say is, this whole thing better work, or we'll lose our heads."

* * *

About midmorning, after making sure no one was around, Caratacus slipped inside Havgan's hut.

The Druid wore a long, homespun tunic and breeches. A gold triskele hung from a thick chain on his chest. They sat on straw mats in front of the little hearth's dim firelight. As Caratacus told him of Fiona's discovery and revealed his plan, Havgan tugged on his trimmed but graying beard. "Have no fear, Caratacus," he said when he finally answered, "I will learn the truth if Ibor and his Druids were involved. Despite their oath of secrecy, there is always someone who can't keep their mouth shut."

"You think so?" Caratacus asked.

A mischievous smile appeared through his whiskered lips. "I have been a Druid for nearly thirty-five of my forty-six years. I can see their weaknesses, especially among the younger ones."

Caratacus winked. "No doubt you can, I should have known better."

"Everyone acknowledges the fact you should be rightful king." He shook his head. "The men of the council are not fools. Adminios is too irresponsible. If you are right, then he is in collusion with the Romans. Ibor was foolhardy in predicting Adminios would be the next king. I would be surprised if he did not know your brother is plotting. You must act quickly. Not only will the Romans overrun our lands, but they will destroy the Druids as they have done in Gaul. Ibor should understand that better than anybody. One of them was an uncle, his father's brother."

Caratacus looked about, saw no one. "When I become king, I swear that I will make you my arch-Druid."

Havgan bowed his head. "That isn't necessary. What I do I would have done for any ruler who serves the people as you do and protects the Druids. Adminios and Ibor must go. Ibor is a disgrace to all Druids."

Late that afternoon, a messenger from King Unig of the Durotrigians, disguised as a merchant, arrived at

Caratacus's home. The prince lived outside the fortress, his holdings on the plain near the edge of the forest. Visitors could come and go with little notice.

The courier informed Caratacus that King Unig was interested in a proposed alliance and requested that a representative be sent for further negotiations. Delighted, Caratacus told the rider that he would personally contact the king when the time was right.

* * *

At dawn the next day, Caratacus and his men left Camulodunum. The first leader they planned to visit and the most prominent was Fergus ap Roycal, senior clan chieftain and councilor who lived near the western border of their tribe. Next to the Druids, he was Cunobelinos's most outspoken and influential councilor.

Late afternoon enshrouded them as they rode through the dark, pine forest. Tall trees frowned on either side of the patchy, snow-covered trackway. A recent wind had stripped the branches of their frost covering and seemed to lean toward one another, black and ominous in the fading afternoon light.

The riders crossed a hurrying brook, flowing through breaks in the snow. Cautiously, the horses picked their way along the graveled bottom, hooves clattering against icy rocks, before bolting up the other side of the bank. Climbing the path up the hill, they arrived at the top where the woods thinned. Beyond squatted a large, open field, lightly dusted with snow, waiting for spring seeding. Multi-fingered strands of fog drifted just above its surface.

In the distance on a low rise stood the small stockade, circled by a narrow moat. Inside sat the longhouse of clan chieftain Fergus ap Roycal. A misty column of white smoke swirled skyward from the home's thatched roof, disappearing in the darkening, slate-gray sky. Smaller outbuildings and corrals filled with livestock clustered around the palisade like fleas on a dog. The baying of cattle and sheep bleating echoed across the countryside. Mixed odors of manure and smoke carried on the chilly breeze.

They crossed the moat's bridge and were met in front of the house by Fergus ap Roycal and four of his guards. He bid them welcome and asked what brought them to his home. Caratacus told him he had urgent news and Fergus waved the men toward his house. Once dismounted, Caratacus and his men followed the chieftain inside.

The chieftain bade them sit on benches at one end of the longhouse, the area he used to entertain guests and for hearing of minor criminal and civil cases brought to him for judgment. Caratacus sat with Tog, Clud, and Donn on his right, while his men stood behind them. Fergus ap Roycal and six of his retainers faced them. Servants came forward and handed every man an earthen cup filled with warm mead and were dismissed.

In the smoky light of a dozen tapers and olive oil lamps, Fergus narrowed his eyes, raised a hand, and motioned towards Caratacus. "Now, tell me your news, it's about your father, isn't it?"

"Aye, and much more," Caratacus said. He reached inside his tunic and pulled out a leather pouch hanging from a string around his neck. Opening the bag, he removed the silver, horse-headed amulet. Even in the pulsating light of the tapers, the three heads sparkled. Caratacus placed it in the upward palm of his right hand.

The chieftain took a swig of mead from his cup, belched, and leaned closer to examine the object. He took another gulp and straightened his back.

"Recognize it?" Caratacus asked as he placed it back into the pouch and shoved it beneath his tunic.

Fergus slowly nodded and grunted. "Hmm, if I remember, your Da gave that to your worthless brother, Adminios." A frown pushed from beneath his bushy moustache. "Where did you get it? Did you kill the bloody fucker?"

Caratacus looked about seeing Tog and Clud raising their eyes. A big grin creased Donn's face.

Caratacus balled his right hand into a fist and struck the palm of his left. "Were that only true, I wouldn't be here."

"Then how'd you get it?"

"Found it."

Fergus glanced to his retainers and back to Caratacus and cocked his head to one side. "Where? You didn't just *find* your brother's good-luck charm."

"I did," Caratacus said in a flat tone, "buried with victims from a human sacrifice."

Fergus cocked his head to one side. "Eh? Only Druids conduct human sacrifice. What does Adminios have to do with it? Did that bastard commit sacrilege?"

"He did." Caratacus revealed information about human sacrifice, including the Druid Ibor's involvement, without telling them it came from Fiona, and about Adminios conspiring with the Romans.

The chieftain took another drink from his cup, but spat it on the floor. "Fucking traitors, both of them. I can see Adminios scheming with the Romans, but Ibor, the old fool is cutting his own throat. The shit-eating Romans will kill 'em sure."

"The strange part of this matter is that Ibor said that he learned Porcius advised Verica against taking over Da's kingdom. He too fears Roman interference."

"That's because the fat bugger has too much at stake like the rest of the traders in our lands."

"Regardless, Ibor must be brought before the council as well as Adminios for his treachery," Caratacus said. "We can't fine or exile him like Adminios, but he can be sent packing to the Isle of Mona. The head of the Druid order will deal with him."

Fergus gulped down the rest of the mead in his cup and wiped his mouth on his sleeve. "Aye, they'll exile him to some remote island. That'll be worse than death for the little spider."

"We'll see if my brother will ride to Camulodunum after he receives Da's command to appear. In the meantime, after I leave here, I will be riding to the homes of the other clan leaders to win their support."

Fergus ap Roycal, a bald-headed, hulking warrior with arms as thick as the legs of most men and powerful limbs to match, stood up, followed by Caratacus. He raised his hand in salute, "I give you my allegiance, Caratacus, son of Cunobelinos, rightful king of the Catuvellaunii and Trinovantes." He lowered his arm.

Caratacus reached out and grabbed Fergus's powerful hand and shook it. The chieftain squeezed it so hard, Caratacus thought he would crush it. "Accepted."

"You say you're going to see the other chieftains?" Fergus asked.

"I am," Caratacus replied.

"Stay away from Cador and Melwas," Fergus advised. "Those whoresons of sows will betray you."

"I'll bypass them," Caratacus said. "But I will see and convince the other chieftains."

Fergus's hand, the size of a ham, tightly gripped the bejeweled, bone hilt of his longsword. His grin revealed a row of black teeth like jagged peaks. "Once you've finished talking sense into their thick skulls, I'll drop by and make sure those fuckers keep their word."

"Yer my kind of man," Donn said.

"That's all some of them understand," Clud added, pointing to his own weapon.

"If I hadn't been so sick," Fergus said. "I wouldn't have missed the Council's meeting when your father proclaimed Adminios King of the Cantiaci. I would've voted against it."

"I knew you would have. I remembered you were absent."

"Aye. Had a terrible fever. Got a big lump in my throat, and my balls felt they'd been smashed by a hammer. They hurt so bad, I couldn't move for two weeks. But I've recovered, and I can back you now."

Caratacus grinned. "I knew I could count on you, Fergus," Caratacus said.

* * *

When Caratacus returned home after convincing the other chieftains, he went to Havgan's home. The two sat on fur rugs across from one another around the center, earthen hearth.

"It happened as you said, Prince Caratacus," the Druid remarked. "There was a human sacrifice, and Ibor predicted Adminios would be king within the year."

Caratacus's chest tightened, heat rushed to his face. He hadn't realized the discovery would affect him so much. *Was I hoping that Fiona's tale was a lie—that a Druid would not violate a sacred oath of silence?* "How did you find out?" Caratacus finally asked.

Havgan gave him a diabolical smile. "I made discreet inquiries among the brethren, especially among the acolytes and novices. They are the most vulnerable, because they are still learning their craft."

"And?"

The Druid pursed his lips. "Despite their training, I found one who hates human sacrifice, no matter what the reason."

"Who is he?" Caratacus asked, his feelings a mixture of relief and surprise.

Havgan stepped to the entrance of his home and looked outside. Apparently satisfied, he returned and sat. "His name is Owen. When I was making queries, not directly, if you know what I mean, I mentioned about the rites practiced by our Druidic brothers in Gaul. I told him how the Romans slaughtered them because of the practice."

"So it bothered him."

"Indeed." Havgan scratched his trimmed beard. "Human sacrifice by the Gallic Druids upset him, but their murders by the Romans even more so. I mentioned that there was the possibility that one day the Romans might invade our lands. Owen started shaking, and I had to calm him. He fears we, too, will be murdered."

"He's right," Caratacus said. "What else?"

Havgan shook his head. "As much I assured him nothing would happen, Owen wept and blubbered about the human sacrifice he'd participated in in the forest near the village of Usk. As you had told me earlier, it was just like the girl, Fiona, described. They killed a young woman and her new born babe—a sacrilege." Havgan paused and took a deep breath. "Only someone of nobility who willingly volunteers is supposed to be sacrificed, and only in great time of danger or famine."

"I agree," Caratacus said.

"Owen was especially alarmed when Ibor proclaimed that Adminios would be king within a year. He was afraid Adminios would kill you and Tog."

The muscles in Caratacus's legs and arms tightened. *Traitor! Does he think by becoming king with the backing of*

*the Romans he will be allowed to rule without their
interference? He will be no more than a puppet, selling out
our people.* Caratacus exhaled several times before calming
himself.

"What is the matter, Prince?" Havgan asked.

"I have heard this story before. But for some reason,
when it is described by a Druid, who witnessed the killing,
it upsets me more. For me, the word of a Druid holds more
credibility than that of a peasant."

Havgan nodded. "You will find Owen a creditable
witness."

"Then he will testify against Ibor and Adminios?"

"He will, but I had to promise there would be no
reprisals against him."

Caratacus focused on the Druid's dark eyes. "You can
assure Owen there won't be. He is only an acolyte and had
no choice but to participate."

"I also promised the young man the Supreme Druid
Council on the Isle of Mona would also forgive him."

Caratacus nodded. "All right, now it's a matter of
waiting for Adminios to answer the king's summons. He
may have to send another command warning to either
show up or he'll be brought before him in chains."

Havgan jabbed a finger toward Caratacus. "It might be
better for all of us if he were brought here in shackles."

CHAPTER 32

The morning after Caratacus had returned from his journey to see the chieftains, he visited his father at his home. The main room of the longhouse was well lit by torches and pleasantly warmed by the central fire, where broth bubbled in a black cauldron and venison roasted on a spit, slowly turned by one of Cunobelinos's serving women.

The walls were fitted with ornate, Roman tapestries depicting hunting scenes. Near the embroidered pictures hung the king's spears, shields, and other weaponry.

Suspended from the thatched ceiling were bunches of herbs used for food and medicinal purposes. In the same area strips of venison, beef, and fish were also suspended so they could be preserved and gain flavor from the smoke and warmth drifting up from the hearth.

As usual, Ibor was present, sitting with them on a low stool by the fireside. The fluttering light gave the priest's cobwebbed face the vision of some craggy demon from the underworld, and his long, white tunic changed continually from light to dark like a specter in the moonlight. The Druid spent ever more time with the king as his mental condition deteriorated.

Caratacus glanced at his father. Cunobelinos's heavy furs covered his drooping shoulders. The skin was drawn over his gaunt face. Intermittently, he spat splotches of blood onto the hard-packed floor. He stared blankly as if into a void. Spittle dripped from the side of his slightly opened mouth.

Caratacus turned to Ibor, who slowly shook his head. His father's condition was growing worse. The last time he had seen him was eleven days earlier, before he left on his journey to visit the clan chieftains. *I must replace Da sooner than I planned.*

A servant girl brought the three cups of corma beer and handed one to Caratacus, Ibor, and the king.

Once she withdrew, Caratacus, knowing he could not speak his mind in front of the Druid, decided to create a ruse to throw Ibor off guard. He wasn't about to tell them it was Adminios who was in collusion with the Romans.

"We have heard that you visited the king's clan chieftains, Prince Caratacus," Ibor said. "Is that true?"

"Aye, to gather information."

Cunobelinos slowly lifted his head and seemed to focus on Caratacus. "Information? Journey?"

"Yes, Da, both."

The king turned to Ibor and back to Caratacus, his eyes staring into space.

"What information were you seeking?" Ibor asked.

"Although you told me in an earlier meeting that Porcius had tried to discourage Verica from scheming with the Romans, rumors persisted that he hasn't stopped."

"Why did you see the chieftains? Did you believe they might have received news that we had not?"

"That's what I needed to learn for myself. I spoke to them and they, too, had heard rumors." He didn't tell Ibor that he had sent spies to Verica's fortress at Caleva to follow up.

"Then you still don't know for certain if the rumors are true."

"No, not yet," Caratacus said. That part was true.

As Caratacus spoke, he noticed Cunobelinos's face brightened, more alert. The faraway look in his eyes seemed to be replaced by a knowing glow that he was aware of his surroundings. The king's mouth closed tight. *How long will he remain clear-minded this time?*

"Is that all?" Ibor asked.

"No, I sent a message to Unig, king of the Durotriges proposing an alliance."

Ibor gave Caratacus a withering look. "What? You did this without first getting the permission of the Council?"

"Unig you say?" Cunobelinos said.

"Yes, Da," Caratacus said.

"Why did you do this? You realize this could be considered an act of treason," Ibor said.

"If Verica is planning to attack us, an alliance with King Unig would give us the winning edge in any fight with Verica's army. In turn, we agree to help him defend his lands should the Romans invade." He glanced to Ibor, who glared back, and then to Cunobelinos, now alert. He coughed more spots of blood.

The prince twisted his fingers, realized what he was doing, and stopped. "The chieftains have agreed to ratify a proposal to be sent to Unig if approved by you, Da. This can be done at the same session when Adminios answers your summons."

Ibor gestured. "You still should have told the king beforehand. It is his decision to make such a proposal, not yours."

"You mean, *your* decision," Caratacus snarled. "I did ask Da, but his mind was clouded—he did not understand what I told him," Caratacus lied.

"I don't remember you telling me anything," Cunobelinos said.

"It was when I visited you the day before I left. I came to your home, don't you remember?" Caratacus asked.

"No." The old king shook his head.

Another lie. Caratacus depended on his father's failing memory to help him here.

Ibor's cruel mouth formed into a sneer and his bony hand touched the crescent-moon amulet that hung on a gold chain upon his chest, the symbol of his authority. "You still should have made me aware."

Caratacus gripped the hilt of his dagger hooked to his waistband. "I don't have to tell you everything, Druid."

Ibor jabbed a finger, resembling a claw, in his direction. "Be careful of what you say."

Caratacus sighed. *For now I should play the fool.* He released his grip, lowering his hand to his side as he viewed the priest. Then he studied his father.

"As arch-Druid, Ibor commands respect," Cunobelinos said in a strong voice.

"I mean no disrespect, Ibor," Caratacus finally answered turning his head toward the priest, "but I have the right to confide in my father and visit him when I want."

"You still should have consulted me," Ibor said. "If you believed this was a matter of grave urgency."

Caratacus raised a hand in disgust. "There wasn't time! Now, I suggest you send out messengers and tell them to be here in five days time. Adminios has already received the king's command to appear."

"So far he has not," the king said.

"Then I suggest you send another messenger ordering him to appear, Da."

"Indeed," the king said. "And I will include a warning. If he fails this time to answer our summon, I will send an army to bring him back in chains."

"Wisely said, Da. It's his kingdom where the Romans are most likely to land."

Ibor shook his head. "I'm not fully convinced they will invade."

"Nevertheless," Cunobelinos interjected, "we cannot take the risk." He looked at Caratacus. "We will do as you advise, Son."

Tight lipped, Ibor stared at Cunobelinos and back to Caratacus. "I believe you are making a grave mistake."

It is you who has made the grave mistake, Druid. I will see that you pay for it.

* * *

On the sixth morning, the day of the special Council assembly, Clud, Donn, Havgan, and Tog arrived at Caratacus's home for a meeting of their own. They journeyed separately to avoid suspicion. The prince lived outside the fortress, his holdings on the plain near the edge of the forest. A small, circular, defensive bank and wooden palisade enclosed the home. The inner yard near the house contained several structures including lean-to-sheds for stables and dens where his blacksmith and other craftsmen worked. Three oval, thatch-roofed buildings for storage and quarters for servants and warriors, when he required their services, straddled the base of the fence.

Most of the Council members had arrived earlier the same morning for the session, which was expected to start at noon in the Great Hall. Caratacus wondered if despite Fergus ap Roycal's assurances to keep the members in line, word had leaked out?

Ornately carved timber pillars held up the roof and circled the room. Several small torches, ensconced on the columns, radiated a guttering light, casting wavering shadows, leaving the outer margins of the room in darkness. The firelight from the enclosed hearth glowed red on a stream of smoke that coiled sinuously toward the ceiling hidden in the darkness above. The group huddled about the central hearth, warming themselves, drinking mead.

Tog peeked through the door cover outside one more time before the meeting began. Caratacus couldn't take a chance that Ibor had spies hidden in bushes at the forest's edge, watching his place. Tog shook his head.

Near one side of the entrance huddled three servant women by the domed oven, built into clay walls framing the lower part of the house. Jutting from the wall above the baking area hung a square, oak plank that deflected the heat and smoke toward the roof where it was absorbed in the thatch covering. To the other side of the opening stood a tall loom.

Dana touched the side of her wiry auburn hair and pulled on the gold, strand earrings, each with which formed the gold images of arching dolphins. Her long, fingered hands dropped to her sides, and she smoothed her fringed, bright-blue, and silver-striped tunic. When she saw Caratacus staring at her, she stopped and gave him a tight-lipped smile.

Rhian turned toward the entrance and back to the others. The twin gold necklaces around her neck and the two around her wrists tinkled. Her flaxen hair, twisted into a long braid, dropped to the small of her back. A paste made from the herb ruan reddened her cheeks. She furrowed her eyebrows, darkened with berry juice, and scratched the tip of her nose. Rhian wore a long tunic covered by a red and gold, checkered cloak with little bells sowed into the fringe that draped her tall frame. The garb reminded Caratacus of one she wore years ago when she encountered him in the corral the morning after he won the race during the festival of Lughnasa.

Donn huffed loudly while Clud and Tog rubbed their hands together in front of the fire. Havgan, clothed in the long, white, ceremonial tunic of his office, staff in hand, stood near Caratacus, sober faced.

The prince nodded to everyone, and they all looked in his direction. He stood in front of a series of wooden chests, bound in leather, used for the storage of clothing and valuables. "Now that everyone is here," Caratacus said, "it's time to go over plans one last time."

Caratacus faced Havgan. "Is Owen ready to testify?"

"He is," Havgan answered.

"What has Ibor been doing since he was told about a possible alliance with the Durotrigians?" Caratacus asked.

Havgan pinched his eyebrows together and tightened his lips. "As we all know, he does not like it. He has not said a word, but I'm certain he has sent a messenger to the arch-Druid of the Durotrigians to verify the matter."

A mischievous grin formed on Caratacus's lips. "He'll be surprised to learn I sent word proposing an alliance before we left to see the chieftains."

"So you really want to ally with the Durotrigians?" Rhian asked.

"Absolutely," Caratacus replied. "If Adminios is in league with the Romans, we will need all the allies we can muster."

Tog grunted. "We should kill Adminios instead of exiling him."

"I agree," Caratacus said. "But it isn't our tribe's way— exile is worse than death—a man without his tribe accounts for nothing. No other nation will accept him."

"Except as a mercenary," Donn added.

"The Romans will use him," Rhian said.

Caratacus wiped the palm of his hand along the right side of his breeches. "You're right, but only for their own evil purposes. In any event, we have to raise an army and defend our lands against their invasion."

"Aye, it would be in the Durotrigian king's interest, too," Clud said.

"What about yer father?" Donn asked. "Will he be having his wits about him when the council meets? If not, the session could be voided by the High Council. Ibor could declare it closed."

"When the session opens, Ibor will speak for Da," Caratacus said. "Ibor is unaware of my plan to replace both him and Da."

Caratacus thought for a few moments and looked from person to person, all of them waiting for him to speak. "You remember Da's condition when we saw him at dinner three nights ago?" Caratacus, along with Dana, Rhian, Tog, and his wife had dined with the king that evening in order to further ascertain his deteriorating condition.

The three nodded.

"He looked so poorly," Dana said. "He was alert one moment and in a daze the next."

"Your father is hopeless, Caratacus," Rhian said.

"He's like an empty eggshell," Tog added.

"I agree. The time has come for him to step down." Caratacus motioned to the men. "When we are finished here, Tog, Clud, Donn, and I will ride to the fortress and meet privately with the chieftains who will support me. Once everyone is present in the Great Hall, we will open the meeting with a discussion of the proposed alliance. Knowing Adminios, he will be impatient to get on with the matter and will probably go along with it."

Clud snorted then frowned. "If he shows up."

"I think he will," Caratacus said. "Once Adminios agrees, I will call upon Fergus ap Roycal to declare Da incompetent and ask the Council to vote him out as ruler."

Tog spat. "Knowing that Adminios and Ibor will object."

"Let them—the vote of the Council is final." Caratacus turned toward Havgan. "Even the Druids can't overturn their decision. Then Fergus will nominate me as king and the Council will declare me as such."

"Adminios will challenge ye—be ready fer a fight," Donn said. His hand gripped the hilt of his sword.

Caratacus waved his hand about the room. "Let him. I'm placing our warriors at strategic locations around the hall."

"But Adminios's men will be there, too," Tog said.

"My warriors will be in position before he arrives," Caratacus said. "And so will Da's retainers—they have pledged their swords to me. Our men will far outnumber Adminios's bodyguards."

Dana turned toward Caratacus. "Wouldn't it be better to wait until you have accused Adminios of conspiring with the Romans?" she asked. "Then it would make more sense when the Council declared your father incompetent and yourself king."

Caratacus remembered how politically astute Dana had been during the welcoming feast after he and his army had arrived in Eburacum to fight the Caledonians. *Although she would deny it, Dana, like her sister, Cartimandua, has an eye for political intrigue.*

Finally, he answered. "As long as Ibor speaks for Da until we level charges of Adminios conspiring with the Romans, it might work. Once that is done, then we can charge Ibor of unlawful sacrifice and conspiring with Adminios and the Romans."

"Then will you make your move?" Clud asked.

Caratacus nodded. "I will charge Adminios with treason."

"Which he will deny," Dana said.

Caratacus balled one hand into a fist and smacked the palm of his other hand. "Let him! He'll choke on his own lies!"

CHAPTER 33

Caratacus and Tog stood about four paces ahead of Clud, Donn, the captain of Cunobelinos's retainers, and six guards as they waited in front of the Great Hall.

Adminios and his entourage rode across the muddy ground toward them, passing several storage buildings and cattle pens. Three days earlier, Caratacus had learned from Ibor that Cunobelinos received word from Adminios. He would arrive within four days in answer to the king's summons. In turn, Ibor sent word to all the king's councilors to be present when Adminios arrived.

The noon sky was a cobalt blue, the freezing sun sitting as if in judgment of its subjects above Adminios's retinue. Adminios and his men were bundled up in heavy, woolen cloaks that fell to the knees, similar to those worn by Caratacus and Tog. Patches of smoke from the village's homes drifted in the air mixing with the pungent odor of dung from the livestock pens.

Besides his fur coat, Adminios wore a vested tunic of costly silk and tartan, woolen trousers. Apart from his long mustache, which proclaimed nobility, he was clean shaven. As a further sign of status, a gold torc circled his neck. A bronze broach fastened a cloak of fine wool to his right shoulder. A golden, sun-wheel medallion hung down the front of his chest over a shirt of iron-ringed mail covering his tunic. Gold bracelets jangled around his wrist, and a bejeweled longsword hung from the right side at his waist.

A protective formation of mounted warriors, similarly attired but plainer, now in muddy clothing, rode on both sides of him and at his back. His retainers wore bronze helmets and carried thrusting spears, symbolizing status as free men.

Despite the cold, the shivering populace flocked to the area outside the moat that surrounded the king's holdings to view the riders.

Tog pulled on his drooping moustache and farted. "So our dear brother decided to *bless* us with his presence after all."

Caratacus smirked. "Obviously the threat of being brought to Camulodunum in chains didn't set well with him."

"I'm surprised the fool didn't put up a fight, he has an army behind him," Tog said. He spat.

"Fishermen and farmers are poor warriors. Only his retainers are real warriors." Caratacus grimaced. "Most likely his advisors told him to come here peacefully. They probably figure he's going to become the next king of these lands anyway."

Tog's mouth twisted into a crooked frown. He turned about, nodded to Clud and Donn, then back to Caratacus. He whispered, "The Council better back you on this one. I want to see the look on his ugly face when he's charged with treason."

"So do I." Despite assurances by the chieftains, Caratacus was still guarded about the chances of the Council expelling Adminios and Ibor from the kingdom.

"That messenger of yours better be telling the truth," Tog said, pulling Caratacus from his thoughts.

"If you mean about the Romans gathering on the Gallic Coast, he is," Caratacus said. A messenger arrived at his home earlier this morning warning him of the forces building up along the shoreline of Gaul for a possible invasion.

"We'll see if the mad Emperor Caligula will actually cross the channel," Caratacus said.

Tog scratched his stubbled chin and pulled on his drooping moustache again. "You'll gather the army when this mess with Adminios is finished, won't you?"

"I will, but first, let's get through today."

Adminios passed through the crowd and drew up before the Great Hall. He dismounted from a sweaty and mud-spattered horse, whose harness was richly decorated with small, bronze plaques representing human heads. His arch-Druid, who had ridden at the back of the column of warriors, pulled up beside Adminios, slipped off his horse, and walked at his side. They approached Caratacus and Tog.

The lips of Adminios's flushed face twisted in hate. Even from several feet away, his breath reeked of strong wine. Probably Roman, Caratacus thought.

Adminios crossed his arms over his chest. His watery eyes scowled under black, beetle brows. He slurred, "Why are you here and not the king to greet me?"

"You dare order our father, your king, to wait for you out in the cold when you are late?" Caratacus answered, his voice full of contempt.

Adminios belched, dropped hands to his sides, and shook his head like a wet dog. "I am a king, too, he should greet me."

Tog gestured toward the hall. "Our father is the *high king* and grovels before no one! He has commanded you to appear before him at once so the Council session can get under way."

Out of the corner of his eye, Caratacus noticed Clud and Donn nodding heads as they grabbed the hilt of their swords.

"My men and I are hungry and thirsty—"

Caratacus cut off Adminios. "You can eat later!" Caratacus motioned to the captain of Cunobelinos's retainers and back to his older brother. "Follow him, he'll show you where to stand near Da."

"I don't need his lackey to lead me, I know my way." Adminios turned and staggered through the entrance, followed by his arch-Druid and warriors.

Caratacus nodded toward the captain, who entered the adjacent side door. Earlier, Caratacus had given him instructions to alert his and the king's men, who were guarding the interior, once Adminios had arrived.

The older brother and his retinue walked into the huge meeting room with its lofty interior.

Caratacus and Tog waited until Adminios and his party had entered before following them inside.

Smoke spiraled upward from the center hearth and seeped through the closely packed, thatch roof. Thicker than a man's thigh and soaring up nearly five times a warrior's height, pillars supported the heavy, roof beams.

Tapestries with elaborately worked designs hung on the walls. Smells of unwashed bodies permeated the room.

Knee-high, wicker screen dividers, spaced far apart at the hall's back, narrowed into a "V" shape. They were like spokes of a wheel funneling to a hub, the center being the fire pit, which circled the hall. A member of the High Council, a clan chieftain, and his retinue occupied each section with Fergus ap Roycal and his people in the section closest to the king.

Cunobelinos sat in his Roman curule chair upon a low, wooden dais several feet above the floor, Ibor at his side. Behind him and on both sides of the dais were four of his armed retainers. Caratacus and Tog stood in front of their father between one set of dividers with Clud, Donn, and a dozen warriors, who had entered earlier. Adminios and his group gathered in the section to the left.

Although Caratacus had persuaded the chieftains of the council to back him, he still had reservations they might change their minds. *I pray the gods they are still behind me. They could lose their collective nerve.*

Dressed in his ceremonial long, white tunic with a gold, quarter-moon disk, a symbol of his authority, hanging down on the chest, Arch-Druid Ibor stepped forward. In the pulsating torch light, he formally opened the session. "In the name of our high king, Cunobelinos, I welcome all who are present for the king's session. In the name of the gods, whom I dare not mention. In the name of Camulos the sacred god who watches over his namesake, our fortress Camulodunum, may the decisions rendered on issues brought before the Council today be just and wise. This session is now open."

Caratacus stepped one pace toward the king. He spoke to the Council regarding the proposed alliance with the Durotrigians and its importance to Cunobelinos and Adminios's kingdoms.

A murmur rumbled through the clan groups behind him.

"If Verica is scheming with the Romans to invade our lands," Caratacus continued, "then we need all the allies we can muster." He paused and glanced at Adminios and back to the council. "The Durotrigians, like the Cantiaci, are primarily a seafaring people. They have few warriors compared to most of the southern tribes and would face the brunt of any invasion by the Romans. We must defend ourselves by defending them."

Adminios hiccupped and snorted. "Where did you get this information? I've received no word."

"We have," Cunobelinos said in a lucid moment. The chieftains turned in his direction as if surprised. The old king raised a hand and gestured toward Adminios. "Your brother doesn't lie."

With a slight bow, Caratacus acknowledged his father and focused on Adminios. "Your kingdom is directly in their path, Brother. I urge you to agree to the alliance so we can send representatives to the Durotrigians to finalize the plan."

Adminios leveled his bloodshot eyes in a fixed stare on Caratacus. "Then why haven't I heard anything?"

"Haven't you?" Caratacus challenged. "Either your spies are inept or they are lying to you."

"The fact remains," Fergus ap Roycal spoke as he eyed Adminios, "we need your agreement to the proposal. We must defend all our kingdoms."

Ten of the twelve chieftains voiced their agreement. Only gap-toothed Cador and broken-nosed Melwas disagreed. Their protestations were overridden by the councilors. A loud murmur of concurrence erupted throughout the crowded hall.

Adminios huffed, and his mouth crimped in annoyance. "All right, I'll agree to it, but I still believe it's a waste of time—there won't be any invasion."

"Don't be so sure," Fergus ap Roycal said with an edge of impatience in his voice.

"Then the majority are in agreement?" Cunobelinos asked in a weak voice. He squirmed in his chair, his head drooped, eyes going blank.

"Aye!" the members of the High Council shouted in agreement.

Caratacus and Fergus ap Roycal turned their heads in the direction of the High King. Caratacus glanced sidelong at Fergus ap Roycal and caught a knowing look. *We have to move fast if we are to take Adminios by surprise.* He nodded to the chieftains on his right as Fergus did the same to the leaders on his left.

"Now, can I leave and get something to eat and drink?" Adminios belched again and turned in the direction of the hall's main entrance.

"There is another matter that the High Council must address before we adjourn," Caratacus said.

Ibor raised an eyebrow and looked to Cunobelinos. "My King, do you know what he is talking about?"

"I do." Cunobelinos's eyes brightened and he gestured with a veiny hand to Caratacus. "Proceed."

This is it. Now. Caratacus's heart hammered and seemed to rise into his throat at the same time his stomach tightened. Outwardly, he showed no sign of fear. He faced Adminios across the wicker divider, narrowed his eyes, raised his arm, and pointed. "Adminios, King of the Cantiaci, and Son of High King Cunobelinos, I hereby accuse you of treason."

A gasp erupted throughout the chamber.

Adminios flinched, his face and body turned rigid.

"You conspired with the Romans to invade the lands of southern Britannia," Caratacus continued, "and planned to overthrow the high king. What say you to these charges?"

A sharp intake of breath rippled among the throng. "Traitor!" came shouts from behind Caratacus.

Caratacus glanced about seeing many faces turning hard with anger. They raised their fists. But his father's hands trembled, his eyes glazed over, and his face resembled a blank page.

Caratacus swallowed and turned to Adminios. "Let him speak."

For a moment, Adminios remained speechless. A scorching look crossed his reddening face before he apparently regained his senses. "Who are those who accuse me of dealing with the Romans?"

Adminios's party murmured words of support.

"Besides myself, I have several witnesses," Caratacus answered and lowered his arm to his side.

The king's councilors looked at one another. Their supporters spoke among themselves. One of them waved a hand airily. "Bring on your witnesses!"

"You lie—they lie!" Adminios shouted in a clear voice, as if sobered by the accusations.

"Do I? Do my witnesses lie? I think not." Caratacus gestured to the members of the Council and then the meeting place entrance. "Even as I speak, the Romans are moving three legions from the River Rhenus in Germania to Gasoricum on the Gallic Coast."

A roar flashed through the hall like a thunderclap. "Invasion!" someone cried out. "Then we fight!" More shouts of support followed.

A space of about twenty heartbeats passed before the noise in the room subsided.

Adminios shook his head. "What invasion? I know nothing of this."

"Now who is lying?" Caratacus said. In a slow, deliberate voice he continued, "Your kingdom is on the coast, and my messenger rode in this morning with the news."

Adminios's eyes searched the room. He seemed to focus on one of his retainers.

Caratacus caught the look and motioned to the king's men. Two of them rushed toward Adminios's man and grabbed him before he could resist.

Several of Adminios's supporters moved towards Caratacus's guards.

Caratacus raised his hand in his older brother's direction. "Call off your dogs, Adminios. My warriors and those of the high king outnumber yours. They won't hesitate to kill yours if they take one more step."

"Stop!" Adminios roared. Once his men returned to their positions behind him, he turned to Caratacus. "Your charges are lies! I would never betray our people."

Caratacus barely controlled his rage. "We know the Emperor Caligula is with the Roman Army at Gasoricum on the Gallic Coast. You didn't warn us. Why?"

Adminios curled his mouth into a sneer. "As king of the Cantiaci I don't have to answer your questions."

As his face came alive once again, eyes alert, Cunobelinos said in a low growl, "You *will* answer your brother's questions, Adminios." He raised a hand, curling it into a fist, then lowered it into his lap. "As your king and father who placed you on the Cantiaci throne, I order it."

Surprised, the vast majority in the hall murmured the king sounded like his old self. They shouted their support for Cunobelinos.

Adminios licked his lips and gulped. "My people told me nothing of this."

"Oh, you mean to say that Porcius, who has been seen at your court, didn't say a word?" Caratacus asked in a scathing tone.

"The Roman pig said nothing about an invasion," Adminios answered.

"Rubbish! You are planning an invasion of our lands with the Romans," Caratacus said. He twisted his head about, eyes raking the room, locking eyes with one member of the Council at a time, then back to Adminios. "My spies followed one of the Romans seen at your court across the channel through Gaul to the legion camp on the River Rhenus where Roman troops were gathering. Then they shadowed him and two cohorts, advance forces, back to Gasoricum. Soon afterwards, three legions arrived at the same place. Now they are building landing barges for invasion—you deny this?"

"Porcius left my court and traveled to Verica's lands—he said nothing before leaving about Romans crossing the channel," Adminios answered through clenched teeth. "Roman merchants come to my court all the time asking for trading agreements. I didn't conspire with any Roman to invade our lands."

"It happens that two of my men, dressed as traders, were in your court when you sent the Roman away, the one they followed to Gaul and Germania." Caratacus turned toward the entrance and back to Adminios. "They are now waiting outside and will testify as to what they observed. Shall I bring them in to bear witness?"

"I know many of your warriors on sight, your spies wouldn't have fooled me," Adminios said.

A knowing grin formed on Caratacus's lips. "Not these, I recruited them after you became king. These men come from the north, the land of the Brigantes, where my consort, Dana, is from. Once I call them forth, you will recognize them as traders that were in your court."

A ripple of low cries went through the room. "Bring in the witnesses!"

His eyes full of contempt, Adminios searched the hall, his features cloaked in defiance.

"However, before I call the witnesses," Caratacus said, "I have something to show you, Brother. I'm sure you'll recognize it." He pulled from a leather pouch hanging from his waistband the silver, three-headed horse amulet. He turned to the members of the High Council and held it up so they could view it. Then he turned back to Adminios. "This was given to you by Da, do you deny it?"

Adminios froze as he stared at the object. "It's mine, but ... but it was stolen from me."

From the back of the room someone said loudly, "If it were stolen, then my mum is a virgin."

A roar of laughter shook the building.

Adminios's nostrils flared, and he puckered his brows.

Caratacus smiled before he sobered and asked, "When was it stolen?"

Adminios glanced to his retainers who stood about the hall. They were outnumbered by the king's, Caratacus's, and Tog's warriors.

Caratacus turned around and spotted Donn, his father-in-law, who stood quietly behind Caratacus with Tog and Clud. The veteran warrior narrowed his eyes as he placed a calloused hand on the hilt of his sword.

Adminios glanced to his Druid advisor, who nodded, and to Ibor, who hovered by the king. Then back to Caratacus.

"I repeat," Caratacus said. "When and where did you lose the amulet?"

"Tell him!" Cunobelinos growled.

"I don't remember," Adminios answered, his voice little more than a whimper.

"Why didn't you tell Da?"

Adminios jutted his chin forward. "Why should I? I'm a grown man, I don't have to tell him anything. Besides, I sent my men out to search, they didn't find a trace."

"You said you didn't remember when or where it happened."

Adminios's mouth quivered. "That's right. What does this have to do with the charges against me?"

"You witnessed an act of human sacrifice and placed a curse on me that included my murder," Caratacus accused.

A loud gasp echoed through the meeting place followed by cries of, "Traitor!"

"That's a lie!" Adminios shouted. He looked about and toward his retainers for support.

Caratacus turned to Ibor. "He aided you. This Druid is known for his Roman sympathies."

Another eruption of voices in the hall mixed with shouts of, "Blasphemy!"

"How dare you accuse me of such a lie?" Ibor protested. He looked to Cunobelinos. "I hate the Romans, they killed my fellow Druids in Gaul."

"It's common knowledge that you're taking bribes from the Roman, Porcius," Caratacus said.

"Where is your proof?" Ibor motioned about him with a hand. "Bring forth your witnesses to the sacrifice and the false charges of bribery at once!"

"The proof is in my discovery of the amulet that belongs to Adminios. It was buried with the bones of a decapitated body of a woman and her baby. I have witnesses to the discovery." He motioned to Tog, Clud, Rhian, Dana, and his warriors. "One of your own acolytes, Owen, has offered to testify against you."

A terrible silence enveloped the room. Ibor twisted his head about as if seeking support for his acts. Eyes filled with contempt stared back at him. For the space of a few heartbeats, he bowed his head before raising it again. He faced Caratacus. "You need not bring forth your witness," Ibor growled. "I will not lie about my involvement with your son, Adminios." He pressed his lips together and bowed his head as if in resignation. "I did perform human sacrifice on his behalf."

A murmur went through the audience in the Great Hall.

"You lie!" Adminios shouted. He looked about the room. "Ibor lies." Adminios's voice weakened.

Ibor raised his head, his eyes focused on Adminios. "Do I? I have been working with Porcius and the Romans. I promised them Adminios would be king of these lands."

"My spies learned the same thing," Caratacus said. "You were negotiating a favorable trading agreement for Adminios and the Romans."

Cunobelinos turned and glared at Ibor. "You admit you are negotiating behind our back?" Ibor nodded.

"You were my trusted advisor and friend. Why did you do this?" Cunobelinos asked, his voice filled with disappointment. "Any dealings by Adminios for the Cantiaci are to be tied directly to us, the Catuvellaunii and the Trinovantes, as part of our federation of tribes."

"Because ... because not only would the agreement be favorable to the Romans, but I ... I would benefit."

"Traitor!" Caratacus accused. "You would sell out our people for Roman gold. You are a disgrace to the people of this land and the Druids."

"Disgrace! Disgrace!" echoed through the hall.

Havgan stepped forward from behind Caratacus. He raised his hand and silence descended on the gathering. He turned to Ibor. "Why are you admitting to these charges now?"

Ibor's face clouded. "I can no longer lie. I am old and tired of all this court intrigue."

"You realize the penalty is banishment?" Havgan asked.

"I know, and I will leave Camulodunum as soon as this meeting ends and journey to the Druid center of learning on the Isle of Mona."

"Your wait ends now," Cunobelinos announced. "I hereby banish you from our lands for all time. What the Supreme Druid Council does to you on the Isle of Mona is their business. Get out of my sight!"

The king focused his eyes on Adminios. "My Son, you have brought shame and disgrace to our family and our people. You are no longer fit to be king. I hereby banish you from our lands as well. You are now a man without a tribe and family. Be fortunate we have not sentenced you to death."

Adminios shook his head. "How could you do this to me, Da? You know exile is worse than any death!"

"You deserve the worst, my Son. Your betrayal of the people—your betrayal of me has broken my heart. Now, leave us!" Cunobelinos's eyes glazed over, a blank stare crossed his face.

The king's men roughly grabbed Adminios, and as they were dragging him from the hall, he turned his head and shouted at Caratacus, "This isn't over. I swear by the gods I dare not name, one day I will use your skull for a drinking cup. This kingdom will be mine!"

CHAPTER 34

The day following Adminios's banishment, Caratacus led a band of loyal warriors to Durovernum, capital of the Cantiaci. Word ran ahead that he had expelled his older brother from the kingdom. When Caratacus arrived at the hill fort, he met little resistance from warriors originally pledged to Adminios. Quickly, they swore allegiance to Caratacus's service when he declared himself king of the Cantiaci.

A week later, when Caratacus returned to Camulodunum, he held a council meeting with fellow chieftains, including Fergus ap Roycal and Havgan, now arch-Druid. They voted unanimously to declare Caratacus king.

* * *

Overnight, the last snow of winter fell: clean, white, and powdery. A frozen noonday sun followed Caratacus, accompanied by Clud, Tog, Donn, Fergus ap Roycal, and nine other loyal chieftains and warriors as they rode toward his father's home.

Not only had the fresh snow covered the roofs of Camulodunum's hovels, shops, and muddy streets, but also its fetid stench, making it almost livable.

The entourage found the palisade wall surrounding Cunobelinos's compound and house ringed by warriors clothed in heavy furs. Unsheathing their longswords, they silently challenged Caratacus's approach.

"Stand aside for your new king," Tog ordered as steaming breath huffed from his mouth. They crossed the short causeway and halted before the tall, bronze-plated gate. All eyes turned to Caratacus.

"Don't waste your lives. My father is no longer ruler," Caratacus said to Cunobelinos's guards.

The grizzled officer in charge stepped forward through the entrance. "By whose authority have you been made king?" he challenged.

"By the High Council," came the reply from the hawk-nosed, senior clan chieftain, Fergus ap Roycal, who sat high on his mount next to Caratacus. "He was lawfully voted and elected as custom dictates. Now step aside before I take your ugly, fucking head!"

The captain recognized the chieftains accompanying the new king. "We have no quarrel with the son of Cunobelinos," he said gravely. He glanced to the troops on the timbered wall, motioned with his head, and raised his sword in allegiance.

"Hail, King Caratacus, Son of Cunobelinos!" he roared. The warriors echoed his words.

Caratacus entered his father's home alone. In the dim light, he saw Cunobelinos huddled next to the big, open hearth, bundled in fetid-smelling wolf skins. His pallid face had assumed the texture of thin onionskin. Tiny blue and red capillaries fanned across his face like streams of a river delta, and his deep, sunken eyes seemed fixated on the glowing fire. Not long ago, he was still a wolf of a man. *It's as if Da had offended the gods, and now they are punishing him for his transgressions.* He could think of no other reason for his father's rapid aging.

The old king didn't hear his son approaching. "Da, it's me," Caratacus called.

"Who?" The old king rolled slowly in his furs and stared at his son without recognition.

"Do you know me?" Caratacus asked.

Cunobelinos winced. His mouth moved silently. He brought a trembling hand to his mouth and looked about. "I ... know you ... young man. I've seen you before ... haven't I?" He drew his index finger from his mouth and pointed, spittle spider-webbing from it. He dropped his hand to the side and stared at the fire. Forgetting the question entirely, he reinserted his finger to massage his gums.

For the space of four heartbeats, Caratacus hesitated. "Da ... it's time you abdicated."

"Abdicate what? Go away!"

303

"You're no longer fit to be king."

"King? Yes ... that's it ... I'm going to be king now that Tasciovanos ... you know him?"

Caratacus nodded. He was Cunobelinos's father.

"He's dead ... my father's dead," the old king said as his voice quivered and trailed away.

Although hopeless, Caratacus continued. "I'm the new king, Da, the rightful heir to the throne. I have the backing of the Tribal Council, and Druids. Adminios is out!"

Cunobelinos stared blankly at Caratacus, spittle dribbled down the sides of his mouth. "You say you're who?"

"I'm sorry, but you're too old and feebleminded to rule." Caratacus shook his head. *I'd rather die in battle than to end my days like Da.*

"Havgan, come here," Caratacus barked in the direction of the entryway where the Druid hovered.

"Yes, Great King?"

Caratacus turned his head toward Cunobelinos. "See that arrangements are made for my father to live what remains of his life quietly. He is to be given the honor due a great king."

Caratacus and his retinue returned to the Great Hall.

A short time later, Havgan, who had replaced Ibor as arch-Druid, appeared at the meeting place, followed by lesser Druids and acolytes.

"Is he settled?" Caratacus asked from the throne in which he now sat. The council members who stood below him turned their eyes on the priest.

The chieftains opened a passageway for Havgan, who came before Caratacus. "He is, High King. Your father is sleeping soundly in your old quarters."

Caratacus scanned the chamber, his eyes momentarily focusing on each of the nine councilmen, who in turn nodded. Satisfied, he spoke. "Very well, there remains one more step to make it official. You know what that is."

Havgan glided to the bejeweled, bronze, ceremonial shield hanging on the wall near the throne. He unhooked the leather holding straps and brought it to Caratacus. "As chief Druid and lawgiver," he solemnly announced, "I now transfer this shield, lawful symbol of your authority, into your possession and proclaim you King of the Catuvellaunian, Trinovantes, and Cantiacian people. Rule well, my King, and may all the gods, whom I dare not mention, watch over you."

Caratacus motioned for Tog, Clud, Donn, Fergus ap Roycal, and the rest of his chieftains to approach. "My father agrees that I am to be king," he proclaimed loudly. "Now we must deploy the army. Soon the Romans will invade our lands."

* * *

It was late afternoon, the sky a sunless gray, an icy breeze swept off the blue-black waters of the British Channel and stung Caratacus's face like a whip. His eyes watered, and he rubbed them with the back of his hand. He pulled his cloak tighter about his shoulders. From his mount, he peered down the enormous folds within the white cliffs of Dubris toward the stony beach nearly two hundred feet below. The sea raced landward and exploded against the shore in a cascade of towering foam, hissing so loud that it echoed in Caratacus's ears. Squawking, squealing seagulls skimmed the surface while curlews scurried along the water's edge dodging the incoming waves. Not far away, the tiny port of Dubris sat within an inlet.

Caratacus raised his head, eyes gliding across the rising swells toward the distant coast of Gaul shrouded in a foggy haze. He turned to his entourage, including Tog, Clud, Donn, and thirty escorting retainers, hovering behind him on their mounts. One of the warriors carried the king's pennant, a scarlet flag with the image of a wolf embroidered in gold, snapping in the wind from the top of a hardwood pole. All his men had hunkered down in their saddles. They braced themselves against the blustery currents that roiled up the cliff's edge to the chalky plateau where they gathered behind the king.

From the back of his gelding, Tog raised an eyebrow as if asking a question. Caratacus shook his head and faced the channel once more. *I know you maggoty Romans are out there. When will you cross? I dare you to fight us!*

After Caratacus had been proclaimed king, he set about planning and organizing defenses for the impending

Roman invasion. He ordered the chieftains of the King's Council to return to their holdings and raise levies for the army. Within ten days, he started deploying warriors along the coast, primarily along the Tamesis and the River Medway estuaries, near the ports of Rutupiae, and Dubris, which faced Gaul across the channel. Although not certain this was where the Romans intended on landing their forces, his spies had learned these were the most likely places.

Yet it puzzled Caratacus why the Romans would attempt an invasion in the early spring. The frequent storms that swept the channel this time of year were a recipe for disaster. He pictured hundreds of transport ships filled with hundreds of legionaries sinking or crashing on Britannia's rocky shoreline. His warriors would slaughter any survivors who managed to come ashore. How he would enjoy that. Then again, why wouldn't he expect Emperor Caligula to order his troops to cross in such rotten weather? Caratacus had received reports that Caligula had made his favorite horse, Incitatus, a consul of Rome, second only in power to himself. The emperor also lived in habitual incest with his three sisters and prostituted them out to his closest friends. Disgusting. He also made a public spectacle of himself by dancing on stage with low-life entertainers. Caratacus shook his head and concluded that Caligula had truly lost his mind. However, Caratacus refused the risk of remaining unprepared.

Thirty thousand warriors had been gathered from the tribal lands. Another twenty-five thousand from the southern tribes, including the Durotrigians, were expected to arrive within a matter of another ten to twenty days. Would they be in time to fight the invaders? And how long would they stay? It was early spring, and food supplies stored for the winter ran low throughout the land. If the Romans did not come soon, so his forces could destroy them on the beaches, food stuffs would be exhausted. His allies would abandon him and return home to plant their crops.

The sounds of fast-approaching hoof beats pulled Caratacus out of his thoughts. He twisted about as a scar-faced rider halted before his brother. "I have news for the king," the warrior said.

Caratacus motioned the rider to his side. "What is it?" Caratacus growled, annoyed at being disturbed.

Smelling of horse sweat, his face and clothing splattered in mud, the messenger hesitated for the space of a heartbeat.

"Report!" Caratacus ordered, "I don't have all day."

"Yes, Sire. Your wife, the Lady Dana, had a miscarriage, the baby died."

Caratacus jolted. For a split second he closed his eyes. His breath whistled through his nostrils. He clenched his fists, the knuckles turned white. *No, not Dana! This can't be happening. Will I never have a child that lives? Gods! Calm yourself! You must not show weakness of any kind.* Caratacus opened his eyes, took a deep breath, and allowed the tension to drain from his body.

The warrior stared at him.

Caratacus motioned with his head. "Go on, man."

He scratched his broken nose and continued, "The lady will recover, Sire. The midwife says she has a fever, but that's to be expected."

"How long ago did she lose the baby?" Dana had been with child for nearly five months.

The messenger glanced in the direction of the white ball of a sun that attempted to pierce the gray sky, and to Caratacus. "About three days ago. I've ridden all day and into the night for the last couple of days and stopped only when it got too dark. Nearly killed four horses to get here fast as I could."

Caratacus huffed. "Do you know if the child was a boy or girl?"

"Don't know, Sire, the midwife didn't say. The Lady Rhian, who was with her, told me to ride to your camp immediately."

"Very well." Caratacus waved the rider away. He motioned for Tog, Clud, and Donn to join him.

He told them the news, and the three in turn gave him their condolences.

"Tomorrow morning," Caratacus said, "I'm returning to Camulodunum too see my wife."

His companions looked at one another, apparently startled and perhaps curious about his decision.

"There are those who would see my leaving now as a sign of weakness. It is the king's duty to stay with his men in time of war." He narrowed his eyes and stared first at Tog, then Clud and Donn. He grasped the handle of his dagger. "Any one of you feel that way?"

Tog shook his head. "No, Brother, we know you better than that."

"Aye, if'n anybody says differently, I'll slice off his bloody head," Donn said. He grabbed the hilt of his sword.

Clud looked toward the channel. "Don't think you're going to be bothered with what anybody thinks, leastways not for awhile. Storm's a brewin' out there."

Caratacus and the rest turned to the channel looking toward the southwest. A wall of ugly, black clouds were moving quickly their way. Swells, now rising to the height of a tall man topped by large, foaming whitecaps, rushed toward the beach.

"In this case, the weather has become our ally," Caratacus said. He turned to Tog. "I'm placing you in command of the army while I am away."

Tog grinned. "You can count on me, Brother, I'll make damn sure things run smoothly while you're gone."

"I know you will," Caratacus said. He raised a hand toward his father-in-law. "Donn, you will be Tog's second-in-command."

"I be honored. Ye couldn't pick a better man fer the job than yer brother," Donn said.

"We're still expecting more warriors to arrive," Clud said, "what about their deployment?"

"I'll take care of that," Tog said, "we've been over plans about it already."

"That's right," Caratacus said, "but we'll discuss it further tonight."

Caratacus motioned to Clud with his head. "You'll come with me along with an escort of my warriors."

"Right," Clud answered.

Caratacus waved to the detail of warriors behind them to move closer. He explained the situation to his retainers.

"We set out tomorrow for Camulodunum at dawn, storm or not."

* * *

The next day as Caratacus and his party journeyed home along the muddy trackway in misting rain, he wondered if Dana would bear another child. If she could not, should he dissolve their relationship, which was his right? He shook his head and futilely attempted to wipe the water that dropped from the edge of his hooded cloak down onto his face and neck. No, he realized he loved Dana too much to return her to her father in Eburacum. He had received word that he was dying and Cartimandua was expected to replace him as ruler of the Brigantes. Dana would be murdered by her sister. Even if she failed to have a child, he would never send her back to certain death.

Caratacus had sent a rider ahead to let Rhian and Dana know he would soon arrive home. When he had started raising an army to defend against a possible Roman invasion, Caratacus placed Rhian in charge of defending the fortress of Camulodunum in his absence.

He and his entourage arrived late on the second day. The rain had turned into a drenching downpour about an hour before they arrived at his home. Caratacus and the men were soaking wet, shivering, teeth chattering, and miserable in general. Strands of smoke seeped through the straw roof of Caratacus's house, disappearing in the rain. As eager as he was to see Dana, he also looked forward to getting out of the deluge and into a warm, dry house.

Once his party arrived in front of the house, Caratacus turned to Clud and told him to dismiss the escorting warriors for the night and that he could leave as well. "I'll see you in the morning, old friend," Caratacus said.

"Aye, I'll see you then, in drier condition, I hope. I pray the Lady Dana will recover."

"As do I."

Caratacus dismounted and handed the reins to an awaiting groom, who quickly led the horse to the nearby stable. He headed for the front porch of the house, the entrance protected by a series of sewn, goatskin hides. Entering the house, he felt the heat of the fire burning in the center hearth and found the interior illuminated by several smoky candles and olive-oil lamps. He spotted Rhian by the hearth, her flaxen hair knotted into a single braid that flowed down the center of her back. She wore the tartan tunic and breeches of a warrior and a dagger hung from a leather belt around her waist. He pulled off his cloak and tossed it to a slave, who quickly approached and took it from him.

At the same moment, Rhian got up from a stool by the hearth, grabbed a towel nearby, and ran up to him. "Good gods, you're soaked, come to the fire and warm yourself before you get the lung sickness."

"I want to see Dana," he said.

Rhian violently shook her head. "Dana isn't going anywhere, and she will be all right. Take off those clothes." She handed him a linen towel. "Take this and dry yourself by the fire."

For the space of a heartbeat, Caratacus glared at her, annoyed that she would order him about. But the more he thought about it, she made sense. "All right, the last thing I need is to get sick."

Once he had dried himself and changed his clothes, the heat returned to his body, and he relaxed. He turned to where Rhian stood, hugged and kissed her. "Thank you," he said.

"For what?"

"For using your common sense to see that I got out of my wet clothes."

"I'm being selfish," she said.

"Selfish?"

"I don't want either you or Dana to die—it seems I have to take care of both of you." She smirked. "I'm happy you arrived so soon, Dana will be pleased."

He looked beyond Rhian's shoulder at the enclosed goatskin cubicle where Dana was bedded down.

Rhian stepped back and, for a split second, peered in that direction and then at Caratacus.

"How is she?" he asked.

"Dana will recover, but still feels very low about losing the baby."

Caratacus nodded toward the enclosure. "I will see her. Now."

Rhian stepped ahead of him and led the way.

He entered the enclosure, which smelled mildly of vinegar. In the dim illumination provided by three candles, Dana rested on the bed-pallet, dressed in a plain bed tunic, bundled in several wolf-skin blankets, her face drawn and pale. She opened her eyes upon Caratacus's approach.

"Caratacus," Dana mumbled in a low, scratchy voice, "is that you?" She attempted to pull her blankets from her body and raise herself upon her elbows but fell back moaning.

He drew closer, going down on one knee next to her. Rhian knelt beside him.

"It's me, Dana," Caratacus said. "I came as soon as I could."

"I'm so ... happy you're ... here." Dana twisted her head toward Rhian. "Thank you, Rhian."

"For what?" Rhian asked.

"You ... you sent for Caratacus." Dana closed her eyes for the space of about five heartbeats before opening them again.

Caratacus turned to Rhian and touched her shoulder. "My thanks, too."

Rhian nodded. "You had to be told about her. Neither of us expected you to return, but thank Mother Goddess you came."

"Yes," Dana said. Once more she attempted to raise herself but failed.

Caratacus and Rhian, who went to the other side of the pallet, simultaneously leaned over, placed several furs behind her back, and raised her to a sitting position.

Caratacus nodded his thanks to Rhian and turned to Dana.

"I'm so sorry, Caratacus," Dana murmured.

"About what?" He knew what she meant.

"I lost ... lost your child."

He shook his head. "No, don't. It couldn't be helped. Right now it is more important you get well. We can think about having another one later."

Dana's body shook, her face twisted in a grimace. Tears welled within her eyes, and quietly, she wept.

Caratacus looked across Dana to Rhian, who motioned with her head toward Dana's hand. He took it into his and found it warm, free of fever. He gently stroked it.

About five minutes later, Dana's sobbing tapered off. Rhian gave her a linen cloth to wipe her face.

"Thank you … for staying with … me, both of you," Dana said. "I acted like … a silly fool."

"You're not a fool," Caratacus said in a gentle voice.

"Dana, it's only natural," Rhian said. "I know how you feel."

"You're so … kind, Rhian, you've been … through this, too."

Dana turned to Caratacus. "What if I … I can't have … another baby? You … you wouldn't send … me back to Eburacum, would you?"

Caratacus narrowed his eyes and frowned. "Never, Dana, never. Under no circumstances will I ever send you back there. This is your home, forever."

To return you would mean certain death at the hands of your scheming bitch of a sister.

Slowly, a smile crossed Dana's pale face. "Honestly?"

"I wouldn't say it otherwise, you are part of my family," Caratacus said.

"It's true, Dana, you are," Rhian said, looking at Caratacus.

"I'm so happy," Dana said in a fading voice. "I'm so tired." She closed her eyes.

Caratacus and Rhian nodded to one another. Together they removed the blankets holding Dana up and allowed her to lie back on the bed-pallet. The two stood and went outside. They sat by the hearth on stools with a small table between them. A female slave was banking wood in the fire pit. Rhian ordered her to bring them mead and dismissed her once she and Caratacus had been served. For a moment, they quietly sipped their drinks.

Rhian placed her cup on the table. "As you can see, dear Husband, Dana will need time to recover—not only her body but her mind."

"That's why I didn't ask her about the miscarriage. Tell me what happened."

She pinched her light eyebrows together as if pondering what to say. "I was riding home after inspecting the defenses of the fortress when one our slaves approached me outside of the compound. He said Dana was sick and needed my help. Quickly, I made my way to the house, and when I entered, I found her sitting by the hearth doubled over in pain. I asked what was wrong, and she said she was bleeding between the legs."

Caratacus cocked his head to the side. "Between the legs?"

"Yes. I knew what that meant—a miscarriage. I helped her to bed, ordered a servant to bring towels to lay beneath her. I ordered another one to fetch the midwife. She arrived and gave Dana an awful tasting potion to stop the miscarriage, but it didn't work." Rhian paused, shaking her head.

"Go on, Rhian," Caratacus said.

She touched her face and continued, "We placed her on the birthing stool. There wasn't anything more we could do to stop the unborn child from coming out of Dana's womb." Rhian stopped again, her lips tightened into a thin line. She shook her head.

This must be very painful for her. "Please, go on."

Rhian nodded. "The pain was so terrible, Dana screamed and passed out."

"You don't have to go into all the details," Caratacus said. "I presume it came out in a bloody mess." He remembered this same thing happening to Rhian in the past.

"Yes," Rhian said in a wooden voice.

"Could you tell if it was a boy or girl?"

"I'm afraid not, Caratacus," Rhian answered in little more than a whisper, "it was too small. I'm sorry."

"But it was five months along, couldn't you determine what it was?"

Rhian shook her head and sighed. "The child was underdeveloped. Perhaps it had already been dead in Dana's womb, but she never complained."

Caratacus exhaled. For the length of about eight heartbeats, he turned his head away to hold back tears.

There is nothing I can do about it now. He tried to put on a sober face and turned back to Rhian.

"What happened to Dana?"

"Even though she was unconscious, thank the Mother Goddess she was breathing. The midwife said she would recover. We cleaned her, placed towels between her legs to stop the bleeding, and put her in bed. She had a fever. When she woke up, the midwife gave her another potion to bring it down." Slowly a smile appeared across Rhian's bowed lips. "Don't worry, Caratacus, Dana will recover, I'm sure. I know what she is going through."

"Aye, I remember the pain and sadness you experienced, Rhian, I'm sorry for both of you."

"Don't, Caratacus, it is long over for me. Now I pray that Dana will one day bear you a child."

He peered into Rhian's apple-green eyes. "Even if it is a daughter, not only will I love and accept her, I will see that one day she succeeds me as queen and ruler of our people."

CHAPTER 35

Four weeks had elapsed since word of Adminios's banishment had reached Porcius and Verica. Now the Roman found himself hiking along the muddy pathway to the home of King Verica for the meeting that Porcius had requested, no, begged the ruler for. The Roman invasion appeared imminent—was Verica planning to defend his realm or ally with them?

The rain had stopped about a half hour before, but slate-gray clouds had not diminished, and the Roman feared more were on the way. The chill from the icy wind stabbed his pudgy face like dozens of tiny daggers. He pulled the woolen scarf across his bejowled face and his oil-skinned cloak tighter against his shoulders.

As he waddled his heavy bulk between the standing puddles of water, he reflected on the month's past events. Porcius had been staying at Verica's capital, Caleva, when news came that Adminios had been expelled. Both he and Verica received reports that Caratacus was preparing defenses against a Roman landing. Word had reached them that Caratacus had deposed Cunobelinos and was now king. He was planning to overrun Verica's kingdom. Although Porcius feared that Caratacus might attack Verica's lands, he wasn't too concerned. He had known Caratacus since he was a youth and figured the new ruler would consider the danger from the Romans his first priority. Besides, Porcius wasn't ready to rejoin the Romans yet. Caligula might still murder him. Porcius was aware Emperor Caligula had journeyed with the Roman Army from the Lower Rhenus to Gaul in preparation for the invasion of Britannia. He had received word that the real reason Caligula had traveled to Legionary Headquarters at Moguntiacum, Germania, was to execute Lentulus Gaetulicus, commander of the Upper Rhenus garrisons. He had been planning to assassinate the emperor and replace him with Marcus Lepidus, widower of Caligula's dead sister, Drusilla. Both men died by the sword.

Months before, Porcius had discovered that Adminios had sent a secret message to the mad emperor pleading with him to launch an invasion against Britannia. In turn, Caratacus's brother had supplied Caligula with vast amounts of economic and military information on the British tribes. Porcius had known Caligula was already secretly planning an assault across the channel long before Caratacus's older brother made his request. However, unforeseen problems had been posed by logistical difficulties. The switching from an essentially land campaign across the Rhine, to a major seaborne operation across the British Channel had delayed the planned invasion. But for how much longer?

Porcius arrived at Verica's private chambers off the Great Hall. After salutations, they sat across from one another next to a smoky, open hearth. Despite the cold breeze, the door flap was left open for extra lighting. Porcius's pudgy hands gripped tightly around the bronze cup of warm calda wine offered to him by a servant. He took a grateful sip of the wine, feeling its warmth as it traveled down his throat. Beneath his oil-skin cloak and scarf, Porcius wore a heavy, woolen tunic and breeches with a fur cloak covering him from shoulder to his arthritic knees. He leaned slightly forward as he studied the scar-faced, slit-mouthed king, who looked fiercely at him.

Dressed similarly, except for the outer coat, Verica was clothed in a tunic of silk, trimmed in gold, with a fur robe hooked at the shoulder by a sapphire encased gold pendant.

"What brings you here?" the king asked Porcius in a gruff voice. He waved away strands of smoke from the hearth's fire.

"Now that Caratacus is king, you realize that our positions here in Britannia are untenable," Porcius said.

Verica gulped his calda from a gold cup and belched, his breath reeking of decay and rot. For the space of a heartbeat, Porcius crinkled his nose and held his breath.

"You don't need to remind me, Roman," Verica said. "I know your Emperor Caligula has granted Adminios asylum, the traitorous dog."

"Caligula may be emperor, but he is not mine," Porcius said.

"What do you mean?" Verica growled.

Porcius took the cup in his hand and examined it for the space of three heartbeats before answering. "He'll kill me if I return to Rome. And do you know how? I'll be forced to run alongside his carriage, while he gleefully watches, until I drop dead. He's done the same to other senators. Why do you think I came here?"

"Because you are here, my people think I am in the moneybags of the Romans."

Then why haven't you expelled me? He sipped his drink. "Aren't you? If Caratacus invades your lands, you will have no choice but to fight or flee to Rome."

A black-toothed grin appeared through the king's bushy, graying mustache. "Caratacus has no time for me. He is preparing for the invasion. When that time comes, I will ally myself with Rome."

"You will have no choice." The dark eyes in Porcius's fleshy face squinted. The smoke from the hearth changed direction on the breeze filtering through the entry, drifting his way. He rubbed his watery eyes. "If you don't join Rome as a client king, your people will be enslaved, and Rome will kill you."

"I know." Frowning lines etched Verica's scarred forehead. "Being a client king is like a whore getting in bed with a high-paying customer."

Porcius held out a hand as if it were obvious. "At least the customer pays for her services, and Rome is generous."

Verica snorted. He took another swill of calda and wiped his mouth on the sleeve of his tunic. "Still, I must think of my people first."

You mean yourself first. Porcius's face remained sober. "Indeed, we still don't know if Rome will invade." He leaned closer. "By now you should realize Caligula is unpredictable. He has been known to start many projects but fails to finish them. He may change his mind at any moment. If that happens," Porcius paused, "Caratacus and his brother will come after your lands. They haven't forgotten how you retook the Atrebatic lands from their uncle, your old enemy, Epaticcos."

The king jabbed a hand with a finger pointing in Porcius's direction. "The lands rightfully belonged to me. They were mine to reclaim." He dropped his hand to his side.

"True, but Caratacus is ambitious," Porcius answered in a resolute voice. "He is determined to expand his territories and plans to one day rule all southern Britannia."

Verica shook his head and slammed a hand against his huge thigh. "Not while I live! I haven't forgotten he killed my son in battle." His mouth twisted into a crooked frown.

Neither have I, nor that your son kidnapped me at Bagshot Heath! If it hadn't been for Caratacus, I probably would have been murdered by that young madman. Porcius decided to let it pass. He and Verica had too much at stake to open old wounds.

A warrior entered the room and informed the king that a messenger had arrived with important news.

"Bring him in," Verica ordered. The warrior departed.

The charcoal-haired, young courier, clothed in a green and yellow, tartan tunic and beige and white, striped breeches with a longsword at his side, entered and stood stiffly before the king, looking straight ahead.

For a few seconds the king studied him. "You are Bran, son of Madog, are you not?"

"Yes, Great King."

He nodded in approval. "A great warrior. All right, what do you have for me?" Verica demanded.

Appearing a little more at ease, the young man spoke. "Great King, the Emperor Caligula and the Roman Army have withdrawn from the coast of Gaul."

Porcius sighed in relief as his body relaxed. *Thank Jupiter. This is not the time for another Roman conquest.* His muscles tightened again. *Now Caratacus will turn his forces against Verica.*

A smile crossed Verica's face. He gestured to the young messenger. "Don't stand there like a fool, man, give me the details."

"The Roman Army mutinied," Bran said. He described how the soldiers refused to board the transport ships for the invasion. Enraged by their actions, Caligula made the troops collect seashells along the Gallic shoreline in parade dress. "Then the emperor did something strange." Bran paused and shook his head as if in disbelief.

"Go on, don't stop now," Verica said, impatience creeping into his voice.

Bran nodded and shrugged. "He waded out into the surf with a sword in one hand. Then he slashed at the waves with it a dozen times. He yelled that he was victorious over Neptune and Britannia."

Porcius gasped. "Truly, he has gone mad."

"If he wasn't already," Verica added. He turned to Bran. "Continue."

The runner explained that Caligula ordered the legions to withdraw from Gaul and return to their camps on the River Rhenus, and the emperor returned to Rome.

"What about Adminios, brother of Caratacus?" Verica asked the man. "Was he with Caligula?"

"He followed the emperor to Rome," Bran answered.

After Verica dismissed the messenger he scratched his scarred nose and turned to Porcius. "Thank the gods, whose names I dare not say, Rome is no longer a threat."

"Perhaps not," Porcius said. "But now, Caratacus is sure to set his eyes on your holdings. What are you going to do?"

Verica's calloused hand, the size of a ham, grabbed the hilt of the bejeweled dagger tied to his waist. "I will stand and fight."

"Is that wise?" Porcius questioned. Sweat poured down his back and heat rushed to his face. "Think about it. Through his alliance with the other southern tribes, his warriors outnumber yours nearly three to one. Those are forces he was going to use against the Romans. Now he will bring them to bear against you. Surely, you cannot win."

Verica raised his left-hand palm up and slapped a curled right fist upon it. "I'm twice the man Caratacus is, and my warriors have no equal in all of Britannia. I dare him to invade my kingdom. We will destroy his army, and he will die by my hands!"

* * *

By the ninth day after receiving the news of the Roman withdrawal from the Gallic coast, Caratacus had formed plans for the invasion of Verica's lands. He discussed them with Clud, Tog, Donn, and the clan chieftains, including Fergus ap Roycal in the Great Hall back in Camulodunum. It was early April, and now that the threat from invasion was over, he had withdrawn his warriors inland, most being sent home. His planned attack on Verica would have to wait until early summer when food supplies were more readily available. They had been exhausted while waiting for the expected Roman landing. His only consolation was that he knew Verica's stores were in no better shape than that of his forces.

Upon returning home from the meeting and during the evening meal, Dana, who had fully recovered from losing their baby, advised Caratacus to beware of the ambitions of Cartimandua. "You know Cartimandua is father's favorite. He is old and not well. Soon, he will be with the gods."

Caratacus sat on the wolf-skin rugs near the hearth with Rhian on his right and Dana to the left. He took the time to finish chewing a piece of bread and think about his reply. After taking a swig of mead to wash down the food, he finally answered, "I am aware of the situation."

"I'm afraid my sister will succeed him on the throne," Dana said. She straightened out her rust-colored work tunic and wiped bread crumbs from her sleeve. "She is very evil and a manipulator."

"You're right," Caratacus answered, "but what about her husband, Venutios, he's with Cartimandua. It's up to him to control her."

Dana sighed, glanced to Rhian, who frowned, and back to Caratacus. "He does not have rights to the succession, only Cartimandua can succeed her father."

Rhian nodded in support of Dana and took a bite of goat stew, the tangy scent filling the room.

"The Council can vote for anybody they want to replace her father when he dies," Caratacus said. He sipped from his cup.

"I know, Husband, but I doubt they will," Dana said. "She wields great influence over them."

"What do you want me to do about it?" Caratacus asked, gesturing with his goblet, sloshing mead.

Dana shook her head as if growing impatient. "Is it true she wants to ally with the Romans?"

"It is," Caratacus said. He had received information from spies that Rome had offered her gold, land, and other luxuries if she would agree to an alliance.

"She craves power beyond anything else," Dana said.

"I know, but the Romans have withdrawn," Caratacus said. "When and if they actually decide to invade, I will deal with Cartimandua at that time."

"Isn't it best you do so now rather than wait before she forms an alliance with Rome?" Rhian asked. "My heart tells me this is something she will do."

Dana nodded. "I agree with Rhian."

Caratacus turned his head toward Rhian. "Maybe, but right now my eyes are on Verica. By early summer, we will have enough supplies on hand so I can recall my warriors and allies to take the field against that maggot. I have sworn to avenge Uncle Epaticcos's death and reclaim the lands that once belonged to him."

Rhian pulled back the strands of flaxen hair that had fallen across her right eye, then motioned toward Caratacus. "Then do so, Husband. But Dana is right, Cartimandua must be dealt with sooner than later."

"I will in time. Right now, Verica is our kingdom's greatest threat. He must be destroyed!"

END OF PART I